VALENTINA
MANDARIN

The Alchemist's Tango

Based on True Events

ISBN: 979-8-218-81158-7 (Paperback)
ISBN: 979-8-218-81159-4 (Hardcover)

Library of Congress Control Number: 2025920699

This is a work of historical fiction. The author in no way represents the companies, corporations, or brands mentioned in this book. The likeness of historical/famous figures have been used fictitiously; the author does not speak for or represent these individuals. All opinions expressed in this book are fictional.

Valentina Mandarin
c/o Registered Agents, Inc.
7901 4th St N, STE 300
St. Petersburg, FL 33702

www.valentinamandarin.com

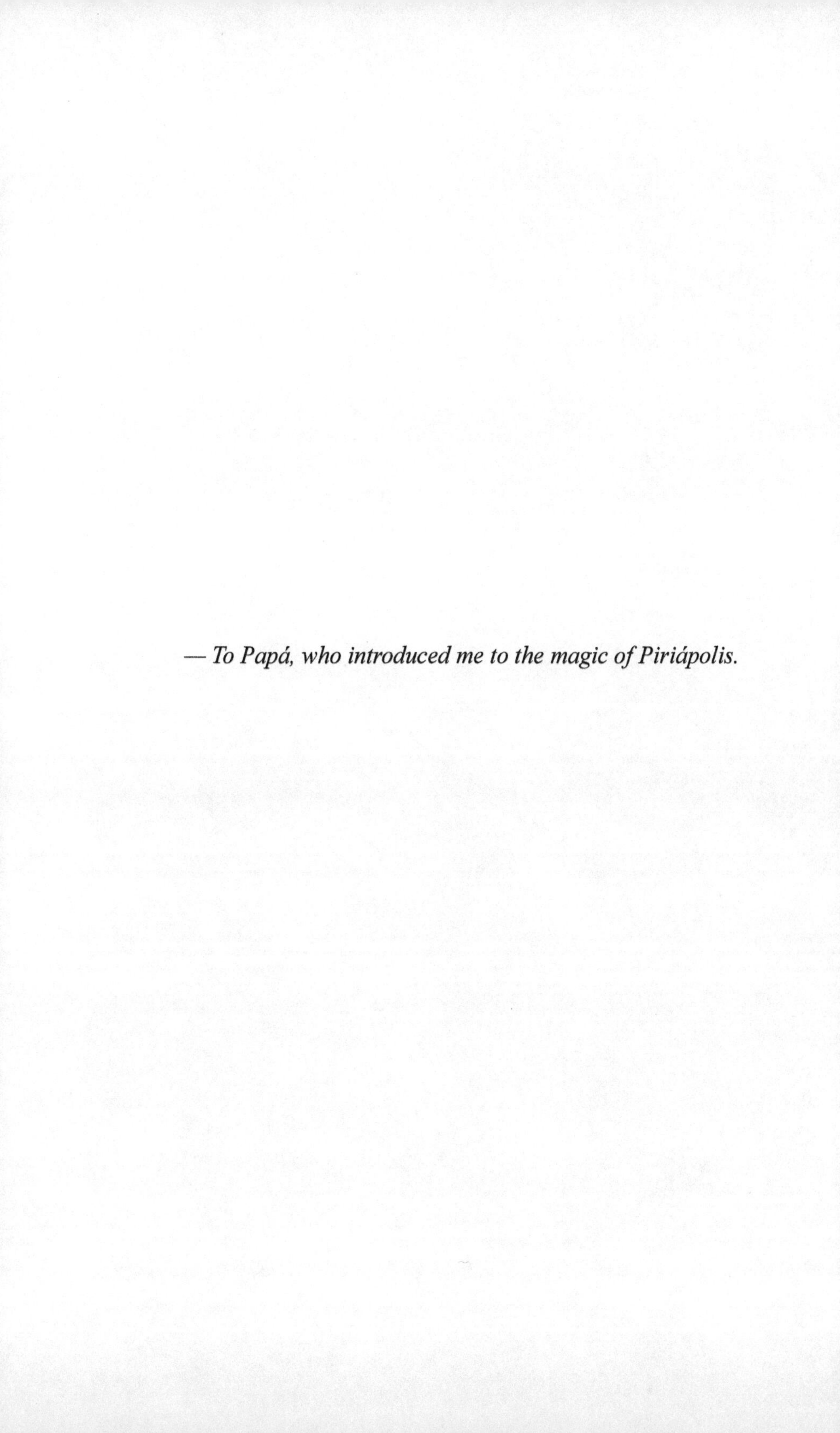

— To Papá, who introduced me to the magic of Piriápolis.

Introduction

The first time I saw the Argentino Hotel in Piriápolis, Uruguay, the Atlantic wind was heavy with salt and memory. My father's eyes gleamed as though we had stepped into a story he had been telling me all my life. For as long as I could remember, he had spoken of this place. The grand hotel where, as a boy from a dusty *barrio* in Salto, he had once competed in a national chess tournament. He described the chandeliers and marble, the lavish tables laden with more food than he had ever seen, and beyond the terrace, the endless ocean; his very first glimpse of the sea. It was here, he told me, that he first felt the stirrings of a larger destiny.

He told the story with a kind of reverence, as though that grand seaside hotel held the keys to his own becoming. It was his very first glimpse of another kind of life: one of beauty, of possibility. It was there, surrounded by Francisco Piria's vision made stone, that my father began to believe that he, too, could reach beyond the life he had known. If a poor boy could sit at a chessboard in such a place, perhaps he could cross the ocean itself. That single moment, set against Piria's creation, propelled him toward the United States, and in time, gave me the life I would inherit.

Nearly three decades later, I finally returned to Uruguay, and at last my father was able to take me to the place he had spoken of all my life. We stood together in Piriápolis, before the Argentino Hotel, at the very point of origin of our family's emigration story. Walking its marble halls with him was like stepping into the legend that had silently shaped us both.

It was on the grounds of Piria's castle that he told me, almost conspiratorially, of the deeper legend: of Francisco Piria, mocked in his lifetime for his wild ideas, who had turned a barren stretch of coast into a world-class resort. And of Carmen Ruiz, the mysterious woman who stood beside him in his final years, shrouded in whispers. *Was she his lover, his daughter, his muse?* No one seemed to know. However, in the ambiguity, I felt something stir inside me. Somehow, I knew I had stumbled onto a story that had been waiting for me. There were pieces of a puzzle: *a woman, a castle, an unfinished church standing in ruins.* A legend wrapped in mystery. It felt less like discovery than recognition, as though it had been waiting for me to unveil the secrets left hidden for almost a century.

From that moment, I devoured every scrap of information about Piria I could find: books, articles, forgotten archives, even whispered anecdotes that survived in family lore. And yet, in all the literature, I found Carmen's name conspicuously absent. Piria's life was recorded in stone and story, yet Carmen's had all but disappeared. In a world where women's voices are so often silenced, I began to feel an almost sacred responsibility to give her back her voice, to let her speak again through the veil of time. To imagine her not only as an appendage to Piria's myth, but as a woman with her own longings, choices, and courage.

I turned to the tools I knew best. Using the instincts I had honed as an unofficial genealogist—another gift I inherited from my father—I began to trace names through church registers, ship manifests, birth certificates, and brittle pages tucked away in municipal files. Every fragment became a thread, and I followed them obsessively, weaving together the outlines of a story that refused to stay buried.

In this search, I found myself drawn deeper into the very current that had once inspired my father. Piria was not only a builder of castles; he was also a student of alchemy. His symbols and inscriptions still hide in the stones of Piriápolis, reminders of a truth the alchemists always knew: that transformation begins from within. This became my revelation too. I realized that my work was not just to tell a love story, but to teach people about a different kind of alchemy: not one based on physical elements, but Spiritual Alchemy. How we, like Piria and like Carmen, can transmute pain into beauty, doubt into faith, and longing into creation.

In bringing Carmen's voice forward, I wanted to honor both her resilience and Piria's vision, but also to offer something larger: a way for others to see themselves in the dance between ruin and rebirth, between dream and reality. My hope is that readers will not only rediscover a forgotten piece of Uruguayan history, but also awaken to their own power to transform, to build, and to dream.

And as Uruguay approaches the Bicentennial of its Independence, I hold close Carmen's own words—words that reach across time with the same fire that first drew my father to the Argentino Hotel, and me to the story I was always meant to tell:

"Uruguay, this beautiful country which welcomes all your noblest ambitions, will soon be celebrating. The traditional festival that recalls the liberty which has been as beneficent to you as to all of us. You must therefore cooperate, so that the land may be adorned yet more splendidly for her double golden wedding. It is not necessary that anyone suggest what you should do for this glorious anniversary. Your own hearts, and the affection you bear her, will tell you what we hope from you."

Valentina Mandarin

iv

Acknowledgements

There are so many people whose love, guidance, and generosity have shaped this journey, and I am deeply grateful to each of them.

To my **Abuela Rosa**, who first introduced me to tango by filling the kitchen with song each and every day, planting the earliest seeds of this passion in my heart.

To **Dr. Aldo Cusumano**, who took me to my very first *milonga* when I was just fifteen, and never stopped believing that I would one day find my voice as a tango singer.

To **Darlindo "El Gato" Correa**, for the priceless gift of bringing me a signed copy of Carmen's *Tan-gó*, traveling all the way from Montevideo to place that treasure in my hands.

To **Norma Fernández** and **Carlos A. Pascual**, for your open hearts, warm hospitality during my stay in Uruguay, and for sharing with me the gift of Carmen's book, *El Hijo Ajeno*.

To my stepmother, **Jessica**, for donning her English Teacher hat and bravely reading (and proofreading!) my very first, very rough draft.

To my sister, **Michelle**, for her constant encouragement and for reminding me—again and again—to let go of self-limiting beliefs, embrace transformation, and step boldly into my divine purpose.

To my mother, my first guide through the world of **spiritual alchemy**, who showed me that transformation begins within.

To my father, whose stories of the magic of Piriápolis enchanted me from childhood, and whose faith in me inspired me to publish this tale.

And finally, to **Francisco Piria and Carmen Ruiz (Piria)**, whose extraordinary lives lit the path that led me to follow my own dreams.

With gratitude as well to: **Yaraví Roig, Marcia Collazo Ibáñez, Jorge Floriano, María Belén Baptista, Marisol Nicoletti,** and **Allan Coctel**—your contributions were incredibly helpful and more inspiring than words can express.

"'Francisco!' I exclaimed, 'That was my name in another life,' I said, remembering.

And at that moment I saw unfold before me a vision of the series of past lives that had previously transpired, all of them lived parallel to the one person I had always held so dear, that kindred spirit, that soulmate, inseparable from mine."

— Francisco Piria, 1898

Chapter 1

Carmen marched briskly through the winding streets of Montevideo, her heels striking the worn cobblestones in a sharp, steady rhythm. A newspaper was rolled tightly under her arm like a weapon, her grip clenched around it as if holding it any looser might allow the paper to flutter away on its own like a Tero bird and cry the headline out loud from the rooftops.

Faces blurred past her, none stopping, none greeting her, only staring. She didn't expect them to welcome her. Not after the scandals. Not after everything.

Carmen inhaled deeply as she turned down a narrow alley, the familiar scent of urine, brine, and beer clinging to the air. Her face was stone. She would not give them the satisfaction of seeing her tears fall.

Barrio Sur breathed with its usual life. The late afternoon sun stretched long shadows across the faded facades of the pastel *casitas* in amber and dust, wrought iron balconies were draped in fluttering laundry, rusted gates creaked open and shut, and voices rose like steam from kitchen windows.

Barrio Sur talks. It always talks.

"*Is that Carmen?*" the neighborhood women whispered, as they peered out from behind clotheslines of laundry and through shuttered windows and cracked doorways.

"*Unbelievable. Showing her face around here, after the scandal and shame she's put her mother through, imagine!*"

"*Hm, looks like she's filled out around the hips. Must be pregnant and back now to beg for help, I'd wager.*"

"*Hmph. I wouldn't be surprised. Like mother, like daughter.*"

The hushed whispers didn't pierce so much as cling, like burrs on the hem of her skirt. Familiar. Predictable. Still sharp.

Carmen kept her eyes forward. Her chest tightened, her breath shallow. The paper under her arm felt heavier with each step, as if soaked in the weight of her past, her shame, and the cruel satisfaction of strangers.

She had fled the newsstand like a bird in flight, as if the ink itself had scalded her skin. Though she hadn't returned to Barrio Sur in months, her feet had instinctively carried her towards the weathered tenement she had shared with her mother since they'd first arrived there from Buenos Aires with little more than a suitcase and hope. The sanctuary of its worn walls called to her like a prayer now, away from the eyes of a city that watched too closely and forgave too little. Her old room, the thin curtain drawn, the door latched, the world kept firmly at bay, was the only place she could let the weight fall, let the tears come. Not in the street. Not in front of them. But behind that door, where no one could see her unravel.

The old men of her *barrio* sat out front in weathered chairs, *mate* in one hand, *cigarillo* in the other, their chessboards balancing precariously on matchbooks to steady them on the uneven surface of the sidewalks laid with Portuguese paving stones. Their murmurs followed her like smoke.

"*You know, I hear she likes her men like she likes her wine. Aged and with a bit of a kick!*"

"*Che, we veterans may have some miles on us, but hey, so does she, from what I hear!*"

The faint sound of a sad tango song playing over an old phonograph floated out through the narrow, barred windows of one of the little townhomes, its bittersweet melody weaving through the street like a ghost.

Carmen's steps faltered, her breath catching in her throat. She furiously fought back another overwhelming wave of grief, but the music, *that* song, peeled back her composure like fragile lace. The notes carried with them the memory of the night she and Francisco had first met.

Her grip on the newspaper tightened. Ink smeared across her fingers.

The scent of simmering soups, *guisos* and fresh-baked bread curled through the air, grounding her in something real, something old. A simpler time, a time before the world had been consumed by war and plague, and before the chaos and harsh realities of adulthood had come bearing down like a stern disciplinarian to quickly snuff out the carefree joys of childhood.

The laughter of children playing *fútbol* barefoot in the street echoed around her as she passed, their joyful cries rising like music against the fading light. They chased each other with the boundless energy of those who had not yet known real sorrow, their scuffed knees and shining eyes untouched by the weight of the world. She paused just long enough to see them, to remember when she had been one of them, running barefoot through these very same streets. Wild, grinning, invincible. The memory softened her, just for a breath.

She turned the final corner. Her mother's house came into view. Narrow, weathered, familiar. *Her sanctuary. Her shame. Her inevitable fate.* Her vision blurred, but she would not crumble yet. Not where they could see.

She ducked her head and reached for the latch on the wrought iron gate. It stuck, as it always had, but her hands worked quickly, trembling only once. The paper clutched to her chest like a shield, she pushed through the door and stumbled inside.

The latch clicked shut behind her.

And only then, behind the curtain, behind the wood, behind the familiar walls of her childhood, did Carmen allow herself to shatter.

She slammed the door shut behind her, her back pressing hard against it as her knees gave way. The first sob ripped through her chest without warning. A raw, unfiltered cry pulled from somewhere far deeper than sorrow. The tears she had fought all afternoon came fast now, bitter and hot, blurring the room around her.

"Carmen? *Qué te pasa?*" Her mother's voice snapped sharply through the silence.

Carmen blinked hard, her vision swimming as she tried to make sense of the dim, flour-dusted space. The only light came through the slats of the narrow shuttered windows, casting long shadows over the worn linoleum floor.

There stood her mother, hands sunk deep in a bowl of dough, apron streaked with flour, the cast iron pan crackling with bubbling grease beside her. The air was heavy with the scent of hot lard and anticipation. Friday afternoon, always for *torta fritas*, always ready for the market.

Carmen had prayed to find the house empty, to grieve in peace.

But of course, her mother was there. Always there.

She tried to catch her breath, leaning her head back against the doorframe, her body trembling from the effort of holding herself together.

"*Qué te pasa, m'hija?* Say something!" her mother barked again, quickly sliding the scalding pan off the fire, the hiss of oil filling the room.

Carmen opened her mouth, but only air came out. Until finally, the truth spilled through sobs.

"He's… he's *married.*"

The words dropped like stone.

Saying them aloud made it worse. More real. Her chest convulsed, and another wave of despair overtook her. She covered her face with both hands, tears slipping through her fingers like something shameful.

Her mother didn't flinch. She stood still, arms crossed now. Her eyes narrowed, not in surprise, but expectancy. Carmen could feel her mother's reproach in the silence between them.

"How do you know?" her mother asked at last, voice low but sharp.

"I saw it…" Carmen choked, pulling the crumpled newspaper from under her arm with a trembling hand. "I saw it in the periodical, *Mamá*!" She thrust the dreaded paper forward with a trembling hand.

Her mother wiped her hands on her apron and took the paper, unfolding it with care. Her dark eyes scanned the front page. There it was, in bold, final print:

PIRIA, TYCOON, WEDS EUROPEAN HEIRESS IN PRIVATE CEREMONY.

She handed the paper back with a shrug, her fingernails still caked with dough. "*Y qué esperabas, eh?* What did you expect, that he would marry *una botija cualquiera*? A poor girl, like you, from the slums?"

She turned her back and resumed kneading, her thick hands folding the dough with the same brutal efficiency she applied to life.

Carmen collapsed onto one of the mismatched chairs at the wobbly dining table, the newspaper slipping from her grip and landing on the floor like a final insult. She buried her face in her hands, her voice muffled through her fingers.

"I don't know," she wept. "I don't know what I expected."

Her mother didn't answer.

The words on the page blurred as tears welled in her eyes, hot and sudden. *He's married.* The phrase echoed in her mind like a cruel refrain, louder than the clang of the *hielero's* bell as he pushed his cart down the street outside the kitchen window. It rang through her like a church bell tolling for something lost.

She picked up the paper to read the caption again, slowly this time, as if the words might somehow shift and rearrange themselves into a different meaning. But there it was, stark and merciless in black and white:

Don Francisco Piria, esteemed developer and statesman, wed Austrian heiress María Emilia Franz in a private ceremony held in Vienna early this morning, following a swift courtship during one of Piria's many expeditions to Europe.

Carmen's stomach twisted. The page trembled in her hands as she traced the delicate, distant smile of the woman in the photograph. Poised, perfect, a vision from another world. A world Carmen had only ever brushed the edges of.

She stared at the photograph, her jaw tightening as her eyes moved over every curated detail. The delicate fan tucked at the woman's waist, the way her mouth was drawn into a demure smile, as if she were born knowing how to pose for the world's approval.

The caption below the photograph was brief, but it said enough: *Doña María Emilia Franz de Piria.*

Carmen's stomach twisted. *De Piria.*

She set the paper down suddenly, as if handling something that might burn her. The ink was beginning to smudge beneath her trembling fingers, over the woman's broad, powdered face. She wasn't beautiful, but she didn't have to be. *She was legitimate.* A lady of society. Proper. Approved. The kind of woman whose worth didn't need defending, whose name opened doors rather than raised eyebrows.

Had they been courting this whole time? Carmen thought, a sick feeling crawling into her throat. She felt the sting behind her ribs. Not jealousy, exactly, but something colder.

She tried to reason with herself. The woman looked older, heavy-set, distant. She didn't seem like the type to inspire Francisco's fiery speeches or wistful glances. And yet, there she was. Wearing the name that Carmen had only ever dared to imagine beside her own.

The image of the only man she had ever loved, now off somewhere celebrating his wedding night with his new bride, pressed against her heart like a quiet vine of thorns. Each breath carried its sting, each thought a subtle ache, the kind that lingers long after the wound is made.

The memories they had shared, the dreams they once held together, now felt like hollow echoes, like laughter in an empty room. *Had it all meant nothing?*

She tore her eyes away from the page, suddenly sick to her stomach. "I can't even bear to look at their faces! It can't be!" She yelled, springing up from her seat.

She stormed across the room, her skirt swishing violently around her ankles. "She looks like a bloated peacock stuffed into lace!"

Her mother didn't flinch. Her gnarled hands pounded the dough with steady, punishing rhythm, flour dusting the sleeves of her housedress. "You act surprised," she said coldly, never lifting her gaze. "As if men like that ever choose girls like you in the end."

"*Mamá!*" Carmen barked, glaring at her mother.

Her mother continued to furiously knead the dough, not taking her eyes away from her work. "I told you!" She exclaimed matter-of-factly, raising her brows for emphasis, "I *warned* you not to get involved with that man. But no, you don't listen! You're *just* like your father. Always with your head in the clouds. Chasing after things that'll never last."

Her mother launched into one of her well-worn tirades, this time about Carmen's father. How he had run off with a Brazilian woman when Carmen was barely three. How her own life might have turned out differently, better, if she hadn't gotten pregnant so young. If she'd married someone else. Someone with more sense.

The words poured out with practiced bitterness, each sentence kneaded into the dough like an old grievance kept warm on the stove. Carmen didn't flinch. She'd heard this monologue a hundred times, each version dressed in fresh resentment. Her mother had a remarkable talent for turning any story, any sorrow, any moment, especially Carmen's, into something that ultimately circled back to herself.

"It's that you never listen, Carmen! You're *just* like your father," she repeated, her voice sharp with frustration. "I warned you about getting involved with a man who would only bring you trouble, but you never take my advice. Look where it's gotten you! Caught up with that *Piria*, thinking he's different," she scoffed.

"Men like that don't marry for love. They marry for power, money, appearances! They're all the same, Carmen, you were just too blind and too *foolish* to see it. What good has it gotten you now, Carmen? *Eh?* Now that you've wasted the last few years of your youth? You should just be thanking God that *viejo* didn't get you pregnant!" Her mother slammed the dough down one final time.

Carmen stood paralyzed, the familiar sting of her mother's words piercing through her, cutting deeper than she cared to admit. She clenched her jaw, refusing to let the hurt show.

She knew better than to imagine she could ever expect to receive any sort of maternal comfort or motherly affection from her own mother. Carmen had heard these rants countless times before, each one a painful reminder of her mother's own disappointments projected onto her. In her mother's eyes, love, especially love outside the confines of class and convention, was a reckless indulgence that could only lead to heartbreak. Carmen knew her mother had been just *waiting* for the moment she would return, humbled and ready to admit that she had been right all along, and she hated giving her the satisfaction of proving her right.

Suddenly, she felt dizzy. Her mother's scolding and the smell of hot lard in the tiny, sweltering kitchen became overwhelmingly stifling, and she felt like she was suffocating.

"I'm going!" She said, exasperated, turning on her heel and heading for the door.

"Oh! So you're going out there to go hit the sauce, eh? *A chupar vas! What else is new!*" She heard her mother shout as the door slammed shut behind her.

Carmen hurried away back along the familiar streets of Barrio Sur, her steps quickening with a sense of urgency, her heart weighing heavy at the thought of losing Francisco for good. She pulled on the little cloche hat she had grabbed on her way out, tugging it down low over her eyes to hide any evidence that she had been crying.

Her dark hair, trimmed into a soft, fashionable bob, framed her face in gentle waves. She wore a navy walking suit, its fitted jacket cinched neatly at the waist, the tonneau skirt skimming just above her ankles, and a pair of sensible heels that clicked with intention across the pavement. Even in grief, Carmen looked composed. Deliberate.

Life hadn't afforded her luxury, but she had mastered the art of elegance through precision. As a seamstress by trade, she understood that clothing could speak before a woman ever opened her mouth. Her garments, though modest, were always impeccable. Hems aligned, seams reinforced, fabrics pressed with a meticulous care born of both pride and necessity. A simple cotton dress, tailored to perfection and adorned with a handmade brooch or scarf, became something quietly striking in her hands. Her appearance was more about dignity than about vanity. It was her armor. In a world that judged women by wealth or pedigree, Carmen used her craft to claim visibility. Her clothing was more than fabric and thread; it was a testament. Each stitch, an act of quiet rebellion. A refusal to be diminished. A way of saying, without ever raising her voice: *I'm here, and I matter.*

She hurried down the cobblestone streets, her head bowed low, hoping to conceal the paths of hot tears that still marked her cheeks. The weight of her mother's sharp words still clung to her, the sting of judgment cutting deeper than she had expected.

She felt around in her little jacket pocket for her handkerchief, and wiped her nose before quickly hiding it back in its place as she turned the corner.

Her mind was a whirlwind of thoughts and emotions as she replayed the last conversation she had shared with Francisco over and over in her mind, thinking of all the things that she could have said, or that could have gone differently.

The finality of it all settled in like a slow, heavy fog. Francisco was no longer a possibility, no longer a lingering hope or daydream she could run back to. He was married now; that truth loomed, undeniable and unchangeable. What she mourned was not only losing him, but the version of herself that had existed in his eyes. The woman he had recognized before she had learned to recognize herself. It was a quieter grief than heartbreak, yet deeper in its cut, the ache of losing the only person who had ever believed in her dreams without asking her to shrink or apologize for them.

Carmen's steps led her instinctively down toward the river, the soothing rush of water calling to her like a balm for her restless spirit. As she reached the intersection of the streets of *Durazno* and *Convención*, she paused, taking a moment to catch her breath.

She looked out over the Río de la Plata, its murky waters churning and swirling, reflecting the dark turmoil inside her. The vast expanse of the estuary, where the river met the sea, seemed to stretch infinitely. Carmen felt her shoulders begin to loosen, the sight of the slow-moving water shimmering under the late afternoon sun seeming to offer a quiet sense of solace.

As she gazed at the river's expanse, a familiar story floated to the forefront of her mind, one that had circulated for years in her *barrio*. It was the story of a young woman, not much younger than herself, who had been cast out of her home by her father, after getting pregnant as a result of a foolhardy love affair with a married neighbor. Rejected by her family and shamed by the whole *barrio*, the girl had found herself with nowhere to turn. In her despair, she had walked down to that very riverbank one cold winter night, where she had thrown herself into its frigid, murky depths. Her pale, mangled body had been discovered by the town fishermen at dawn, twisted up in the jagged river rocks. Her tragic fate had become a cautionary tale, a whispered warning passed down through generations, from mother to daughter.

"You should be thanking God that viejo didn't get you pregnant!" Carmen's mother had snapped, the words laced with both anger and disdain. Her voice echoed in her mind, relentless and unforgiving, each syllable like a slap against her already bruised heart. Carmen's chest

tightened. She tried to focus on her breathing, willing herself to let go of the hurt, but it clung to her like a stubborn shadow. She thought of Francisco, of his kindness, of how he had spoken of her dreams not as impossibilities, but as inevitabilities. And now, the echoes of her mother's words threatened to tarnish those memories, to reduce them to nothing more than a mistake she should be thankful to have escaped.

Was that really how her mother and everybody saw her? As a foolish woman, naïve and reckless, only chasing after silly delusions? A pariah who only deserved to exist as long as she kept quiet and didn't get herself pregnant?

Carmen shivered at the thought. She could almost see the shadow of the girl in her mind's eye, standing where she stood now, torn between despair and defiance. Though her own troubles were of a different nature, she felt a profound kinship with the girl. A shared experience of wrestling against a world that left so little room for women like them to breathe.

Carmen inhaled deeply, steadying herself. She couldn't let herself fall into the same despair as the girl from the story. No matter how stifling her mother's expectations, or the *barrio*'s ever-watchful eyes, Carmen knew deep in her bones that she couldn't surrender her dreams so easily. There was a fire in her. A quiet, enduring flame that had kept burning through every whispered judgment, every disapproving glance, every sermon disguised as concern. She knew she wasn't made for silence or smallness. They could try to shame her, box her in, make her doubt herself, but she would not bow. As she gazed out over the horizon, she knew she needed to find a way to move forward, to focus on her own path now. Despite the weight of her anguish making each step feel like a monumental effort, she took a deep breath, letting the warm, briny air fill her lungs, and forced herself to keep walking.

As she moved further into the heart of *Barrio Sur* and through the plazas, the rhythmic sounds of *candombe* drums filled the air. A group of drummers had gathered on a street corner to practice for the upcoming *Carnaval*, the infectious beats from their *tamboriles* serving as a swift rhythm for Carmen's measured footsteps.

Montevideo was a mosaic of little *barrios*, each neighborhood a reflection of the diverse waves of immigrants who had arrived on its shores, bringing with them their cultures, traditions, and languages.

The cobblestone streets of the Ciudad Vieja echoed with the whispers of Spanish settlers and African drummers, while the sprawling *mercados* of Villa Muñoz bustled with the Yiddish chatter of Jewish shopkeepers alongside the melodic cadence of Italian vendors hawking their wares.

In La Aguada, smokestacks loomed over modest homes, their plumes a reminder of the industrial backbone that had brought jobs to so many laboring-class immigrants from Europe.

Meanwhile, the leafy streets of Pocitos told a different story, a place where wealthier newcomers from France and Britain had settled, building elegant homes that overlooked the glittering Río de la Plata.

Every *barrio* had its own rhythm, its own stories. Tango floated through the air of working-class neighborhoods like La Unión, where immigrants from Andalusia and the Basque Country danced alongside *criollo gauchos*.

In the *barrio* of Porteño, artists and poets gathered in cafés, weaving together the city's multicultural spirit into verse and melody.

Carmen had always felt at home in this tapestry of cultures. Though her own family had come from Buenos Aires years ago, Montevideo had embraced them like it had so many others, folding them into its patchwork of identities. She had arrived as a child, her mother seeking opportunity across the river, but it was here, among the winding streets and humble *conventillos*, that she had truly grown up.

Barrio Sur, a living memory of old Montevideo, had become a part of her identity, woven into her soul like the intricate rhythms of the *candombe* drums that echoed through its narrow, cobbled streets.

The sounds of Barrio Sur had become the soundtrack of her life: children playing in the streets, their resounding laughter cutting through the melancholy of daily struggles, the barks of the stray dogs running rampant, the chatter of women scrubbing clothes and gossiping in shared courtyards, the echoing voices of men debating politics around smoky *parillas* in the fading afternoon light, and, above all, the pulsing beat of the *tambores*.

Each *barrio* held its own charm, but also its own set of eyes and ears, ever watchful. Carmen knew well that any slip or scandal would be swiftly carried from house to house, across plazas and over steaming gourds of *mate*.

The German baker on the corner would murmur it in passing to his customers. The Polish seamstress would pause her stitching to shake her head in disapproval. The Lebanese grocer, fluent in gossip as much as in commerce, would recount the tale with a knowing smile to the Italian mason who lingered at his counter.

In the small *barrios* of Montevideo, anonymity was a luxury few could afford, and privacy was as fleeting as the afternoon breezes that swept in from the Río de la Plata. It was a city where the past and present intertwined in a tapestry of woven tales, where the walls seemed to hold the secrets of generations. Every corner of the city hummed with the stories of those who had built lives from the ground up, crafting neighborhoods that bore the imprints of faraway homelands.

For Carmen, living in Montevideo was both sanctuary and burden. A city alive with rhythm and breath, yes, but also one that *watched*. It knew her. It remembered everything. Her footsteps echoed in a place that did not forget.

"*Ragazzi, venite qui a mangiare!*" a tired-looking woman shouted in Italian from a shadowed doorway, her voice sharp and maternal, the weight of a hefty baby balanced on her hip. A tangle of children paused their game of *La Farolera*, their laughter still clinging to the cobblestones as the woman herded them inside with the firm authority of someone long accustomed to chaos. As Carmen passed, the woman glanced at her up and down with a tight-lipped smile that was more observation than greeting.

Her face was lined and strong, carved by years of endurance and grit. And in her eyes was something sharp, something *knowing*. A recognition of ache. Of stories carried behind the eyes, unspoken but impossible to hide.

Carmen held her gaze for a moment. And in that moment, she wondered: *could this woman see it?* The restlessness beneath her skin? The way her thoughts ran wild, looping in endless circles around a man she was trying to forget?

She kept walking.

The streets, the alleys, the cafés, they all conspired against her. Every block bore the weight of a memory. Every turn brought back a detail: the way Francisco had once reached for her hand in silence, or the warmth of his voice when speaking about futures they'd never live to see.

She passed small taverns where men shared *mate* in old gourds, conversation rising and falling like song. Tobacco smoke curled from hand-rolled *cigarillos*, rich and sweet. The scent caught her off guard. It was *his* scent. The comforting, smoky balm of his pipe, the way it used to wrap around her in quiet moments, like a fog of belonging.

And then: *a violin.*

The melody swelled from a street corner like something pulled from the past. A tango. Slow, mournful, haunting. Carmen's chest tightened.

She still knew the steps.

Still remembered the way his arm curved around her waist, the rhythm of his breath against her temple. The way the world had always quieted when they danced, as if time bent in reverence to their connection.

Even the harbor, glimpsed through a break in the buildings, stirred something deep. The sea, glinting beneath the fading light, still held his voice in it. Plans of distant places they would travel to together.

But they wouldn't.

She stopped at the edge of the street, the wind lifting her hair as if to remind her she was still here, still standing. The memories, vivid and unrelenting, washed over her not as ghosts, but as proof.

Proof that it had been real.

She paused at a small plaza where the trees leaned into the breeze like old women whispering secrets, and the setting sun spilled gold across the weatherworn stones. Montevideo pulsed around her, its walls steeped in memory, its heartbeat steady beneath the noise.

Carmen closed her eyes.

Not to retreat, but to stand still in something deeper. She let the wind embrace her like a mother, let the scent of sea and stone and fresh bread fill her lungs. The sound of a distant *bandoneón* drifted from a window above, faint but unmistakable. A sound that belonged to her, to the city, to everything she'd survived.

The memories came, not as sorrow, but as substance. The echo of Francisco's voice, the weight of his gaze, the impossible hope stitched between their silences. Yes, what they had was gone, but it had been *real*. And like the city that had seen her through every version of herself, it had *shaped* her. Not broken her.

She drew her strength from the same cobblestones that had felt her footsteps since girlhood. From the sea that kept moving no matter who stayed or left. From the shadows and light that lived side by side on every Montevidean street.

She opened her eyes, not softer, but sharper.

The past had carved her.

But it was *this city* that had made her indestructible.

With a deep breath, she opened her eyes and continued walking, determined to find her own path through the labyrinth of memory and longing.

Chapter 2

The streets of Montevideo were bustling as Carmen finally turned the corner into the town square of the Ciudad Vieja, the street cars dinging and whirring their way past bicycles, pedestrians, motorcars, and the occasional horse and carriage clattering over the cobblestones, their drivers calling out to pedestrians to make way. The smell of horse manure and of burning coal, steam, oil, and smoke greeted her, each competing to overtake the other.

The fishermen and merchants hawked their wares from stalls that lined the streets, their voices blending into a symphony of commerce.

Across the expanse of the cobbled Plaza Independencia stood the Gateway of the Citadel, a silent sentinel between eras. A threshold between the Old World and the New World, where the weight of history brushed against the new breath of progress.

Carmen hadn't known where she was headed to when she had left the house, only that she needed to go somewhere, anywhere, that still felt like hers. And somehow, her feet had led her to the only place that ever had: the Madreselva.

Carmen had first discovered the Madreselva when her childhood friend, Nicolás, had landed a job as a busboy at the club, shortly after they had both graduated from secondary school. Eager to show off his newfound place in the adult world, Nico had invited Carmen to stop by in honor of her eighteenth birthday. She had run into him by chance at the bakery one morning, her fingers fumbling over a few tarnished coins as she tried to afford a loaf of bread.

"Come by tomorrow," he'd said, flashing that familiar lopsided grin, all boyish charm and mischief. "It's nothing fancy, but it's got *soul,* Carmen. You've just got to see for yourself. Hey, I'll even get them to pour you a drink for your birthday," he said, wiggling his thick eyebrows suggestively.

Carmen had hesitated, fidgeting with the cuff of her blouse. "Nico, you know I can't just go waltzing into a club *alone.* People would talk. And my mother…she'd *never* let me hear the end of it, if she didn't kill me first."

At the time, Carmen had felt conflicted by Nico's proposition. At seventeen, she had just started to glimpse the expanse of life beyond the narrow streets of her *barrio*: a mix of hope, curiosity, and the yearning to step beyond the boundaries of her small, familiar world.

Nico's invitation had stirred something bold in her, but even then, she knew the cost of boldness. The rules may have been unwritten, but they were enforced all the same: with whispers, with shame, with silence. And Carmen had always been painfully aware of their weight.

In Montevideo's conservative climate, where everyone knew everybody else's business, the very idea of a young woman stepping out unescorted after dark was seen as nothing short of scandalous, if not outright disgraceful. The streets, with their dimly lit corners and whispering alleys, were no place for a woman of so-called respectable standing. Everyone knew that only one kind of woman wandered alone after dark. The kind whispered about behind closed doors and judged in open ones. In a *barrio* like hers, a single stroll alone beneath the moonlight could unravel a reputation thread by thread. And Carmen knew it all too well.

And then, for Carmen, there was the matter of her mother's steadfast moral principles. Ever since Carmen's father had left them, leaving a void too vast to fill, her mother had sought refuge in the church, immersing herself in the structured solace of Catholic devotion. It had become the cornerstone of her life, a guiding light in a world that had suddenly felt too dark and uncertain to bear.

For as long as Carmen could remember, her mother's expectations were as clear and rigid as the carved pews of the parish where they worshipped every Sunday. Modesty, piety, and obedience were virtues her mother emphasized with fervor, and she fully expected Carmen to embrace the same values.

A woman's dignity is measured only by her piety. Without it, you might as well be naked in the streets, she would say.

To her mother, the world outside their small home was brimming with temptation and sin, particularly for a young, unwed woman like Carmen. Bars, or any other places her mother deemed to be of *"ill-repute"* were entirely out of the question. Such establishments were dens of vice where loose women, drunken men, and illicit music tangled together in ways her mother refused to even speak of. *And to go there alone for the sake of meeting up with a man?* That would have been a scandal beyond redemption.

Carmen knew this all too well, which was why she hadn't breathed a word of Nico's invitation to her mother. The very idea of Carmen venturing out into the night, unaccompanied, to a place like the Madreselva would have sent her mother into a fervent storm of disapproval.

But there had been something about Nico's infectious enthusiasm that had been hard to resist. He had made the Madreselva sound like a magical place, a hidden corner of the world where music and passion reigned supreme, where the rules of propriety and class seemed to blur beneath the veil of night.

As she mulled it over later that afternoon while writing in her journal, Carmen couldn't help but wonder what it might feel like to experience that kind of freedom. For once, to step out of the neat, constraining lines of her life and into a world of spontaneity and possibility.

"Madreselva…" she whispered to herself, tossing the name around on her tongue. The name even *sounded* provocative, carrying a rebellious thrill that she couldn't quite shake.

She imagined herself there, bathed in candlelight, the soft hum of music curling through the air like smoke. She could almost feel the starched crispness of the table linens beneath her fingertips, hear the low murmur of conversation blending with the clink of glasses and the faint, sweet tang of cigar smoke drifting lazily overhead.

It would be her first real taste of a world beyond the narrow borders of her daily routine, a fleeting glimpse of the kind of life she had only ever encountered in the pages of books.

Stories had always been Carmen's only refuge. Novels, poetry, philosophy, they were her maps to other worlds, an escape hatch from the quiet monotony of her days. Every evening, she would devour books as if starving, losing herself in tales that carried her across oceans and eras. Stories that introduced her to women who dared to live, and men who challenged fate. Between the lines, she found courage, rebellion, longing, and the possibility of something more.

And when the stories of others no longer quieted the ache inside her, Carmen turned to her own words. She wrote with fierce devotion, spinning poems and fictions where she was no longer the obedient daughter, or the weary seamstress. On the blank page, she became bold and brilliant. Defiant, daring, and free. Her little writing desk, worn and ink-stained, was her secret doorway. And through it, she stepped into a life she had not yet lived, but refused to stop imagining.

Yet, there were moments when the call of the world outside her window felt too strong to resist. The oppressive stillness of her small tenement room, the suffocating weight of expectation, it all pressed down on her like the heavy summer air. Sometimes, the freedom of the night, with its cool breezes and starlit skies, seemed to promise something she couldn't quite name, but desperately longed to reach.

Nico's invitation hung in the air, tempting her, as if she were a bedouin, lost and starving in the desert, and his proposition a bright, juicy lure, dangling before her in a lush, forbidden oasis. Montevideo's lively nightlife and the allure of the unknown beckoned her now, promising a taste of the excitement and new adventure that she desperately craved. Yet, her mother's stern warnings echoed in her mind, a constant reminder of the risk of condemnation and the boundaries she was expected to adhere to.

"If only I were a man," she thought glumly, her fingers trailing over the spine of her well-worn journal. Carmen envied the ease with which men like her friend Nico, or her cousin, Rafael, moved through the world. They had the freedom to wander the city streets, to linger in the company of friends, to indulge in drinks and dance with anyone they pleased, women or men, without a second thought.

Rafael, a tall, thin, effeminate young man with a penchant for gossip, had always been Carmen's best friend and favorite cousin. As a man, and with his charismatic, easy going demeanor, Rafael's world was one of open doors and boundless horizons, while hers felt hemmed in by propriety and caution.

She imagined him now, his carefree laughter echoing through the bar's smoky air, his charm lighting up every room he entered. And yet, here she was, a young woman relegated to the shadows, her desires tethered by the expectations of what it meant to be *respectable.*

She thought back to her mother's solemn admonishments, the words heavy with unspoken fears: *"A young woman out in the night invites trouble,"* her mother would say, her voice like a locked door. It wasn't just a warning, it was a decree, drawn from a world that had little mercy for women who dared to step outside the lines.

But Carmen yearned for more than safety; she craved life itself, the kind that pulsed through the streets of Montevideo after dusk, like the seductive sound of the *bandoneón*.

As she stood by her window, the cool night breeze carried with it the faint sound of music and laughter. As Carmen gazed out at the flicker of gas lamps in the distance, her envy of Rafael turned into resolve. For once, she wanted to be the one with stories to tell.

Let the gossips wag their tongues, she thought decisively. *If this city has adventures to offer, why should they only belong to the men?*

Despite all her mother's warnings and the weight of societal expectations, the temptation to defy them, even just once, was strong. Her eighteenth birthday felt like a threshold, a moment brimming with quiet defiance and possibility.

The Madreselva called to her, not for its glamour, but for what it represented: a portal out of the ordinary, a glimpse of something electric and free. It would be her first brush with the world she'd long dreamed of, where the humdrum routine of her reclusive life in the *barrio* gave way to something extraordinary.

Carmen made up her mind: *she would go.*

But she knew better than to venture out alone. Respectability was a currency, and hers would already be worn thin. If she were to cross that invisible line and enter the night on her own terms, she'd need to carry at least a sliver of plausible decorum with her. And as it turned out, it was Nico—playful, careless Nico—who had handed her the perfect excuse.

"Look, it's simple," Nico said, snapping his fingers like the answer was obvious. "Your mother's let you out before, hasn't she? Like the time you and Rafael went to see *The Peace of 1904* at the Salón Rouge? Just tell her he's taking you to the cinema again. Say it's his birthday treat for you. Then he brings you to the Madreselva instead. Who's going to question you for spending your eighteenth birthday with your dear old cousin?"

It wasn't a bad idea. Her mother had indeed allowed Rafael to escort Carmen on select, tightly supervised outings in the past, his presence as a male relative adding just enough veneer of propriety to make the arrangement palatable. She knew it would mean lying to her mother, but it was the only solution.

Rafael would know just how to appeal to her mother, who had always seemed to favor him over Carmen. She also knew that her mischievous cousin would likely leap at the chance to escort her, especially if it involved defying her mother's strict rules. Rafael, with his charming smile and devil-may-care attitude, also knew the ins-and-outs of all the clubs around town, which made him the perfect companion for Carmen's first foray into Montevideo's bustling nightlife.

"Fine," Carmen said, exhaling as though she'd just made a dangerous pact. "But only if Rafael agrees, and only for a little while."

"That's my girl!" Nico grinned, rapping his knuckles lightly on the nearby countertop. "Trust me, you won't regret it."

The next day, the morning sun hung low, casting a soft, golden light over the worn cobblestones of the quiet streets of Barrio Sur. Carmen and Rafael sat side by side on the front stoop of her house, their legs brushing slightly as they passed the *mate* gourd back and forth. The earthy aroma of *yerba* mingled with the distant scent of horse manure from a nearby courtyard.

Their mothers were off at church, whispering their sins into the darkness of the confessional. In their absence, the *barrio* held its breath in a hush of peace, the kind that wrapped around them like a shawl.

She hesitated, fingers tapping her skirt, eyes fixed on the steam curling up from the gourd in Rafael's hands. She'd been turning Nico's invitation over in her mind all night, and now, in the calm of morning, with Rafael beside her, the question felt too ripe to ignore.

"Rafa," she began, trying to sound offhand, "you doing anything tonight?"

He raised an eyebrow, passing the *mate* back to her. "Tonight? Nothing tragic. Why, what are you plotting?"

She smiled into the cup, watching the herbs swirl like secrets. "Well... it is my birthday."

He grinned. "Of course, *boluda*, I said happy birthday this morning, remember? I was going to tease you about finally catching up to me."

She nudged him with her elbow, emboldened now. "Thanks. But...well, Nico invited me to the Madreselva tonight. You know, the new club where he works. He says it's nothing fancy, just music and dancing, but...I don't know, I thought it might be fun." She lifted the *mate* to her lips, drawing slow, careful sips through the silver *bombilla* until it gave that familiar gurgle of air, signaling it was empty. With a soft sigh, she handed it back.

Rafael took it gingerly, tilting it in his hand like a crystal ball. His lips pursed in exaggerated thought as he leaned back against the stucco wall, lips pursing in mock thought. "The Madreselva, *eh*? Word is it's got spirit. New place. Bit rough around the edges, but alive."

"I'd never go alone, of course," she added quickly. "And you know how my mother is. She'd call both the police and the priest."

He let out a low chuckle. "*Ah*, so that's what this is," he said, giving her a sidelong glance. "You want me to sneak you out like some runaway nun, *eh*?"

Carmen looked at him, eyes wide with mock innocence. "Maybe."

Rafael raised an eyebrow, feigning deep contemplation as he folded his arms and leaned lazily against the wall. "Hmm… I don't know, *Carmencita*," he said, drawing out the words with playful drama. "You? Out gallivanting around town?" Rafael gasped theatrically, clutching his chest as if she'd just confessed to a grave sin. "What would the knitting circle say? *Ay, Dios mío*, your dear mother might summon the Holy Ghost itself to smite me right where I stand!"

With a wicked grin, he reached for the cast iron kettle and poured more hot water into the *mate* gourd, his movements exaggeratedly delicate, like a priest performing a sacred rite. The comical look on his face made Carmen laugh despite herself, her earlier nerves easing just a little.

She met his eyes, serious now. "*Dale*, please, Rafa. Just this once. I want to see that side of the city, the side you always talk about. Where no one's pretending, and people live like they mean it."

He sighed, theatric and loud, like she'd just asked him to carry her on his back across the Pampas. "You make it impossible to say no, you know that?"

"Is that a yes?"

Rafael paused to take sips of *mate*, savoring the suspense, then a sly grin crept across his face. "Fine. But if your mother finds out, you better be prepared to do all the talking while I do the running."

Carmen laughed, her heart lifting. "Deal."

"Alright then," he said, reverently pouring another stream of hot water into the *mate* and handing her the gourd with a mischievous glint in his eye, "tonight we enter the forbidden underworld. But you owe me, *Carmencita*…big time."

She smiled, cradling the warm *mate* in her hands. "You won't regret it."

But even as she said it, a flicker of doubt passed through her. Tonight wasn't just about fun. It was about crossing a line she'd always been told never to approach. And there was no turning back once you stepped into the fire.

"Anyway," Rafael said with a wink, nudging her lightly, "it's about time you spread your wings. Who knows, maybe one of us might finally snag ourselves a handsome bachelor."

It was a joke laced with truth. Carmen smiled, but the warmth in her chest was laced with a quieter ache. Rafael's romantic preferences were a secret kept between them, tucked beneath his charm, quick wit, and the easy confidence he wore like armor. In a country where conservative expectations ruled with quiet brutality, his truth could cost him his life.

In Montevideo, to be different was to be in danger. Carmen knew it in her bones. The whispered gossip. The sudden silences. The way entire lives could be shattered by a single cruel accusation. Rafael had never said it outright. He didn't have to. She had seen it in the way he looked away when men spoke of women like trophies, in the way he flinched when someone asked why he wasn't married yet. How she wished they lived in a world where he could be free to love without caution. But for now, all she could do was walk beside him, quietly loyal, fiercely protective; his silent ally in a world that wouldn't understand.

Back on the stoop, Rafael shifted gears with a grin. "We'll just tell your mother we're going to dinner," he offered breezily. "Not a lie. We'll eat something. We'll laugh. Just… not exactly the version she's picturing."

Carmen gave a half-smile. "That'll work. As long as we're together, she won't ask too many questions." She paused, then added softly, "I hate lying to her, Rafa. But if she knew the truth… you know she'd lock the door behind me."

Rafael nodded, more serious now. "*Ya sé*. But sometimes, *prima*, you have to choose your own freedom. You're not wrong for wanting one night that belongs just to you."

As Carmen prepared to leave that night, a flutter of nervous anticipation stirred beneath her ribs. She'd chosen her dress carefully: something simple, elegant, the kind that whispered confidence rather than shouted it. It hugged her in all the right places but left nothing boastful behind.

She didn't want to stand out.

Not yet.

She wanted to slip into the night like ink into water. Present but unnoticed, free to observe, to feel, to breathe without explanation. Drawing too much attention might invite questions. From the room. From her mother. From herself. And tonight, she needed freedom more than approval.

She waited nervously by her bedroom window until she saw Rafael walk up. As she paused at her bedroom door, her hand hesitating on the doorknob, she could almost hear the clucking of tongues and see the disapproving stares of the matrons who sat knitting on their stoops by day. She shook her head, silencing her own thoughts.

The pull was too strong to ignore now.

She was determined to see this through.

When Carmen stepped into the front room to answer the knock at the door, her mother was in the kitchen, hunched over a simmering pot of lentils. The scent of garlic and onion hung in the air, mingling with the low clatter of the wooden spoon against the pot.

"*Mamá*," Carmen called out casually as she opened the door to reveal Rafael, who was already grinning. "Rafael and I are going out for dinner tonight."

From the stove, her mother turned, spoon still in hand, eyes narrowing. "*Ah si,* and I suppose you think I was born yesterday?" Her tone was laced with suspicion as she wiped her hands on her apron and studied the pair of them, eyes sharp as a hawk's.

"*Mamá*, it's just dinner," Carmen replied, trying to keep her voice light, measured. "Rafael's coming with me. You know I wouldn't go alone."

Rafael stepped in with practiced ease, his charm warm and theatrical. "Hola, *Tía*," he said, striding forward gallantly to kiss his aunt on the cheek. "Nothing scandalous. I'm just taking her to that new *café* near the plaza. I hear they have *milanesas* almost as good as yours."

Her mother sighed, turning back to her pot with deliberate slowness. The wooden spoon resumed its orbit. "You know how people talk, Carmen."

"I promise to return her at a very respectable hour," Rafael said, pressing a hand to his chest with mock solemnity.

Carmen offered a small smile. "Rafael just wanted to treat me," she said softly. "After all, it's still my birthday, *Má*."

Her mother didn't flinch. Her brow arched higher. "*Ah, claro.* Because the cake your aunt made, the candles, and your whole family singing to you this afternoon wasn't enough for you, *no*? You always need more. Always chasing something." She shook her head in disapproval.

Then she turned, pointing the spoon like a weapon. "You," she said, eyes locked on her daughter, "still live under this roof. You may think you're grown, but don't think for a *second* you're too grown to forget what decency looks like. Girls wandering around at night earn themselves a reputation they can't wash off."

Carmen held her mother's gaze, calm, composed, but unyielding. No roll of the eyes, no defensive words. Just quiet resolve.

"You only turn eighteen once, *Má*," she said gently. "Please, I'll be careful. And I'll be home soon."

Her mother didn't reply. She turned back to her lentils, stirring in slow, heavy silence.

It wasn't submission. It was control. The kind her mother could recognize, even if she didn't like it. A silence settled between them, thick with everything neither of them was willing to say.

Rafael cleared his throat again, this time more awkwardly. "We'll be back before the bread rises, *Tía,* I swear it."

Her mother studied them both for a long moment, her eyes narrowing just slightly. Then she exhaled, the sound sharp as steam escaping a kettle.

"I swear, the two of you will be the death of me," she muttered. Then, reluctantly: "Fine, go. But if I so much as hear a whisper from the neighbors, *just one*, you'll both be peeling potatoes until your fingers blister."

"Got it, *Mamá,*" Carmen said quickly. She flashed Rafael a frantic look, seized his arm, and tugged him toward the door before her mother could change her mind.

Her mother muttered something under her breath, returning to the pot with a dramatic huff.

"And you better not drink!" she shouted after them.

"I won't!" Carmen called back just as the door slammed shut behind her.

Outside, the cool night air met the flush of her cheeks like a blessing. She exhaled, shoulders sinking. "Well," she said, "that went better than I expected."

Rafael grinned, looping her arm through his. "Easy. She didn't even throw the spoon at you this time. Now, let's enjoy the night. *Your night.*"

Carmen clutched her purse a little tighter, her steps quick and quiet beside him. Her heart was racing, not just with nerves, but with something else. Excitement. Freedom. The sense that something new might be waiting just around the next corner.

The streets of Barrio Sur were alive at night in a way they never were during the day. Above her, the stars pulsed in the Montevideo sky like notes from a distant song she had not yet learned the melody to.

The *barrio* stoops, normally vantage points for gossiping families and watchful elders, now sat empty. Their stern mutterings were replaced by the faint strains of a guitar drifting from a distant courtyard, mingled with the sounds of laughter and conversation and the clopping sound of horseshoes and carriage wheels along the cobblestones.

The air was thick with the scent of grilling meats from the *parrillas* and the faint, intoxicating aroma of aromatic beers and wine. A lone lamplight flickered on the corner, casting long shadows that seemed to dance along the walls. Carmen walked quickly, her eyes scanning the street ahead. Each step felt like a small rebellion, a quiet assertion of her own will against the rigid confines of propriety.

"Don't worry, *prima*, you're not alone," Rafael laughed, sensing her unease and giving her arm a reassuring squeeze. "We'll have a great time."

Carmen nodded, taking a deep breath to steady her nerves. Wrapping her shawl tightly around her shoulders, stepping forth into the cool embrace of the evening, her footsteps soft against the paving stones.

"*I'm really doing this,*" she thought to herself.

The confidence Carmen had carefully stitched together throughout the day was beginning to unravel at the seams. A flicker of doubt tightened in her chest, and the thrill of rebellion started to slip into the edges of panic.

She turned to Rafael, her voice low, threaded with apprehension. "Rafa… what if my mother finds out we're going to a nightclub? You know how she gets about these things."

Rafael offered her a crooked, reassuring smile, the kind only cousins could give when bound by shared secrets and impossible mothers. "Oh, I know, *prima*. You know my mother's the same way," he said, rolling his eyes. "If she had it her way, I'd be in bed by nine and married to a girl from the church choir."

They both laughed.

He touched her arm gently. "*Mira*, Carmen, sometimes you've got to take a few risks. Live a little. Bending the truth isn't the same as breaking it." He offered a reassuring smile. "We'll stick to the plan. We say we went to dinner, and maybe that we caught a show at the Teatro Solís. Harmless."

He gave her a wink. "She doesn't need to know every detail. Not everything has to be confessed to earn forgiveness."

Carmen nodded, her shoulders easing slightly. "You're right. It's just…people talk." She glanced ahead, voice dropping to a murmur. "And you know how she is. To her, places like the Madreselva are nothing but dens of sin and scandal."

Rafael chuckled softly, shaking his head. "The older generation always thinks joy has to be paid for in guilt." He turned to her then, eyes lit with something tender and true. "But tonight… I think you'll see it for what it really is. The music, the dancing, it's not about vice. It's about belonging. About connection. It's a celebration of life, Carmen. And there's nothing sinful in that."

Carmen had wrestled with the guilt of her decision. The idea of sneaking out to the Madreselva, of stepping into a world her mother would never condone, was both thrilling and terrifying. She respected her mother, loved her even, but she also longed for something more than the cloistered life that her mother seemed to envision for her. Her mother's life, marked by early motherhood and a loveless marriage, was a constant reminder of what Carmen desperately sought to avoid. The weight of her mother's choices, the unfulfilled dreams, and her daily struggle constantly loomed over Carmen like a dark cloud.

But as they turned a corner, the lilting strains of music suddenly drifted out into the night like a promise. Candlelight flickered behind windows, laughter hummed beneath the melody, and for a moment, the heaviness in Carmen's chest began to lift.

Rafael glanced at her with a knowing grin. "Looks like we've found the place."

As they neared the club, Carmen slowed, letting the moment stretch. Twinkling lights framed the doorway, casting a warm, amber halo over the sidewalk. The door stood ajar, and from within, the sultry strains of tango music drifted out: *bandoneón*, piano, and violin mingling in a bittersweet melody that seemed to beckon her inside.

The name *Madreselva* curled across the front window in gold paint, catching the flicker of the gas lamps like fire on glass. Through the panes, Carmen glimpsed shadows dancing, glasses clinking, laughter rising like smoke in the candlelit haze. The air buzzed with something alive, an energy that tugged at her chest like a secret waiting to be claimed.

Her mother would never understand. This was a world built on pulse and pleasure, not permission. And yet, as Carmen stood at the edge of that glowing threshold, something deep inside her stirred. This wasn't just rebellion. It was freedom.

They're going to judge me no matter what, she reminded herself.

She drew a breath, straightened her spine, and stepped toward the music.

The moment Carmen stepped through the door of the Madreselva, the world tilted. The scent hit her first: sweet smoke, spiced wine, and something darker, like secrets steeped in old wood. Then came the music: a sultry pull of the *bandoneón* that seemed to rise from the floorboards themselves, wrapping around her spine like a silk ribbon drawn taut.

"Ah, it's a *milonga*," Rafael said with a grin, as they stepped into the Madreselva and took in the scene unfolding like a secret meant just for them.

Everything shimmered: the low amber lights, the gleam of polished shoes gliding across the floor, the flicker of candlelight reflecting off coupe glasses held by women in slinky dresses.

A *milonga*, a tango dance party, was already in full swing.

The dancers moved like they were born inside the music: close, deliberate, burning with an intimacy that made Carmen's breath catch. It wasn't just a dance. Each step seemed like a dare, a seduction, a story whispered skin to skin.

Rafael leaned in and whispered, "Well, *Carmencita*, welcome to the *forbidden side of the city*."

But she hardly heard him. Her eyes were fixed on the floor, on the woman in the blue dress whose heel hovered just above the ground before slicing back like a blade. On the man guiding her like a shadow that belonged to her body, not his.

Carmen clutched her purse, its strap digging into her palm, but her heart was soaring. She had imagined a hundred versions of this moment. None of them had looked like this. And yet, somehow, it felt like the first time she was standing exactly where she was meant to be.

Rafael wove deftly through the crowd, guiding Carmen to a small table nestled at the edge of the dance floor. From there, the entire room unfolded before her like a stage, and she couldn't look away. Couples floated past in seamless harmony, their bodies tethered in a tension that was both tender and charged. The air shimmered with heat and longing. The dancers didn't just perform; they confessed. In every lean and pivot, they surrendered pieces of themselves, unapologetically alive in their desire. It was beautiful. Brazen. And it stirred something in her, something wild, quieted too long by duty and doubt.

Something beginning to wake.

As Carmen and Rafael settled into their seats, they were greeted by a familiar face. Nico, who had just finished clearing up another table's glasses, spotted them and rushed over, his face lighting up with excitement.

"*Hola,* you made it! I'm so glad you decided to come," Nico exclaimed, pulling Carmen into a quick hug and shaking Rafael's hand enthusiastically.

Carmen smiled, feeling the warmth of Nico's genuine happiness. "We couldn't resist your invitation, Nico. This place is amazing, it's even more lively than I imagined."

Rafael nodded in agreement. "The atmosphere here's great. We're glad we came."

Nico beamed with pride. "Isn't it? I knew you'd love it. I'm telling you, this place has a special kind of magic. Let me get you both something to drink. Tonight's on me!"

As Nico slipped away toward the bar, Carmen took a cautious glance around the room. The club was filled mostly with men and a scattering of middle-aged couples, none of whom she recognized. Aside from Nico, she was easily the youngest person there. And yet, no one stared. No one seemed to notice her at all.

The air buzzed with music and motion, the dancers utterly absorbed in the rhythm, their bodies attuned to the beat and to each other. Conversations were quiet, movements deliberate. It was as if the entire room breathed in time with the *bandoneón.*

For a moment, Carmen exhaled, her nerves giving way to something steadier. In a place so alive with sound, she found unexpected comfort in being invisible.

Rafael leaned in, his voice low and edged with something like reverence. "I'm glad Nico convinced us to come. The *milongueros,* they're a breed of their own," he said, tilting his chin toward the dancers. "You know, the *milonga* is really a form of quiet rebellion, if you think about it."

Carmen turned to him, curiosity dancing in her eyes. "Rebellion?"

He nodded, his smile softening into something thoughtful. "Think about it. Tango was born in the shadows. *El tango criollo.* Out of the docks, the *conventillos,* the brothels. Back when the *barrios* were alive with immigrants and outcasts. Africans, *gauchos, mestizos…* people with nothing but rhythm in their blood and stories in their bones. They weren't invited into the gilded salons, so they created their own spaces, their own rules."

Rafael tilted his chin toward the dance floor, his voice dropping as though the moment deserved reverence. Couples glided past, their bodies close, movements sharp and tender all at once.

"Look at them," he murmured. "Every step, every pause, it's more than just a dance. It's…a way of saying: *we're still here. We feel, we dream, even when the world would rather forget us.*" His gaze softened, almost wistful. "Tango takes all the grief, the hunger, the longing…and turns it into something beautiful. It's survival set to music."

Carmen felt his words settle inside her like music she'd always known but never fully heard. "You're right, it's not just a dance," she whispered. "It's a language."

Rafael's grin returned, wicked and warm. "Exactly. And we speak it, you and I. We've got that same deviant spirit running through us, *prima,*" he said with a wink.

She felt a flush of exhilaration rise in her chest, a quiet bloom of recognition. Before she could reply, the band shifted tempo. The music softened into something tender, but no less magnetic. On the floor, a new group of dancers met in a deliberate embrace.

Carmen turned, caught in the spell once again.

The dancers moved with such grace and purpose, their faces lit with quiet intensity. For the first time in a long time, Carmen felt a deep, comforting sense of belonging, as if the music itself was inviting her to step into its world.

Her fingers absently traced the fringe of her shawl as the thought settled into her bones, a slow warmth blooming in her chest. Here, surrounded by music and movement, by people who wore their passion, defiance, and history openly, she felt something she hadn't allowed herself to feel before: *possibility.*

Her gaze swept across the room, catching the glow of laughter, the rhythm of feet in motion. Her eyes sparkled with something just beginning to stir.

"Nico was right," she said softly. "There *is* something magic about this place…"

Nico returned with two glasses of wine, placing them on the table with a flourish. "Here you go, our finest Malbec, in honor of our *Carmencita's* birthday. If you need anything, just wave me down."

"*Gracias*, Nico!" Rafael laughed, lifting his glass toward her. "Happy birthday, *prima*. Tonight is all yours."

Carmen raised her glass in reply, her smile soft but radiant. "*Chin-chin*! To new experiences… and unforgettable nights."

The first sip spread through her chest like warmth uncoiling. And as she set the glass down, the spell of the room swept her away. The music was a current, carrying her deeper, its rhythm pulsing through the floorboards. She watched the dancers glide past in seamless harmony, their bodies whispering in gestures and glances. It was more than movement, it was communion, as if each couple shared not only steps but a single breath.

Carmen felt her own breath catch, drawn into their orbit, spellbound.

It stirred something deep within her. Awe. Yearning. The dizzying thrill of possibility. Yet beneath the wonder was a thread of doubt. She wondered if she could ever move like that. So boldly, so sure of her own body, so fluent in a language she had only ever watched from the margins.

The thought both thrilled and terrified her.

"Do you want to dance?" Rafael asked, as though plucking the thought straight from her mind. His smile carried that familiar teasing spark, daring her to say yes.

Carmen hesitated, her pulse quickening. A wave of self-consciousness rose up, tightening her chest. "I don't know if I can dance like *that*," she confessed, her voice almost lost beneath the music.

Rafael leaned closer, his tone gentle but insistent. "Don't worry. Nobody's born knowing. You just have to listen. Feel the music, let it take you."

His words stirred a memory. Carmen had learned a few tango steps once, though not like this, not with the elegance she saw gliding across the floor.

She remembered laughing with her cousins in the street, their bare feet tracing patterns in the dirt as music drifted down from open windows. The adults sat in doorways smoking, talking, watching, while the children twirled each other with wild, clumsy joy until the sun disappeared and the *luciérnagas*, or fireflies, that they called *bichitos de luz* started appearing for them to chase around in the dark like fleeting dreams. It had been playful then, unpolished, but the rhythm had stayed with her. Now, under the spell of the *milonga*, that rhythm stirred again, waiting.

It wasn't unusual to see friends or family members pairing off on the floor, or even to see two men dancing together out on the floor.

Far from taboo, it was a tradition rooted deep in the early history of tango. Carmen remembered Rafael explaining it once, his voice low with pride as they watched the couples moving in precise, passionate sync.

"See those two?" Rafael nodded toward a pair of men locked in an intense embrace, their brows furrowed with concentration. "They're practicing. Tango is built on communication and trust, a conversation without words. To lead, you first have to know what it means to follow. To follow, you have to feel how it is to lead. Only then can the dance speak clearly."

Carmen nodded, understanding the importance of that kind of practice. It wasn't just about mastering the steps; it was about building a silent conversation with your partner. The thought made her smile, knowing that the dance floor was a place of both learning and connection.

Rafael turned to her then, hand outstretched. "Come on, *prima*. Your turn."

With a deep breath, Carmen took Rafael's hand as he led her toward the dance floor. Carmen felt her breath catch as the music swelled around them, the rhythm pulsing through her veins.

The emotive voice of the *bandoneón* was raw and aching, weaving through the air like a thread of memory, binding her to something greater than herself. It was impossible to resist. The music called to her, daring her to surrender, to let go of everything and simply lose herself in the music. Carmen closed her eyes for a fleeting moment, feeling the pull deep in her chest. It was the cry of *her people*: of their joys, their sorrows, their struggle, their endless search for something just beyond reach.

And tonight, she would answer it.

She took a breath, squared her shoulders, and stepped onto the dance floor.

As she and Rafael began to move, she focused on the rhythm, letting the music flow through her. Her steps were tentative at first, but gradually, she found her footing, her body responding instinctively to the beat. Rafael's steps were light yet assured, his frame steady but never rigid. His hand rested gently against the small of her back, guiding her with effortless precision. With each turn and pivot, Carmen's confidence grew, and the world around them blurred into the haze of music and movement. Suddenly, it was as if they were children again, twirling and laughing together with glee. The weight of expectation, of propriety, of the world outside the *milonga* melted away, leaving only the sheer joy of movement.

Carmen caught Rafael's eye, and he grinned, an impish, knowing smile that caused a bubble of happiness to float up in her chest. She couldn't help but laugh as he spun her effortlessly, the room a blur of light and music around them. For a fleeting moment, it was as if nothing else existed. No worries, no heartaches, no expectations.

Just the simple, present moment.

The sensation was intoxicating. The music guided their every movement, threading through her like electricity, until all thought fell away. And for the first time in what felt like forever, Carmen surrendered completely: to the rhythm, to the moment, to the fierce, undeniable pulse of her own heart.

Rafael must have sensed her shift, offering her a grin as they twirled. "You're a natural, *prima*," he said, his voice steady against the rise and fall of the *bandoneón*.

She smiled back, her heart soaring. For the first time, she let herself believe it might be true. Maybe she *was* a natural, not just at dancing, but at stepping beyond the careful borders of the cloistered life she'd been expected to lead.

Despite the rigid expectations pressing in from the world outside, the Madreselva offered Carmen another reality altogether, one where expression wasn't just tolerated, it was celebrated. The weight of her daily life, with its unspoken rules and quiet constraints, seemed to loosen at the threshold. In its place came something rare and intoxicating: a steady hum of freedom, alive beneath her skin.

The Madreselva and the secret pulse of the *milonga* had claimed her, subtly at first, and then completely, the allure of the dance weaving itself through her spirit until she was no longer the shy observer lingering at the edge of the floor, but part of the rhythm itself. A familiar face in the shadows, a presence moving in time with the music.

For Carmen, the tango became more than just a dance. The floor became a sanctuary where stories unfolded without words, where each embrace carried a new role, a new beginning. Slowly, the tango had stitched itself into her heart like an embroidery, each step a thread, each night another pattern in the fabric of who she was becoming. In that world, Carmen found her place.

The *Madreselva* had become Carmen's escape ever since.

Chapter 3

The late afternoon sun slanted through the storefront windows of the Madreselva, casting golden light across the floor and a soft shimmer of dust in the air. Carmen stepped inside, the weight of Francisco's marriage still fresh, like a bruise that hadn't yet surfaced.

It was early. The club was just beginning to stir awake for the night. Cherrywood tables, polished to a soft gleam, stood unclaimed, each one a tiny stage awaiting its story. The air held a hushed stillness, thick with the scent of old wood, aged wine, and the faint trace of yesterday's music.

It was a place that had once felt like a sanctuary. And yet today, it felt like walking into the memory of something that used to be hers.

It had been months since Carmen had stepped foot in the Madreselva, but Nico, who had been promoted to barkeep some years ago, didn't look surprised to see her as he looked up from wiping down the shiny mahogany bar top as Carmen sauntered into the club. She sensed a look of pity in his eyes.

"Pour me a cup, would you, Nico?" I'm going to the Ladies' Room."
She said, trying to sound upbeat as she made a beeline for the restroom.

A record played softly over a phonograph in the quiet bar. A solitary older couple Carmen didn't recognize practiced their tango steps silently, their eyes closed and their cheeks pressed together, feeling the movements.

The sunlight filtering through the storefront windows cast long shadows across the room. To Carmen, the dance floor felt strange and desolate in the harsh afternoon light, lacking the usual warmth of the flickering glow of candlelight and the vibrant energy of the *milonga*.

Carmen took off her hat as she stepped up to the vanity mirror. Surprisingly, she looked alright. She had often been told that she possessed a strong, arresting kind of beauty. Less delicate flower, more carved marble. Her face bore the proud lines of a Roman statue, all sharp cheekbones and quiet intensity. But it was her eyes that truly set her apart. Those hazel eyes, mercurial and expressive, shifting in hue with her every mood. In moments of joy, they sparkled golden; in sorrow, they deepened to the turbid color of the storm-tossed Río de la Plata.

At twenty-eight, she might not have been the most celebrated beauty in Montevideo, but there was something arresting about her. An effortless allure in her features, a warmth in her manner, and a quiet confidence in her stride that often made people look twice. People noticed her. Even when she tried to go unseen, she was the kind of woman that turned heads, though she never seemed to revel in the attention. Carmen wore her beauty like armor, not ornament. It had always been that way.

She smoothed her hair and gave her cheeks a quick pinch for color, a reflex born from countless nights spent freshening up between *tandas*, when the club pulsed with music, laughter, and watchful eyes. But now, the club lay dormant, its usually vibrant energy tucked away in silence and shadow. She paused, suddenly aware of the motion's futility. There was no crowd, no curious glances to return, no partner waiting by the floor. It was just Nico. Old habits, it seemed, were slower to fade than music.

Carmen returned to the bar and slid smoothly onto one of the red leather bar seats, where Nico had a little glass of Merlot waiting for her. "Hey, I heard about Piria," he said, genuine concern filling his big dark eyes, "I'm really sorry. This one's on me, ok?"

"Thanks, Nico." Carmen said, nursing the glass.

Carmen's mother was wrong, she actually rarely ever drank anymore, and she certainly didn't enjoy the feeling of being drunk. It had only taken one time for her to learn that lesson the hard way.

For Carmen, dancing had always been her truest escape, the only one she ever really longed for. There was something transcendent in the way the music rose around her, the aching sweetness of the *bandoneón* and the sweep of violins pulling emotion from deep within her chest. The melodies always seemed to move through her like a current, guiding her limbs without thought, each step lifting her higher, until she felt almost weightless, untethered. But today, she was thankful for the opportunity to drown her sorrows.

She peered over the rim of her glass, watching the old couple on the dance floor. It had been there, five years earlier, at the Madreselva, that she had first met Francisco, she thought darkly.

Ghosts from her memory seemed to fill the room, and it was as if she could see the club exactly as it had been that night. Couples had filled the dance floor, twirling and swaying to the seductive strains of tango music from the live band playing on a small stage in one corner of the club. The room had been buzzing with energy as people danced and chatted, sipping on their glasses of red wine.

Through tireless practice and an almost instinctual grace, Carmen had come to embody the essence of tango: its tension, its yearning, its fire.

By the time she had turned twenty-three, she had become one of the most sought-after partners on the *milonga* circuit, admired not only for her technical precision, but for the emotion she bled into every step. Each movement spoke of sorrow, of defiance, of dreams stitched into the soles of her shoes.

When Carmen danced, the room shifted. Conversations hushed, eyes turned. Every flick of her wrist, every sharp pivot or slow sweep of her leg carried a raw, magnetic force. She didn't just follow the music, she channeled it, as though the rhythm lived beneath her skin.

She danced not to please, but to speak, her movements a language all their own. Men lined up for *tandas* with her, drawn not only to her precision but to the fire she brought to every step, as if the music had been written in her bones.

Over time, necessity had taught her to spot the gleam in a man's eye before he even reached for her hand, the kind that had nothing to do with the dance. She could parry false praise with a single raised brow, sidestep suggestive remarks with a flick of her skirt. She knew too well that gallantry often wore the mask of entitlement. Her mother's words echoed like a curse she couldn't quite shake: *Men only want one thing,*

Carmen. Don't be naïve enough to think otherwise. The warning had taken root, winding itself tight around her sense of self until it became both shield and scar.

So she moved through the *milonga* with elegance but no invitation, her cool detachment a perfume no one could breach. A polite smile here, a nod there, a turn that left admirers chasing shadows. She never lingered after a dance, retreating instead to her perch near the bar, where Rafael's banter and Nico's dry humor formed her safe harbor. She never accepted drinks from strangers. A drink was never just a drink, she knew that well.

Instead, over time, she had learned exactly how to wield the attention. She wore her beauty like a shield and her silence like a blade. Let them look. Let them whisper. She owed them nothing. Not her time, not her laughter, and certainly not herself. If they asked her to dance, she would dance, but not to charm. She danced to learn.

Each *tanda* became a study in nuance. Every partner was a new dialect in the language of tango: some led with assertive precision, others with a subtle, fluid grace. Carmen absorbed it all, the firmness of a shoulder, the tempo of a breath, the whisper of a cue in the tightening of a hand. She learned to yield without disappearing, to follow without surrendering herself. Each time she stepped onto the dance floor, she was deliberate. Elegant. Unreachable. And in that, there was power.

The *milonga* had been at its peak that night, the music thick and slow, like honey poured over candlelight. The scent of wax, wine, and perfume lingered in the air, curling into every soft breath between songs.

Carmen stood at her usual spot near the bar at the back of the hall, arms folded loosely, her expression composed, distant, a slight sheen of sweat cooling on her collarbone. The last *tanda* had left her breathless, her pulse still echoing faintly in her ears. Rafael, ever gallant, ever in motion, had stepped away to work with one of the younger dancers, patiently guiding him through the mechanics of the cross-step. Carmen watched them for a moment, a soft smile playing at the corners of her mouth. Rafael danced the way he lived: lightly, without ego, full of warmth and mischief. It was never about being seen, it was about feeling alive.

She turned, eyes sweeping the room with ease, until, across the salon, a glance caught hers.

A *cabeceo*. A head tilted slightly, just enough to make the invitation to dance unmistakable.

Not one of the regulars. Not the familiar crowd of neighborhood dancers and their well-worn habits. He was young. Immaculately dressed. Clean-shaven, with slicked hair and a navy suit that looked newly pressed. He stood at the edge of the dance floor, back straight, chin slightly raised as he surveyed the room like a man familiar with attention.

Carmen didn't respond immediately.

She tilted her head just subtly, watching him. There was something familiar about him. Not his presence, exactly, but the echo of it. She remembered him from another *milonga*, a few weeks ago, when Rafael had wanted to check out *El Alma del Sur*, the smoky salon tucked behind the old hotel near the port. The young man had danced with nearly every woman there, sharply, confidently, and just a little too loudly.

Martín? Marcos? She couldn't remember his name. Only that he'd been introduced with a bit of a flourish by someone who clearly thought well of themselves. A visiting instructor, maybe. Or someone who wanted to be.

She remembered watching him that night, his flawless posture, the flourish in his steps, the slight tension in the way he clasped his partners' backs. He danced like he knew exactly what tango was supposed to look like. But not what it felt like.

Still… she hadn't danced in this *tanda* yet, and the band had just started playing one of her favorite songs. And she was curious. Curiosity was a weakness of hers.

She gave the smallest nod. A gesture so subtle only those trained to see it would catch it. He smiled instantly, smug in the quiet way some men wore certainty, and crossed the room toward her.

"*Buenas noches*," he said, offering his hand like he was extending an invitation to a stage, not a dance.

"*Buenas*," she replied coolly, placing her fingers in his.

Let's see if you lead as well as you look, she thought.

He led her onto the floor with the kind of theatrical flourish that made Carmen instinctively tense, and placed his hand at her back, guiding her into the embrace with just a bit more pressure than necessary.

Technically, he was flawless. His posture was perfect, his steps crisp. But he pushed. He steered her like a passenger, not a partner. Every movement felt dictated, not shared. She tried to inject softness into her steps, to carve space for the music to breathe, but he rushed through the silences. He overled, underlistened. And whenever she dared to add the smallest flourish of her own, he tightened his hold in subtle correction.

His fingers gripped, not guided. He moved with the certainty of someone who had practiced steps to perfection, but forgot to learn the woman in his arms.

Carmen felt herself drifting. Not into the music, but out of the moment. Her face stayed composed, elegant. But inside, she was already walking away.

By the end of the first song, she knew the rest of the *tanda* would be endured, not enjoyed.

He didn't notice.

When the final note faded and they stepped apart, he guided her back over to her spot by the bar without asking, and lingered beside her.

"You dance very well," he said, smoothing his lapel like he expected the compliment to be returned immediately. "Not bad for someone who's clearly self-taught. You're the seamstress, right?"

Carmen arched a brow, one corner of her mouth twitching.

He continued without waiting. "You're light on your feet," he said as they stopped, brushing an invisible wrinkle from his jacket. "But I could tell you haven't trained formally at the *Academias*. You know, you'd be something remarkable with a little real training," he added. "You've got the natural sensuality, it just needs discipline. I'd be happy to coach you sometime."

She turned to him then, gaze steady. "And what would I be without your discipline, I wonder?"

He didn't catch the tone.

He leaned one elbow on the bar, angling himself to keep her hemmed in. "Don't worry, I'll make you look good. It's easy for a woman to look good when she's following a man who knows exactly what he's doing."

Carmen kept her eyes averted towards the edge of the dance floor, where Rafael was still conversing with his last dance partner, letting the silence stretch before she spoke again.

She gave him a slow, elegant blink, then tilted her head ever so slightly, her expression unreadable.

"*Ah*," she said lightly, crossing her arms. "And here I thought we were both dancing."

She took a sip of her water without breaking eye contact, letting the silence fill with its own verdict.

Nico, polishing glasses just behind the bar, choked back a laugh.

The young man's smirk faltered.

He chuckled, missing the point entirely. "A woman needs a strong lead. You give her too much space and the whole thing falls apart. Of course, when you've practiced with the best it becomes second nature. You know how to lead with precision, how to control the floor."

"Is that what you were doing out there?" she asked, tilting her head. "Controlling it?"

He nodded with pride. "Exactly. You have to command the energy of the space. That's what separates an *aficionado* from a social dancer."

"Strange," Carmen said, her voice cool and composed as she turned slightly away, "I always thought the best leaders knew how to listen."

She didn't wait for a response.

Instead, she reached over the bar, where Nico, ever watchful, ever wordless, was already sliding a small glass of Malbec her way. Their eyes met briefly. He raised a brow in quiet question.

Carmen gave him a little nod, small, but clear: *I'm alright.*

Nico said nothing, only gave her a subtle tilt of the head and moved to serve another guest, like a shadow slipping across the floor.

She took a slow sip of the wine, letting its warmth settle low in her chest, grounding her. The wine was bold and dry. No frills. No sweetness. Just the truth, in full.

Unlike him, she thought.

Men like him weren't dangerous, not exactly. But they didn't see you. They saw the image of you. The one they could mold into their rhythm, their story.

He smirked, as if amused. "That's where we differ, I think. I lead. Always have. In business, in dance. It's what sets me apart."

"You're very proud of yourself," she said, voice dry as cracked parchment.

He laughed, but there was a flicker of something uncertain in it. "Shouldn't I be? Women always tell me I'm the strongest lead they've danced with. It's why people remember me."

He said it without irony, clearly expecting her to agree. To offer some small admission of awe or gratitude. She didn't.

She leaned in, close enough that only he could hear her next words. "Listen, *eh…*"

"Marvin," he said.

"Marvin," Carmen echoed, her tone deliberate. She set her glass down with slow precision, the faint clink of crystal punctuating the silence. Then, leaning in just enough to let her words land, she said, "Let me give you something worth remembering: *not every man who leads knows where he's going.*"

His smile faltered, only slightly, but she was already walking away to join Rafael, who had just finished his conversation with his partner.

Behind her, the young man was still lingering, likely trying to calculate whether he'd just been dismissed.

He had.

As she passed the mirror near the bar, she caught her reflection: spine tall, face calm, eyes still burning.

Not every invitation is worth accepting, she reminded herself.

She made her way toward the far side of the bar, where Rafael was laughing with someone over a glass of beer, the rim already smudged from conversation. His presence, like always, was a balm. Warm, steady, familiar.

But then, midstep, she felt it.

Like a subtle change in music. The sensation of a thread being pulled.

A glance.

She shifted her gaze and found him, their eyes locking from across the room.

Dressed elegantly and seated at a private table on the mezzanine level at the far side of the dance floor, sat a man she didn't recognize outright, yet who somehow stirred within her a strange familiarity.

He was older, but not ancient, silver streaking the edges of his hair, a trimmed beard softening an otherwise commanding face. He wasn't laughing. He wasn't surrounded by women. Wasn't trying to be noticed.

But he was watching.

Not hungrily.

Not arrogantly.

Just… intently.

He was conversing with a man standing next to his table and they seemed to be looking in her direction.

Rafael pulled her in gently by the elbow at the bar, his voice low, meant only for her. "He's been watching you all night, you know."

"Has he?" Carmen replied, feigning disinterest, but she couldn't help it. Her eyes flicked back toward the far end of the room.

Yes.

He was still watching her.

Not staring, not leering. Just *present*. Composed. Like a man listening to music only he could hear.

"Who is he?" she asked, her voice quiet, edged with curiosity she didn't bother to disguise.

Rafael grinned, tilting his glass toward the gentleman. "Are you kidding? None other than *Francisco Piria*."

Carmen's brow lifted slightly. Of course she'd heard the name. Who hadn't? The eccentric businessman, the merchant-turned-industrialist, a man with money, strange ideas, and a flair for drama. Some said he built cities. Others said he disappeared for months chasing dreams that belonged in novels. A man who could fund an opera and vanish before opening night. The newspapers were always circling him, and so were the whispers.

But Carmen didn't buy into gossip. She had learned long ago that the louder the story, the emptier the truth. In her neighborhood, storytelling wasn't just a pastime, it was an art form. It was a place where gossip spread like wildfire and rumors took on a life of their own, each tale more embellished than the last.

From the elderly *abuela* who spun tales of days gone by to the mischievous *niños* who concocted fantastical adventures, everyone had a story to tell and an eager audience to listen. It was a place where reality blurred with fiction, where the line between truth and exaggeration was often obscured. And yet, there was a certain magic in the air, a sense of camaraderie and community that came from sharing stories and weaving dreams together.

"Haven't you heard?" Rafael went on, "Apparently he's buying up land left and right, I heard he's developing a new resort hotel around here somewhere. They say he's some kind of sorcerer, you know. A wizard or something."

Carmen snorted softly. "I've heard the name, of course, but what do you mean, he's a *wizard?* Rafa, don't be ridiculous." Carmen scoffed, smirking coyly as she reached over to grab the glass of water Nico was handing to her across the bar, nodding at him in thanks.

"I'm serious," Rafael said, eyes twinkling. "They say he built a whole town on the coast, carved it out of nothing. Designed it like some kind of spiritual map. Numbers, symbols, geometry. People say he lines up buildings with the stars. Hotels with hidden floors. A shrine hidden in the hills."

"Sounds more like a man with too much money and too much time on his hands," she replied, though something in her stomach tightened.

"Hey, Marí, isn't it true what they say about Piria?" Rafael asked, nudging their friend María Rodino, a plump middle-aged woman sitting at the bar, engaged in lively conversation.

María, with her sparkling eyes and infectious laughter, was already on her third glass of wine. She was gesturing animatedly as she recounted a particularly amusing story, her words occasionally slurring but her enthusiasm undiminished. Her husband, Antonio, a stout man with a hearty laugh, was nursing a tumbler of whiskey, his cheeks flushed and his eyes twinkling with the effects of the alcohol. They had been chatting with another couple, but María whirled around on her barstool at the chance to engage in some juicy gossip.

"Piria? Oh, yes! They say he's an *alchemist*! They say he doesn't age, you know. That he went to Europe to study hermetics. That he writes with invisible ink and signs his business deals with moon phases!" María chortled. Her round face was very flushed, and she was clearly a little drunk. She and her husband's love for good wine and strong spirits was well-known among their friends, who had grown accustomed to their lively, sometimes boisterous presence at social gatherings.

"Rafa, have you heard the latest?" María asked, leaning in, her eyes alight with mischief.

Rafael arched a brow, clearly humoring her. "Ah, Marí, you know how the grapevine works in this town. What scandal has our wealthy recluse stirred up now?"

"Well," she began, lowering her voice for effect, "Marta, you know, the florist at the Mercado del Puerto, swears Piria's been buying up rare herbs. They say he's using them to brew potions and conduct strange experiments in the hidden laboratory of his castle."

Carmen scoffed, rolling her eyes. "Potions and experiments? Marí, you know people love spinning tales about the rich. It's probably nothing."

María smirked. "Oh, *querida*, you're far too skeptical." She turned toward Rafa, ignoring Carmen's dismissal. "Don't you remember the rumors a few years back? About him turning lead into gold? Alchemists do exist, you know."

Rafa widened his eyes in exaggerated wonder. "Yes, yes, very mysterious indeed!" he said, his tone dripping with mock drama.

Carmen laughed, shaking her head. "Marí, your imagination is running wild. If anything, the man's just buying herbs for trade."

"Well," María countered slyly, "the whispers say otherwise. They claim he's searching for the philosopher's stone."

Rafael chuckled. "The philosopher's stone! Now that's a tale straight out of a novel. As if he's not rich enough already!"

María leaned closer, her voice dropping to a conspiratorial whisper. "It's not just about seeking wealth, Rafa. They say what he's after is *eternal life*."

Rafa lifted his brows, playing along. "Eternal life, you say? Could it be true?"

María nodded gravely. "That's what people are saying. And some even believe he's already achieved it."

"Oh, Marí, you always bring the juiciest stories," Rafael said with delight.

María sipped her wine, her eyes glinting. "Laugh if you want, but there's something strange about that Piria. I'm not the only one who thinks so, the whole city is buzzing with curiosity."

Carmen rolled her eyes again, though this time with less conviction. "He's eccentric, that's all."

"Maybe," Rafael allowed, tilting his chin toward the far side of the room. "But look at him."

And she did.

Don Francisco hadn't moved. Still at his table. Still watching, not with ownership, but with presence. With awareness.

"There's something strange about him." Rafael murmured, nursing his beer.

Carmen said nothing. Because Rafael was right. There was something curious about him.

She stole another look at the handsome older gentleman, admiring him from afar. He didn't look like the other big shots who wandered into the Madreselva once in a while, eager to collect dancers like trophies. He wasn't loud or pompous. He wasn't flashing a gold pocket watch or scanning the room for something to own. He just sat there, composed, relaxed, a glass in hand, watching the dancers not with hunger, but with thoughtful, quiet attention.

Amid the blur of dancers and the shimmer of candlelit shadows, their eyes found each other again across the room.

He was still a stranger, yet something in his gaze stirred a quiet recognition in her, an inexplicable pull she could neither name nor resist. Even from a distance, he carried a gravity all his own, a presence that felt carved from stories left untold. He drew her as the tide draws the shore: subtle, inevitable, unrelenting. With every heartbeat, the invisible thread between them tightened. In the golden wash of candlelight, his dark eyes glimmered with mystery.

Then, almost imperceptibly, he inclined his head: a *cabeceo*, the traditional gesture, an invitation spoken without words. A question posed in silence.

Carmen's pulse fluttered. She knew the ritual well; she had been invited before by other men in the same manner, their glances woven into the unspoken language of the *milonga*. Eyes met, a nod given, the silent thrill of acceptance. But this—his—was different.

It wasn't just an invitation to dance. It felt like a call.

She hesitated, for just a second. Enough to remind herself she could say no. She could retreat behind her wall of wit and distance. Shake her head. Decline with grace. Walk away. But something in her body moved before her mind could protest. Her eyes softened, barely, and her chin dipped, tilting her head in a slight nod back, accepting his proposal.

Yes.

The gentleman rose from his table, murmured a quiet excuse to those around him, and began moving toward her. His unspoken invitation lingered in the air, heavy with promise.

"Rafa… he's coming this way," Carmen whispered, her voice barely audible over the music. Her cheeks burned, her pulse leaping with every step that closed the distance between them.

The orchestra's prelude deepened, the *bandoneón*'s low cry threading through the room like smoke. Rafael sucked in a sharp breath.

"Go on! This is your chance to investigate!" he urged, giving her a playful shove toward the floor.

Heart hammering, Carmen rose to meet him at the edge of the dance floor. The air between them crackled with a strange inevitability, a magnetic pull neither seemed able to resist. Step by step they drew closer, until at last they stood face to face, only inches apart. In that suspended moment, the dancers, the music, the candlelit crowd, all of it seemed to dissolve. The world narrowed to just the two of them, caught in the quiet gravity of a single gaze.

"*Señorita,*" he said, nodding his head nobly and extending his hand.

His voice rumbled in a smoky, baritone timbre. His commanding presence exuded a timeless charm, and his eyes seem to hold the secrets of a thousand stories. In that fleeting, electric moment, Carmen felt eager to uncover the mysteries hidden within those enigmatic eyes. She nodded, silently placing her hand in his. His hand felt warm and secure as he gracefully guided her out to the dance floor.

The band launched into a passionate tango, the first notes of the *bandoneón* curling through the air like incense rising from an altar. As they stepped onto the floor, time seemed to bend around them. The music slowed, cloaking the room in a soft veil. The crowd receded into shadows, the lights melted into a golden blur.

What remained was a sanctuary of rhythm and breath, where all that was left were the space between their bodies, the haunting cry of the *bandoneón*, the brush of their shoes against the floor, and the steady thunder of their hearts.

She draped her left hand over his shoulder, steadying herself, while he placed his hand lightly at the small of her back. Not possessive. Not coaxing. Just present. When she set her right hand in his, she felt the steadiness there, the patience, the way he seemed to wait, not to lead, but to listen.

The melody deepened, and they began to move. Their steps unfurled in quiet harmony, gliding in time with the bittersweet pulse of the music. He danced with the grace of a man who had long mastered the language of the body. Though his temples carried silver, his movements were assured and elegant. Each step, each pivot was a question and an answer, given in the same breath. He did not drag her forward; he met her, matched her. He held when she yielded, released when she pulled away. Like he knew the fortress around her heart and had no intention of storming it, only to waltz at its gates until she decided to open them herself.

And for a few heartbeats, Carmen forgot. She forgot the weight she carried, the careful distance she kept, the years of silence folded into her chest. In his arms she was only breath and movement, fire and surrender. She, who had spent so long guarding every glance and gesture, felt her edges blur, her defenses softening. In his arms, there was tension, but not the kind that threatened. It was the pull of curiosity, the spark of recognition, like two untold stories brushing against the same page for the first time.

For a few precious minutes, there was no past, no future, no poverty or privilege. There was only the *bandoneón*'s pulse, and the exquisite illusion that they were flying.

The *tanda* ended before she realized it was over.

As the final note echoed through the room, they both stood sharing a breathless, lingering gaze, their breaths heavy, the chemistry between them palpable.

Carmen stepped back, her breath catching at her ribs, a slight warmth brushing across her cheeks.

She couldn't meet his eyes just yet. Not because she was shy, she never let herself be that, but because something had shifted during that dance. Something small, quiet, and dangerous.

She had danced a thousand *tandas* before: casual, forgettable, automatic. But never like that. Never with someone who really listened through the music instead of just moving to it. This man didn't lead with force; he invited. Like every step was a question. Every pause, a promise not to rush her.

For some reason, that scared her more than if he'd tried to control her.

He held her hand for a moment longer than necessary, his touch lingering like a song that didn't want to end. Then, gently, he let go.

"That was extraordinary." he said, looking into her eyes.

"Yes, it was." Carmen said breathlessly, forgetting herself for a moment, her voice husky.

"Francisco Piria de Grossi," he said, tipping his head nobly and extending his hand, palm open, waiting, not assuming.

She hesitated a beat, then placed her hand in his. "I'm Carmen. Carmen Ruiz de Suarez."

"It's a pleasure, Señorita Carmen." he said, gazing at her with a warm smile. His voice, deep and resonant, carried an innate magnetism, and she couldn't help but be drawn in. His hand was warm and strong, and Carmen felt a deep sense of familiarity as he took her hand in his.

He didn't kiss her hand, thank God, but he held it gently with an elegant bow, just long enough to make her pulse skip before releasing it.

A sense of self-assuredness and charisma seemed to emanate from Don Francisco, and he moved with a graceful and confident stride that belied his age. As they stepped off the dance floor, he gestured toward his private table, adorned with a flickering candle and two glasses poised, waiting for company.

"Would you do me the honor of joining me for a drink? I feel we must toast to the beauty of the tango we just shared."

Carmen didn't respond right away. Her lips curved into the hint of a smile as she tilted her head, eyes narrowing just enough to make him wonder. "You always talk like that?"

He smiled, low and warm, like a secret shared only with her. "Like what?"

"Like you're a character in some old novel." She smirked.

Francisco chuckled, the sound low and effortless, like he wasn't at all offended. "Maybe I am," he said, his dark, brooding eyes twinkling with amusement. "And maybe you just stepped right into the middle of it."

She liked that he didn't flinch. Liked that he could meet her sharp edges without trying to smooth them over.

Still, she tilted her chin, testing him.

"I don't usually take drinks from strangers."

"Then it's fortunate we've already met."

"A *tanda* hardly makes us friends."

He nodded slowly, not disagreeing. "No, but it's a start."

She studied him then: his face, marked by the subtle lines of age, told a story of a life well-lived. His skin, though weathered by time, retained a healthy and sun-kissed complexion, hinting at a life filled with adventure and experience. The little flecks of black in his silvery-gray hair, the patience in his posture, the way he waited for her to come to him rather than trying to pull her in. It wasn't a tactic. That's what made it worse. It was sincerity.

And sincerity made her nervous.

She narrowed her eyes, pretending to think it over. She looked past him, where couples had returned to the floor, slow and smoldering under dim golden light.

She could slip away right now, pull Rafael out the door and disappear down the street like she always did, back to safety, to silence. But her feet didn't move.

She wasn't sure what held her there, whether it was his voice, the softness in his eyes, or the echo of their last step together on the floor. In that moment, a thousand questions danced through her mind, a whirlwind of intrigue and fascination.

Who was he? She wondered. What stories did his heart hold? What secrets did he carry beneath that handsome façade? And what was a man like him doing at the *Madreselva*, of all places?

She blinked, lips twitching despite herself. She could have said no. Should have. But her feet moved before her doubt could catch up, and suddenly she was following him back to his table.

She told herself she was only doing it because her friends had told her to. That it was just one drink. Nothing more. It wasn't like she hadn't played this game before, conversing just enough to keep the mystery alive, always knowing when to draw the line. She'd get the gossip, and then go back to the safety of the sidelines.

She looked back at Rafael and María, their eyes wide as they watched her walk off with their mysterious villain.

They made their way up to his table, where Francisco gallantly pulled out her chair. He waited for Carmen to take her seat, and then followed suit, taking his place across from her, his dark eyes gazing back at her in the candlelight.

Carmen shifted uncomfortably as she sat across from him, careful to smooth her skirt and sit straight. She was used to spinning across the dance floor, laughing with Nico and teasing her friends at the bar. But there, on the small platform of the mezzanine, unease crept into her chest. The chair beneath her was too soft, the tablecloth too crisp, too white, untouched by wine stains or careless elbows. From this perch, the Madreselva seemed distant, as though she were peering into someone else's world.

"I want you to try something of mine," he said, tipping a dark, fragrant liquor into her glass. The liquid caught the glow of the candlelight, rich and amber. "It's a cognac, from grapes grown in my very own vineyards. Made with the same care as the best in Europe." His voice rumbled low, steady, as his dark eyes glimmered in the flicker of the flame. "I think you'll like it."

Francisco poured the cognac with the kind of ease that said he'd done it a thousand times before. His hands didn't tremble. His movements were smooth, almost reverent.

She watched him, unsure of how to sit, how to be. *What the hell was she doing?*

He was too old. Too rich. Too something she didn't even have a word for. And she was… well, she knew exactly what she was. A poor seamstress from Barrio Sur. A girl who smelled like cheap soap and old fabric, who had learned the tango barefoot outside on dirt roads while wild dogs ran around, nipping at her heels.

Then he handed her the glass, and for a moment, their fingers touched.

"To the dance that speaks the language of the heart, and to new connections forged in its passionate embrace." he toasted, raising his glass to her.

Carmen clinked hers against his. "And to walking right into old novels."

His deep laugh rumbled softly in his chest. She liked the sound of it more than she meant to.

They drank in silence for a moment. The *milonga* swirled around them, dancers drifting past like ghosts, music humming through the walls, laughter blooming like flowers in the background. But at their table, time slowed.

As they sipped, their eyes met in a shared moment of quiet appreciation.

Francisco's eyes were arresting. Deep and discerning, they burned with a quiet intensity that spoke of years lived and lessons learned. There was a gravity to them, a kind of knowing that made it hard to look away.

When his gaze met hers, it was as if he saw straight through the layers she so carefully wore. It unsettled her, the way he looked at her, not with possession, but with perception. And yet, despite the discomfort it stirred, Carmen couldn't help but be drawn in. There was something in that gaze that made her feel both exposed and seen.

"I have to say, I couldn't help but be captivated by your radiant energy on the dance floor tonight. What brings you to this *milonga*, *Señorita* Carmen?" he asked.

Carmen lifted her glass, letting the rich cognac catch the glow of the candlelight, like an amber gem held between her fingers. She didn't answer right away. She was good at that, making silence feel like a choice.

Her eyes flicked toward him, sharp and unreadable, the corners of her mouth tugging upward in the ghost of a smile.

"What makes you think I came looking for anything at all?" she replied.

Francisco returned her look with quiet ease. "Everyone comes to the *milonga* looking for something," he said. "Even if it's just to forget."

That made her smile, for real this time. "Well then, maybe I came to forget that I've got nothing worth remembering." There was no bitterness in her tone, just a simple truth polished by use.

But Francisco didn't flinch. He leaned in slightly, folding his hands on the table as if her words deserved a place between them. "I don't believe that," he said. "Not for a moment."

Carmen arched a brow. "Forgive me, Don Francisco, but you've known me all of five minutes."

"And yet," he said, "I've seen how you carry every step like it means something. That kind of fortitude doesn't come from nowhere."

She hesitated, the cognac suddenly tasting stronger. She wanted to say something clever, to laugh him off like she did with everyone else. But the way he looked at her, like he wasn't asking for performance, just presence, unsettled her.

"I come here because I like the music," she said finally with a shrug, her voice quieter now. "Because dancing feels like... freedom. Like I get to be someone else for a few minutes."

Francisco nodded slowly as he savored a sip of the cognac. "You know," he said finally, setting his glass down, "you're very good."

She froze slightly, eyes narrowing. "At dancing?"

He tilted his head. "No, at hiding. But yes, also at dancing."

Her first instinct was to run away. Retreat into her armor. *Not this again. Another man who thinks he's figured me out.* But she didn't.

She looked down into her glass, taking a long sip. "I'm not hiding anything."

She expected him to play the same old game. A clever man with careful eyes, speaking like he was peeling back layers no one else could see. Like he was the first one to notice she was more than just pretty steps and quick wit. They always thought they were special. That they could name the truth of her before she'd spoken it.

But Francisco didn't press. He didn't smirk, didn't gloat as others might have. He said nothing. Just sipped his drink, gazing at her quietly with those same dark eyes.

She hated that. Hated how his silence felt like permission. Like he was letting her lie, but not believing it. That quiet steadiness that made it hard to tell if he was actually trying to seduce her, or just listening. Somehow, that unsettled her more than flirtation ever could.

"You don't know me," she said quietly.

"No," he answered, just as soft. "But I'd like to."

Something twisted in her chest, and she looked away, turning her gaze out towards the dance floor. A knot she thought she'd buried under years of knowing better.

Something about him was disarming, gentle without being weak. She wanted to turn away. Wanted to tell him to leave her alone. But instead, she asked, "What exactly is it that you think I'm hiding?"

He didn't hesitate.

"A burning fire. With a fortress built around it."

Her breath caught. She turned her head slightly, just enough to see the quiet certainty in his eyes. No one had ever said something like that to her before.

She met his gaze then, really met it. And what she saw there wasn't pity or curiosity. It was recognition. As if he'd built a fortress, too, once. As if he knew the architecture from the inside.

There was a depth in his expression, a stillness that hinted at a life lived fully, privately, and perhaps painfully.

For a moment, neither of them spoke. The noise of the *milonga* faded into the background. And in that quiet, Carmen felt it: the strange sensation of being seen, not just clearly, but kindly.

It was terrifying.

So she took another sip and smiled with a tilt of her head, slipping back into her mask.

"Careful, Don Francisco. You're starting to sound like a man who wants to save someone."

"And you, Señorita Carmen," he said gently, "sound like a woman who's convinced she doesn't need saving."

This time, she didn't smile. Not right away. But something in her chest cracked a little, just enough to let the music back in. Maybe it was the way he said her name like it mattered.

She shifted the conversation gently, her eyes narrowing with curiosity. "And what about you?" she asked. "What brings a man like you to a place like this? It's not every night someone of your...stature wanders into the Madreselva."

Francisco's smile unfolded slowly; wry, knowing, as if he'd been waiting for the question. He took a measured sip of his cognac, then let the glass linger in his hand, its amber contents catching the candlelight.

His gaze drifted toward the dance floor, where bodies moved in rhythm beneath the flicker of worn chandeliers.

"I came here for the same reason you do, I suppose," he said. "To escape. To feel something that isn't buried in numbers or boardrooms or long, echoing halls filled with empty conversation."

Carmen tilted her head, intrigued despite herself. There was something disarming in the way he said it; too honest, too human for a man who carried himself like a figure out of a more polished world. She leaned back slightly, studying him.

She raised an eyebrow. "And what is it exactly you're trying to escape?"

He looked at her then, not with a flirtatious glance, but something quieter, more reflective. The kind of look that didn't reach for attention, only truth.

"Expectation," he said simply. "Legacy. The kind of success that looks good in the papers but feels empty when you're alone."

Carmen blinked, caught off guard. She hadn't expected the walls to come down so easily. People like him usually guarded their vulnerability like a safe: hidden, locked, and buried beneath layers of performance. But Francisco offered his like a quiet invitation.

"Shouldn't you be at some grand ball tonight," Carmen asked, arching a brow as she leaned back in her chair, "waltzing with a Countess in pearls, instead of here with me?"

Francisco chuckled, low and warm. "You're right," he said, swirling the cognac in his glass. "I could be at some private salon, where everything tastes expensive and means nothing."

He glanced toward the floor, then back to her.

"I've danced with women like that: elegant, graceful, practiced. Lovely partners. But they move like porcelain, with each step counted, all while trying to keep every hair and ornament in place." He paused, the flicker of candlelight catching in his dark eyes.

"They don't dance with their *soul*," He said, his dark eyes earnest. "Nothing like how we danced together here tonight."

Her throat tightened. The words landed with the weight of something too real. She glanced down at her glass, suddenly aware of how close she'd let him. And Carmen, for the first time in a long while, didn't know what to say. So she drank instead. And didn't notice how close her glass was to empty.

Out on the dance floor, the music shifted. A new *tanda* began. Something slow and aching.

"Tell me," Francisco said, his tone light but sincere, "beyond tango, what else stirs you, Carmen? What are your passions, outside the dance floor?"

She tilted her head, eyes narrowing just slightly, that familiar calculating glint flashing beneath her lashes. The kind of look she wore not for vanity, but protection.

She leaned back, trailing her fingertip slowly along the rim of her glass, letting the silence stretch just enough to make him wonder. She wasn't stalling because she didn't have an answer, but because she wasn't sure she wanted to give it.

"Why do you want to know?" she asked finally, a wry curve tugging at the corner of her mouth. It wasn't quite a smile, more like a challenge dressed as charm. "Most people are only interested in what I can do out on the dance floor."

Francisco chuckled, unbothered by the deflection. "I'm just trying to get to know the woman I'm talking to, beyond the music."

She glanced at him then. She felt a flicker of something. Vulnerability? Temptation? It passed quickly, replaced by the familiar tilt of her chin; pride, carefully disguised as indifference.

"I write," she said finally, softly. "Mostly for myself. Notebooks full of things I never show anyone."

He didn't respond right away. He didn't need to. His stillness was permission enough to keep going.

"Poems, little scenes. Fragments I scribble down when I can't sleep." She took a sip of her drink. "Sometimes I think it's the only place I ever tell the truth."

Francisco's gaze deepened, his smile fading into something quieter, more reverent.

"And what do you write about?" he asked gently.

She shrugged, but there was a weight to it. "The things I don't say out loud. The things I feel when I'm dancing but can't name." She let out a soft breath, eyes fixed on the candle's flame between them.

Francisco's expression didn't change; he didn't pity her or flinch. He just listened.

"I write about pain, mostly. Things I don't understand until I write them down," she continued, her voice low, steady. "Of why people leave. Of what it means to stay. Of why some of us build walls, and others spend their lives trying to tear them down."

Her eyes flicked up to meet his. "Of the weight a single word can carry. Of how silence can be louder than shouting."

She gave a short laugh, soft and bitter. "I know, it's not very cheerful."

Francisco shook his head. "It's honest," he said. "Which is rarer than cheerful."

Carmen watched him for a beat, her guard relaxing just slightly.

Francisco's mouth curved, not in humor, but with something closer to reverence.

"A writer and a tango dancer…" he said slowly, as though tasting the thought. "It's rare enough to master one art, but you live in both. Both speak of a deep connection to the human soul."

His eyes glimmered with curiosity as he leaned forward, intent on her in a way that felt disarming, as though he were seeing her more clearly than anyone had before.

"I'm intrigued to know, as a writer, do you have any favorite authors or books that have left a lasting impression on you?" He asked, gazing at her intently with those deep, penetrating eyes.

Carmen paused to reflect. "Well, the poetry and essays of Esteban Echeverría have always resonated with me. I've always been very moved by his poem *La Cautiva.* One of my very favorite lines is: *The harmonies of the wind speak clearer truths than philosophy vainly attempts to teach.*"

"Ah, yes, Echeverría," Francisco asserted, "One of the lines that has always stuck with me comes from his essay *El Matadero: Perhaps the day will come when it will be prohibited to breathe fresh air, take a walk or even chat with a friend, without permission from the competent authority.*"

Carmen studied him for a moment, caught off guard by the depth of his response. Something in her began to loosen, her defenses softening just enough to let the silence between them settle. It was rare, this kind of stillness, like standing in a room where no one was pretending.

"It's chilling, isn't it?" she said quietly. "How Echeverría was warning us about totalitarianism long before the word even existed. He saw it all coming: the blind obedience, the way fear gets dressed up as patriotism." Her voice carried both awe and unease as she spoke, her mind turning over the brutal imagery of *El Matadero*, a story written nearly a century before their time, yet hauntingly familiar.

"It's almost prophetic," she continued. "Especially now, with all the tension between the *hacendados*, the wealthy landowners, and the cattle farmers, the *estancieros*. The story doesn't feel like history, it feels like a warning we still haven't learned to heed."

"Indeed," Francisco said, leaning in, his eyes sparkling, "Tell me Carmen, what inspires you to write?" he asked, taking a sip of his drink.

She let out a soft breath, eyes fixed on the candle's flame between them. "Sometimes," she said, "I write about beauty. The kind that sneaks up on you when you least expect it. A song that stops you in the middle of the street. The way someone looks at you like they see something worth saving."

Her voice caught faintly at the end, and she masked it with a sip of cognac.

She was quiet for a moment. "I suppose I'm inspired by life itself, really. By people and their stories, the weight of their heartbreaks, the beauty in their resilience. And, of course, by tango. It tells its own stories through movement and music: of longing, loss, desire, and defiance."

"Yes, well, tango is truly a language spoken in silence, understood only by those willing to feel rather than speak. It's no wonder it inspires you." Francisco's voice was velvet over steel, warm, sincere, but with an undertone of quiet insistence that made Carmen's chest tighten.

Francisco leaned in slightly, his eyes never leaving hers.

"Well, I hope you keep writing," he said, his voice low and deliberate. "Because that's exactly the kind of beauty the world needs more of."

His gaze lingered, steady and intent. "And I believe, *Señorita* Carmen, that passions like yours aren't meant to be stifled. They're meant to be pursued."

Carmen's breath hitched, just enough that she felt it. The way he said it, not as a motivational platitude, but as a truth forged through fire, unnerved her.

She forced a smirk. "You say that like it's simple."

"It's not," he replied easily. "But it's essential."

She looked away, her gaze drifting to the flickering candlelight between them. The words she usually wielded so easily felt tangled now, caught somewhere between fear and yearning.

"Where I come from," she said quietly, "dreams aren't something you chase. They're something you outgrow." Carmen said, looking down into her glass.

Francisco said nothing for a moment. Then, softly: "And yet here you are. Still dancing. Still writing. Still burning with everything you're trying not to say."

She looked up sharply, eyes narrowing. "Well, now you're starting to sound like one of my poems, Don Francisco."

His laugh came warm and unguarded, a sound that seemed to linger between them. "Then perhaps," he said, leaning ever so slightly closer, "it's time you let the world read them."

Carmen stared at him, feeling that familiar tug inside her, the part of her that wanted to bolt, and the part that wanted to believe.

"Why does it matter to you whether I chase anything at all?" she asked.

Francisco's expression softened, but there was a gravity in his voice when he spoke.

"Because when I see someone carrying a light like yours, I can't help but hope they'll stop hiding it." He paused. "And maybe... because I remember what it's like to need someone to believe for you, before you believe for yourself."

Carmen looked at him, something breaking and blooming all at once in her chest.

"You see, Carmen, the beauty of our dreams is that they have a way of guiding us towards our true purpose. Dreams show us where the soul wants to go. They're not illusions, they're invitations. Find inspiration in the everyday, and let those experiences find their way into your writing. You already have a rare gift: the way your words breathe passion, especially when you speak of tango, is nothing to shy away from. With patience, with devotion, I have no doubt your dreams will not only endure, but take flight."

Carmen stared at him. Her lips parted slightly, but no words came. Not right away. Compliments she could brush off. Flattery she could sidestep. But this, this quiet affirmation, landed somewhere deeper, somewhere raw.

She laughed, softly, to cover the way his words landed.

"The thing is, Carmen, brilliant people don't come around often. And when they do appear, the world quickly tries to bury them before they realize how brightly they're burning."

Carmen felt her breath catch.

"Don't let it bury you," he added softly. "Let it fuel you instead."

For a long moment, she said nothing. Just sat there, staring at the man who saw straight through her without asking permission. And to her own quiet surprise, she wasn't angry.

She was inspired.

At that moment, a gentleman approached the table, leaning to whisper something in Francisco's ear. His expression shifted slightly as he listened to the whispered words, before turning to Carmen with a regretful smile.

"I'm afraid my partner and I are being called away to tend to an urgent matter," he said, rising with an apologetic smile. Taking her hand gently, he bowed his head just slightly. "Forgive the sudden departure, I've truly enjoyed our conversation and the pleasure of your company."

"Likewise, it's been a pleasure meeting you, thank you Don Francisco."

"The pleasure was all mine, *Señorita* Carmen. I hope our paths cross again someday soon." Francisco said, his expression sincere.

With a final nod farewell, he placed his tophat on his head and grabbed his cane, casting one last glance over his shoulder at Carmen before gracefully departing.

As Francisco disappeared through the crowd, his silhouette swallowed by smoke and music and the shifting tide of bodies, Carmen sat frozen for a moment. She couldn't quite place the feeling, but something had stirred within her. Something deep and quiet and long asleep.

She stayed seated at the little table for a moment, lost in her own thoughts, absently tracing the rim of her glass with one fingertip. The music had faded into background noise, and her mind wandered. Back to the dance, to his eyes, to the unspoken words lingering in the air like perfume.

Suddenly, a burst of laughter and hurried footsteps pulled her back to the present. Rafael and María appeared like a whirlwind, practically bounding up to her with wide grins and flushed cheeks.

"Carmen, *querida*!" Rafael sang, sweeping in with theatrical flair as he snatched a chair from the next table and spun it around, straddling it with casual elegance. His eyes sparkled with mischief. "So, how'd did it go? We need every detail about your encounter with the mysterious

Francisco Piria. Was he as devastatingly charming as they say? Did sparks fly? *Dale*, don't be stingy…spill!"

María leaned in beside him, her grin practically glowing. "Yes, tell us everything! Is it true he's an alchemist? Did he slip you a potion?"

Carmen laughed, unable to help herself. Their excitement was infectious. "Alright, alright. *Tranquilos*, both of you," she said, waving a hand as a playful smile tugged at her lips. "Let's not turn this into a melodrama. It was just a conversation, nothing more."

Rafael and María exchanged a look. The kind that made it clear they didn't believe a word of that.

"Oh, come on, Carmen," Rafael said, nudging her arm. "You're *glowing*. That's definitely not a 'just a conversation' glow."

María gasped dramatically. "Was it your drink? Was it enchanted? Did he speak in riddles? Did he ask your star sign while stirring a mysterious elixir?"

Carmen rolled her eyes, laughing. "I hate to disappoint, but no. No potions, no riddles, and certainly no sorcery. He was polite. Thoughtful. We talked, we laughed a little…he was a gentleman, that's all."

Her cheeks warmed, a blush she tried to wave off. But her friends were already leaning in, grinning like cats with cream.

"Right," Rafael said knowingly, tapping his finger against his chin. "There may not have been any mention of alchemy, but something was definitely bubbling…and don't even try to deny it, Carmen, because I can see *chemistry* from across a room."

The three of them burst into laughter, the sound spilling warm and easy between sips of wine. The teasing flowed as naturally as the music drifting through the room, Rafael and Marí sparring with playful jabs that only deepened their bond. Carmen smiled, letting their chatter wash over her—tales of reckless romances, half-true scandals, rumors whispered like contraband over steaming gourds of *mate*.

But as laughter echoed around her and music curled through the air like smoke, she felt something shift. She couldn't shake the edges of something unfamiliar tugging at her; a quiet flutter beneath the ribs, a warning, or a promise. Something dangerous, maybe. Or something true.

Carmen didn't sleep that night.

She lay in her narrow little bed, staring at the water-stained ceiling of her room, the old fan clunking in rhythm with her heartbeat.

Outside, the city murmured its usual lullaby: stray dogs fighting in the alley, muffled music from a neighbor's radio, the occasional drunken shouts of someone stumbling home too late. But none of it felt familiar. That dance had done something to her. It had opened a door she hadn't meant to touch.

She kept seeing his face. Hearing his voice.

"A burning fire. With a fortress built around it."

Damn him for saying that.

Damn him for seeing it.

She rolled over, pulling the thin sheet tighter over her body, as if it could guard her from whatever had stirred inside her on that dance floor. Francisco had looked at her like she was a mystery worth solving, not a problem to be fixed. And that was dangerous. That was worse than flattery. Because part of her wanted to believe him.

That was the part she had to shut down.

She wasn't used to being seen the way he saw her, like she was worth something. Like she wasn't just another girl with good legs and quick feet. And she didn't trust it.

Carmen rose from her bed, grabbing her old journal. Careful not to wake her mother, she quietly pulled out a chair and sat by the kitchen window.

She opened the shutters, the street outside her window was hushed now, all the city's restless breath stilled beneath the velvet dark. She could faintly smell the sweet fragrance of the night blooming jasmine climbing up along the outside of the house as the late night breeze whispered gently through the wrought iron bars safeguarding the window.

She kept replaying the memories of her evening encounter with Don Francisco over and over in her head, her mind and body still swirling with a whirlwind of emotions. An electric feeling seemed to buzz through her, and she hugged her arms tightly to her chest.

She thought of how their bodies had moved together so rhythmically as one, how his mysterious dark eyes had seemed to captivate her, how they seemed to have gazed right into her very *soul*. She thought about the ease and comfort she had felt in his presence. There had been a deep sense of familiarity and connection between them, as if they had been old friends.

No one, not even her mother, knew about the secret she guarded closest to her heart: her dream of being a writer. Even she herself had dismissed it, brushing it off as a foolish indulgence, a pastime meant for quieter moments and nothing more.

But somehow, Francisco's presence had stirred something dormant within her. His questions, his quiet intensity, had unsettled her, not with judgment, but with possibility. For the first time, she found herself truly considering the ambitions she had long buried beneath duty and doubt.

"Dreams show us where the soul wants to go," Francisco had said, that voice of his like worn velvet and old wine. *"They're not illusions, they're invitations."*

She had laughed at the time, deflecting with her usual sharpness. But the words had followed her home like perfume clinging to her dress.

She stared out at the empty street, one leg tucked beneath her. *What dreams?* She'd taught herself not to have them. In her world, dreams were dangerous. Dreams made people soft, made them wait for things that never came. She had learned early to want less, expect less, to make herself small in order to survive.

But something had shifted. She had felt it in her chest, in the way her feet had moved when she danced, in the way her body had leaned ever so slightly toward him, against her better judgment. Like a door had cracked open. Just a sliver. But enough for air to slip in.

And now she couldn't stop wondering.

What if this wasn't a mistake?

What if this, he, the dance, the invitation, wasn't a detour...but a beginning?

She hated how the idea took root. Hated how it made her feel like a girl again, foolish and wide-eyed. But beneath the fear, beneath the old armor and sharp wit, something else stirred.

Hope. Or something dangerously like it.

She lit a single candle on the kitchen table, the flame flickering as if it, too, were restless with wonder. The house was quiet, save for the soft scratch of her pen as she leaned over her worn notebook, the ink flowing as freely as her thoughts.

She didn't write about him exactly, not his name, not his face, but she wrote about the feeling. The spark. The strange electricity that seemed to settle beneath her skin the moment their eyes met.

She wrote:

September 1912 —

There are moments that do not ask for permission. Moments that breathe. Moments that lean in close and whisper secrets to your spirit. They arrive unannounced, shifting the air and shaking the bones, demanding to be remembered. Like a storm wrapped in silk, or a stranger whose glance knows the shape of your soul.

Tonight, I met a moment.

She kept writing all through the night, her passion fueling her creativity until the pale light of day filtered in through the curtains. Finally, she set her pen down, content that she had somewhat captured the essence of her evening. The magic, the emotion, the inspiration.

She closed her eyes.

Maybe meeting Francisco was a sign. A guide. A mirror held up to a self she'd long stopped looking for. And maybe, just maybe, the universe wasn't mocking her by crossing their paths.

Maybe it was pointing the way.

And though she would never admit it, not yet, not even to herself, Carmen had already begun to wonder what it would mean to follow that light.

Chapter 4

Carmen woke with a start to the sound of the front door creaking open and then slamming shut. Her mother, back from Sunday Mass. Heavy footsteps echoed in the main room, followed by the rustle of a shawl being thrown over a chair, the clatter of keys on the table. The house filled with a tension she recognized all too well.

Her mother was in one of her moods.

Carmen lay still for a moment, staring at the ceiling, bracing herself. Life with her mother had always been a delicate dance between affection and alienation, a pendulum swinging wildly between tenderness and reproach.

There were days when her mother was quiet and distant, retreating into a shell of stoic resignation. On those days, Carmen wandered the house like a ghost, careful not to disturb the silence. Other days, warmth would bloom like sunlight through a cracked window. Her mother would laugh over *mate*, telling stories from her youth, teasing Carmen with surprising gentleness. In those rare and precious hours, Carmen felt what it might be like to be truly loved.

But then there were the dark days, the ones where her mother's gaze hardened, where every word Carmen spoke was a provocation. Days when Carmen felt less like a daughter and more like a burden. As if her very existence was a mirror held up to her mother's regrets.

Carmen never knew which version of her mother she'd wake up to. The uncertainty made every interaction feel like walking a tightrope, one misstep away from collapse.

It was a strange thing, to love someone so fiercely and still feel like a stranger in their presence. But that was the rhythm of their life together: a cycle of hope and disappointment, closeness and withdrawal, like the tide washing in and pulling away before she could find her footing.

And today, judging by the sharp movements and muttering from the next room, the tide was already pulling back.

"*Carmen!*" Her mother's voice cut through the morning stillness like a blade. Sharp. Shrill. Inevitable.

So it begins, Carmen thought grimly, blinking herself awake. She sat up, eyes still heavy with sleep, and slipped into her dressing gown. Her bare feet padded across the cool floor as she shuffled into the main room.

She hadn't even crossed the threshold before the storm broke.

"Carmen Elena, what is this I hear about you being seen with *Don Francisco Piria* last night?" her mother cried, her voice rising with every word. "Have you completely lost your sense of decency?"

Her mother stood rigid, her hands shaking as she yanked the kerchief from her head. Her copper-brown eyes, already fierce, seemed to burn red when she was angry, and this morning, they were blazing.

"It's bad enough you've stopped going to Mass, and that you're out gallivanting around town with strange men at those clubs, at those hours. But now *this*?" she spat. "You've become the talk of the *barrio*, Carmen. Is that what you wanted? To be a spectacle?"

Carmen froze, her jaw tightening. She didn't answer right away. Years of tiptoeing around her mother's moods had trained her in the art of silence; measured, deliberate, strategic.

Of course the news had already spread. In a town like this, gossip moved faster than facts. Someone must have run their mouth. Maybe one of the old market women, or Marí with her flair for drama. And her aunt, always ready to stir the pot, wouldn't have hesitated to fan the flames.

Carmen could already hear the rustle of lace fans and the hiss of whispered speculation threading through the pews at Mass. It never mattered what really happened. Truth was always the first casualty in the court of public opinion, especially when a girl like her dared to step out of line.

It hadn't taken long before her mother had caught wind of the truth: that her daughter had been slipping out to dance most weekends.

The gossip had spread through the narrow streets of Barrio Sur like wildfire, fanned by idle tongues and sharpened by judgment. Every whisper was another cut, wounding her mother's pride and chipping away at Carmen's already precarious reputation.

"Did you hear about Carmen?" one neighbor would murmur to another, loud enough to be overheard. *"Out at night, dancing in those dens of sin like some shameless harlot. Her poor mother must be heartbroken."*

"It's no surprise," came the reply. *"A girl without a father? What do you expect? If she were my daughter, you'd better believe I'd knock that nonsense right out of her."*

Carmen knew too well what it meant for a woman to step into the night. In the eyes of the world, such a woman wasn't just bold, she was dangerous. Suspect.

A woman seen unaccompanied after dark was immediately branded: looking for trouble, or worse, *available for it.*

She had seen them, of course, those forgotten women of the night. The ones who moved like ghosts through the city's underbelly, cloaked in perfume and shame. The ones who slipped through the umbral corners of Montevideo, where decency turned a blind eye and sin was bartered in whispers. Women who, by choice or circumstance, had been pushed to the margins, their lives unfolding in the hush of alleyways and curtained rooms.

She'd heard the men talk, too, at family barbecues, on street corners, in the drunken lull of Sunday evenings. They spoke of the *putas* with lewd certainty, like they were commodities, not people. A quick fix when wives were pregnant or sick, or just too weary to fulfill their "wifely duties." Their vulgarity came wrapped in laughter, in smoke, in bravado. Carmen had always turned away from it in silence.

Everyone knew the rumors. There was a brothel somewhere on the seedy fringes of the city. And across the river in Buenos Aires, the cabarets and *casas de tolerancia* were said to sprawl endlessly, their crimson lights drawing ships like moths to flame.

But the Madreselva was not that kind of place.

Nico kept a sharp eye on everything. The moment he caught wind of anything suspicious—drunken troublemakers, shady transactions, wandering hands—he'd shut it down. Quietly. Firmly. The club had its pulse, but it also had its code.

Still, the weight of judgment was always waiting outside, heavy and suffocating.

Carmen always made sure Rafael walked her home each night. Not just for protection, but because it gave the gossips one less excuse to sharpen their knives.

But the rumor mill was still ruthless. People still whispered behind her back, their eyes lingering on her a little too long.

Carmen had heard the whispers before, noticed the sideways glances from older neighbors, the narrowed eyes of shopkeepers who would suddenly go quiet when she passed.

Respectable girls stayed home.

Respectable girls went to Mass on Sundays.

Respectable girls didn't waltz into *milongas* with the hem of their skirt brushing their ankles and fire in their eyes.

To the old guard, tango was more than music. It was a symbol of everything they feared: vice, violence, moral decay. Born in the working-class *barrios*, in brothels and crowded taverns, tango's raw rhythms and intimate embrace had long been dismissed as vulgar. It belonged to dockworkers, immigrants, Black musicians; the invisible threads of a society the elite refused to see.

But change was creeping in. With universal suffrage newly granted to all men over thirty, the voices of the working class were growing louder. Their customs, once mocked, began to emerge from the shadows. Even the *milongas* were transforming, no longer just dens of sin, but sanctuaries of identity and expression.

Carmen heard whispers that tango had even reached Paris, where the same elite who scorned it at home now found it exotic and chic. A bitter irony, but also a sign that the tide was turning.

Still, in Barrio Sur, the old judgments clung like smoke. Progress moved slowly, threading its way through music and fashion, while the older generation clutched tradition with white-knuckled fear. Carmen lived at the fault line, caught between a past collapsing and a future not yet born.

Every time she walked through the streets, the whispers followed. She kept her chin high. Let them talk, she thought. They always have.

Because Carmen didn't dance to be seen.

She danced to survive.

Over the years, her mother's resolve had begun to erode. The world was shifting faster than she could hold it still, and piece by piece, her iron will had softened into weary silence. What had once been fierce proclamations and sharp-edged judgments had dwindled into muttered resignations, the quiet laments of a woman watching the old ways slip through her fingers.

But the news of her daughter dancing the tango in the arms of one of Montevideo's high society was not just a disappointment. It was humiliation. Public, flagrant, unforgivable. That wasn't progress. That was scandal. And it cut deeper than any changing law or foreign fashion ever could.

The whispers had already made their way through the tightly woven streets of Barrio Sur:

"Did you see Carmen Ruiz? With the alchemist? And at a milonga, no less. Shameful."

"I always said that girl had too much imagination. Look where it's gotten her."

"They say he's dabbled in the dark arts. It's no wonder, all the ungodly convene in those kinds of places."

And of course, the neighbors had plenty to say to her mother directly.

"Really, Carmen!" her mother snapped, voice quivering with restrained rage. "Don't you understand that your choices reflect on our name? It's one thing to sneak off to those clubs, but to be seen entangled with a man like *Francisco Piria*? Do you have any idea what people are saying? You've thrown yourself into impropriety!"

Carmen stood her ground, her voice calm but firm. "I don't see what the fuss is about. Don Francisco was respectful. We shared a drink and conversation, nothing more."

"Nothing more?" Her mother's voice sliced through the air like glass. "You think this is just about a conversation? People *saw* you, Carmen. You know how it works here, no one waits for facts. The moment they catch a whiff of scandal, they write the ending themselves."

Carmen opened her mouth to respond, but her mother pressed on, voice rising with fury.

"You may be too naïve to see it, but men like Francisco Piria don't concern themselves with girls like you. He comes from a world that feeds on spectacle. And you—" she jabbed a finger toward Carmen, "you were just the entertainment for the evening."

"You're wrong," Carmen snapped, defiance flaring in her chest. "Don Francisco treated me with more dignity than anyone else in this town ever has. He listened. He saw me."

Her mother let out a bitter, humorless laugh. "*Saw* you? Please. Don't mistake attention for respect. Men like him don't *see* girls like you, Carmen. They use them. And when they're done, they throw them away like scraps."

Carmen felt the heat rise to her face, but her mother wasn't finished.

"Wake up. You think parading around at night with strange men makes you admirable? Makes you free?" Her voice dripped with contempt. "No one respects a girl who makes herself easy. And Piria? He may flirt with the gutter, but he builds statues for the ones who keep their place."

Carmen's throat tightened as her mother's words echoed through her mind, sharper than any slap.

Her mother had always known exactly where to cut.

It wasn't the first time they had clashed. Her mother had long disapproved of Carmen's choices, her defiance, her dreams. But this time, something had fractured. This wasn't just anger. It was rejection.

The wound bled silently beneath her ribs, raw and aching.

She tried to steady herself, clinging to a memory that felt like a lifeline: Francisco's gaze, steady, tender, unwavering. In his eyes, she hadn't been an embarrassment or a mistake. She had seen respect there. Possibility. A vision of herself untainted by judgment.

Surely, he couldn't have seen her the way her mother did, like something shameful, something disposable.

No. Their encounter had felt real. It had transcended rules and reputation, slipping past the heavy chains of expectation like light through a cracked door.

And yet, the question still gnawed at her: If he saw her so clearly, then why did it all hurt so much now?

The tension in the kitchen was thick enough to choke on, simmering beneath the hiss of the kettle and the sharp clatter of dishes. Carmen and her mother stood on opposite sides of the small, worn space, two immovable forces, both unwilling to bend.

Their voices had started low, clipped. But now they crashed like waves against stone, the old house echoing with things too long unsaid.

"I don't want to live a life built on fear and silence," Carmen said, her voice calm but resolute. "I have dreams of my own. And I won't let your shame, or society's ridiculous rules smother them."

Her mother's face hardened, voice rising like a whipcrack. "*Sos una ilusa, Carmen!* Get your head out of the clouds! You think a man like that could ever love a woman like you? No, *m'hija*. Men like that will use you. And when they're done, they'll throw you aside like trash. Keep dancing around town like some *brisca*, some tramp, showing your ankles and your ambition. See where that gets you! And don't you dare come crawling to me when you find yourself ruined and alone!"

The words struck like slaps, but Carmen didn't flinch. Her jaw tightened. Her spine straightened. And when she finally spoke, her voice didn't tremble, it burned:

"You know what? I'd rather be judged by people who never dared to dream than spend my life shrinking to fit a mold I never chose. You want me silent. Invisible. But I won't disappear. Not for you, not for anyone. If I get burned for standing in the light, then *so be it*."

A heavy silence fell between them.

Still groggy from sleep, Carmen flinched. For a split second, she thought her mother might actually reach for the rolling pin on the counter and bring it down on her skull.

Instead, her mother scoffed, snatching her purse from the chair.

"Suit yourself," she snapped. "I'm going to your aunt's. Stop standing there like a useless lump and pay the landlord before we end up in the street. You're lucky I even still let you live here."

Her mother's eyes raked over her, barefoot, still in her nightgown, with undisguised disdain.

But Carmen didn't move. Not yet. She stood her ground, the heat of her defiance still flickering in her chest. Because no matter what her mother believed, Carmen couldn't deny what had happened between her and Don Francisco. That connection had been real. And nothing, not fear, not gossip, not even her mother's rage, could unmake that truth.

But deep down, she knew the truth.

She was afraid.

Afraid he'd be there again. Afraid he wouldn't.

She didn't go back to the *milonga* that night. Nor the weekend after. She told herself it was the money. That the hem of her only decent dress was fraying, and she couldn't afford to buy the materials to mend it. She told herself she was tired, that her sewing work was piling up, that she had better things to do than play around in someone else's world.

So she stayed away. She made herself busy. She practiced alone in the kitchen, humming tango under her breath while the pot simmered on the stove. She tried not to think about the way his hand had rested on her back, warm and steady. Or the way he had waited for her answers without pushing for them.

She tried, but it didn't work.

Because even as she pulled away, part of her already knew: he'd gotten under her skin. Into the quiet places. And if she wasn't careful, he'd find the fire she spent years trying to bury. And then she'd have no choice but to run.

A couple of weeks later, Carmen returned to the Madreselva.

The air buzzed with the usual energy, the rustle of satin skirts, the low murmur of greetings, the familiar strains of a *bandoneón* warming up in the corner. But beneath the music and motion, there was an edge of restlessness in her. A quiet anticipation she tried not to name.

She wore the same shoes. The ones she'd danced in with him. Her hair was pinned the same way, loosely, like it might fall free with one well-placed turn. She told herself it was coincidence. Habit. But every time someone entered the room, her eyes darted toward the door.

Francisco didn't come.

She danced one *tanda*, then another, distracted. Her steps sharp, elegant, but missing the soft connection she'd known with him. Her mind wandered to his voice, his gaze, the way he had listened like every word she spoke had weight.

Still, he didn't come.

By the end of the second set, Carmen was no longer dancing. She stood by Rafael and Marí at the bar, nursing a glass of Malbec, pretending she wasn't watching the door. Pretending she wasn't unraveling just a little.

She kept her ears open as the latest gossip swirled around the bar, but there was no mention that Francisco Piria had been spotted at the *Madreselva* since.

With each passing moment, Carmen couldn't shake the nagging doubt that perhaps her mother had been right all along. Had her encounter with Piria been nothing more than a fleeting moment of amusement for him, as she had warned? Had she allowed herself to be swept away by a fantasy that had never truly existed?

She hated that she cared.

It made no sense, this feeling in her chest. They had shared one drink. A couple of laughs. A few glances that stretched longer than they should have. And yet, something in her had opened around him, uninvited.

She pulled her shawl tighter around her shoulders, her gaze drifting to the little table where they'd sat together, where she had let herself be seen.

Was it all in her head? A charming night. A wealthy man with poetic words and too much free time. Maybe he'd simply moved on. Maybe she was foolish for thinking it had been anything more.

Francisco lived in a world of polished wood and books with gilded pages. He had probably grown up with pianos in every room and was used to women who wore perfume that cost more than her rent. Meanwhile, she had grown up counting coins to buy bread and dodging men who looked at her like she was something to take, not something to learn.

She sat there long after the music faded, her heart quiet but restless. She wouldn't cry. She wouldn't chase.

But she would remember.

The way he had looked at her like she was a story waiting to be told.

The way, just for one night, she had let herself believe she was worthy of being written.

That was the problem. She had believed him.

And Carmen knew she couldn't afford to believe in people like that.

Because sooner or later, she knew the music stopped. And people like Francisco Piria always left when the lights came on.

Chapter 5

Carmen returned to the *Madreselva* most nights now. Not always to dance, sometimes just to watch. To breathe in the scent of old wood and wax, to let the music wind itself around her like a shawl. Her feet moved differently these days. Lighter. As if her soul had grown out of its cage and slipped into her steps.

But she didn't expect to see him anymore.

Three weeks had passed and Francisco had not returned.

She tried to convince herself it didn't matter.

The *milonga* had thinned to shadows and soft murmurs by the time Carmen reached the bar, ready to say goodnight to the evening, and to the foolish hope she'd been carrying like a secret beneath her coat.

Nico, wiping down the polished wood counter with a rag worn soft from years of use, glanced up just in time to catch the weight in her eyes.

He tilted his head, the corners of his mouth tugging into something between a smile and a sigh. "Come on, *amiga*, spill it. You've got that look."

Carmen blinked, feigning innocence, but her shoulders betrayed her with a small slump.

She hesitated, then let out a quiet breath. "Do you ever feel like someone walked into your life just to rearrange everything?" she asked, her voice barely louder than a whisper.

Nico gave a small laugh, but it was kind. "Yeah. And sometimes they don't even bother sweeping up after the mess they make."

Carmen smiled faintly, the kind of smile that hurt a little at the edges. "And then you're left to pick up the pieces, wondering if you imagined it all."

Nico's expression softened. He poured her a splash of something warm and golden, sliding the glass toward her. "You know, some people don't come into your life to stay, they just come in to shake the walls, to open windows you didn't know were nailed shut."

Carmen raised the glass slowly, the weight of it grounding her. She nodded, murmuring, "*Salud,*" before taking a quiet sip.

The liquor was smooth, its warmth curling down her throat like a quiet consolation. Carmen let the silence stretch for a moment, letting the sting settle, not from the drink, but from the truth of Nico's words.

She looked at him, grateful. "How did you get so wise, huh?"

He shrugged with a smirk. "Comes with the territory."

Just then, two familiar figures appeared through the crowd: Rafael, grinning ear to ear, and María's husband, Antonio, waving as they made their way to the bar.

"*Bo,* Carmen!" Rafael called, his eyes sparkling with mischief. "We're heading to Café La Giralda for a bite. Come with us! Marí's coming too, and maybe a few of the others."

At the mention, Carmen felt her heart lift. La Giralda had always been one of her favorite places in the city; warm and bustling, steeped in the hum of voices and the clink of glasses.

She could already imagine it: the scent of rosemary and pepper drifting from the kitchen, the comforting crackle of wood-fired ovens.

There, the *fainá a caballo* came out crisp and golden, chickpea flatbread laid like a crown over a slice of pizza. The *choripán* arrived still sizzling from the grill, tucked into crusty Italian bread and dripping with sharp green *chimichurri*. And for dessert, there was always temptation: homemade *helados* in glass dishes, or her weakness, *postre alpino*: layers of chocolate sponge cake and dulce de leche, clouds of chantilly cream, the whole thing glossed with ganache and a scatter of chocolate sprinkles.

But La Giralda was more than just food. An evening there with Rafa, Marí, and the usual circle meant stories and laughter, the kind that loosened the knots inside her. For a few hours at least, it was a place where the heaviness of her thoughts could dissolve into warmth and light.

Marí swept up to the bar like a gust of wind, her presence brightening the dim corners of the room. She spotted Carmen near the counter and grinned, eyes gleaming with mischief.

"Carmen, *mi amiga,*" she said, linking her arm with hers. "You're far too young and beautiful to be hiding in a dusty bar all night. *Dale, vamos.* You can always mope with Nico another time. Tonight is for music, *chisme,* and La Giralda's *empanadas,* and don't act like you're strong enough to resist those. Plus, Antonio's paying. So really, it would be rude not to go."

Carmen let out a soft laugh, her resolve already melting beneath Marí's charm. The thought of savory *empanadas,* clinking glasses, and the familiar comfort of shared laughter tugged at her like a gentle current.

"Alright, alright," she said, offering Marí a grin and shooting Nico an exaggerated look of apology. "I surrender. But only because you mentioned the *empanadas.*"

"*Eso!*" Marí beamed, already tugging her toward the door. "You'll thank me later."

With a final burst of laughter and clinking glasses, the group spilled out of the Madreselva and into the night, their spirits lifted like lanterns in the dark.

Café La Giralda welcomed them in a rush of sound and scent. The supper club pulsed with life: music spilling from the stage, voices overlapping in a cheerful din, and the warm, smoky aroma of *habano* cigars swirling through the air like incense.

Excitement crackled between them as they stepped into the chaos. Their eyes danced over the crowd, taking in the vibrant scene and the blur of motion, as dancers spun past dining patrons.

"Over there!" Rafael called, pointing toward a table being vacated near the center of the room. "They're getting up—move fast!"

Laughing, they threaded their way through the crush of bodies, sidestepping flouncing skirts and swaying couples, ducking past waiters balancing towering trays of steaming *milanesas* and bowls of fresh pasta.

Familiar faces from the Madreselva greeted them with raised brows and toasts mid-sip, and for a moment, the whole night shimmered with possibility.

At last, they reached the coveted table, just as the previous occupants stood to leave, coats in hand and laughter still lingering. With a brief exchange of smiles and murmured thanks, Carmen and her friends slid into the warm, worn chairs like victors claiming a small but meaningful prize.

The moment they sat, the pulse of Café La Giralda enveloped them. The air vibrated with music and motion, a kaleidoscope of life and color. Carmen's eyes swept across the room. Bohemians in fraying scarves leaned in close over half-drunk bottles of wine, their conversations animated and full of secrets. Elegant couples swayed on the small dance floor, their bodies moving in rhythm to the band's playful tango, while the bartenders in crisp white jackets worked like magicians, conjuring drinks with practiced flair and knowing glances. Patrons from every corner of the city filled the room: poets and painters, dockworkers and dreamers, all gathered under the same low-hung strings of colored bulbs that cast a soft, golden hue over everything.

It was loud, alive, and utterly intoxicating. As the music swelled and the tempo quickened, Carmen felt herself exhale, truly exhale, for the first time in weeks.

As the group settled into their table, the waiter approached with a warm smile, ready to take their drink orders.

"Would anyone care for an *aperitivo* to start?" he asked, his voice polite and attentive.

Marí's husband, Antonio, perked up at the suggestion, a gleam of excitement in his eyes. "Do you have *Kola Indiana*?" he asked eagerly.

The waiter nodded, his smile widening. "Certainly, sir! Our bar makes a fabulous *Cocktail Kola Indiana* with the kola tonic and rum. Would you like one?"

Antonio's face lit up with delight as he eagerly placed his order, the anticipation evident in his voice. "Yes, please. Make it two, one for me and one for Marí. I need to perk this one up before I have to carry her home." He teased, pointing his thumb over at his wife. María feigned a scowl, giggling as she playfully grabbed her husband's arm.

The waiter nodded in acknowledgment before turning to the rest of the group, his pen poised expectantly. "And for the rest of you?"

Carmen glanced around the table, her friends exchanging nods and murmurs of agreement. "I'll have Hesperidina, tonic and lemon," she said.

Rafael followed suit, his eyes twinkling with excitement. "*Fantastico!* Same for me, *por favor.*"

As they waited for their drinks, Rafael leaned in close to Carmen, a mischievous twinkle in his eye. "Carmen, have you noticed?" he whispered, his voice barely audible over the music. "There are some very good-looking men here tonight."

Carmen laughed, the sound spilling out before she could stop it. A faint warmth rose to her cheeks as she arched a brow at him. "Oh, really?" she teased, feigning innocence. "I hadn't noticed."

Rafael chuckled, his grin widening. "Come on, Carmen," he chided, "don't tell me you're still thinking about *the alchemist*."

Carmen laughed at Rafael's teasing, though a faint heat rose to her cheeks at the mention of Francisco. "Who said anything about him?" she countered lightly, lifting her glass of water as if to hide her smile. "I'm just here for the music, the company…the ambiance, nothing more."

Rafael raised an eyebrow, his expression one of mock disbelief. "*Claro*, sure you are," he teased, nudging her playfully. "But seriously, *Carmencita*, you're a catch. Don't waste your time pining over that *viejo*. You know, maybe it's for the best. You don't want to get caught up in that world. Who knows what kind of complications that could have brought?"

"You think so?" Carmen asked.

"Absolutely. Trust me, *prima*, you're better off without getting sucked into all the drama of high society."

As the server returned with their drinks, Antonio's eyes lit up with anticipation. "Ah, just in time," he exclaimed, his voice filled with excitement as he reached for her glass. "*Chin-chin*, everyone!"

"*Chin-chin!*" they chimed together, their glasses clinking as laughter rippled between them. The table quickly filled with chatter and playful debate until, at last, they agreed on a spread of their favorite dishes to share, each choice met with more teasing, more laughter, the kind that made the night feel boundless.

"Let's start with some *empanadas* and *morcilla*, shall we?" Rafael suggested, his eyes alight with enthusiasm.

Carmen nodded in agreement. "And maybe some *provoleta* as well," she added, her mouth watering at the thought of the cheesy dish served with vibrant *chimichurri* and grilled slices of Italian bread.

The server jotted down their order with a polite smile before melting back into the whirl of the crowd, the hum of voices and clatter of dishes rising in his wake.

Carmen leaned back in her chair, her shawl slipping from one shoulder as Antonio lifted his glass once more, the candlelight catching in the rim like a spark.

"Well, if you ask me, the real excitement this year wasn't at the *milongas*, but on the field."

"Oh, don't start," Marí groaned playfully, sipping her cocktail. "We've barely made it through one night without you turning it into a sermon about *fútbol*."

But Antonio was undeterred. "It's worth a toast! *Nacional* took the championship again. Twelfth season of the *Primera División*, and they've proven they're still the kings of the field."

Rafael raised his glass with mock solemnity. "To *Nacional*," he said, grinning. "May their egos grow only slightly larger than Antonio's."

Laughter erupted around the table, and even Carmen joined in. Though *fútbol* had never held her interest, the warmth of their banter was infectious. She lifted her glass, sipping slowly as she watched them with quiet amusement.

"I don't know much about *fútbol*," she said with a small smile, "but I know enough to say I never see Rafael this animated outside a *milonga*, unless he's talking about sports."

"That's because *fútbol* and tango are the soul of this country," Rafael declared, placing a hand dramatically over his heart. "One teaches you how to move, and the other teaches you how to live."

"And both," Marí chimed in, raising an eyebrow, "give men an excuse to cry when they lose, whether it be on the field, or in love!"

Laughter spilled around the table, and for a moment Carmen let the weight she carried slip from her shoulders.

The air swelled with the scent of sizzling spices and warm pastries, their voices weaving together like music, bright and easy. Stories and jokes tumbled back and forth, but every so often their gazes darted toward the kitchen door, anticipation rising like steam from the ovens.

At last the server appeared, arms laden with a tray of golden *empanadas*, bubbling *provoleta*, and platters of *morcillas* still hissing from the pan. The table broke into cheers, hands reaching eagerly as the feast was set before them.

"*Qué rico!*" Marí exclaimed, her eyes gleaming as she plucked an *empanada* from the tray, steam curling from its flaky crust.

Carmen's grin widened, her appetite waking at the sight of the spread. "This looks amazing," she said, the heaviness of the day already softening in the glow of good company.

"Wine for the table, and a whiskey for me," Antonio declared grandly, already leaning forward with his fork. He speared a piece of *morcilla*, dropped it onto a slice of bread, and shoved it into his mouth with unabashed gusto.

Carmen took a bite of an *empanada* and closed her eyes. The buttery crust gave way to tender beef, sweet caramelized onion, and the subtle sweetness of roasted peppers, a burst of flavor that transported her instantly.

She was back in her *abuela*'s kitchen, small and barefoot on a tiled floor, watching sauces bubble on the stove while the scent of spices danced in the air. Sunday afternoons had smelled like this, full of comfort, memory, and the music of her family's laughter. With each bite, the years fell away. For a moment, she wasn't a seamstress or a fallen woman, just a girl cradled by tradition, tethered to something enduring and familiar. She lingered on the final bite, savoring it like a secret.

Laughter tumbled over the clatter of plates, and wine poured as quickly as stories were told. The joy of good food, seasoned with friendship and noise, wove a kind of warmth that settled deep in their bones, as if for that night, nothing outside their circle could touch them. But the light chatter paused when suddenly a familiar figure appeared at the entrance of the club.

Marí leaned forward, eyes narrowing. "Wait… is that Nico?" she whispered, nudging Antonio.

Carmen turned, eyebrows lifting in surprise. "It is." She watched as he stepped through the doorway. "He usually disappears right after his shift at the Madreselva. I've hardly seen him out this late."

Rafael raised his glass with a grin. "Well, well. Maybe the night's finally tempting him out of hiding."

As Nico approached, weaving through the tables with his usual quiet ease, Carmen felt a smile tug at her lips. He was dressed as always, gray newsboy cap slightly askew, thermos tucked under one arm, *mate* gourd in hand like a badge of identity. There was something grounding about him. In a room full of change and noise, Nico was a constant. Familiar. Solid.

And tonight, even his presence felt like a small kind of gift.

"*Che, fantasma!*" Antonio bellowed in greeting, his eyebrows lifting in surprise as they watched Nico approach their table, "What are you doing here?"

Carmen and her friends exchanged smiles of greeting as Nico made his way around the table, gently bumping cheeks with each of them and planting air kisses in customary greeting.

Nico shrugged, his expression casual. "Oh, you know, just felt like getting out for a change," he replied with a nonchalant shrug. "Thought I'd see what all the fuss was about."

"What a treat," Carmen remarked with a smile, her eyes twinkling with warmth as Nico took a seat next to her. "I rarely get to see you on the other side of the bar."

Nico chuckled, nodding towards the dance floor as he took a sip from his *mate* gourd through the silver *bombilla*. "I'm surprised you're not already out there taking names."

"Some of us enjoy savoring a moment, Nicolás. Not everything's a race to the dance floor." She said, smirking over the rim of her glass.

"Savoring, huh? You mean stalling. Admit it, you're just waiting for the orchestra to play your dramatic entrance song." He teased, a sly grin playing at his lips.

"And why not? A woman deserves a little flair. Besides, I can't go out there and outshine everyone too early. I have to give them time to warm up."

Nico laughed. "*Ay, Dios…* with that ego, it's a wonder there's still room on the dance floor for anyone else."

"Well, someone has to keep *your* poor fragile pride in check."

"You wound me, Carmen. Truly. I should charge you for emotional labor."

"Add it to my tab." Carmen quipped, raising her glass with a grin. "I'm really glad you came out tonight, Nico," she said with a warm smile. "You hardly ever come out with us."

Nico paused, his fingers tracing the rim of his *mate* gourd. "It's not that I don't want to," he said quietly. "It's just that nights like this…drinks, food, pretending everything's fine…it's a luxury. And I'm not exactly swimming in spare change these days."

Carmen's smile faltered for a second. She knew things had been tough for him, but he rarely admitted it out loud. Hearing it now, said so plainly, tugged at something tender inside her.

She reached across the table with a soft chuckle. "Well, lucky for you, Antonio's footing the bill tonight. You can get the next round, once we're both rich and wildly successful."

She nudged his foot playfully beneath the table. "Deal?"

A strained smile tugged at the corners of Nico's mouth. "Deal."

He set down his *mate* and reached for the matchbook nestled inside the clean ashtray. With practiced ease, he drew a hand-rolled *cigarillo* from his shirt pocket, striking the match and lighting it in one fluid motion. The flame flickered briefly in his eyes before he exhaled a slow curl of smoke, his silence saying everything he didn't.

As the waiter returned with the next round of drinks, Marí raised her glass in a toast, her voice ringing out above the din. "To friendship, love, and the best company in Montevideo!" she declared. Antonio joined her, their glasses clinking loudly, spilling a bit of wine onto the tablecloth.

"*Chin-chin!*" everyone echoed, raising their drinks in unison.

As the evening wore on, Antonio, buoyed by the warmth of his whiskey, regaled the table with tales of his youth, each story more exaggerated than the last.

"Ah, to be young again," Antonio began, his words slightly slurred but his smile wide. "Back in the day, I was quite the troublemaker. There wasn't a street in Montevideo I didn't roam or a scheme I didn't try to pull off."

Marí, seated beside him, rolled her eyes playfully. "Oh, here we go," she teased, nudging him. "Antonio's greatest hits."

Antonio chuckled and took another sip of his whiskey. "You laugh, but it's true! Like the time I snuck into the old Teatro Solís after hours. I must have been about seventeen. My friends and I wanted to see if the rumors about it being haunted were true. We got inside, and sure enough, the place was pitch dark and eerie. We were creeping around backstage when suddenly, a spotlight flicked on by itself. We nearly jumped out of our skins!"

"What happened next?" Rafael asked, his eyes alight with intrigue, always the lover of a good scandal.

Antonio grinned. "Turns out, it was just the night watchman messing with us. He had heard us sneaking in and decided to give us a scare. We bolted out of there so fast, I think we set a new record for the 100-meter dash!"

Encouraged by the laughter and applause from his friends, Antonio launched into another story. "Then there was the time we decided to try our hand at fishing down at the *Escollera Sarandi*. We were a bit older then, maybe twenty. We didn't have proper equipment, just some old nets and a lot of optimism. We had this brilliant idea that we'd catch enough to sell at the *mercado* and make a small fortune."

Carmen shook her head, laughing, already knowing where the story was heading. "Oh boy, I can't imagine that went well."

Antonio laughed heartily. "You could say that. We ended up tangling ourselves in the nets more than catching any fish. And to top it off, we got chased away by the local fishermen who didn't appreciate us amateurs trying to muscle in on their territory. We were soaked and penniless by the end of the day."

Antonio's voice softened as he concluded his story. "You know, those were simpler times. We didn't have much, but we had fun. We made memories that have lasted a lifetime." He took a deep breath, setting his glass down with a determined clink. "But these days, things are different. The world is changing, and not always for the better."

María, sensing the sudden edge in her husband's tone, laid a hand gently on his arm. "What is it, Antonio?"

Antonio leaned back in his chair, brows knitting. "It's the government, Marí. Batlle and his damned monopolies," he muttered. "They dress it up as reform: stability, fairness, protection for the people. But give the state that much power, and sooner or later it all rots. You know what happens to the small shops, the men scraping by? They get crushed under the weight of the state's appetite."

Carmen, who had been turning her glass slowly in her hands, finally spoke, her voice calm but firm. "Don Pepe's done good, Antonio. He's given workers rights they never had, pushed for women to have a voice. That matters. Sometimes change has to come from above."

Antonio's scowl softened into a frown. "Maybe. But when the state runs everything, what's left for the rest of us? Bureaucrats can be as cruel as any landlord."

Rafael, leaning forward with a spark in his eye, jumped in. "But look at the other side, when the railroads and utilities are left to the vultures, it's worse. Corporate greed isn't any gentler, *hermano*. At least Batlle is trying to keep the bones from being picked clean."

Antonio snorted, but didn't argue. He pushed the plate of morcilla toward Nico. "*Che, boludo*, you've been quiet. What do you think?"

Nico took his time, slicing the *morcilla* and spreading it onto a crust of bread. He chewed, swallowed, and only then spoke.

"It's all about how it's managed. Do it right, and maybe the poor get a fair shake. Do it wrong, and the whole economy buckles." He glanced around the table, his tone more weary than passionate. "Batlle's right about one thing though, the gap between rich and poor is killing us. If nothing changes, we're all screwed."

A silence settled, punctuated by the clink of cutlery. Then Nico sighed, his shoulders slumping. "In any case, politicians… they don't live where we live. They don't stand in line for bread. They don't worry about rent. They make decisions from up there in their ivory towers and leave us to choke on the dust."

The table fell into a thoughtful hush, each person drifting into their own reflections. For Carmen, Nico's words struck like a note held too long, vibrating in her chest. She thought of the *barrios*, of the *milongas*, of neighbors who clung to song and verse when politics gave them nothing else.

As the conversation shifted, she let herself simply listen. Nico's voice carried the easy rhythm she knew so well, weaving stories of unpaid bills, patched-together jobs, the endless game of stretching one paycheck into three. There was always some new obstacle: tips that barely covered a meal, repairs that cost more than they should, but somehow he softened the weight of it with humor, turning complaint into anecdote.

What struck her most wasn't the struggle itself, but the way he bore it: never bitter, never mean. Even with so little, Nico always found a way to give, whether it was his last coin pressed into another's hand, or the quiet gift of staying up until dawn, listening, keeping company. It wasn't wealth that defined him, Carmen thought, but a generosity of spirit that no law, no government monopoly, could ever regulate or extinguish.

As the band at Café La Giralda paused to change sets, a current of murmurs spread through the crowd. As a young artist took the stage, Rafael's eyes widened in recognition. "*Mirá vos*, it's Eduardo Arolas!" he exclaimed, his voice filled with excitement.

Carmen followed Rafael's gaze, her curiosity piqued by the mention of the up-and-coming tango artist. She watched as Eduardo Arolas took his place on stage, his *bandoneón* cradled in his arms, with a sense of quiet confidence.

Beside him stood Tito Roccatagliatta, the renowned violin player whose virtuosity was unmatched in their era. Vicente Pecci, with his imposing presence and masterful command of the flute. And on the guitar Emilio Fernández, his fingers poised to unleash a torrent of melodies that would captivate the audience's hearts.

Together, they formed a formidable quartet, each musician bringing their own unique talents and skills to the table.

Carmen felt a thrill of anticipation course through her veins as the first notes of their performance filled the air, weaving a tapestry of sound that transported her to another time and place.

As she listened to the haunting melodies of Arolas's song, *Una Noche de Garufa*, her attention was captured by the evocative rhythm, her body swaying instinctively to the music as she watched the couples on the dance floor move with grace and passion.

"So Ruiz, are you ever going to get up and dance, or are you going to sit there nursing that drink all night? I've seen snails cross the *avenida* with more urgency." Nico teased.

Carmen let out a soft laugh, shaking her head. "Is this your version of a charming invitation?"

"Oh no," he said with mock seriousness. "This is a full-blown rescue mission. *Dale, Carmencita*. One dance. You're not going to solve the meaning of life at the bottom of that glass."

Carmen blinked, nearly choking on her sip. "Excuse me?" she said with a laugh, setting her glass down. "*You?* Dance? I thought you were all talk and no rhythm, Fernández." In all her years of knowing Nico, Carmen had never once seen him get on the dance floor.

Nico clutched his chest in mock offense. "I'll have you know I've got rhythm in abundance. It's the humility I struggle with."

She arched a brow, trying not to smile. "So why now, after all this time?"

"Because I've been doing you a favor, obviously," he said, the corners of his eyes crinkling with amusement.

Carmen arched a brow, her mouth twitching at the edges. "A favor?"

He nodded solemnly, taking a slow sip. "Of course. Sparing you from falling madly in love with me. Would've ruined your whole life."

She let out a soft laugh, shaking her head. "You're impossible."

Nico offered his hand with a dramatic flourish. "Shall we?"

With a breath of laughter, she placed her hand in his. "Alright, barkeep. Let's see if you can keep up."

As they stepped onto the dance floor, a flicker of hope seemed to dance in Nico's big brown eyes.

Dancing with Nico felt different from the familiar embrace of her usual partners. His steps were hesitant, his frame stiff, his weight shifting a beat too late. Where others glided, he stumbled; where the seasoned dancers conversed in silent precision, Nico seemed to fumble for the language. Carmen felt the tension in his shoulders, the effort in every movement as he tried—too hard—to match the music.

And yet, there was something disarming about it. He wasn't trying to dazzle her, or command the floor with bravado. He was simply there, earnest and determined, his big brown eyes flicking nervously toward hers, searching for reassurance. Carmen found herself smiling in spite of the awkwardness, trying to let herself relax into Nico's arms, so that her body would respond instinctively to the rhythm of the music and his movements. But just as she began to lose herself in the moment, her breath suddenly caught in her throat.

Amidst the swirling crowd, she thought she caught a glimpse of a familiar figure: a distinguished-looking man with salt and pepper hair and a top hat making his way through the swarm of people crowding the bar.

Her pulse quickened as she struggled to make sense of what she was seeing. Could it really be him, or was it just a trick of the light, a figment of her imagination?

Francisco? Carmen's breath caught, her heart skipping at the thought of his sudden, impossible presence.

The jolt broke her focus; her steps faltered, her movements losing their flow. The music pressed on, but she stumbled through it, her mind racing as her eyes swept the room, desperate to catch another glimpse of him in the crowd.

Sensing her hesitation, Nico slowed, then stopped altogether. His brow furrowed as he searched her face. "Carmen… what is it?" he asked, his voice low, threaded with concern.

She shook her head quickly, as if the motion could banish the unease rising inside her. "I thought I saw someone," she murmured, barely above the music. "But…it was probably nothing."

Nico followed her gaze, scanning the dimly lit room. His eyes landed on the man she had spotted. For a moment, the resemblance was uncanny: the posture, the profile, a fleeting impression that might fool the heart before the mind caught up. But then, as the figure turned, the illusion shattered. The man lacked the polish, the refinement, the quiet magnetism that made Francisco Piria unforgettable.

Recognition flickered across Nico's face, followed by a shadow of disappointment.

Carmen's chest tightened. Guilt pricked at her, sharp and unwelcome, as she realized her sudden distraction had broken the fragile magic of their dance.

"I'm so sorry, Nico," Carmen whispered, her voice filled with regret. "I didn't mean to spoil the moment."

Nico shook his head, offering her a reassuring smile. "It's alright, Carmen," he replied, his voice gentle. "Let's take a break and regroup."

Carmen and Nico returned to the table, where Antonio was still mid-rant about the latest political scandal. Without missing a beat, he roped Nico back into the fray, gesturing animatedly with his wine glass as if the fate of the nation depended on it.

Rafael leaned in, his tone low and teasing. "So," he murmured, a mischievous glint in his eye, "when are you finally going to give poor Nico a chance?"

Carmen blinked, caught off guard, then felt the flush creep up her neck. She let out a small laugh, more out of surprise than amusement. "Rafa, please," she said, shaking her head. "Nico and I practically grew up together, we're basically brother and sister."

Her words were light, but she felt the need to say them clearly. The thought of Nico as anything other than a friend had simply never occurred to her, not because he wasn't kind or charming, but because their bond had always existed in a different register, one rooted in shared history, not romantic possibility.

Rafael arched a skeptical brow, a sly smile tugging at his lips. "Are you sure about that?" he said, voice low with mischief. "Because I've seen the way he looks at you when he thinks no one's watching."

Carmen rolled her eyes and waved him off. "Rafa, please. You know I love Nico, but not like that."

Rafael tilted his head, curious. "Why not? He's funny, loyal, kind of charming when he wants to be…"

She laughed softly, then sighed. "Because he's cynical to the core. Always expecting the worst, always half a breath away from some personal disaster. Besides, I think he's just heard too many sob stories at that bar. He's completely convinced that love is just a setup for disappointment."

Rafael nodded slowly, his teasing smile fading into something more thoughtful. "That's fair," he said. "Still… he does light up when you walk into a room."

Carmen's gaze drifted toward Nico, who was deep in conversation with Marí and Antonio. His hands moved animatedly as he spoke, his eyes bright with conviction, and Carmen couldn't help but smile. There was something comforting about him, something familiar in the rhythm of his voice, the easy warmth he carried wherever he went.

He caught her eye across the table and offered a gentle smile, one laced with a quiet affection that made her chest ache, not with longing, but with something more complicated. They had always shared a closeness that defied easy explanation: part history, part loyalty, and part unspoken understanding. In many ways, Nico would have been the obvious choice. Safe, constant, no sharp edges or storms. But that was just it. She had seen what comfort could curdle into. She had watched her mother shrink beneath the weight of duty, watched love wear itself thin on the spindle of routine. A marriage of obligation, not passion. A life where dreams gave way to dust. And though Nico was dear to her, a confidant, a lighthouse through many of life's darkest moments, he wasn't her fire.

She didn't want a love that merely kept her warm. She wanted one that could set her soul ablaze. To settle with someone just because it made sense was, to Carmen, its own kind of heartbreak. A soft, slow fading. And she wasn't ready to disappear.

As the group's conversation meandered through the labyrinth of politics and personal reflections, it inevitably turned to the topic of Francisco Piria and his ambitious projects.

Antonio, swirling the last of his third drink, broke the lull at the table. "Speaking of progress and control," he muttered, "have you heard what Piria's up to now? Redeveloping half of Montevideo, they say. New *barrios*, boulevards, everything planned down to the last brick."

Marí leaned in, curiosity sparking. "I've heard he's buying up land like it's candy at a *feria*."

At that, Nico, who had been unusually quiet, slammed his palm flat against the table. "And who pays for it?" His voice was tight, bitter. "It's always the same. Men like Piria talk about vision, about progress—but it's profit, nothing else. They build castles while half the city can't even afford bread."

The sudden sharpness in his tone silenced the group. Carmen studied him, surprised at the depth of his anger.

"Nico," she said softly, "you've never been quick to judge a man's character."

He raked a hand through his hair, his expression raw. "It's not judgment, Carmen. It's watching children sleep on sidewalks while men like him drink champagne in their marble halls. It's not fair. It will never be fair."

His words sank heavy between them. Even Rafael, who loved debate, was slow to respond. "Still," Rafael said at last, cautious, "Piria wasn't born rich, you know. He came up from nothing. Maybe that gives him a different perspective. Maybe he actually remembers what it feels like to struggle."

"That makes it worse," Nico shot back, his voice low but hard. "Climbing the ladder only to kick it out from beneath the rest of us? Just because he came from the same mud doesn't mean he hasn't forgotten it."

Rafael shrugged, stubborn. "I've seen the drawings, Nico. Schools, parks, clean water. If he can make that real, maybe it helps more people than it hurts."

Carmen finally set down her glass, her voice steady but thoughtful. "Both of you are right," she said. "Inequality is real, it's everywhere. But so is the possibility of change. Maybe men like Piria use progress to line their own pockets, but progress can still open doors. Education, art, a chance for ordinary people to feel seen. If his projects create that, isn't it worth something?"

Nico's gaze fixed on her, dark and questioning. He poured more hot water into his *mate* gourd. "And what about the strikes, Carmen? The food lines? The women pawning their wedding rings to buy coal? Tell me what use your parks are to them."

Carmen met his challenge, not flinching. "I don't deny the suffering. I see it every day. But people need more than just survival. They need hope. They need spaces to gather, to create, to be reminded they're part of something larger. Without that, all we have is despair. And despair builds nothing."

The table went quiet again, but this time the silence was thick, alive. Nico's jaw tightened, and yet for a flicker of a moment, Carmen thought she saw him soften, just a little, at her words.

"Listen to her!" Antonio guffawed, "She's had one brush with the elite and she already thinks she's one of them!"

Carmen felt her cheeks flush slightly as laughter erupted around the table. Finally, she spoke, her voice calm but tinged with sadness. "You all know that's not true," she said quietly. "I may have had a brief encounter with Don Francisco, but I would never forget who I am or where I come from."

Antonio waved her off with a dismissive gesture, his laughter still echoing in the air. "Oh, come on, Carmen," he said, his tone mocking.

"Don't take yourself so seriously. We all know you're just a humble *barrio* girl at the end of the day."

Carmen bristled slightly, her smile tightening as she set her glass down a little more firmly than intended.

There was laughter around the table, but the comment hit differently, too familiar, too dismissive, like a reminder of a past she'd worked hard to rise from without ever disowning.

"I am," she said, her voice calm but edged with steel. "But that doesn't mean I have to stay boxed into everyone else's idea of what that means."

Marí blinked, sensing the shift, while Carmen shot a warning look at Antonio, who merely raised his hands in mock surrender.

He leaned in, drawing everyone's attention. "Do you all remember the time Carmen tried to organize a 'formal dinner' in the middle of Barrio Sur?"

Marí and Rafael exchanged amused glances, ready for one of Antonio's classic tales. "Oh, I remember that," Rafael said, laughing. "Carmen must have been what, seven or eight years old?"

Antonio nodded. "Exactly. She had just read about these grand dinner parties in one of her books, and decided that the kids in the neighborhood needed a bit of *culture*. So, she went around collecting scraps of old fabric to make napkins and convinced everyone to dress up in their parents' clothes."

Rafael laughed. "But the best part was the 'entertainment.' Carmen decided we needed music, so she got me and a couple of the other older boys to play makeshift instruments. A pot and a pan as drums, a broomstick with a string as a guitar. It was a sight to see."

Antonio chuckled. "And then there was Carmen herself, sitting there in an oversized hat and her mother's old shawl, holding her teacup with the pinky out, like she was the Queen of England! Classic Carmen, always acting like she was better than everyone else, and everyone always went along with it because she was just so darn bossy."

Antonio's indulgence for whisky was a double-edged sword, bringing both laughter as well as the potential for turmoil, and he could sometimes come off as careless and rude when he drank.

Carmen felt a surge of frustration rise within her, but she bit back her retort. Instead, she met his gaze with a steely resolve, refusing to let his words diminish her worth or undermine her confidence.

Antonio continued in his drunken rant, "You know, it just seems like everyone wants recognition and validation and we're all on this endless pursuit of always seeking admiration from others instead of finding fulfillment within ourselves. It's like we're turning into a society of narcissists," he slurred, trying to take a swig of his drink and realizing that his glass was empty.

Nico nodded in agreement as he put a cigarette between his lips, lighting it expertly with a match from his pocket. "Exactly," he replied. "Sometimes, the true rewards of hard work are found in the journey itself, not just the destination," he said soberly.

At that moment, the waiter returned to their table, and Carmen couldn't help but feel a sense of relief at the interruption. Antonio nudged Nico playfully, a mischievous grin spreading across his face. "Come on, Nico, let's get you a real drink," he urged, teasingly. "Why don't you put that *termo* away for once and join us for a change?"

Nico shook his head. "Thanks, but I think I'll pass," he replied, declining Antonio's offer with a dry smile. "The *morcilla* must have disagreed with me," he said flatly, exhaling plumes of smoke through his nose.

Antonio raised an eyebrow, his expression one of mock disbelief. "Blaming the *morcilla, eh*?" he teased, his voice laced with amusement. "Let's get you some *Arazá*, that'll fix you right up!" he declared.

"*Ay, si*!" said María, "You know, it has *marcela* in it, Nico, it'll help settle your stomach!"

"Actually, I think I'm going to head home," Nico said at last, his voice carrying a weary edge. He stubbed out his cigarette in the ashtray, the gesture sharp, final.

Carmen's concern flickered immediately. "Are you sure you're alright, Nico?" she asked gently, leaning toward him.

He offered her a faint smile, gratitude softening his tired features. "*Sí*, Carmen. *Todo bien*. Thanks. I'll see you all later."

She watched him go, a pang tugging at her chest as his figure disappeared into the crowd. The memory of their awkward dance replayed in her mind, mingling with guilt. She couldn't shake the sense that she had let him down somehow. Tomorrow, she promised herself, she would stop by the bar to check in

"You know," Rafael said, glancing at his watch, "we'd better get going too. It's nearly three." He rose from his chair, brushing off his jacket. "Come on, Carmen, I'll walk you home."

Relief fluttered through her, lightening her shoulders. "*Buenas noches*, Antonio. *Chau*, Marí. Thank you for treating us, it was so good to catch up." She leaned in, brushing a kiss against each of their cheeks before rising to join Rafael.

Marí's eyes sparkled, her cheeks flushed with wine. "Take care, you two. Get home safe," she said, her voice bright with genuine warmth.

"*Gracias*, Marí," Carmen replied, her voice soft but sincere. "We'll see you at the Madreselva."

With final kisses and waves, Carmen and Rafael slipped toward the exit. Behind them, the laughter and music of the café spilled into the night, fading into memory as they stepped into the quiet streets.

As they stepped out of the supper club, the contrast between the warm, lively atmosphere inside and the dark, quiet streets outside was stark, and Carmen suddenly appreciated Rafael's company all the more.

It was a cold, moonless night, and the thick darkness seemed to envelop the streets like an inky cloak. The few street lamps that dotted the street corners flickered feebly, the dim glow barely penetrating the thick veil of darkness that shrouded the night. The dim lights cast long, eerie shadows that danced and swayed with the whispering night breeze, lending an air of mystery to the deserted streets.

The street cars had already stopped running, and the only sounds that broke the silence were dogs barking in the distance and the occasional echo of footsteps muffled by the oppressive stillness of the night.

A trio of drunk men stood loitering by a lamp post, their rowdy laughter cutting through the night air. One of the men violently hurled a paper bag containing a glass bottle against the facade of a nearby building, causing it to shatter loudly.

Carmen instinctively moved closer to Rafael, linking her arm with his, finding solace in his reassuring presence. His statuesque frame offered a sense of protection that she welcomed wholeheartedly, and she couldn't help but feel a sense of relief knowing that Rafael was always by her side, his presence serving as a shield against the uncertainty of the night.

Rafael must have sensed her apprehension, and he squeezed her arm gently, offering her a supportive smile. "Don't worry, Carmen," he said softly, his voice a comforting whisper. "I've got you."

Carmen nodded gratefully, her nerves beginning to settle as they walked briskly past the group of men, the strong smell of booze permeating the aura surrounding them.

Once they were safely out of earshot, Carmen let out a sigh of relief, her shoulders relaxing. "Thank you for always walking me home, Rafa," she said, her voice tinged with gratitude.

Rafael smiled warmly, squeezing her arm gently. "Anytime, *prima*," he replied, his tone reassuring. "We've got to look out for each other in this city."

As they walked side by side, the gentle rhythm of their footsteps and the quiet hum of the city around them provided a soothing backdrop to their conversation.

"Rafa," Carmen began hesitantly, glancing at her cousin, "I can't help but feel bad about the way Nico took off tonight."

Rafael looked at her with a mixture of concern and curiosity. "Oh, well, you know how moody Nico is. Why, did something happen between you two?"

Carmen exhaled, her breath lingering in the cool night air, a faint mist rising from her lips. "I don't know," she murmured, "I got distracted during our dance, thinking I saw Piria walk in, and I think Nico noticed. He's probably spent years building up the courage to step out onto that floor, and there I was, moving like I didn't even want to be there."

"I'm sure he's fine," Rafael said with a smirk. "He's probably just feeling like a *boludo*, kicking himself for waiting so long to make his move. And now he knows he doesn't stand a chance."

Carmen's brows knit, her voice softer. "Do you really think he feels that way?"

Rafael's smirk faded. He nodded, this time with sincerity. "Of course he does, Carmen. I mean… compared to someone like Piria?" He gave a small shrug. "Worldly, mysterious, practically a legend. Poor Nico's probably feeling like he brought a paper kite to a storm."

Carmen looked away, a quiet guilt blooming quietly in her chest.

She had never meant to make Nico feel small. Never meant for the moment between them to feel like second place. He had offered her something gentle, honest, and she had drifted, distracted by the thought of a man from a world so far removed from their own it might as well have been another life.

But even now, she couldn't shake it.

As they walked together through the quiet streets, Carmen found herself lost in thought, reflecting on Rafael's words.

Whatever Francisco had stirred in her, it was not a comparison. It was a question she hadn't yet learned how to answer.

Perhaps Antonio had been right.

Had meeting Francisco truly shifted something in her? Tilted the axis of what she thought she wanted?

It felt possible, no, *inevitable*, that something had been stirred. A seed planted. Not of romance alone, but of restlessness. Of wanting more than the familiar rhythm of her days. More than measured stitches, evening dances, and polite futures.

With a final embrace and parting smile for Rafael, Carmen slipped back into her house, the door clicking softly behind her. The night pressed close, thick with questions she wasn't ready to name.

Later, curled beneath her blanket with the wind rattling the shutters like an old memory trying to get in, Carmen lay still, eyes fixed on the ceiling. The darkness offered no answers, only space to think.

Had she outgrown her own definition of adventure?

Once, it had meant late nights at the *milonga,* whispered laughter in the stairwell, the thrill of being wanted, but never caught. It had meant surviving, striving, dancing in defiance of gravity and expectation.

But now…

Now, adventure felt quieter. Heavier. Less about escape and more about *becoming,* something fuller, more honest, more real.

And for the first time in a long while, she wondered, not with fear, but with quiet anticipation, what her life might look like if she let herself want something else.

Something *more.*

Chapter 6

The first light of morning crept softly through the lace curtains, casting delicate patterns across the wooden floor. The wind had stilled sometime before dawn, and the house felt unusually hushed, like it too was holding its breath.

Carmen stirred beneath the blankets, her limbs heavy with sleep, her thoughts already trailing behind her into waking.

She didn't rise right away.

Instead, she lay there a moment longer, eyes half-open, watching the light shift across the ceiling. There was no rush, no list of tasks running through her mind yet. Just the echo of last night's thoughts.

Had something in her changed?

The question still lingered, but it no longer felt like a burden.

It felt like a doorway.

She finally rose, wrapping her shawl loosely around her shoulders, and padded barefoot into the kitchen, the familiar ache in her feet after dancing all night. The floor was cold against her feet. Grounding. Comforting.

As she lit the small stove and set water to boil, she glanced toward the little notebook on her windowsill, the one where she jotted dreams and thoughts she didn't always understand. She hadn't written in it for days.

She picked it up and opened to a blank page.

For a long moment, she just stared at the paper, unsure what to say.

And then, quietly, she wrote:

"Something is shifting. I don't know where it leads yet. But I want to follow it."

She closed the notebook.

The kettle began to hum.

Outside, the street began to stir, vendors opening their carts, children running late for errands, the ordinary beginning of another ordinary day.

But Carmen felt it. Today wasn't quite the same.

After a few sips of *mate* and a few more scribbles in her notebook, she stepped out, her work apron folded under one arm, the quiet rhythm of her footsteps blending into the soft stir of the waking city.

Usually, her walk to the atelier was brisk, practical, just a stretch of cobblestone between home and duty. But today, everything felt... softened. Slowed. Like the city had slipped into a different tempo and invited her to follow.

The streets of Barrio Sur were still stretching awake. The sky was soft and gray, the kind of sky that pressed close to the rooftops and made the air smell faintly of rain and ironed cotton. A few shopkeepers were lifting their metal gates, sweeping out yesterday's dust. A baker arranged loaves on a wooden tray in his window, their crusts still steaming. A boy ran past with a bundle of letters tucked under one arm, whistling a tune she couldn't place.

Normally, Carmen would have walked with purpose, with her shoulders forward, thoughts already tangled in the hours ahead.

But today, she moved slower.

She let her fingers brush the brick walls as she passed. Paused at a corner where the jasmine spilled over a rusted iron fence. Listened to the uneven rhythm of the city, the distant clang of a streetcar bell, the soft murmur of water being poured from a second-story window.

She took a different route than usual, letting her feet wander down side streets where iron balconies still dripped with dew, and the laundry lines swayed gently like quiet dancers between the buildings. She passed a florist opening her shutters, the scent of crushed eucalyptus spilling into the street. A stray cat darted across her path, then sat and watched her like it had been waiting.

And all the while, something inside her was loosening.

She didn't feel lost.

She felt unfastened.

Like the version of herself that had clung so tightly to certainty had taken one small, brave step back.

At a corner, she paused beneath an old *jacarandá* tree, its fallen petals lilac against the cracked pavement. The color caught her breath a little, reminding her of a silk bolt they'd just received at the dress shop, one that she had run her fingers over like it held magic.

The rain had barely begun, more mist than downpour, brushing against Carmen's shawl as she turned onto the narrow alleyway beside the atelier.

The building was modest. Two floors of pale stucco, its window boxes overgrown with trailing ivy and last season's dead lavender. But inside, it carried the scent of fabric and oil. It was a place where hands knew what to do before minds caught up. A place of making.

She unlocked the back door with her brass key, stepped inside, and closed it quietly behind her.

The city's gray softened instantly, replaced by warm wooden floors and shelves stacked with bolts of fabric in shades of seafoam, garnet, and bone. Light filtered through the row of narrow windows, catching dust in the lace curtains.

The air was heavy with the scent of fabric and thread, mingling with the faint aroma of old wood and dust. Rows of sewing machines lined the walls, the mechanical clanks that usually filled the air with their steady rhythm were now silent.

Carmen exhaled.

She liked this hour, before anyone else arrived. When the atelier felt like a secret. She crossed the room, placed her shawl and folded apron on the long cutting table, and paused.

Her fingers brushed the record player tucked beneath the window.

She hesitated only a moment before selecting the old tango record she'd brought from home, the one with the scratch near the beginning of Elsie Janis' *El Choclo*. She set the needle gently. The hiss came first, then the bright sound of the violin, singing softly through the quiet.

She stepped out of her shoes.

The floor was cool beneath her stockings.

And then she danced.

Not for anyone. Not for applause. Just for herself. Just to feel the music trace the outline of her again.

She moved through the empty workshop, the fabric on the shelves her only audience. Her steps were slow, fluid, deliberate. A breath forward. A pause. A pivot. The ache of the melody stitched into her ribs.

She had never married, not because she couldn't love, but because she had learned to love the silence between steps. The freedom to move without permission. To feel without explanation.

As the melody stretched into quiet, she stood still in the center of the room, eyes closed.

The city waited outside. The women would arrive soon, and she would pin hems, adjust bodices, and laugh when the measuring tape caught in her hair. She would return to her role.

But on that quiet morning, she was not a seamstress.

She was still *Carmen Ruiz*: dancer, dreamer, untamed and unclaimed.

And she smiled.

The last note of the tango hadn't fully faded when Carmen heard the soft click of the atelier door opening behind her.

She didn't flinch.

She only turned, slowly, still barefoot, one hand loosely at her hip, the other brushing a curl from her cheek.

"Sorry," came a voice, light and shy. "I didn't mean to interrupt."

It was Francesca, the youngest of the seamstresses. Seventeen, maybe eighteen. All long limbs, calloused fingertips, and curious eyes that missed nothing. She held a bundle of muslin pressed against her chest like a shield, her cheeks flushed from the chill outside, and maybe something else.

"You're early," Carmen said, calm as ever.

"I wanted to finish the pleats on the blue skirt before Sylvia comes in," Francesca replied, eyes darting around the room, then back to Carmen. "Were you… were you dancing?"

Carmen nodded, reaching for her shoes. "Just a little practice before the day begins."

Francesca hesitated in the doorway, then crossed the room slowly, her voice softer now. "It was beautiful."

Carmen gave a small smile as she sat at the workbench. "It's only beautiful when no one's watching."

"I was watching," Francesca said. "And it was."

Carmen didn't reply to that. Not with words. She began unrolling a bolt of raw cotton, fingers steady, movements efficient.

But Francesca stayed rooted in place. Then, gently: "Do you think…you could teach me sometime?"

Carmen looked up.

Francesca met her gaze, not with girlish infatuation, but something deeper. Earnestness. Longing. The kind that Carmen remembered from her own girlhood, before she knew how the world would try to press it out of her.

"Tango?" Carmen asked.

Francesca nodded. "Not the way they teach it in the plazas. The way you move. Like it comes from the heart."

Carmen studied her for a long beat. Then, without looking away, she reached over and turned the record back to the start. The Victor Orchestra hissed to life again, and Carmen stood barefoot in the center of the workshop, the fabric of her dress swaying faintly with her breath.

She extended a hand.

Francesca blinked. "Now?"

"There's no better time," Carmen said. "But I warn you, it's not about looking pretty. It's about learning to hold your own weight."

Francesca placed the bundle of muslin on the table and stepped forward.

"Alright then, I think I'm ready."

Carmen smiled, not soft, but steady. Approving.

"We'll see."

And just like that, the atelier became a ballroom again.

Two women. Barefoot. Finding the music not in their steps, but in themselves.

Carmen and Francesca were mid-step, their movements slow and careful, Carmen guiding her with the lightest pressure at the shoulder blade, Francesca trying not to overthink the rhythm, when the door burst open with the unmistakable jangle of the atelier bell.

"*Dios mío*! What is this?"

Both women froze.

Sylvia, the head seamstress, stood at the doorway, her sharp features framed by the stiff gray collar of her coat. Her arms were already halfway crossed, brows drawn together in a way that could pleat fabric from across the room.

Francesca immediately took a step back, cheeks flaming. "We, I was just…"

"I know what you were just doing," Sylvia said, closing the door behind her with a soft thud. "Dancing, when the thread hasn't been sorted and the hem samples are two days behind? Is this a dance hall or a workshop?"

Carmen didn't flinch. She straightened, graceful as ever, barefoot still. "I got here early. Francesca was here early too. We had a few minutes."

Sylvia's eyes narrowed. "Minutes better spent preparing orders than twirling around barefoot. This is not the theater, Carmen."

Carmen bent slowly to slide her shoes back on. "You'll have your orders by the end of the day. You always do."

"That's not the point," Sylvia snapped, then paused. Her voice softened, but only slightly. "You set the tone here. These girls look up to you. If you lose sight of the work, so will they."

Carmen stood again, shoulders level. "I haven't forgotten the work," Carmen said evenly. "But if these girls follow what I do, then I hope they also learn to find time to breathe between stitches."

That hung in the air.

Even Sylvia didn't respond right away.

Finally, with a tight motion, she set her bag down on the counter. "Don't be ridiculous. We're not here to *breathe*, Carmen. We're here to deliver what's been promised. Not all of us have the luxury of... morning *tangos*." Sylvia muttered.

Carmen said nothing.

Sylvia turned her sharp gaze to Francesca. "Go on, *niña*. Hemlines don't stitch themselves."

Francesca looked to Carmen, uncertain, then down at her feet as if embarrassed by her own body. Her shoulders curled in, as though trying to become smaller again.

But Carmen, without speaking, reached down and passed her back the measuring tape.

"Go on," she said with a wink. "We'll dance again."

Francesca nodded, just once, and took the tape like a secret.

As she disappeared toward the back of the workshop, Sylvia busied herself with inventory notes, muttering numbers under her breath. The music had faded, and the moment was over.

As the workday settled in, Carmen moved toward the cutting table and pulled the measuring tape from around her neck, wrapping it around her fingers.

The rhythm of the day returned, measured not in music now, but in stitches, chalk lines, and the hiss of steam from the pressing iron.

Carmen stood at the cutting table with her sleeves rolled, pinning the pleats on a dove-gray skirt meant for a senator's wife. Something conservative, unremarkable, but expensive in its restraint. Her hands worked deftly, but her mind drifted, her gaze slipping now and then toward the glass-paneled wall that divided the workshop from the storefront.

From behind those panes, like images on a flickering screen, elegant women passed in and out: always gloved, always powdered, always wrapped in fur or feather or the perfume of old wealth. They drifted through the storefront room with practiced grace, trailing silken hems and soft laughter, turning their heads only just enough to be admired.

Carmen watched them the way a traveler might study birds through a window. Curious. Detached. Not envious, but aware.

There had been a time when she'd imagined herself as one of them, if only in the quiet privacy of childhood. She remembered watching women like them walk past her on the boardwalk at the *Hotel de los Pocitos*, parasols in hand, their hats tilted just so, their heels tapping rhythm on the planks. She'd imagined their lives: filled with poetry, champagne, and slow afternoon dances in parlors gilded with gold.

She knew better now.

She'd sewn the boning into their corsets, the stays into their bodices. She'd fitted their waists too tight, hemmed their skirts to hide bruises or swelling or stubborn aging. She'd heard their sharp whispers through the curtain, their dismissive laughter when they thought the working girls weren't listening.

They lived wrapped in satin, yes, but they bled just the same. Only quieter. And more expensively.

Still, Carmen couldn't help but admire them sometimes. Not for their refinement, but for the performance. How easily they wore roles that Carmen had never learned to play.

She returned her attention to the skirt beneath her hands, carefully folding the next pleat.

"Carmen," came Sylvia's voice from behind her, sharp and clipped. "Señora Paiva's fittings have been moved up an hour. You'll have to finish the collar yourself."

Carmen nodded, not looking up. "It'll be done."

She could feel Sylvia's eyes on her back for a moment longer before the older woman retreated into the bustle of the workroom, calling out instructions to Francesca and the others.

Carmen glanced once more toward the front.

One woman, standing at the mirror, was laughing, head thrown back, mouth red as a crushed rose, veil pinned perfectly in place.

Carmen didn't envy her.

But she wondered what it would be like to laugh like that, with no need to impress, no fear of unraveling.

She shook the thought loose, picked up her needle, and bent again to her work.

Outside the glass, the women danced through their rituals.

And inside the workshop, Carmen stitched the world back together, one careful seam at a time.

Her thoughts were momentarily disrupted by Sylvia again, appearing in the doorway.

"Carmen," Sylvia called, her voice as crisp as the pleats she'd just inspected, "bring that new damask sample up to the storefront. Señora Delgado wants to see the pattern under the light."

Carmen nodded in acknowledgment, lifting her foot from her sewing machine's treadle, using her right hand to gently pause the balance wheel from turning and stopping the machine.

She rose from her seat and made her way to the front of the shop, gently cradling a yard of the fine silk fabric folded in her arms. A pale champagne with a rose-gold vine motif that shimmered differently every time it caught the light. Imported. Precious. A fabric that would never touch the skin of anyone who worked back there.

As she crossed the threshold into the plush, sunlit storefront, the air changed instantly.

Cooler, perfumed. Brighter.

Walls lined with bolts of silk and taffeta, floral arrangements placed just so, the scent of bergamot and pressed linen clinging to everything. It felt like walking into a painting. Or a performance.

And then, there they were.

Señora Antonia Delgado, one of the atelier's most prominent and particular clients, stood by the gilded mirror with her gloved hands folded in front of her, her chin slightly lifted in practiced assessment. Draped in dove gray silk and pearls, she radiated the serene authority of a woman who had never once needed to explain her place in the world.

Beside her stood Isabella, her daughter.

Carmen knew her age only because someone had mentioned it once in passing: nineteen, maybe twenty. But she looked younger. All flushed cheeks and high-waisted satin, her beauty effortless, feathered with privilege. Her hair was pinned in soft waves, her gloves pristine, her perfect satin slippers barely scuffed from the street. She turned as Carmen entered, and her gaze, polite but indifferent, passed over her as one might glance at a vase or a curtain being drawn.

Carmen felt the difference between them instantly.

Not in worth. But in weight.

She could feel the callouses on her fingers against the silk she held. Could still smell the starch of the workshop on her sleeves, the faint iron of the needle she'd been threading moments before.

She crossed the room with composure.

"Ah yes, here we are!" exclaimed Sylvia, quickly plucking the fabric from Carmen's arms. As Sylvia explained the intricate details of the fabric, Señora Delgado examined it with keen interest.

She stepped closer, adjusting her lorgnette, running her fingers lightly over the pattern. "Mm. Yes. Better in daylight, isn't it?"

"Much," Sylvia replied, keeping her voice smooth.

Isabella drifted closer, her hands clasped loosely behind her back. "It's lovely," she murmured, mostly to her mother. "Do you think it would work for the reception dress?"

"Perhaps," Antonia said. "Though with your coloring, darling, something cooler may suit you better. This is rather soft."

Carmen remained silent, but she couldn't help it.

Somewhere inside her, the comparison whispered itself.

She knew what Isabella's life likely held: piano lessons, garden parties, weekends at the coast. She'd probably never danced in a crowded *milonga* with sweat clinging to her neck, never stitched her own hem at midnight by candlelight. She'd never had to endure the taste of stale bread, or scrub her laundry in a shared courtyard while sleazy old drunk men ogled her backside.

And yet, Carmen did not envy her.

Not exactly.

But she felt the space between them like the cold edge of glass.

Polished on one side.

Pressed against the other.

"Thank you Carmen!" Sylvia snapped, dismissing her. She thrust the fabric back into her arms without as much as a glance in her direction.

As she passed the mirror near the entrance, she caught her own reflection.

Dark eyes. Loose tendrils of hair. Fingers still stained faintly with ink and chalk dust. No pearls. No silk.

As Carmen stepped through the curtain and back into the workshop, the murmur of silk and perfume still clinging faintly to her skin, she heard it. Clear, careless, and entirely intended to be overheard:

"It's a shame, you know. She's actually quite pretty, that girl, but dressed so frumpy. You should really consider requiring your staff to be in uniform."

Señora Delgado's voice, elegant and effortless, floated behind her like the last note of a piano played too sharply.

Carmen froze, just for a breath. Her fingers gripped the edge of the table, knuckles whitening slightly against the polished wood.

She didn't turn around.

Didn't offer a reply.

She didn't need to.

The workshop around her continued as if nothing had been said: Sylvia leafing through fabric invoices, Francesca carefully pressing a bodice seam, the quiet hum of machines murmuring their steady rhythm.

But something inside Carmen tightened, then steadied.

Frumpy.

Not untalented. Not rude. Not incompetent.

Just not dressed for their stage.

She sat back at her machine, adjusting the needle with calm precision, her hands steady, her spine straight.

Let them wrap themselves in silk.

She worked with her hands, not her father's name. She knew how to make beauty, not just wear it. And she carried her elegance in silence, not lace.

Still, the words lingered. *Actually quite pretty*, as though it were a discovery, not a fact. As though her worth needed permission to be visible.

Carmen began moving her foot on the pedal. The machine whirred to life, louder than a whisper, sharper than a glance.

And with each stitch, she reminded herself: she didn't need any sort of garment to be unforgettable.

She was already stitched into rooms they could only buy their way into.

Chapter 7

It was nearly midnight before Carmen and Rafael finally arrived at the *Madreselva*, Carmen's hair still faintly perfumed with starch and steam from the day's work. The *milonga* was in full bloom, with lace and satin drifting across the floor like poetry in motion, and laughter curling through the air like cigarette smoke beneath the flicker of amber lights. The wooden boards echoed with the sharp rhythm of heels, the hush of soles, the silent push and pull of bodies surrendering to the music in close embrace.

Carmen paused at the threshold, letting the pulse of the room steady her. Here, in the warmth of sweat and violin, she always felt like herself again: softened, grounded. But tonight, something still weighed on her.

She spotted him near the end of the bar. Nico, busy slicing limes with that casual precision he always had. His sleeves were rolled to the elbow, forearms dusted with salt and citrus, his dark curls falling forward as he worked. He hadn't seen her yet.

Carmen walked over, heart tight, brushing a stray curl from her cheek.

"*Hola*," she said softly.

He looked up, surprised for only a beat. Then came the familiar half-smile, the guarded kind he wore when he wasn't sure which version of someone was walking toward him.

"Look what the wind swept in," he said, setting down the knife. "You just get off work?"

"Yes," she breathed. "Barely made it. I had to work overtime to get a last minute order out for the Chancellor's wife. Some gala, or something." She rolled her eyes.

He reached for a towel, drying his hands. "What can I get you?"

"Nothing. Not yet." She hesitated. "Listen, Nico…."

He put down the towel and set aside the cutting board, giving her his full attention. "*Que pasa*?"

Carmen folded her arms, unsure where to put her hands. "About last night. At La Giralda…"

Nico gave her one of his usual boyish smirks, trying to wave it off.

But she didn't let it slide. "No, I mean it, Nico. I'm sorry," she said.

Nico arched a brow, amused. "For what?"

"For spoiling our only dance. You deserved better than that."

He exhaled slowly, the grin softening into something gentler as he leaned his elbows on the bar.

"Listen, Carmen," he said, his voice quieter now, "don't mention it. It's nothing, really. No hard feelings."

"I mean it," she said. "You've always been good to me. I didn't mean to make you feel like a placeholder."

"You didn't," he replied after a moment. "Or, you know, maybe you did. But I get it."

She looked at him, brow furrowed. "What do you mean?"

"You've always been chasing something bigger than this," he said, waving vaguely at the bar, the floor, the crowd. "I knew it before you did."

Carmen swallowed. "I didn't know I was leaving anything behind."

"You don't have to explain, Carmen. Some people dance to forget. Others dance to become. I think you're the second kind."

She smiled faintly, and let out a breath she didn't realize she'd been holding.

"I hope you find whatever you're dancing toward," he added, then gave a soft shrug. "And, hey, if you ever need a drink along the way, you always know where to find me."

She nodded, touched. Then, with one last grateful glance, she turned back toward the floor.

"Hey, wait," Nico said. "Someone left something for you earlier this afternoon."

Carmen blinked. "For me? Who was it?"

Nico shrugged. "A bicycle courier. Didn't say who it was from."

He reached beneath the bar and handed her a carefully wrapped parcel. It was wrapped in plain brown paper and tied with twine. Her name was written across the front in a deliberate, elegant hand.

Her pulse quickened.

"You gonna open it?" Nico asked, leaning on one elbow, curiosity alight in his eyes.

Carmen gave a cautious smile. "Eventually."

But the weight of it was already pressing against her palms, more than just paper and string.

She moved to a little empty table near the back of the hall, heart thudding as she untied the knot of twine and peeled back the wrapping.

A book.

Worn leather binding. Gilded edges. Faintly scented with time and dust.

Thus Spoke Zarathustra by Friedrich Nietzsche.

She ran her fingers over the embossed title, eyes narrowing. Then she noticed the thin envelope tucked inside the cover, sealed with crimson wax. Pressed into the surface was the faint outline of a winged lion, encircling the words: *Ex nihilo nihil fit.* No initials, just the clean press of intention.

She opened it carefully. Inside was a letter, neatly folded. The paper thick and textured, as though meant to last.

October 1912 –

Carmen,

Forgive my absence. I have been in Vienna these past weeks, attending to an unexpected matter of business, urgent and unrelenting. The kind that insists on one's full attention and leaves no room for the things that truly matter.

I've chosen this book not because of its philosophy, which is often misunderstood, but because of its courage. Zarathustra walks alone, searching for truth not given to him by the world, but discovered through the fire of his own becoming.

You remind me of him.

You carry a flame, even when the wind howls against it. And though you may not know it yet, your solitude is not emptiness, it is preparation.

For the dance. For the words. For the life you are slowly writing into existence.

You once said you write to make sense of pain. I wonder if, in time, you might also write to make sense of joy.

–F.

Carmen stared at the page for a long time. Her hand trembled just slightly as she refolded the letter and slid it back between the pages of the book.

She glanced around the room. The music, the murmuring laughter, the swirl of bodies on the floor all seemed to dull to a hush, and she felt, for a moment, as though she were suspended between worlds.

She must have read the letter a dozen times that night, in the quiet of her room. Once quickly, as if afraid of what it might awaken. Again, slower, like a melody she was trying to memorize. Then again, each time a little deeper, until the words stopped feeling like his and started feeling like her own.

She ran her fingers across the edge of the paper, already softened at the fold. His handwriting was elegant, deliberate. A man used to being precise. But there was something vulnerable in the letter, a hesitation between the lines. Francisco had seemed composed, cloaked in the confidence of someone who'd long ago learned to command a room. And yet here, in ink, he seemed… tentative. Human.

She let the words flicker in her mind, again and again. Then she reached for her notebook.

Carmen sighed and sat back in her desk chair. The window beside her was cracked open, letting in the chill of the night air, along with the distant whistle of a midnight train. She wrapped her shawl tighter around her shoulders and stared down at the blank page in front of her.

She picked up her pen, and for a long moment, did nothing.

Then, softly, tentatively, she began to write.

Not a letter. Not at first. Just fragments. A flicker of memory, the warm press of his hand at the base of her spine. The echo of the *bandoneón* during their first dance. The weight of his gaze as he asked her about her dreams. She wrote in half-thoughts and incomplete sentences, letting the language break apart and reform like waves on a shore.

She didn't stop to edit. She didn't try to be clever. She let the ink spill the truth of what she hadn't dared speak aloud:

Sometimes, I feel like I'm both the flame and the moth. I want to be seen, but it terrifies me. You saw me. And I hated you for it. And yet, I wanted more.

A pause. Her breath caught. She kept going.

There is a girl who dances because the world is too loud. Who writes because the silence is worse. Who thinks she's too much and not enough, all at once.

Her pen hovered for a moment.

To be luminous is not to shine for others,
but to burn in the dark and still call it holy.
To carry your name like a prayer,
even when no one is listening.

I am not waiting to become.
I already am.

The ink bled slowly into the paper, like truth. Like a vow.

And outside, somewhere across the sea, she imagined him. Francisco. Perhaps tracing constellations from his window or pacing the marble halls of his hotel in Vienna, holding her name in silence like a secret promise.

She hesitated, pen hovering, and then turned to a fresh page.

This time, she began a letter she had no intention of sending.

November 1912 –

Francisco,
You don't know this, but I've spent my whole life trying to build a wall no one could climb. And you…
You didn't climb it.
You knocked. Waited.

And part of me wanted to open it.
Another part ran.
You must know by now: that part always wins.

But now I wonder what would happen if, just once, it didn't.

–C.

She stared at the letter, unsure if she felt lighter or more exposed. Then, without thinking, she tore it from the notebook and folded it, tucking it between the pages of *Zarathustra.*

In any case, the parcel had no return address. She had no way of knowing where Francisco was by now, or where in the world he could be next.

As she closed the book, she caught her reflection in the darkened window. Her hair loose, her eyes tired but bright, like embers that refused to die.

Carmen leaned back, cradling her notebook in her lap.

She had written.

For the first time in weeks, she had written not to impress, not to escape, but to feel.

And that, she realized, might be the first true step toward something. Whether or not Francisco ever saw it…

The fire was lit again.

That night, Carmen didn't sleep so much as drift, slipping between layers of memory, emotion, and something else she couldn't name. The letter, the book, the writing, all of it still humming in her body like a dance that hadn't ended.

She lay curled beneath the woven blanket on her narrow bed, the notebook still open on her desk across the room, pages fluttering gently in the breeze from the cracked window.

And then…

She dreamed.

But it wasn't like her usual dreams. It wasn't scattered, or senseless. It was vivid, almost tactile, as if someone had stitched reality into her sleep.

She was back at the *Madreselva.* The lights were lower than usual, the shadows heavier, as though the club itself were half-asleep. A *bandoneón* cried from somewhere out of sight. The music was slow and aching, a melody soaked in longing.

She stood in the center of the empty dance floor, barefoot, wearing a violet-colored dress she'd never seen before but somehow recognized. The hem brushed her ankles, catching on each step.

Then, he was there.

Francisco.

Not just the idea of him, but him. His dark eyes soft, his posture as still and grounded as he had been on that first night, though in the dream he looked younger, or maybe just unburdened. He said nothing. He simply held out his hand.

Carmen didn't hesitate. Not this time.

Their palms touched.

And as they moved together, it wasn't just tango, it was like every conversation they hadn't had was unfolding through their steps. Every silence. Every almost. Every unspoken confession.

He spun her, gently, and when she turned back into his arms, she whispered something she couldn't remember the moment she said it, but it made him close his eyes, press his forehead to hers, and exhale like he'd been holding his breath for years.

The music faded.

The lights dimmed further.

And Carmen woke with a start.

The room was still dark. Early morning.

She sat up, breath shallow, her skin prickling. Her heart was beating hard, not from fear, but recognition.

She knew that dream. Not as a fantasy, not as invention. It felt like a memory. Or a glimpse of something that could be. A parallel life slipping through the cracks of this one.

Still dazed, she slid out of bed and crossed the room.

The book sat where she'd left it.

She opened *Zarathustra* to the spot where she'd tucked her unsent letter, and pulled it out. Her handwriting looked different now. Softer. Less afraid.

Then she turned the page in her notebook and wrote three words at the top:

I saw him.

And underneath, she began writing the dream as if it were real. The violet dress. The ache in the *bandoneón*. The forehead touch. She described it all with aching precision.

Because maybe, just maybe, it wasn't just a dream.

Maybe it was a message. A memory from the soul.

A sign.

Outside, the first light of dawn crept across the rooftops of Montevideo, like warm, golden honey being poured over the tiled rooftops.

And Carmen wrote, as if the fire in her had never gone out at all.

Chapter 8

Carmen had never minded being poor.

She wasn't the type to be dazzled by gaudy displays of wealth or dripping jewels. Those things felt hollow to her. Loud declarations of importance that masked something empty and deeply insecure.

She'd grown up with threadbare linens and chipped enamel cups, and yet nothing ever felt lacking. Her mother had taught her that pride had little to do with money, and everything to do with how you carried yourself in the world.

She could sew a hem in candlelight, cook a full meal from next to nothing, and walk into any room with her head held high, even if her shoes were worn thin and her dress had been mended twice over.

What mattered to Carmen was warmth. Familiarity. The quiet rhythm of a day well spent. She found her contentment in the faint sound of music drifting in through the window, the scent of simmering stew in the air, the golden sunlight streaming through the curtain's edge as she stood at the sink washing clothes.

Her little kitchen, with its cracked linoleum and water-stained ceilings, held more peace than any grand hall ever could.

It was here, surrounded by humble things, that she felt most herself. The old wood-burning stove, its blackened surface bearing the marks of countless meals cooked over the years. The pots and pans hanging from nails driven into the wall. The few faded photographs of her grandparents. The little altar shelf in the corner above the folding table, home to her mother's statuette of the *Virgen de los Treinta y Tres*, and her holy prayer cards depicting *El Sagrado Corazón* and *Padre Nuestro*.

Simple. Familiar.

Steam curled around her face as she leaned over the sink, the scent of soap and fabric rising from the worn basin.

She didn't mind the work. It gave her hands something to do while her mind wandered.

Her fingers worked methodically, scrubbing at the sweat-darkened collars and underarms of her blouses. Her good ones. The ones not good enough to impress Señora Delgado.

That's what she did mind. What gnawed at her late at night when the city was silent and her hands were still, was being *underestimated*. Pity. Assumptions. The quiet patronizing looks from people who thought they knew the shape of her story just by glancing at her shoes.

She pressed a damp sleeve between her palms, twisted, and watched the water drip back into the basin.

She had always lived between worlds. Too sophisticated and independent to fully fit within the modest, traditional life her mother expected of her, yet too unpolished and poor to belong to the glittering circles of people like Isabella Delgado.

That in-between space was a lonely place to live. And though she wore her pride like a shield, she often found herself wondering where, if anywhere, she truly fit.

Carmen didn't believe in fairy tales. But sometimes, on quiet afternoons like this, when the city breathed slowly and the world outside felt far enough away, she let herself believe in a different kind of royalty.

Not one born of blood or name, but of fire. Of grace. Of a girl who came from nothing but who chose to walk like she came from everything.

A queen of her own making.

Not the kind in storybooks, helpless in towers, waiting to be rescued or redeemed. No, she imagined herself as a queen of fire and roses. Crownless, barefoot on marble floors. A queen who ruled with her eyes, with the way she held her spine straight even when the world pressed against it.

In that moment, she was no longer just a seamstress. She was a goddess, a woman capable of capturing the heart of any man who dared to love her. A woman who inspired poetry and songs, who could bring even the most powerful men to their knees. She imagined herself in the arms of a passionate lover, someone who saw her not just as a queen, but as a woman of depth and complexity.

The thought made her smile.

She dunked another blouse into the soapy water, the rhythm of her work softening into something almost ceremonial. Rinse. Wring. Pin to the clothesline out the window to dry.

She rinsed the last blouse and turned off the tap. Water dripped from her wrists, trailing down her forearms like glass threads. Somewhere in the distance, children shouted, an engine rumbled.

Carmen allowed herself to revel in the moment, savoring the feeling of contentment that washed over her. Her needlework lay in a pile on the kitchen table, a reminder of her reality. But her fantasy left a lingering sense of empowerment.

Suddenly, the quiet rhythm of the afternoon was broken by the low, mechanical growl of a motor. The unfamiliar sound rolled in through the open window. A deep, steady rumble that stood out sharply from the usual background hum of the neighborhood. Too mechanical to be a cart, too smooth to be a delivery truck. It grew louder, then slowed, then stopped just outside her door.

She froze, heart suddenly alert.

Her daydream scattered like drops across the floor.

No one she knew drove a car. Not on her street. Not in her world.

Carmen moved to the window and pulled back the curtain.

A gleaming silver motorcar stood parked on the street outside her house. And beside it, removing his gloves, brushing road dust off his shoulders, stood none other than *Francisco Piria.*

He exuded an air of elegance, which seemed remarkably out of place against the backdrop of her squalid little neighborhood.

Carmen stood there, frozen, her breath caught somewhere between her ribs and her throat. Her pulse surged in her ears like waves crashing against the shore.

What in the world was he doing here?

How had he found her?

For a brief moment, she wondered whether she was seeing things. If the weight of missing him had conjured his image from memory and longing. But no. He was real. Standing there. On her doorstep. Francisco Piria.

Her chest tightened with panic.

She wasn't ready. Not for this. Not for him. She had told herself that the letter, the book, the dream, had all been closure. A final chapter. That he had been a flash of meaning in a dark corridor. A brief, blinding moment that couldn't possibly belong to her real life. A door that had opened just wide enough to glimpse possibility… and then shut.

But now that door was standing in front of her. Waiting.

She dried her trembling hands on a dish towel, the familiar scent of the simmering stew grounding her in the reality of her small kitchen. Then, with effort, she turned off the burner, smoothed the front of her dress, and crossed the room. Her fingers hovered on the doorknob, hesitating, bracing, disbelieving, before she finally opened the door.

By the time Francisco had come around to the front of the car to step up on the curb, Carmen was already waiting.

"Good afternoon, *Señorita* Carmen." Francisco greeted her, as he doffed his driving cap, removing it and holding it earnestly in his hands.

Carmen felt a flicker of surprise, her composure wavering beneath the weight of his presence. His eyes—dark, magnetic—had the same intensity that had unsettled her from the first moment they met. His posture carried an effortless authority, graceful yet commanding, as though the very air bent slightly toward him.

Her pulse quickened despite herself. Curiosity mingled with caution.

"*Señor* Piria," she said at last, her tone cool, laced with disbelief. "How unexpected. How did you manage to find me?"

She leaned into the doorframe, crossing her arms, her expression hovering between amusement and warning.

He smiled, the curve of his mouth tempered with charm. "Please— Francisco," he corrected gently. "I asked a friend to make some discreet inquiries at the Madreselva. One of the regulars was kind enough to mention where you lived." He gave a small shrug, almost boyish in its humility. "I trust it wasn't too presumptuous of me."

Carmen wasn't surprised that he had found her so easily.

The gossips never sleep.

They're always watching. Always whispering.

Probably one of the old men at the corner table who can't dance anymore but remembers everything.

She observed Francisco intently as he stood there, his hat held earnestly in his hands.

To his credit, he looked hesitant. Careful. As if he sensed there was a line he might've crossed, even if he didn't mean to.

That softened her. A little.

Because most men would've looked pleased with themselves. Like finding her was a game, and winning meant possession. But Francisco?

He looked like someone who understood he had found a gate, not a door. And that it might not open just because he knocked.

She studied him. The lines around his mouth, the candor in his voice, the sincerity that made it hard to breathe. He didn't carry flowers or say anything rehearsed. He had only his presence. That quiet gravity she had come to recognize as truth.

"I have to admit, I had lost hope of ever seeing you again," Carmen said finally, her voice composed, though her fingers tightened in her palm. "It certainly is a surprise to see you here."

"I hadn't meant to disappear," he said. "Vienna kept me longer than planned. I trust you got my letter?"

"Yes," she responded, nodding once. "And the book."

Francisco didn't look smug. Didn't look like he thought he'd earned something. He looked... tentative. Almost as if he wasn't sure whether he had overstepped a boundary.

And that's what made her pause.

Because the men she was used to wouldn't have cared. Would've said her name like a trophy, not a question. Would've shown up with expectation, not apology.

Francisco didn't assume. He stood there, waiting for her to decide the next move.

She wasn't sure what she meant to say next. Whether to invite him in for stew or send him away. But the words clung to her throat like something unfinished.

So instead, she asked, quieter this time, "Why are you really here?"

"I was wondering if you would care to join me for a ride today," Francisco said, his voice low, measured, with that ever-present undertone of restraint. "I promise it will be an experience you won't forget."

Of course he said it like that. Like a line from a book left half-open beside a glass of wine. Always deliberate. Always just poetic enough to tempt her, but never so bold as to trap her.

An experience I won't forget, she echoed silently.

That could mean anything. And coming from him, it probably did.

Carmen hesitated for a moment, torn between her curiosity and the unexpectedness of the invitation. Her first instinct was to say no. To retreat behind sarcasm or suspicion. But something about the way he stood there, unguarded, slightly uncertain, made her hesitate.

"Forgive me. If I've overstepped, please say so... I'll leave." There was a hint of disappointment in his eyes.

Carmen studied him for a moment longer, her expression cool. She let the silence stretch, taut with possibility.

Her gaze flicked past him, down to the curb where the motorcar waited. It didn't belong on her street, and neither did he. Not really. But here he was. Asking, not taking.

She considered her reflection in the car's windowpane. Hair pinned back in a hurry, blouse slightly damp from where she'd been doing laundry, hands still smelling faintly of lavender soap. Hardly the picture of a woman ready to go spinning off into the unknown.

She looked tired, maybe. Or maybe just *real*. No lipstick, no perfume, no polished mask to hide behind.

She thought, absurdly, of the women Francisco probably spent time with in Vienna. Silk-slick and polished, with voices like music and fingertips like porcelain. Women who wore gloves even when they didn't need to.

And yet, here he was.

Not asking for perfection. Not asking her to become anything more than what she was, standing barefaced in her own doorway with the day still clinging to her skin.

A couple of neighbors, including the garrulous *viejita* on the corner, had started to poke their heads out to see what was going on, and Carmen thought she had better make up her mind.

"Yes, I suppose I could join you…" Carmen said finally, nervously eyeing the strange contraption he stood next to.

Francisco's lips parted, just slightly. Not a smile. Not relief. Something softer. Grateful.

"I can't be back too late," she warned.

"You have my word," he replied.

She grabbed her bag and her shawl from the hook on the wall and stepped outside, letting the door fall shut behind her.

Then, with that same dry elegance she always carried like a blade hidden behind her smile: "You're lucky I find surprise charming," she quipped, as she stepped off the front stoop.

The sleek, polished metal body of the silver motorcar gleamed in the sunlight, like something out of a dream she hadn't asked to have. It looked out of place here. Too polished. Too foreign. Like Francisco himself.

She'd seen cars before, of course, but she'd never actually ever sat in one. Certainly never been invited into one by a man like him.

The automobile's design was a mesmerizing blend of curves and angles, its long hood leading to a glass windshield and a plush, luxurious, open air cabin. Large, circular headlamps, like the eyes of a giant insect, adorned the front, giving it a peculiar and otherworldly appearance, like some sort of strange spacecraft from one of her Jules Verne novels.

Francisco, ever perceptive, caught the flicker of hesitation in her eyes. He said nothing, only opened the passenger-side door and extended his hand with an old-world grace that felt more like an offering than a gesture of habit.

She hesitated for a moment before taking his hand and accepting, as she stepped gingerly into the car. Her skirt rustled as she gathered it slightly and slid into the passenger seat. The leather was cool beneath her fingertips, the smell of old wood polish and warm tobacco clinging faintly to the interior.

The entire vehicle sat surprisingly low to the ground, and she was a bit frightened as she peered at all the intricate knobs and gauges on the vehicle's dashboard. She sat upright, hands folded in her lap, gaze fixed ahead like a passenger boarding a ship and unsure of the tide.

A few of the neighborhood boys who had been kicking a worn leather soccer ball down the street now stood clustered at the edge of the curb, wide-eyed and grinning as they gawked at the gleaming motorcar. One of them nudged another with his elbow and whispered something, and all three burst into stifled laughter.

Across the street, Doña Teresa, who hadn't missed a single piece of gossip since Carmen was a child, stood beneath her doorway with arms folded and a knowing expression. Her eyes swept over the vehicle, then narrowed sharply on Carmen inside it.

Carmen sank slightly into the seat, her spine stiff.

She wasn't embarrassed by *him*. Not exactly. It was the eyes. The watching. The unspoken stories already forming on people's tongues.

She could already hear it: *"Did you see her? In that car?"*

"She always thought she was better than the rest of us."

"She's selling herself, you know."

"A girl like that doesn't get a ride like that for free."

Carmen pulled her shawl tighter around her shoulders, more for armor than warmth.

They didn't know anything about living a life outside the prison they created for themselves.

The bars weren't made of iron. They were made of habit. Of bitterness. Of the small, petty pleasures that came from tearing someone else down just to feel taller for a moment.

They stayed behind their curtains and gates, clinging to pride like it could keep the roof from leaking, convincing themselves that sacrifice made them righteous and suffering made them pure.

And they certainly didn't know *her.*

She didn't look at them, didn't offer a wave, not even a glance toward the gathering cluster of murmuring mouths and squinting eyes.

Let them talk.

Let them twist it.

They could have their stories. She would write her own.

Francisco walked around the front of the car and hopped into the driver's seat beside her, pulling on a pair of leather driving gloves and gripping the large wooden steering wheel. His sleeves were rolled up, revealing strong brown forearms dusted with silver hair,

"Ready?" he beamed excitedly.

"Yes, I suppose I am." she replied nervously.

"I believe in experiencing life to the fullest, Señorita Carmen. And today, I want to show you a world beyond Montevideo. A world of beauty and magic."

He expertly cranked the engine to life, manipulating a bewildering array of levers and knobs, and the car purred to life like a contented beast. Puffs of steam and the scent of burning fuel rose into the air, a symphony of industry and innovation.

The motorcar rumbled as he eased it into motion, the boys stepping back with theatrical flair, whooping and laughing as the tires rolled past them.

A few of them tried to run and keep up with the automobile, but were quickly left behind, holding onto their hats and staring after them in awe, their mouths agape.

Carmen could still feel eyes on her as they turned the corner and pulled away from the block. Her stomach twisted. Not with shame, exactly, but with the old, familiar ache of not belonging. Of knowing that, to most, this moment looked like something it wasn't. Like wealth reaching down to pluck her out of her world. Like seduction dressed up in horsepower and leather seats.

But Francisco didn't try to touch her. Didn't speak for a while. He just drove, giving her silence where others would have filled it with flattery or noise.

And slowly, the tightness in her chest began to ease.

She leaned her elbow against the window frame, letting the wind loosen a strand of hair from behind her ear, and watched Montevideo pass by. Familiar streets and narrow alleyways fading into something unknown.

They drove through the city, past the old harbor, down into the dim curve of the Rambla. She looked around in amazement as the city's bustling streets and grand architecture faded into the distance.

The clamor of the urban landscape, with its ceaseless flow of people and vehicles, gradually gave way to the tranquil countryside, where open fields and rolling hills stretched as far as the eye could see. The contrast was striking, as they left behind the noise and chaos of the city for the serene beauty of nature.

Carmen marveled at the vast, open spaces, dotted with patches of wildflowers and grazing cattle. The air was fresher here, carrying the faint scent of earth and greenery, a welcome change from the urban smog.

The vibrant hues of verdant green seemed to stretch on for miles, painting a picture of stillness and tranquility that filled her heart with a sense of peace. It all felt so surreal.

"It's like a dream," Carmen marveled.

Carmen stared out at the horizon, the coast stretching endlessly ahead. The motorcar rumbled steadily beneath them, but in that moment, everything else seemed still.

"Life can be a dream if you dare to dream it, Carmen," Francisco said, his voice soft above the sound of the wind rushing through the open windows.

She turned to look at him.

He was watching her. Not with expectation, but quiet curiosity. That ever-present calm he wore so well. And just the faintest tug at the corner of his mouth, like he already knew she would roll her eyes at something so sentimental.

And she did.

She laughed.

Not the small, practiced kind she used to deflect compliments or soften uncomfortable truths, but a real one. Bright, unguarded, and a little surprised by its own weightlessness.

"Life can be a dream," she echoed. "But not everyone wakes up in the same reality, Don Francisco."

He didn't argue.

He didn't have to.

He just kept driving, the silence between them no longer filled with distance, but possibility.

"I've thought of you often in the time we've been apart," Francisco said finally, his voice low, unhurried. "I have to say, your passion and unique intelligence left quite an impression on me during our first encounter."

The words settled in the air between them like a slow-falling feather. Graceful. Intentional. Impossible to ignore.

Carmen didn't respond right away.

The words felt like a soft weight against her ribs. Too much and not enough, all at once. Like something she'd longed to hear and feared believing. She kept her gaze on the road ahead, pretending to focus on the blur of shoreline and sky.

Passion. Intelligence.

Words that had so often been turned against her. Flung like accusations or dismissed like inconveniences. From him, they sounded different. Not like flattery. Not like seduction. But recognition.

And recognition was more dangerous than desire.

"Most men remember what I look like, not what I say," she replied, her tone light, but her fingers curled slightly in her lap.

Francisco glanced at her. Not surprised, not offended.

"I'm not most men, Carmen," he said quietly.

Carmen gave a soft laugh, one without humor. "No. You're not."

For a few breaths, neither of them spoke. The wind whispered past the windows, and the road curved gently along the coast. The sea glittered with the last light of day, endless and indifferent.

She turned her head just slightly, looking at him out of the corner of her eye.

"I didn't realize I had left that much of an impression on you," she said at last, keeping her tone light, even as something stirred beneath it.

He looked at her then, really looked. "You made it impossible to forget, Señorita Carmen."

That silenced her. It wasn't the compliment that caught her off guard. It was the *tone*. The sincerity. As if he hadn't just remembered her, but *carried* her with him, like a poem half-memorized and recited under breath.

And so she said nothing. Not because she didn't have something clever to say, but because for the first time in a long while, she didn't want to hide behind cleverness.

Just let the quiet stretch out between them, warmer now. Not heavy. Not tense.

Just full.

Of what had been said.

Of what hadn't.

Of what still might be.

The motorcar rumbled steadily along the winding coastal road, the sea glinting beside them like molten silver beneath the fading light. The wind pulled at Carmen's shawl, teased strands of her hair loose, and carried the scent of salt and eucalyptus into the open air.

Silence with Francisco never seemed to feel empty. There was something about him. Something grounding. As if his presence filled the quiet with a sense of meaning, like the stillness between notes in a song that made the melody richer.

Ahead, the hills unfurled like a secret being revealed one turn at a time.

The motorcar purred along the winding coastal road, the sea stretching out beside them like a sheet of hammered silver. Francisco sat relaxed at the wheel, one hand guiding the machine while the other rested thoughtfully on his knee. Carmen's hair danced in the breeze, the salt air curling its ends as she gazed out at the shifting blue horizon.

He glanced sideways, a smile playing at the corners of his mouth.

"So," he said, his voice low over the hum of the engine, "what did you think of *Zarathustra*?"

Carmen turned to him, her expression thoughtful.

"I'm still... unraveling it," she admitted. "Some parts felt like riddles. But I think that was the point. It doesn't seem like a book you finish, but one you keep going back to."

Francisco nodded, pleased. "Good. If it were too easily understood, it wouldn't be worth much."

"I don't agree with everything," she added quickly. "At first, his idea of the *Übermensch* felt elitist. But then he'd say something so piercing, so true, I'd find myself underlining it twice."

She reached into her bag and pulled out the worn copy he'd given her, its margins now swollen with notes.

"I underlined this one," she said, flipping through the dog-eared pages. "*'One must still have chaos in oneself to be able to give birth to a dancing star.'*" She glanced over at him, the wind tugging at her hair. "That line... it didn't just speak to me. I felt it in my bones."

Francisco's smile curved, slow and knowing, a flicker of admiration lighting his gaze.

"I had a feeling you would," he said softly. "I recognized that same chaos in you, Carmen. I saw it the moment you stepped into that *milonga*." He paused, a faint smile touching his lips. "You didn't just dance, you lit up the room, like a star finding its own rhythm."

Carmen shifted slightly in her seat. She glanced out the window, giving her a moment to steady her breath. Compliments had always made her uneasy, especially ones that saw too much.

But this didn't feel like flattery. It felt like he'd peered straight into her, past every guarded corner, and still found something worth naming. Something luminous.

The road curved ahead, monumental hills beginning to rise in the distance like sleeping giants.

"So, where are we going?" Carmen asked finally, her voice softened by the wind, her eyes still fixed on the horizon.

Francisco smiled, keeping his gaze on the road. "To something I've been building for years. I want you to see it."

She arched an eyebrow. "And what exactly is it?"

He didn't answer right away.

"A dream," he said at last. "One I refused to let stay in my head."

Carmen glanced sideways at him, unsure whether to scoff or fall deeper under whatever spell he was weaving. "You sound like one of those poets who hang around cafes and never pay their tab."

He laughed, and the sound surprised her. Deep and real. "The difference is that I make my poetry come to life. I build what I imagine. I want you to see what happens when dreams become reality. When stubbornness meets sky."

The car crested a ridge, and suddenly, the landscape opened.

There it was.

Francisco slowed the car, his voice low with quiet pride.

"This… is *Piriápolis*," he said.

She drew in a sharp breath as the view burst into sight, wide and wondrous. Cradled between sweeping emerald hills and the shimmering expanse of the Atlantic, stretched out before them a coastal paradise so impossibly beautiful, so carefully imagined, that to Carmen, it really did feel like wandering into someone else's dream. And yet, somehow, it felt meant for her eyes.

A majestic, crescent-shaped bay curved gracefully into the coastline, embraced by rolling green hills that framed the view like a crown. Gentle waves lapped at a ribbon of golden sand, so pristine it shimmered in the sunlight. Along the shore, a palm-lined promenade stretched like a delicate thread, the fronds swaying softly in the ocean breeze.

Carmen had been to Playa Ramírez before, where she'd waded into the murky estuary of the Río de la Plata, its brown-tinted waters muddied by river sediments. But she had never seen the true Atlantic before, not like this.

Now, faced with its endless, impossibly blue horizon, she felt something electric surge through her chest. Exhilaration. Awe. A kind of reverence that silenced her every thought. The sunlight shimmered across the waves like scattered diamonds, the sea stretching out with a grandeur and wild beauty that stole her breath. It was not just a view. It was a revelation.

Carmen stared in wonder as the seaside town unfolded before her as they cruised along the promenade, a vivid tapestry of elegance and leisure bathed in golden sunlight. The beach stretched endlessly along the coast, its sands dappled with colorful umbrellas and dotted with sunbathers who moved with a quiet, unhurried grace.

Men lounged in straw boater hats and striped tank suits, their sleeves brushing elbows, their pant legs grazing their knees. Women strolled the shoreline in Turkish-style bloomers beneath knit frocks, their legs covered in stockings, slip-on sandshoes dusted with grains of sand. Each wore a bathing cap or silk bonnet in delicate hues that matched their ensembles, fluttering faintly in the sea breeze.

Above it all, the cries of seagulls drifted on the wind, mingling with the rhythmic hush of the tide and the distant creak of sailboats bobbing lazily in the bay's sparkling embrace.

And at the heart of it, impossible to miss, rose a grand hotel, poised proudly at the water's edge. The Hotel Piriápolis. Ornate. Audacious. A dream made stone.

Carmen's breath caught.

"*You built all this?*" she whispered.

He nodded. "Stone by stone. Idea by idea."

"But why all the way out here?"

"Because they said it couldn't be done." He glanced at her now, his eyes warm, serious. "Because I wanted to create a place that belonged to no one and everyone. For anyone brave enough to dream."

She was quiet for a long time, her gaze drifting over the still-growing city. She wasn't sure what stirred in her more: admiration, disbelief, or the quiet ache of wanting something she hadn't let herself name.

And then, quietly, almost without meaning to, she said:

"It's beautiful."

He looked at her. Not at the road, not at the resort. At her.

"So are you, my dear, when you're not busy doubting yourself."

Carmen turned her head, just slightly, as if unsure whether to meet his gaze or look away. The compliment hung in the air between them. Unexpected, unadorned, impossible to deflect.

She didn't thank him. She couldn't. Not yet.

She held his gaze for a breath, maybe two, then looked away again, overwhelmed by the vastness outside the window and the strange quiet blooming in her chest.

The car continued down the winding boulevard, the view shifting with each curve, revealing new angles of the dream he had built from dust and willpower. And yet, Carmen felt the real shift happening inside her. Slow, uncertain, but undeniable.

She wasn't sure what this place meant yet. Or what he meant to her. But for the first time in a long while, she wasn't afraid to find out.

As the motorcar climbed the winding coastal roads toward the bluff, the sea glinting far below in shifting shades of blue, Francisco's voice carried over the hum of the engine. Measured, certain, alive with purpose.

He spoke of what his vision could become.

Of extending the palm-lined promenade to embrace the entire curve of the bay, of elegant bathhouses and open-air pavilions, of gardens blooming where dust now gathered. He described an electric lift that would one day carry visitors up the hillside, and a theater by the water's edge that would bring art and music to even the most humble guests.

But more than grand architecture or seaside glamour, it was his talk of people that caught Carmen's ear.

"I want this place to be more than just a tourist destination," Francisco explained. "I want it to be a vibrant community where people from all walks of life can come together to live, work, and play."

Carmen listened, her gaze shifting between the rising skyline ahead and the man beside her. He wasn't boasting. He was building something. With words, with stone, with a kind of conviction she wasn't used to seeing outside of books.

Carmen turned to Francisco, her gaze thoughtful, touched by something deeper than mere admiration.

"That's a beautiful idea," she said quietly. "Creating a place that isn't just for visitors, but for residents to thrive as well, could really set this place apart. Making it about more than just the attractions, but also about fostering a sense of belonging and community."

She paused, glancing out toward the sweeping view of the bay. "Anyone can put up buildings. But giving people a reason to stay… that takes something else entirely."

Francisco nodded, a flicker of gratitude in his eyes at her understanding.

"Exactly," he said, his voice steady with conviction. "I don't just want to build hotels and cafés. I want schools, parks, libraries. Spaces where people can grow roots, not just pass through. Places where children can dream bigger, and neighbors can gather without needing a reason."

He glanced out toward the unfinished city below, then back at her. "Tourism may keep the lights on, but it can't be the whole story. I want people to belong here, to feel proud of what they're part of. Not just workers in uniforms, but partners in something that lasts."

The motorcar wound its way higher along the coastal road, climbing with steady purpose until, at last, they reached the summit. Francisco eased the vehicle to a stop, the engine purring into silence. Without a word, he stepped out and came around to open the door for Carmen, offering his hand with quiet formality.

She stepped out onto the bluff, the wind cool and crisp, tinged with the briny scent of the sea. Her shawl fluttered gently behind her as she followed him to the edge of the overlook.

And then, she saw it.

Spread out below them like a vision made real, the city of Piriápolis unfolded in sweeping, breathtaking detail. Nestled between rich, green hills and the endless sweep of the glittering Atlantic, the town stretched out like a living tapestry. Red-tiled roofs and whitewashed buildings caught the sunlight, gleaming against the blue sky like scattered pearls.

For a long moment, Carmen could only stand there, breathless.

The coastline curved with natural grace, cradling the turquoise sea as waves rolled in, kissing the shore with a rhythm as old as time. Everything shimmered with a kind of quiet magic, as if the land itself pulsed with a hidden energy. Something ancient, something waiting.

"It's incredible," she said at last, her voice hushed with wonder. "You managed to blend nature and civilization so seamlessly. It feels less like something built, and more like something grown. Like this place was always meant to exist."

Francisco smiled at her reaction, a quiet pride flickering in his eyes. "Thank you," he said softly. "It's been a labor of love. Every stone, every line of it."

He turned to face her, the wind catching the edges of his coat as a more reflective expression settled across his face.

"This, Carmen," he continued, gesturing to the expanse before them, "is the culmination of a dream. A dream that first took root the moment I stood on this very bluff."

His gaze drifted toward the horizon, his voice lowering with a trace of nostalgia. "The first time I came up here, I felt something stir in me. Something wild and consuming, like the fevered rush of a lover's first glance. And in that moment... the city appeared in my mind, fully formed. Not in stone, not yet. But alive. In color, in music, in purpose."

He looked back at Carmen then, his expression softened, unguarded.

"I suppose some visions aren't born from logic," he said with a wry smile. "They're born from fire."

Carmen listened closely, drawn in by the quiet conviction beneath Francisco's words.

"I originally named it Heliópolis," he said, a glint of warmth in his eyes. "Greek for 'City of the Sun.' A fitting name for a sunny beach resort, don't you think?"

He paused, smiling to himself as if at an old joke.

"But fate, as always, had other ideas."

His voice took on a note of amusement. "When word of my plans reached the press, they couldn't help themselves. They ridiculed me and my idea. This empty stretch of coast, transformed into a resort city? Madness, they said. And so, half in jest, they started calling it *'Piriápolis'* in the papers. My name, tacked onto the grandiosity of my dream."

He laughed softly, shaking his head. "Mockery, at first. But...the name stuck. And now...well, here we are."

Carmen followed his gaze as it swept across the vista below. So vast, so carefully imagined. In that moment, Francisco looked almost mythic to her, like a monarch surveying his chosen kingdom. Not with arrogance, but with the calm certainty of someone who dared to believe before anyone else could see.

"It seems only right that this place should bear your name, Francisco," Carmen said softly, her voice touched with genuine awe. "Not many people can say they've built an entire city from nothing. Especially not one so full of beauty and purpose. It's incredible to think this all began as an idea in your mind."

She turned to look at him fully, her gaze lingering on his profile, lit by the fading glow of the sun. There was something almost unreal about him in that moment. A man who had dared to shape the world around him, and somehow, succeeded.

A subtle ache bloomed in her chest. Part awe, part something she couldn't yet name. There was a gravity to him, a brilliance that both unsettled and captivated her. How could one man bring something so impossible to life?

She turned to him, her voice hushed with wonder.

"But how?" she asked. "How did you make all of this real?"

Then, with a faint smile tugging at the corner of her lips, she added, "I'm sure you've heard the rumors people throw around, that they say you're an alchemist, that you conjured your fortune through some kind of magic."

She looked up at him, her eyes bright with curiosity. Half teasing, half serious, as if daring him to confess something mystical.

He chuckled, the sound low and unhurried, as he turned his gaze toward her. And there they were again. Those eyes.

Carmen caught her breath.

There was something about them. Dark, fathomless, quietly consuming. They held the weight of things unsaid, as if entire constellations of secrets shimmered just beyond reach. Each time their eyes met, it felt like gravity shifted, drawing her further into something she couldn't explain.

What if he really has enchanted me? She wondered, half in jest, half spellbound by the strange electricity that seemed to hum between them.

"It's funny," Francisco said, amusement laced through his voice as they began walking side by side through the windswept meadow above the cliffs. "People would rather believe in magic than admit what hard work and vision can do. *It must be magic. Alchemy*, they say, because accepting the truth would require facing it. And truth is far less seductive than the illusion of magic. Too plain, too demanding, too ordinary for their taste."

But there was nothing ordinary about him.

And Carmen, still watching the way the light played along the angles of his face, wasn't sure she disagreed.

"The truth is, Carmen, we're all alchemists in our own way," he said, his voice low and reflective. "Once you realize that the essence of life lies in the transformation of our own thoughts, and that with the intention of our hearts, the impossible begins to be within reach."

He paused, letting the breeze carry his words like something sacred.

"You see, wealth, power… they're merely echoes of our inner world. I didn't build this life by chasing gold or acclaim. It all began with a journey inward. With learning to shape the intangible first: *thought, belief, intention*. The rest followed." He looked at her then, his gaze steady. "True transmutation doesn't begin with stone or silver. It begins within oneself."

Carmen walked beside him in silence for a moment, the grass brushing against her skirts as the sea breeze lifted strands of her hair. His words lingered. Too poetic to dismiss outright, too unsettling to ignore.

She had always thought of life as something to endure, to navigate carefully. You survive it, if you're lucky. You don't shape it. You certainly don't transmute it.

And yet…

There was something intoxicating about the certainty in his voice. As if he'd cracked a code no one had ever bothered to write down.

She glanced up at him, her tone quiet but clear. "You make it sound so simple. Like all you need is boldness and belief."

"It's not simple," he said. "But it is possible."

She looked out over the vast blue horizon, her voice thoughtful now, shaded with wonder.

He smiled, a knowing warmth in his eyes. "You see, Carmen, the greatest gift we've been given is *will*. The freedom to choose, to create. Every day, with every thought and action, we're shaping the course of our own lives."

He gestured softly to the world around them, to the city that rose from sea and stone.

"I began with a vision. Not a fleeting hope, but something vivid and complete. I saw it all clearly, down to the finest details, as if it were already real. And with time, step by step, it became truth."

He paused, his voice lowering with quiet conviction.

"You see, our thoughts are like seeds. Once you plant them in the fertile soil of the mind, they begin to take root. If you feed your thoughts with fear, doubt, and worry, that is the harvest you'll reap. But if you fill your mind with visions of what could be, and your heart with gratitude, hope, and purpose, then the world around you begins to bend in that direction."

Carmen narrowed her eyes slightly, her steps slowing as she considered his words. She wasn't one to dismiss ideas outright, but the ease with which he spoke of shaping reality felt... idealistic. Romantic. Even a little dangerous.

"You make it sound so effortless," she said quietly. "As if dreaming were enough to rewrite the world."

Francisco glanced at her, but didn't interrupt.

She continued, her voice more steady now, tinged with the edge of truth. "What about the rest of us? Those of us who don't have land or money or family names? I've known people with dreams bigger than the sky, and they still go hungry. I've watched my mother work herself to the bone just to keep a roof over our heads. She dreamed of a better life too, but dreams don't feed you."

There was no bitterness in her tone, only the weight of reality.

"I don't mean to dismiss what you've built," she added, softer now. "It's extraordinary. Truly. But I've lived in a world where survival comes first. And it's hard to believe that just thinking differently would have changed any of that."

She looked at him, searching his face for something. Proof, maybe, that he understood the cost of dreaming without a safety net.

Francisco listened without flinching, her words hanging in the air with the quiet force of truth. When she finished, he didn't rush to respond. He looked out over the horizon for a long moment, as if remembering a time when it hadn't looked like a dream at all, just a stretch of empty land and doubt.

"You're right," he said softly. "It wasn't easy. And it wasn't instant."

He turned to face her fully, the usual grandeur in his voice replaced by something quieter, more grounded.

"There were years when I couldn't afford to dream either. When I went without meals. Without certainty. There were days when the only thing I owned were the visions in my head, and even that felt foolish at times."

His gaze softened, but didn't waver.

"It's true, dreams alone aren't enough. You first need that unshakable fire inside you, that quiet certainty that *knows* you were meant for something more than what the world's handed you. That's what carries you forward, even when the path is unclear."

Carmen nodded slowly, her gaze drifting out toward the horizon as his words settled deep in her chest.

She thought of the familiar ache she'd carried for as long as she could remember. That silent, burning thread inside her that insisted there was more. That she was more.

But then her thoughts turned to people like her friend, Nico. Dear, complicated Nico, who often moved through life carrying his own quiet wants, but who let the world's rejection weigh him down. Her heart clenched with the thought.

"What about people who carry that spark, but still feel invisible? The ones who keep running into closed doors, no matter how hard they try?" Carmen asked, her voice tight with emotion.

She turned her gaze out toward the horizon, where the last streaks of sunlight were bleeding into the sea. "What about those who long for more, but are too busy just trying to make it through the day to even begin dreaming?"

Francisco didn't answer right away. He watched her, the wind tugging softly at her hair as she hugged her shawl tighter around her shoulders. Then he stepped a little closer, not to crowd her, but to stand beside her in quiet solidarity.

"It goes deeper than just wanting something, Carmen," he said finally, his voice low, grounded. "Your thoughts must align with your deepest values…with your true, God-given purpose. You have to ask yourself: *What is my true purpose? And how can that purpose ripple outward, serving more than just myself?*"

He looked out over the cliffside with her, the two of them suspended in the stillness between sky and sea.

"It's when your intentions are rooted in love, in contribution…that's when everything shifts," he added. "That's when life, the universe, God, the Creator, whatever name you give to the Divine, begins to move *with* you, not against you."

Carmen's brow furrowed slightly, and she folded her arms across her chest, the breeze tugging gently at her sleeves.

"That sounds beautiful," she said slowly, "but the world I've known doesn't seem to reward good intentions." Her gaze drifted out toward the sea, steady and sharp. "I've seen the kindest people broken by bad luck. I've seen selfish men rise while others with generous hearts get left behind."

She turned to him, her voice clear. "So how do you explain that? If the universe rewards service and love, then why does it so often look like it favors power and cruelty?"

There was no anger in her words, only an earnest need to understand. To know if what he said was just poetry, or something she could actually hold on to.

"I want to believe you," she added softly. "But I need to know this isn't just another story we tell ourselves to soften disappointment."

Francisco's expression softened, a faint, almost wistful smile touching his lips. He let her question hang for a moment, the distant rush of the sea filling the silence between them.

"You must understand, life doesn't reward the loudest or the strongest. It rewards those who keep their hearts aligned when no one's watching. Those who move through chaos without letting it poison them. It's not about avoiding pain or failure, Carmen, those will come for all of us. It's about staying true when it would be easier to give in, to harden, to become like the very forces you despise."

Francisco's expression sobered. He turned his gaze back toward the horizon, but his voice no longer carried the smooth cadence of a man used to being believed. It was rawer now. Real.

"There was a time when I lost everything," he said. "Not just money, but my name. My reputation. A business partner I trusted betrayed me, and I was too proud to see it until it was too late. Friends I thought were loyal turned their backs on me. The press crucified me. My late wife took my children and kept them from me. I couldn't even walk through Montevideo without hearing my name spat like a curse."

He paused, his jaw tightening, a shadow passing over his features.

"For three weeks, I slept in an abandoned carriage," he went on. "No home, no allies, nothing left but the stubborn belief that I wasn't finished. That maybe…maybe life wasn't punishing me, but tempering me. Testing how much I could endure before I became who I was meant to be."

His dark eyes lifted to hers then, stripped of pretense or power.

"I've learned something since then," Francisco said, voice steady. "Right before life opens a door, it will try to break you. Everything will seem to crumble at once. Most people turn back here. They second-guess, convince themselves the dream wasn't meant for them. But if you can keep walking when it feels impossible, if you can hold onto your vision even when no one else sees it… that's when the tide turns. That's when things begin to shift."

He smiled faintly, but there was no triumph in it. Only truth.

"I don't believe in fairy tales, Carmen. But I believe in transformation. Because *I've lived it*."

Carmen was quiet for a long moment, his words hanging in the air between them. Heavy, human, and disarming.

She hadn't expected that. Not from him.

She had been braced for idealism. For another sermon from a man who'd never known hunger or shame.

But what she got was something else entirely. Humility. Bruised truth. A glimpse of someone who had once fallen, hard, and chosen to rise anyway.

Her arms slowly loosened around her chest.

"I had no idea," she said softly. "I just assumed..."

She trailed off, unsure of how to finish the thought without admitting how tightly she clung to her defenses. How often she had assumed that men like him, men who wore tailored suits and spoke of destiny, had always lived above the weight of reality.

"That, Carmen," he said softly, his gaze holding hers, "is the purest form of alchemy: not the changing of metals, but the transformation of the soul."

Francisco stooped to pluck a wildflower sprouting from the rocky earth. He rolled its stem gently between his fingers, then held it out to her, a fragile offering.

"To take sorrow," he continued, his voice reverent, "and shape it into something that lifts others... that breathes beauty into the world."

His tone dropped to a near whisper, as if speaking to the wind itself.

"To turn wounds into wisdom," he murmured, "and heartache into something everlasting."

They stood in silence at the edge of the bluff, the wind wrapping gently around them like a whispered lullaby. Below, the sea continued its endless rhythm, waves curling against the shore with the steady grace of something eternal. The sun had dipped lower now, casting the landscape in a soft amber glow that turned every surface to gold.

"Let me share a secret," he said, his tone quiet but firm. "Consistency, aligned with intention...*that's* the key. I took deliberate steps toward my vision each and every single day, even if they were the smallest of tasks. Progress didn't always look impressive, but each action was a declaration: *I'm serious about this. I'm not just dreaming, I'm committed.*"

Carmen turned to him, letting his words sink deep, their weight settling over her like a slow, steady tide. For a long moment, she simply breathed, the silence between them rich and alive.

At last, she spoke, her voice low and measured, shaped by quiet revelation.

"I think I see it now," she said. "It's not only about the dream itself, but the resolve to keep walking toward it, even when the path is lonely, even when no one else believes."

Her gaze met his, steady and unflinching. "It's the small, relentless steps," she murmured, "repeated day after day, that turn vision into something lasting. Something that can't be undone."

"Exactly," Francisco said with a thoughtful nod. "But you must never mistake wealth or power as the end goal. They're only instruments. They can build or destroy, depending on who holds them. Real fulfillment comes from the journey. Who you become through it, the lives you touch, and the legacy you leave behind."

The hillsides were awash with blooming violets, their vibrant purple petals scattered like brushstrokes across the green. Carmen slowed her steps, her gaze drawn to a small cluster growing resiliently between the stones. She knelt slightly, fingertips grazing the delicate blooms as if they held a secret meant only for her.

"I've always felt a little lost inside my own dreams," she admitted, her voice barely above the breeze. "Like they were too big, too far away."

She glanced up at him, a quiet determination beginning to rise in her chest.

"But listening to you, I realize that it's not necessarily about having the whole path figured out. It's about taking the first small step, and then another. And not losing hope, being determined enough to keep going."

Francisco watched her, his expression softening as she spoke.

He stepped closer, his gaze following the violets blooming stubbornly between the cracks.

"You see those?" he said gently. "No one planted them. No one told them the soil was good enough. But they grew anyway. Quietly, steadily. They didn't wait for perfect conditions. They just reached for the light, one inch at a time."

He looked at her then, his voice low but certain.

"You don't need to see the whole garden, Carmen. You only need to trust that something beautiful can come from wherever you choose to begin."

They wandered along the sun-dappled hillsides, the earth beneath their feet soft with spring's awakening. Wildflowers stretched in joyful bursts across the knolls: blues, purples, and soft whites tangled in the tall grass like nature's embroidery. With every step, new clusters appeared, as if the land itself were blooming in welcome.

Francisco slowed his pace, pausing to kneel beside a patch of delicate white blossoms nestled among the green.

"Look here," he said, his voice hushed with reverence. "*Yerba lucero.*"

He ran his fingers gently along the edge of the leaf, as if honoring something sacred. "The indigenous people, the Charrúa, brewed this into a tea. It's said to ease the body and soothe the spirit. Headaches, indigestion... but also grief. They believed the plant knew how to comfort what words could not."

Carmen knelt beside him, her eyes soft with curiosity as Francisco carefully gathered a small bundle of the herb, folded it into a handkerchief, and tucked it into the pocket of his jacket with quiet veneration.

"And this one?" she asked, pointing to a nearby cluster of small, daisy-like flowers swaying in the breeze.

"*Manzanilla*," he said with a faint smile. "For calming nerves, and quieting racing thoughts."

She listened, drawn in by his quiet passion, the way he treated the land not just as property, but as inheritance, living history woven with memory and care.

As he spoke, something stirred in her. Something deeper than just admiration. It was a feeling of connection, not just to him, but to the earth beneath her, to the stories that lingered in every bloom, every breeze.

For the first time in a long while, Carmen didn't feel like she was on the outside of someone else's world. She felt invited in.

"You've given me so much to think about," she said softly, her voice touched with wonder. "More than you know."

"Of course, *querida*. Life is a grand adventure, and you're just beginning yours. Walk it with a purpose, align your intentions with your heart, and the universe will respond in ways you can't yet imagine."

The sun was slipping gently into the arms of the horizon, casting a golden veil across the sea. The ocean shimmered like glass touched by fire, and the sky above them blushed in soft shades of amber and rose.

Carmen turned her gaze from the glowing water to Francisco, then downward toward the city that sprawled beneath them. His dream, made stone. The weight of the day, its revelations and quiet miracles, settled in her chest like a secret too big to name.

The breeze picked up, warm and gentle, tugging playfully at her hair. The air smelled of salt and violets, of sun-warmed earth and possibility.

Without a word, Francisco slipped off his coat and laid it over a soft patch of grass. She watched him, heart thudding quietly, as he lowered himself and gestured for her to join him.

Carmen sank down beside him, knees drawn in, arms wrapped loosely around them. They sat in silence, side by side, as the sun melted slowly into the sea.

And for a moment, with the sky ablaze and the horizon wide open before them, it felt less like a dream and more like the beginning of something real. Something neither of them dared to name just yet.

She looked up at him, her breath catching slightly in her throat.

"Thank you. Not just for your words…but for sharing this part of yourself with me," Carmen whispered, her voice barely louder than the wind. "For showing me a world I never knew existed."

Francisco turned to her, his gaze steady. His face, marked by time and experience, held the kind of strength carved not just by age, but by endurance.

For a moment, they simply looked at each other. Two souls shaped by different paths, drawn together by something neither could fully name.

It wasn't logic that had led them here, nor chance. It felt older than both. As if time itself had been weaving them toward this one breath, this one moment between heartbeats.

Fate, perhaps. Or something deeper.

"My world…" Francisco's voice came low, almost hesitant, as if he were admitting the thought to himself as much as to her. "Before you arrived, Carmen, my world was precise, ordered. Every stone I laid had its place, every plan its measure. It was solid, yes, but lifeless, like a statue." His gaze held hers, unflinching. "And then you came. Suddenly there was breath in it. Color. Fire... you've made it feel alive."

Carmen's breath caught.

The weight of his confession settled between them like a held breath, the silence that followed rich with both anticipation and unspoken meaning.

His dark eyes searched hers, not with urgency, but with reverence.

Her heart, already fluttering from the emotion of the day, now thundered against her ribs like it was trying to break free.

"Carmen," Francisco began softly, taking her hand in his, his touch warm and steady. The setting sun cast a golden glow across his features, softening the lines that time had etched into his face.

Her heart beat wildly in her chest as his fingers brushed against hers. Lightly at first, as if asking permission. The warmth of his touch spread up her arm like fire, unspoken but undeniable.

"From the moment our paths crossed, something about you stayed with me. Something I couldn't quite explain or forget. It was as if your presence left a mark…one that went deeper than reason."

His eyes met hers: dark, unguarded, full of longing.

"Your fire, your fearlessness, has sparked new light into my life, Carmen. Into corners I didn't even realize had grown dim. The way you move, the way you see things. It captivated me. It still does."

The world seemed to pause around them. The breeze, the sea, the fading light, all conspiring to give space to the truth hanging delicately in the air.

"I know we've only just begun this story… and I've tried, truly, to keep my distance. To reason my way out of these feelings. But something about being with you here, like this, makes it impossible. I can no longer pretend."

He paused, searching her face, his voice dipping into something more vulnerable.

Carmen's heart fluttered at his words, their sincerity wrapping around her like a warm, unexpected breeze. For a moment, she let herself linger in the tenderness of his gaze, her own emotions mirrored there, unspoken, but undeniable.

Her first instinct was to run, as she had always done when things grew too big, too beautiful, too close.

But another part of her, a softer, braver part, held her still.

Instead, her lips parted, her eyes softened, and her voice, small, trembling, barely escaped her throat.

"…Francisco…"

And then, gently, she pulled her hands away.

Not in rejection, but in self-preservation.

She stood and turned slightly, her eyes fixed on the horizon, the last light of day flickering across the sea like a question she didn't yet know how to answer.

"But, why?" she asked, her voice low, trembling at the edges. "Why me?"

She shook her head, more to herself than to him.

He stood up to meet her.

Her pulse thrummed in her ears like a warning bell, louder than the hush of the wind or the rhythmic crash of the waves below.

She could feel the heat of Francisco's gaze behind her, but she didn't turn. She couldn't. Not when the fragile scaffolding of her confidence felt ready to collapse beneath the weight of his belief in her.

"There are so many women who would be so much more suitable, more polished, more... belonging to your world, Francisco. I don't come from salons or marble halls. I don't have a family name or wealth or anything that makes sense next to a man like you."

She looked at him then, her eyes filled not with doubt of him, but of her place in his world.

Her world was sharp-edged and practical. Threadbare dresses, whispered judgments, nights spent mending what was broken instead of daring to build something new.

She had spent so long guarding her heart, pretending she didn't care when doors closed or chances slipped through her fingers.

It was safer not to want too much. Safer to keep her dreams folded tightly in the corners of her mind, never quite real, never quite reachable.

But now… here he was. This man who looked at her like she mattered. Not just for her beauty, or her body, or even the way she danced, but for her mind, her spirit, her fire.

And that terrified her more than anything.

Francisco's expression softened as he reached out, his fingers gentle beneath her chin, guiding her gaze back to his.

"I see you, Carmen," he said quietly. "Not where you come from. Not your name. You."

His gaze didn't waver. "And you see me. Not my name, not my title, but me." His voice was steady, but laced with something raw. "And you don't shrink from it. You meet it head-on."

He studied her for a moment, as if committing every part of her to memory.

"You challenge me, Carmen. You inspire me. With your wit, your fire, your refusal to be anything other than exactly who you are. Most women I've known would have *never* left the house without a wardrobe crisis and a dozen second thoughts. They only worry about their hemlines and headlines, about propriety and perception."

He smiled faintly, a trace of awe in his voice now.

"But you…you step into the world as you are. Unafraid. Passionate. Dancing, knowing the world is watching, and daring it to keep up. And that… that is what has captured me."

He paused, his eyes never leaving hers.

"It wasn't something I planned. But I look at you, and I see truth. And somewhere along the way… that truth became the very thing my heart began to yearn for."

Carmen shook her head gently, her brows drawn with uncertainty. "But… what about the years between us? The difference in our lives, our worlds?"

She looked away for a moment, gathering the courage to speak the truth lingering just beneath her fear.

"The people in your world, Francisco. Society… they'll never accept us."

Her voice was quiet, but the weight behind it was unmistakable: she wasn't questioning her feelings, only whether the world would allow her to have them.

"*Mira*, Carmen," Francisco said gently, "the world is always shifting, and the opinions of others, those are the most fleeting things of all. What endures… is love. Connection. The joy we find in the rare moments where two souls truly meet."

He took her hand again, more gently than before. "If we live by their approval, we'll never live at all. The question isn't whether others will approve, it's whether we have the courage to claim what we already know is real, and to believe in it."

Her heart beat wildly, stirred by the pull of something she couldn't name. Part of her longed to believe it, to fall into the warmth of it, to surrender to the wild, blooming feeling that had been quietly taking root in her chest since the first moment they danced.

But fear had a voice too.

What if she wasn't enough for the world he came from? What if he woke one day and realized he'd romanticized the idea of her, not the reality? What if love, no matter how poetic, simply wasn't enough?

Her breath caught, and she looked away for a moment, her voice barely above a whisper.

"I want to believe it," she said. "More than anything."

She turned back to him, eyes wide with the weight of hope and hesitation.

Francisco didn't speak.

He didn't try to answer her fears with grand declarations or promises he couldn't yet make. Instead, he simply reached for her hand. Slowly, gently. Threading his fingers through hers with a tenderness that spoke without words.

His thumb brushed lightly across her knuckles, steady and warm.

No pressure. No urgency. Just presence.

Carmen looked down at their joined hands, her breath hitching slightly. Not from fear now, but from the tenderness of it. The way he didn't rush her. The way he allowed her doubts to exist without pushing them away.

The sky had faded to a soft indigo, the stars beginning to pierce through the velvet above them. And as the night unfurled around them, vast and quiet, something in her heart shifted.

She didn't have all the answers.

But in that moment, she knew. She wasn't alone in the asking.

And maybe, just maybe, that was where love began.

Francisco smiled gently, his eyes never leaving hers as he reached up to brush a tendril of hair from her cheek, his touch feather-light, tender.

"This is only the beginning," he said softly. "Whatever lies ahead, we'll face it together. One step at a time."

He paused, his voice lowering with quiet hope.

"All I ask is a chance. A chance to see where this could lead. Will you walk beside me, on this new adventure, *Carmencita*?"

Carmen's breath hitched in her throat at the sound of her name, *Carmencita*, spoken with such gentleness, such care.

Her heart thudded against her ribs, a quiet thunder of emotion she could no longer deny.

For a moment, she forgot where she was. The hilltop, the sea, the wind whispering through the tall grass all blurred in the background. All she could see was him.

The way Francisco looked at her then, unflinching, vulnerable, certain, made her chest tighten with something too vast to name. Her heart pounded like a drum, loud and insistent, as if trying to warn her and welcome him all at once.

Is this real? she wondered, panic flickering just beneath the surface of her awe.

Does he mean it? Truly? Or am I just another muse for a man who builds dreams out of air and stone?

But the look in his eyes wasn't the fleeting gaze of a man enchanted by novelty. It was something steadier. Something that saw her not as a fantasy, but as a mirror. Flawed and real and luminous.

She met his gaze, and in the depths of Francisco's eyes, she saw it. Not persuasion, but recognition. A love that felt ancient, fated. As though their hearts had known each other long before their bodies ever crossed paths.

A love that defied logic and timelines, whispered not in words but in something older, written in the stars.

With a trembling breath, she gave the only answer her heart had been aching to say.

"Yes," she breathed, her voice a whisper over the wind.

Francisco's eyes softened, and for a moment, he simply looked at her. Truly looked, as if trying to memorize the exact shape of that moment.

He stepped closer, his voice hushed and reverent.

"Then let this be the first step… of everything," he murmured tenderly, cupping her face with an adoration that made it hard to breathe.

Carmen closed her eyes and leaned into his touch, a warmth unfurling inside her like a rose opening to the golden warmth of the summer sun.

In that stillness, her walls quietly slipped away, and finally she let herself surrender.

And then, without urgency, without question, Francisco leaned in, and he kissed her. Gently at first, like a vow.

It was a kiss that asked nothing and promised everything. Soft, searching, and achingly real, as if time itself had stilled to let them find one another in the quiet between heartbeats.

A slow burn.

A promise.

And when they pulled apart, the stars had fully bloomed above them.

The sea sighed below, the earth still beneath them.

And between them something infinite had just begun.

Chapter 9

The weeks that followed unfolded in a hush of golden light, as if the world had slowed just for them. Time took on a dreamlike rhythm, each moment lingering like the final note of a melody: sweet and slow, yet slipping away far too soon.

Their mornings began in Piriápolis, with leisurely walks along the shores of the beach. The ocean provided a soothing backdrop as they walked side by side, their footsteps leaving imprints in the soft sand. Around them, the sunlight spilled like honey over the surf, gilding the waves in light as they rolled in and out with a lullaby's patience.

On weekends, when Carmen's schedule allowed and Francisco wasn't pulled away by business, they found themselves returning to this stretch of shore as if by some unspoken agreement, drawn back again and again by a force neither of them could name. It was as though the tide itself conspired to bring them there, carrying them to the one place where the world fell away and only the two of them remained.

The shoreline became their refuge, a place where the clamor of the world fell away with the tide. Between the hiss of waves and the sweep of sky, they found something rare: privacy, a space where words could flow as freely as the sea.

Here, on the sand, the beach turned into their chapel, their confessional, their canvas. It was in these stolen hours that Francisco revealed the pieces of himself he showed no one else: the boy who once lay awake beneath strange constellations, tracing futures in the dark, dreaming of monuments that might outlast him.

One morning, as the horizon bled pale gold, his voice broke the stillness. "My father was a sailor…" he said, the words heavy, deliberate. His gaze stayed fixed on the skyline. "I lost him to the sea when I was still a young boy."

Carmen turned to him, studying the stillness in his features. The kind of stillness born from wounds learned to be carried, not cured.

"It happened so suddenly," he continued. "No storm. No warning. One moment, he was there. The next… he was gone."

Carmen didn't speak right away. Instead, she let the silence stretch, respectful and unintrusive. The tide whispered against the shore, its rhythm steady and ancient, as if the ocean itself mourned with him.

Quietly, she reached for his hand, her fingers threading through his. His grip tightened almost imperceptibly, like someone startled by the comfort they didn't know they needed.

"I'm so sorry, Francisco," she said gently, her voice steady and low. "You must've had to grow up so fast after that. I know that kind of loss… it leaves a mark."

"It does," he admitted, his eyes still on the water. "It was the first time I realized how fragile life truly is. How powerless we are to stop it from changing without our consent."

Carmen hesitated, then said softly, "I can't pretend to understand exactly what you went through. But I do know what it's like to grow up without a father. Mine left when I was very small. No explanation. Just… absence. It leaves a kind of emptiness, doesn't it? A question that never quite gets answered."

He turned to her slowly, his expression shifting, less guarded now, more open. "It does," he said. "It leaves a hollow space that teaches you how to live without expecting much. But also how to find strength where you didn't think any existed."

They walked on, the sun warming their skin, the sea murmuring beside them like an old companion.

"It's true," she said softly, her voice barely above a whisper. "My mother gave everything she had, but there were nights we still went to bed hungry. I had to grow up quickly, to find ways to help, to stay strong for the both of us. There wasn't space to just… be a child."

"Yes, my mother also did what she could," Francisco went on. "But with my father gone, she found herself with five children to feed, and no income. So she made the impossible choice, and sent me away to live with my uncle in Italy. An uncle I didn't even know. I was barely six years old…I thought it meant she'd given up on me."

Carmen's heart ached at the quiet in his voice. He didn't speak of it bitterly, just as fact, as history he'd grown from.

"I was headstrong," he said, a faint, self-aware smile tugging at the corner of his lips. "Too much fire, they used to say. Maybe my mother thought I'd burn the house down if I stayed."

Carmen smiled faintly, brushing her thumb against his knuckles. "Or maybe she saw the potential in you. That you were the one strong enough to turn exile into destiny."

He glanced at her then, something shifting in his eyes. Gratitude, perhaps, or something deeper.

"My uncle saw that fire in me. He believed only God could temper me," Francisco continued, his voice low, almost reverent with memory. "He sent me away to study at the monastery of San Fantino, in Palmi. I was just a little boy. Too wild to understand discipline, too young to understand why love sometimes meant sacrifice."

He paused, his gaze drifting.

"There I was, alone in a strange place, surrounded by silence and stone walls. I missed my father. Missed my mother even more. I used to lie awake at night, wondering why she had sent me away, and not my brothers. For a long time, I thought it was because I was too much, too difficult to love."

Carmen's heart ached at the confession. She squeezed his hand gently.

She paused, eyes fixed on the horizon, as if the waves might carry away what she was about to say.

"It's a strange thing, isn't it?" she said after a moment. "The way children carry so much weight without knowing how to name it. I didn't understand it either, back then, why after my father left everything suddenly felt so cold, so different. I used to hear my mother crying herself to sleep at night. I used to lie awake at night too, staring at the ceiling, wondering what I'd done wrong, and why love seemed to be something that had to be earned instead of something given."

Her voice faltered, then steadied again.

"One day we were a family, and the next…" Carmen paused again, her voice catching slightly. "I felt like a burden she never meant to carry." She stared ahead, her gaze unfocused. "You know, they say I have my father's eyes…and sometimes I wonder if that's why my mother can't bear to look at me. Like I'm a mirror she didn't choose. I tried so hard to make her love me. But it was never enough."

Francisco didn't speak right away. He looked at her the way someone might look at a wounded part of themselves, tenderly, without flinching.

"I also know that ache," he said quietly. "At the monastery, they made us believe that to be good was to be small. Polite. Devout. Invisible. I thought if I prayed hard enough, stayed quiet enough, became useful enough… maybe then my mother would want me back. Maybe then I could go home."

A hush settled over them. Not the absence of sound, but the presence of something shared.

"It teaches you something though, doesn't it?" he said at last. "Not just how to survive, but how to create. At the monastery, I realized that if I ever wanted a life of my own, I'd have to build it from nothing. No one was going to hand it to me. So I began to imagine. And I held onto that vision, even when everything else was uncertain."

Carmen nodded, the warmth of his palm grounding her.

"I think," she said slowly, "that's why I started writing. I couldn't go back and change anything, but on the page I could create something honest. Something that made sense of it all."

Francisco's lips curved into a soft smile.

"It was that way for me, with books," he said. "The ones hidden in the monastery's corners like they were waiting for someone to notice them. History, myth, philosophy… I devoured them. I began to see the world not through sermons, but through stories. I read about empires built from dust, revolutions sparked by ideas, heroes who bled not for punishment, but for purpose."

He turned to her then, something bright and unwavering in his eyes.

"Somewhere between the pages, at just eight or nine years old, I began to understand that life wasn't meant to be lived on one's knees. It wasn't about martyrdom. It was about rising; not about being a lamb, but a lionheart."

He paused, a quiet fire in his eyes.

"I made a choice to take command of my own story. Not just for myself, but for something that would outlast me. To build with intention, to lead with courage, to create despite fear. That's when everything changed."

They continued walking, the tide whispering against the shore beside them, the sun now fully risen, casting golden light on two people learning how to carry the past without letting it define the future.

"After I left the monastery, it was Palmi that taught me how to savor the quiet joys of life," Francisco continued, his voice steeped in memory. "There, people looked after one another. Not because they had much, but because they understood the value of what little they did have. Every Sunday, the whole commune would gather together. Each person brought a humble dish, and we'd all sit under the open sky, sharing food, stories, laughter… pieces of ourselves."

He paused, the memory softening his expression.

"The neighbors, the bakers, the children darting between the trees…all of them gave me something I hadn't felt since losing my family: a sense of home. There was this warmth, this unspoken understanding... it reminded me that even in the wake of loss, life finds a way to begin again."

He looked to Carmen.

"It was there I learned that the true wealth of a life is measured not in coins, but in connection. My mother used to say: *'a man's riches lie in the friendships he keeps and the love he gives away'*. And she was right."

Francisco turned back toward the horizon, his voice quiet but sure.

"I carried those lessons back with me to Uruguay. Loss left its mark on me, but gratitude shaped what remained. When I returned, it wasn't simply to raise buildings or lay out boulevards. My aim was to create something lasting, a community rooted in dignity, framed by beauty, and strengthened by a true sense of belonging. What I saw in Palmi, I longed to give our people here: not just streets and stone, but the feeling of unity."

"You've done that. You've created so much, Francisco…but you don't have to carry it all alone anymore."

Carmen's voice was barely above a whisper as she turned to him.

"Did you… ever see her again? Your mother?"

Francisco's expression shifted, softened, shadowed. He looked out toward the horizon for a long moment before answering.

"No," he said quietly. "She died of yellow fever when I was ten, while I was still living in Palmi."

The words landed like stones in the silence.

"Before she died, I had told myself that I'd go back someday, and show her what I had become, that maybe then she'd see it was worth it. But I never did get a chance to say goodbye."

He exhaled, the weight of old grief still present but no longer consuming.

"Life had other plans. And some doors, once closed, don't reopen."

Carmen gave his hand another gentle squeeze. There was nothing to fix, nothing to say to undo the ache. Only the quiet gift of presence.

She traced small circles on the back of Francisco's hand, her voice gentle. "Do you have any memories of her?"

Francisco nodded slowly, a flicker of something tender lighting his eyes.

"Just fragments. But the ones I do have… they stay with me." He paused, a faint smile tugging at the corner of his mouth. "I remember she used to dance."

Carmen looked at him, surprised. "Dance?"

"Yes," Francisco said after a pause, his voice carrying a faraway edge as the waves lapped at their feet. "Back when tango was still finding its feet, before it even had a name."

Carmen glanced over, noticing the way his eyes had gone distant, watching not the sea, but something tucked deep in memory.

"We lived in a *conventillo* near the port, in Montevideo," he continued. His steps slowed, the damp sand sinking slightly beneath his feet. "Cracked walls, leaking roofs, the scent of sea salt and the fishermen's latest catch always in the air."

She listened without interrupting, adjusting the shawl over her shoulders as the morning breeze caught it.

"My mother would dance with our neighbors," he said. "Many of them of Congolese descent. Beautiful people…proud, resilient."

He bent to pick up a smooth shell and ran his thumb along its ridges before tossing it gently into the surf.

"It wasn't formal," he went on, a small smile forming. "Not like the salons you see today. It was raw. Spirited. Born of drum beats, longing, and survival."

They walked a few more steps in silence. Seagulls called in the distance.

"They'd gather in the courtyards," he said, "or right there in the dirt streets, barefoot sometimes. Someone would start drumming on a crate. Someone else would hum something low and ancient."

He stopped then, turning slightly toward her.

"She'd lift her skirts just a bit," he said, eyes soft. "Laughing as she spun. No choreography, just joy scraped from hardship."

Carmen's heart swelled at the image: the laughter, the music, the defiance of beauty carved out of nothing.

And in the hush between waves, she could almost hear it too.

His voice softened. "She was radiant when she danced. It was one of the only times she ever seemed free."

Carmen smiled, the image vivid in her mind. "I think I would've liked her."

Francisco nodded, looking at Carmen with a quiet reverence. "I think she would've liked you too."

In the quiet that followed, Carmen understood: Francisco hadn't just built a city. He had built a memory into stone. A promise. A legacy of love that refused to be forgotten.

"Do you ever wonder," she asked softly, "if all of this, the vision, the ambition, the cities you've built, was your way of creating the home you never had?"

Francisco was quiet for a long moment, the rhythm of their footsteps blending with the hush of the waves. "I do wonder," he said finally, his voice low, contemplative. "Sometimes I think… if my father had lived, if my mother hadn't sent me away, maybe I would've followed in his footsteps. Become a sailor. Learned the tides instead of the land. Lived a quieter life, perhaps. One without monuments or maps."

He paused, the wind tugging gently at his coat. "But losing them so young, it shifted something in me. Left a hollow space I didn't know how to name. And maybe, yes… maybe everything I've built since then has been a way of trying to fill it. Not with gold or glory, but with something that feels like belonging. Like permanence."

He looked at her then, the flicker of vulnerability behind his steady gaze. "Maybe I wasn't meant to drift like he did. Maybe I was *meant* to root. To build something that couldn't be taken away in a single storm."

Carmen reached for his hand again, and this time, he held on tightly.

Her voice was gentle, hesitant. "Do you remember him? Your father?"

Francisco's gaze stayed on the horizon, where the sky met the sea in a seamless, shimmering blur. His silence lingered for a beat before he spoke.

"Not really," he admitted quietly. "He was always at sea. I remember his silhouette more than his face… the sound of his boots on the dock, the smell of salt and tobacco on his coat. He'd come home like a ghost. There for a moment, then gone again."

His brows furrowed slightly, a shadow of longing crossing his expression.

"I think I remember his laugh. Or maybe I just want to. My mother used to say I had his spirit. Restless, curious, always chasing the horizon. But he belonged to the ocean more than he ever belonged to us."

He looked down at the sand as they walked. "Sometimes I wonder if that's why I've spent my life building things that won't disappear. Things that stay."

"And you?" Francisco asked gently. "Do you remember your father?"

Carmen nodded, her eyes wandering toward the horizon as they walked. "I do," she murmured. "I remember climbing onto his lap, feeling the scratch of his shirt against my cheek, the soft brush of the blonde hair on his arms. He'd hold the book open with those big hands of his and read aloud, myths of gods and monsters, stories from Greece and Rome. His voice would change for every character, deep and booming one moment, light and playful the next. To me, it felt like he could pull entire worlds out of those pages. I think that's how I first fell in love with books."

She paused, the memory washing over her.

"One night, he took me out to the *campo* and pointed to the stars. He told me their names, the stories written in their light. He had a mind meant for more than the slums and *conventillos* of Buenos Aires. He was brilliant, really. Too brilliant for the life he was born into."

A trace of sadness flickered in her expression. "But he drank," she added quietly. "I remember the scent of whisky on his breath, even as I curled up in his arms. He loved me," Carmen said quietly. "I know he did. But I know love doesn't always save someone from their demons."

Francisco nodded slowly, his expression darkening with quiet understanding. "No," he said after a long breath. "Sometimes love isn't enough. Not when the demons have already taken root."

They walked in silence for a moment, the sea whispering at their feet.

"Some people drown them in drink," he said at last. "Others... in doctrine."

Carmen glanced at him.

"I've seen it," he said, his voice low, almost bitter. "Men so consumed by their idea of salvation, they forget how to be human. They wrap their wounds in scripture, call their suffering sacred. And in the name of God, they punish themselves... and everyone around them. Fanaticism is just another form of escape, only colder. And cloaked in righteousness."

Carmen walked silently beside him, the words sinking deep. She thought of her mother, how piety had become her armor, how pain had become hidden behind a facade of devoutness.

After a pause, she glanced up at him. "You mean your uncle?" she asked softly.

Francisco didn't answer right away. His eyes drifted toward the horizon, where the sky kissed the sea.

"He meant well," he said at last. "But he believed salvation came through suffering. That discipline could shape a soul the way fire tempers steel. What he never understood was that I didn't need to be tempered. I was a little child, one who needed to be held. Seen. Loved."

Carmen's brow furrowed, her voice quiet. "Do you think he truly believed he was helping?"

"I think," Francisco said gently, "that sometimes, believing in a punishing God is easier than forgiving yourself, or others. Easier than facing grief, guilt, or powerlessness."

Carmen slowed her steps, the hem of her skirt brushing the sand. "I think for a long time, I also equated God with punishment. With silence. With being left to suffer and told to call it sacred."

Francisco looked at her, listening, not just with his ears, but with the kind of presence that made her feel gently unraveled, seen.

"I stopped praying when I was little," she confessed. "Not because I didn't want to believe, but because every time I begged for things to get better and they didn't... I thought maybe I wasn't worthy of being heard."

She looked at him, eyes gleaming, not from sadness, but clarity. "I still went to Mass every Sunday, sat in the pew beside my mother like a dutiful daughter. I'd mouth the prayers, kneel when I was supposed to. But eventually, I stopped going. It didn't feel like there was a place for someone like me there. Someone full of questions, full of doubt."

Francisco was quiet beside her, letting her words settle.

"I never stopped wanting to believe," she added. "I just stopped knowing how."

He reached for her hand, gently, grounding her with the simple warmth of his touch.

"And you?" she asked. "Did you ever find your own version of God, after all that time in the monastery?"

He paused, considering. "Not in the God they taught me," he said. "But there were moments. Quiet ones. Reading by candlelight. Watching the rain fall through the cloister. The kindness of an old monk who shared his bread with me in silence. They reminded me that the divine doesn't always speak in thunder or scripture. Sometimes it's in the small, almost invisible acts of grace."

He turned to her then, his gaze steady.

"You know, my connection to God has only grown stronger with time," he said, his voice low. He hesitated, choosing his words with care. "Most of my life, I've been building systems, cities, places I believed could lift people up. I wanted them to be balanced, beautiful, full of meaning. But I realized that even the most perfect design...can be undone by misunderstanding. By fear. By greed. I've seen it too many times."

He turned to Carmen, the weight of experience behind his eyes.

"It made me think about how the Creator must feel," he said, his voice steady. "To gift humanity with beauty, balance, abundance, and then watch as it's twisted. Twisted by fear, by the thirst for power, by the urge to dominate instead of live in harmony. That, I think, is the tragedy of it all: the gift was perfect, but what we've done with it is not."

He looked back at Carmen, something solemn and searching in his expression.

"I used to think if I could just build it all *just right*, design something flawless enough, good enough, that it would hold. That people would see it, feel it, and rise to meet its potential. But even the most divine architecture can't inspire those unwilling to see beauty."

He paused, then added more quietly, "Maybe that's the burden of the creator, whether divine or human. You can give your best: your vision, your labor, your love…but in the end, you must release it. And trust that even if it's misunderstood, that it was still worth bringing into existence."

He let the thought settle before adding, more softly, "I still don't claim to have all the answers. But I truly believe that divinity lives in what we create, how we care, how we choose to show up for each other. That's the closest I've come to real faith."

They walked on in silence for a while, the sand cool beneath their feet, the sea murmuring its eternal prayer beside them. No steeple overhead, no hymn but the rhythm of the tide. But in that stillness, in the presence of one another, something sacred stirred.

It wasn't doctrine that gave Carmen comfort. It was the way Francisco listened without trying to fix her pain. The way the breeze caught the hem of her dress like a blessing. The way the sky opened wide, quiet and endless, as if making room for her story.

Those mornings on the beach in Piriápolis became their own kind of church: humble, wordless, holy. Not a faith of absolutes, but of presence. Of healing. Of beginning again.

But even the most sacred stillness can't hold back the tide forever, and something was already shifting beneath the surface, waiting to rise.

Chapter 10

The first cracks appeared subtly. A lingering glance from a passerby at the Hotel Piriápolis, the whispered curiosity of a servant, a business associate raising an eyebrow too high when Francisco introduced her, not as a guest, but as someone important. The kind of important that didn't quite have a title, yet couldn't be ignored.

Carmen felt it like a draft sneaking under a door: the subtle chill of being observed, assessed, measured against expectations she never agreed to in the first place.

In those rare, golden intervals between Francisco's travels, when it was just the two of them, barefoot on the beach, trading silence and soul, reading her poetry aloud to him by lamplight in midnight cafes, Carmen felt invincible.

With Francisco, the world seemed softer, more forgiving. They moved in harmony, like two notes in a secret melody, sheltered from the noise beyond the garden walls.

But outside their quiet orbit, the world still turned, indifferent and unyielding.

It wasn't a rupture. Not yet. But Carmen could feel something shifting. The blissful cocoon of their beginning was thinning. And outside, the world was knocking.

One morning, after a lingering stroll along the shore, Francisco led her to the Hotel Piriápolis. Its sweeping architecture caught the morning light like a mirage, elegant and otherworldly, a palace seemingly carved from seafoam and sun.

Carmen paused beneath the arched entryway, taking in the marble floors, gilded chandeliers, and the soft murmur of morning guests dining behind heavy velvet drapes. The scent of fresh coffee, warm bread, and citrus filled the air. A soft symphony played in the background, its lilting notes mingling with the clink of porcelain and low murmur of refined conversation.

In the dining hall, white linens stretched across every table like freshly fallen snow. Silver teapots gleamed. Crystal glasses sparkled. And on a long buffet sideboard: platters of sliced fruits, delicate pastries dusted with sugar, cheeses arranged like art, soft-boiled eggs in porcelain cups, and breads still steaming from the oven.

Carmen stood frozen in place for a moment, wide-eyed. She had never seen so much food. She came from a world that meant scraping together loose coins to afford to indulge herself with an empanada at Café La Giralda. Here, before her, was a feast that felt almost mythic.

She hesitated at the entrance.

Francisco offered her his arm, a gentle smile playing at his lips.

"Come, *mi querida*," he said, warmth in his voice. "Let's see what the morning has prepared for us."

She placed her hand in the crook of his elbow, though her fingers trembled slightly. Heads turned as they walked past, the elegant women in tailored dresses and gloved hands taking quiet inventory of Carmen's simple blouse still clinging with salt air, the way her dark curls had sprung loose in the sea breeze and framed her face with unruly grace. There were no harsh words, but the smiles were tight. Too polite. Too practiced.

They were sizing her up. Wondering who she was, why she was with him.

Carmen kept her eyes forward, her chin lifted with quiet dignity. But inside, the old insecurities began to stir. Ghosts of voices that once told her she wasn't enough, that she was meant to shrink, to stay silent, to tuck herself away in some quiet corner of the world and never be seen.

He noticed.

He leaned toward her as they reached their table, speaking low so only she could hear. "The ones who whisper often do so because they've forgotten how to live boldly."

Her chest loosened a little. She took a breath, nodded, and let him pull out her chair.

As they sat, a waiter arrived with a silver tray and an accent Carmen couldn't place. She watched as the man addressed Francisco deferentially, barely glancing her way. The old feeling returned. A sense of being invisible in rooms where power spoke only to power.

But as Francisco smiled warmly at her across the table, she met his gaze and saw only pride reflected there.

"I brought you here," he said softly, "because the world should know your name, not just your face."

Carmen glanced around the room again, at the chandeliers glittering like constellations overhead, at the eyes that still lingered, curious and cautious.

She placed her napkin in her lap with steady hands.

Let them look.

She was still learning how to carry herself in rooms like this. But she knew one thing for certain: she had not come to shrink.

Just as the waiter finished pouring their coffee, a voice drifted toward them, smooth and melodic, like piano notes played with practiced elegance:

"Francisco?"

Carmen turned slightly. A woman approached their table. Poised, immaculately dressed in a high-necked blouse of ivory silk and a sweeping skirt the color of Bordeaux. Her gloved hands clasped a parasol she hadn't needed indoors, but which lent her an air of deliberate elegance.

Her gaze flicked briefly to Carmen, measured, unreadable, and then returned to Francisco with a practiced warmth.

"Amalia," Francisco said, rising from his chair out of courtesy. "How lovely to see you. I didn't know you were back from Paris."

"I arrived last week," she replied, her eyes never leaving his. "Piriápolis seems to have grown since I last saw it. Or perhaps you've made it grow."

Her smile was refined. Almost congratulatory. But there was an undercurrent, a glint of something less generous.

"And this must be…" Amalia turned to Carmen at last, letting the sentence hang like an unfinished note.

Francisco moved slightly, as if to place himself between them. Not out of shame, but as if to control the space.

"This is Carmen Ruiz," Francisco said, with steady pride in his voice. "A very promising local writer. One I've no doubt will soon be published."

Carmen met Amalia's gaze head-on. She offered a polite smile, though something flared in her chest. Pride, perhaps, or defiance.

Amalia's lips curled. "Charmed," she said, though her voice suggested anything but.

Carmen nodded, her tone composed. "Likewise."

There was a pause, just long enough to feel sharp.

"Well," Amalia finally said, turning back to Francisco, "perhaps we'll speak again before I leave. I'm hosting a small salon next Friday. *Poetry and Port.* You're always welcome, of course."

Francisco gave her a diplomatic nod. "Thank you, Amalia."

With a graceful turn, she disappeared through the dining room, the scent of violet perfume lingering in her wake.

Carmen stared down at her coffee cup.

"She thinks I don't belong here," she murmured.

"She's wrong," he said. "But let them wonder, Carmen. You don't have to prove anything to a world that only knows how to measure worth by proximity to privilege. You're not here to fit in, you're here to change the story."

Carmen exhaled slowly, the tightness in her chest easing. The room was still full of eyes, still full of judgment, but beside him, the noise faded. The scent of strong coffee and fresh buttered bread returned.

Francisco leaned in slightly, his tone thoughtful but encouraging.

"Amalia's husband is a well-respected publisher," he explained. "He's deeply connected in the literary world. An ally worth having."

He paused, watching her reaction before continuing.

"It's important, *querida*, that you begin to immerse yourself in these literary circles. Not just for opportunity, but for inspiration. Exposure isn't about vanity, it's about expansion. You have something to say. And the right people need to hear it."

Carmen hesitated, her fingers tightening around the coffee cup. The porcelain felt fragile in her hands, the way she herself felt under so many watchful eyes.

"I don't know if I belong in their world," she admitted, her voice low. Her gaze drifted toward the table where Amalia and the others sat, every gesture effortless, every smile practiced. "They move through every conversation like it's all theater, with polished words, and careful masks. I don't know how to do that. What I feel, what I write… it comes from somewhere raw. Somewhere real. I'm not sure it has a place among those people."

Francisco reached for her hand beneath the table, steadying.

"They've rehearsed how to say things. But you…you have something *authentic* to say. Don't let the gloss intimidate you. What you carry is substance."

Francisco's voice was quiet, but resolute. "I learned early on that there's no better weapon than the pen. It doesn't shout. It doesn't defend itself with fists. It simply stands, calm and clear and undeniable."

Francisco reached into the inner pocket of his coat, withdrawing a slim, timeworn volume bound in deep green linen. He turned it over once in his hand, almost reverently, before offering it to her.

"For you," he said, placing it gently beside her coffee cup.

Carmen blinked, then leaned in to read the cover. *"The Colonel's Family."* Her brow furrowed. "By… Mr. Henry Patrick?"

A soft, knowing smile curved at Francisco's lips. "A name I used when I didn't yet have the right to be bold with my own," he admitted.

Her eyes widened. *"You* wrote this?"

He nodded. "A long time ago. Before anything of mine had walls and windows. Just words and hope."

She turned the book over in her hands, still stunned. "But why haven't you ever…?"

Francisco's gaze softened, his eyes tracing the delicate way she held the book, as if it were something fragile and sacred. "I wanted you to see me for who I am now," he said quietly. "Not for something I once published under another name, in another life."

He paused, searching her face. "And because with you, Carmen, I don't feel the need to prove anything. But I also know how lonely that road can feel, when you're chasing a dream that hasn't yet materialized, when your voice is still trying to find its place in the world."

He gestured gently toward the book. "I thought maybe it was time you knew that I've been there too. That you're not alone."

Carmen looked up at him, the weight of his gesture sinking in. And for a moment, the noisy café disappeared around them, leaving only the space between truth and trust.

Later that evening, back in the modest quiet of her room in Barrio Sur, Carmen sat with the book still resting on her table, the edges of its worn cover catching the amber flicker of her oil lamp. The name Mr. Henry Patrick stared back at her. Formal, distant, nothing like the man who had tucked wildflowers behind her ear or kissed her knuckles with quiet reverence.

She traced her finger over the title, still reeling from the discovery. He had written this long before her. Had built a life of words, of legacy, in silence. And yet, he'd chosen to show her now, not as proof, but as kinship. As a quiet offering: *I've known what it is to create something from nothing, too.*

That gesture stayed with her even as the old voices crept in again. The ones that echoed down the narrow streets of her *barrio*. The whispers she caught at the corner store, the sharp looks from the older women on their stoops, arms folded, eyes narrowed:

"Mirá vos, Carmen Ruiz, suddenly walking arm-in-arm with el Señor Piria."

"Does she think she's somebody now, just because she's been seen at the Hotel Piriápolis?"

"It won't last. Girls like her don't belong in that world."

Their words stung, not because she believed them, but because a part of her still feared they might be right.

She closed the book gently and leaned back in her chair, the scent of ink and old paper lingering on her fingertips. She thought of Francisco's words: *"There's no better weapon than the pen."*

She thought of the breakfast table, of clinking china, of silks and glances, of the way Francisco had introduced her with such quiet certainty, as if her name belonged in that room. As if she belonged.

The memory of judgment still stung, but it had not undone her. If anything, it had lit something inside her.

She dipped her pen in ink and began to write something new. Something true:

Take heart, beloved soul
The world may sneer and cast its stones,
May twist your name in idle tongues
And mock the grace it cannot own.

Let them whisper in their corners,
Let them glare with hollow pride.
What they fear, they seek to tarnish
What they envy, they deride.

But you were not made for their measure,
Nor meant to kneel before their scorn.
You walk with truth stitched in your shadow,
With every wound, more richly worn.

Let their cruelties gather like weather,
You are the storm that will not break.
Your fire is older than their malice,
Your voice, the dawn their dark can't take.

Gather their stones in quiet hands
And lift your chin, beloved soul.

You are still here,
Turning it all into gold.

She paused, the words pulsing on the page like a heartbeat.

Tonight, she wasn't just writing. She was remembering who she was becoming.

Perhaps, she realized, this scrutiny, this friction, wasn't something to hide from. Perhaps it was the fire through which her own voice would be forged.

Chapter 11

The streets of Barrio Sur seemed narrower than ever now, hemmed in not by stone, but by voices. Whispers floated through the laundry lines like smoke, curling in the ears of women who stared a little longer now, and men who muttered over *mate* and cigars.

Carmen had barely stepped foot into the house when the first blow landed, not with hands, but words.

"You come in here with your hair perfumed of smoke and your head in the clouds, while the chores pile up and this house falls apart," her mother snapped, wringing out a rag as though it had wronged her. "You really think a man like that could actually love a girl like you? He'll take what he wants, and when he's done, he'll leave you with nothing but whispers behind your back and shame on your name."

Carmen didn't respond. Her jaw tightened, but she held her tongue. There was no point in trying to explain a kind of love her mother had never known, one that asked for nothing but her whole self.

Instead, she stood in silence, letting the sting of her mother's words settle deep.

She'd known this road wouldn't be easy.

And still, she had chosen it.

As she returned from the bakery with a warm loaf tucked beneath her arm, Rafael stepped out from the shadows of the stoop, arms crossed, expression already drawn tight with disapproval.

"*Prima*," he began, his voice low but sharp, "do you even know what you're walking into?"

She stopped short.

"Do you really think you can survive in that world? With *them*?" He gestured vaguely, dismissively. "Those people will eat you alive, Carmen."

The loaf pressed tighter against her ribs, but she said nothing yet. The truth was, Rafael wasn't just worried, he was afraid. And in his fear, he confused protection with control.

Still, it was Nico's disappointment that cut the deepest.

"You're fooling yourself, *amiga*," he said quietly, not looking up as he polished a glass behind the bar. His voice carried none of its usual bite, just a worn-out kind of sorrow.

He finally met her gaze, the hurt unmistakable in his eyes. "Think about it, Carmen, he's old enough to be your father. What could you *really* have in common, aside from whatever fantasy you've built in your head? One day, you'll wake up, and it's going to break your heart."

Fueled by indignation, she walked home from the bar alone for the first time that night, heart pounding louder than the tango spilling out of every corner.

The gas lamps flickered low, casting long shadows where seedy men lurked with hungry eyes, their murmurs slicing through the silence like blades. In her mind, the voices of the old women rose louder. Whispered judgments sharpened by rosary beads and bitter mouths.

Whore. Dreamer. Fool.

Carmen didn't flinch. Let them talk. Let them hiss from behind their curtains and clutch their pearls.

If they were going to name her a scandal, then so be it.

She'd give them something worth remembering.

The voices still echoed: her mother's scorn, Rafael's warnings, Nico's disappointment. They clung to her like soot.

But when Carmen sat alone at her small writing desk that night, with only the lamplight and the scratching of her pen for company, a different voice began to rise. Quieter. Steadier. Her own.

She opened her notebook to a blank page, stared at it for a long moment, then wrote in sharp ink across the top:

They think I don't belong. So I'll write myself in.

She paused, the words vibrating in her chest.

She could stay silent. Let shame press her back into the shadows. Let the old rules win.

Or she could show up. In all her defiant grace and threadbare truth. Not just for herself, but for every girl like her, told to stay quiet, stay small, stay in her place.

Carmen closed the notebook and stood. She wasn't going to wait for permission.

She would attend Francisco's friend Amalia's *Port and Poetry* event.

That Friday night, the city's literary elite had gathered in the parlor of famed essayist José Enrique Rodó, where the air itself seemed steeped in erudition and smoke. Warm lamplight flickered against polished mahogany, mingling with the heady perfume of cigars and the faint musk of old leather and ink.

Scholars, poets, and publishers moved like seasoned performers through the room, draped in velvet and fine linen, sherry swirling in cut crystal glasses as though language were a blood sport dressed in silk.

Men with spectacles balanced on sharp noses pontificated in measured tones; women replied with practiced poise, their metaphors clever, their critiques wrapped in silk and laced with venom.

Carmen stood at the edge of the gathering, fingers curled tightly around the stem of her glass, willing her breath to steady.

Francisco stood beside her, gracious and composed, greeting familiar faces with effortless charm. Every conversation seemed to reference a name she didn't know, a writer she hadn't read, a place she'd never been: Oxford. Cambridge. Vienna. Florence.

These weren't just places to them, they were seasons of their lives, chapters written in marble and mahogany, bound with lineage and legacy.

And here she was.

A seamstress's daughter from the portside *barrios*. Her university had been thread and hunger, *milongas* and whispered poems written after midnight.

Her syllabus had been the ache in her mother's silence, the rhythm of laundry lines, the smell of hot grease and fresh fish.

She felt like an impostor, draped in borrowed poise, every syllable she spoke weighed down with the fear of being found out.

What was she doing here among these women who had discussed philosophy in salons, dined with publishers, and recited Rilke in French without blinking?

Her dress was modest, carefully chosen, but it might as well have been stitched together from straw for how invisible she seemed. A girl shaped by necessity, now trying to pass in a world built on laurels.

Still, she lifted her chin.

She didn't have their lineage. But she had her own kind of education, carved from survival, stitched with fire.

She just wasn't sure yet if they would see it.

Francisco leaned close. "Just be yourself. Speak from your truth. That's all any real poet has ever done."

She nodded, inhaling deeply, steadying her breath. Tonight, she would not shrink.

Tonight, she would be heard.

Francisco introduced her with an encouraging smile, his hand steady at her back. "This is Carmen Ruiz," he said. "A rising poet from Barrio Sur. You'll want to remember her name."

A few heads nodded. A few eyes drifted.

"She's young," someone murmured near the samovar.

"She's lovely," another said, as if that were the point.

Carmen stood straighter.

When it was her turn, she stepped to the small wooden lectern with her heart pounding. Her fingers trembled as she opened her notebook, the one with frayed edges and corners softened by handling.

She cleared her throat. "This is… called *Born Threadbare*."

Her voice was soft at first, but it grew steadier with each line, her poem stitched with the thread of lived sorrow and quiet rebellion, women she'd known, pain she hadn't learned to disguise:

I come from women
who hem their silence into seams,
who gather the broken edges of a day
and stitch them into bread.

Women who carry too much:
water, grief,
the weight of men who forgot how to love,
in aprons stiff with flour and memory.

My mother wept into dishwater.
My aunt sewed saints into pillowcases.
My neighbors danced barefoot on cracked tiles,
wringing joy from radios and rum.

They taught me that grace
does not glitter.
It frays.
It smells of soap and sweat,
burnt sugar and prayer.

I was born threadbare
but I do not unravel.

Every torn thing in me
is a testament.
Every scar
a verse.

I do not know how to sing pretty.
I sing true.
And that,
sometimes,
is mistaken for rage.

But listen:
can you hear it?
That low hum beneath the noise,
the song of women who stayed standing,
even when the world told them
to kneel?

When she finished, a hush lingered.

The applause came too late and too light. A smattering of polite claps. Raised eyebrows. A few exchanged glances. One woman coughed pointedly into her glove.

"Thank you," she said quickly, stepping back.

No one approached her after the reading. Conversations resumed around her like a tide rising to swallow silence, the soft strains of piano cloaking the subtle murmur of judgment drifting from corner to corner.

She stood still, as if outside the frame of the evening, the clink of glasses and low laughter brushing past her like wind through a locked door.

A publisher with silver hair leaned toward another guest and whispered, "Too raw. Not quite refined."

Another woman, lips lacquered like rubies, offered a thin smile. "She has… passion. But one wonders if it's poetry or simply catharsis."

Francisco tightened his jaw. "Art should unsettle," he said under his breath, but Carmen had already begun to fold in on herself.

Later, in the car, he tried to soften the blow.

"They don't see it yet," he said, taking her hand. "But they will. You wrote from the soul, Carmen. That takes courage."

She didn't answer right away. Her voice finally came, low and flat.

"They stared like I'd spilled wine on their shoes."

Francisco exhaled slowly. "You're not here to be liked. You're here to be heard."

"I'm not sure they even know how to listen," she whispered.

The lamplight behind them faded as they drove on, her hand still in his, but something in her had gone quiet.

"It was one thing," she said quietly, "to face my own *barrio*'s criticism, the whispers, the stares, the scorn. Those wounds, I know. I've carried them all my life."

She paused, pressing the words past the knot in her throat.

"But to stand on the *world's stage*, Francisco? I don't know if I have the strength for that. Who am I to stand among writers who've walked ancient streets, who've debated philosophers over wine? Women who slip into French and Latin as easily as breath, who've never once had to patch their own shoes just to keep going?"

Her voice cracked, just slightly.

"My words are plain, unpolished. They don't sound at all like theirs, all elegant and refined. I wasn't made for salons or lecture halls. And no matter how much I pretend, I don't belong in those rooms."

Francisco was quiet for a moment, the weight of her words settling between them. Then he gently reached for her hand.

"Maybe not," he said. "But perhaps that's exactly why your voice matters."

Francisco's grip on her hand tightened slightly, grounding her, as he slowly pulled over and parked the car on a shadowy side street.

"You know," he said, his voice low and steady, "there was once a boy in Corsica, son of minor nobility but considered little more than a provincial. He didn't speak proper French. They mocked his accent, dismissed his ambition. But he rose. Not because he fit in, but because he refused to shrink."

Carmen looked at him, curiosity flickering through her doubt.

"Napoleon?" she asked.

He nodded. "People only remember his empire. They forget that he was once a boy they laughed at. Or take Sor Juana Inés. A woman. In a convent. Teaching herself Latin in secret because the world thought her gender made her unworthy of knowledge. They couldn't silence her either."

He turned to her more fully now, eyes searching hers.

"You don't write in spite of where you come from, Carmen. You write *because* of it. Your hands carry stories those women in silk will never know. And when you speak, you speak for all the girls who've lived through your pain."

She breathed out softly, her heart aching.

"You're afraid, Carmen," he said gently, "because you haven't yet seen how small the world becomes when you stop fearing it. And how similar people are, once you look past the illusion."

His voice dipped lower, steadier.

"Those people may have their titles, their fancy clothing, but it's all a facade. People wear masks to guard the most tender parts of themselves from being truly seen, to shield themselves from judgment. But beneath all that, we bleed the same, we ache the same, we all hunger for something that makes us feel real."

Then, with that familiar spark in his eyes, half-mischief, half-magic, he leaned in just slightly.

"Come away with me. Just for a while. Let me show you how much more there is to the world than what you've been told to expect."

Carmen blinked, her breath catching.

"Go away?" she echoed. "Where?"

Francisco turned to face her fully, taking both her hands in his, his touch warm and steady.

"How would you like to join me on a trip," he said, a spark in his eye, "to New York?"

The words hit her like a gust of wind off the sea: sharp, dizzying, impossible. The thought of crossing an entire ocean, of setting foot in a place as vast and electric as New York, filled her with equal parts wonder and panic.

"New York?" she breathed. "*The United States?*"

She said it like an incantation, as if the syllables themselves might vanish into smoke.

Francisco gently squeezed her hands, anchoring her.

"I know, it's a big step," he said, voice low with conviction. "But it could be an incredible adventure, for the both of us."

Carmen looked down at their joined hands, her fingers instinctively tightening around his. The invitation shimmered like a dream, but reality pressed in quickly, heavy as ever.

"I don't know, Francisco..." she murmured. "What about my job? The dress shop...Sylvia would never forgive me if I left mid-season. We've got orders stacked to the ceiling."

She pulled her hands back slowly, her eyes flickering with worry.

Carmen exhaled slowly, as her thoughts raced even more.

"I can't just take off, Francisco, it would be madness," she said, her voice wavering. "And it's not just the shop. What about my mother? She needs me to help her make rent. If I disappear for a month, everything would fall apart."

Francisco squeezed her hand lightly, his brow creasing not with frustration, but with understanding.

"We can send her money," he said gently. "From New York. I'll have it wired directly to her. She'd be taken care of."

Carmen stiffened slightly. The offer, though kind, scraped against something raw inside her.

"No. I don't want your charity," she whispered. "I don't want to feel like I owe you."

Francisco reached for her hand again, not gripping it this time, just holding it open between his palms.

"It's not charity, Carmen," he said. "It's an investment. In you. In everything you could become if you only stepped outside the limits the world handed you."

She looked down, heart pounding. Pride warred with longing. Fear wrestled with wonder.

She knew how rare a door like this was. And how often doors like it never opened again.

"I need time. Let me think about it," she said at last.

Francisco smiled. "That's all I ask."

Late that night, Carmen made her way down to the river. She stood at the edge of the old quay, where the Río de la Plata stretched wide and silver beneath a velvet sky, its surface scattered with the flicker of distant ship lanterns, like stars adrift on water.

The air was crisp, salted, and alive with the kind of quiet that made decisions feel permanent.

In her hand, she held the note Francisco had pressed into her hand: a date, a time, a dock number, and nothing more.

No persuasion. No pressure.

Just belief.

She thought of the workshop, of the ache in her fingers and the hiss of the sewing machine. Of her mother counting coins in silence. Of the *milonga*, the perfume of longing and sweat. Of the tight, familiar circle of her life. Secure, but shrinking.

And she thought of the sound in Francisco's voice when he said "*if you only stepped outside the limits the world handed you...*"

The words echoed like an open door. But still, something in her resisted.

It wasn't just fear of the unknown, it was the fear of disappearing inside someone else's life. The thought of running away with Francisco, of vanishing into his glittering world, stirred something more than doubt. It terrified her.

Not because she didn't love him.

But because she wasn't sure who she'd be once she left everything she'd ever known behind.

She thought of what Francisco had told her that day on the bluff in Piriápolis, how the wind had tugged at their clothes, how the sea had stretched wide and endless beneath them.

We have the freedom to choose, to create, he'd said. *With every thought, every action, we shape the course of our lives.*

Now, those words rose within her like a tide.

She couldn't wait for the world to decide who she was meant to become. The choice had to be hers. And in that quiet moment of clarity, she understood.

She had to choose herself.

The fear was still there. But now, it had company: a pulse of courage, wild and unfamiliar, rising in her chest.

She folded the note and slipped it into her dress pocket.

Then, with the dawn barely breaking over Montevideo, Carmen turned from the edge of everything she'd ever known, and began to pack.

Chapter 12

A few weeks later, mist veiled the harbor in a soft blur as Carmen boarded the giant streamliner that loomed ahead like a promise too large to hold in one's hands; sleek, majestic, bound for an entirely new horizon.

The port was teeming with the bustling energy of passengers and crew: trunks thudding onto wooden planks, passengers shouting their goodbyes, the scent of saltwater mingling with the tang of diesel fuel, and the occasional cry of gulls circling overhead.

As Carmen approached the gangway of the ship, her heart fluttered as she gripped her handbag tightly, her legs trembling beneath her as she hesitated at the threshold.

Towering stories above the dock, the ship rose up like a majestic titan of the sea. Every curve spoke of ambition, every rivet a testament to the brilliance of human engineering.

She exhaled slowly, the air sharp in her lungs.

Beside her, Francisco stood in quiet stillness. He didn't speak, didn't rush her, only offered his presence like a steady lighthouse in uncertain waters. After a moment, he reached for her hand, his touch gentle, steady.

She didn't pull away.

"Ready?" He asked softly.

Carmen looked up once more at the towering ship, at the flags snapping in the wind, at the flurry of parting embraces and laughter that carried on the salt-laced breeze.

And she nodded.

Whatever lay ahead, she wouldn't let fear write the ending. Not this time. The world was calling, and she was ready to answer. Not in spite of the risks, but because of them.

The horn bellowed, a deep, resonant sound that seemed to rise from the belly of the sea itself. It rolled over the harbor, stirring gulls into flight and silencing chatter with its solemn promise of departure.

The great streamliner shuddered to life beneath them, mooring lines loosened like the untying of fate. Carmen stood at the railing beside Francisco, watching the dock slip slowly away, the crowd of waving hands and embroidered handkerchiefs shrinking into blur.

Behind them, Montevideo and everything she had ever known dissolved into mist and memory.

Below, the engines churned, a rhythm both thrilling and terrifying. The sea opened before them, wide and glinting, as if the horizon itself had taken a breath.

Carmen pressed a hand to her chest. Not in fear, but in awe.

She looked over at Francisco. He wasn't watching the land recede. His eyes were fixed on her, as though she were the true voyage.

"I still can't believe it," she whispered. "We're really doing this."

He smiled, the wind tugging at his collar. "We are."

And as the ship pushed forward into the open water, Carmen felt something within her rise too. Equal parts hope and defiance.

The past was behind her now.

The future had just set sail.

The interior of the ship gleamed like a palace carved into steel and velvet. Chandeliers swung gently overhead, casting golden light across polished floors and silk wallpaper. Liveried stewards moved with effortless grace, attending to passengers in silk top hats and woolen waistcoats, speaking in clipped accents that made Carmen feel like she'd stumbled into a world just beyond the veil of her own.

Francisco walked beside her through the main corridor, offering a quiet smile as she tried not to gape. Her shoes clicked awkwardly on the parquet floors, her hands nervously smoothing the skirt of her simple gray and white striped summer walking suit.

When the steward turned to her with a bow and said, "*Señorita* Ruiz, allow me to show you to your cabin," she blinked.

"My… *my* cabin?" she echoed, glancing at Francisco.

He simply nodded, as if it were the most natural thing in the world.

The door to her quarters swung open, revealing a suite unlike anything she'd ever seen before. A writing desk by a porthole. A velvet armchair. A bed so plush it looked like it could swallow her whole. Fresh flowers waited in a porcelain vase.

She stepped inside, stunned.

"Get some rest, *Carmencita*." Francisco said gently as the steward led him away.

The door clicked shut behind her with a soft finality. Alone now, Carmen set her small satchel on the edge of the bed, her fingers lingering there as she took in the room. She wasn't sure whether to sit, to cry, or to chase after the steward and beg for a cabin in a lower class.

She was still the girl from Barrio Sur, stitched from scraps, forged by struggle. And yet, here she was, bound for New York City, her name engraved on a brass plaque outside a first-class cabin.

She ran her hand along the curve of the polished mahogany desk, her blurred reflection winking back at her from its lacquered sheen. The comfort was undeniable. So was the disquiet rising in her chest.

Everything around her felt borrowed from another life, one she had long observed from a distance, but never truly believed she could ever inhabit.

She had dreamed of distant shores, of being seen and heard. But she had never anticipated the loneliness of being suspended between two worlds, nor the strange quiet of stepping into luxury and realizing it did not feel like freedom.

Not yet.

Carmen drew a steady breath and lowered herself into the velvet chair, its softness both foreign and inviting.

She would not let discomfort rob her of this moment.

She belonged, not by birthright, but by boldness. Not because the world had opened its doors, but because she had dared to walk through them.

Rising again, she crossed the cabin with quiet resolve, pulled her weathered notebook from her satchel, and returned to the chair. Its fabric welcomed her now.

Then she began to write.

February 1913 –

This room gleams like a borrowed future,
its velvet too proud,
its flowers too soft.
I run my fingers along the desk
and wonder if it knows
how callused hands learn to dream.

Back home,
I was too much
too loud, too bold, too bruised.
Here,
I'm afraid I'm not enough.

But I didn't sail all this way
to wear someone else's name
or sit small in a room
that never asked me to belong.

I came to write.
To live.
To answer the call
of a life I've only whispered about
in the well worn corners of the night.

So here I am,
on a ship bound for the impossible
and still,
very much
me.

As the ship finally glided into New York Harbor days later, Carmen stood at the railing of the deck, her eyes fixed on the iconic skyline that stretched before her.

The ship glided past the Statue of Liberty, her torch raised high like a promise against the pale morning sky, and Carmen's heart leapt.

She clutched the rail, the chill of the sea air brushing her cheeks as the skyline rose from the mist like a dream. A city carved from ambition. New York.

She had imagined it a thousand times. An almost mythical place, pictured in travel posters throughout the streets of Montevideo, written into pamphlets and praised from pulpits: the land of opportunity, the place where destinies could be rewritten and names made from nothing.

But now it was no longer just an idea. It was here. Before her.

She thought of her father, reading her tales of American ingenuity by candlelight. Of her mother's warnings about dreamers who flew too close to the sun.

She thought of sewing late into the night, ink-stained fingers, pages of poetry she was too afraid to share. All of it had led her to this moment.

Behind her, the ship creaked and shifted as passengers gathered their trunks and stories. Ahead, the harbor opened its arms.

Francisco joined her quietly at the railing, his coat brushing hers.

"Well, *querida*," he said, watching her with quiet pride, "welcome to New York."

Carmen didn't speak. She simply nodded, her eyes fixed on the city that shimmered like possibility. For the first time, she allowed herself to believe that she belonged in the story unfolding beyond the dock.

"Look there, Carmen," Francisco said, pointing just beyond the misty haze. "There it is, the Woolworth Building. Tallest in the world."

Carmen followed his gesture. The building rose like a monument to modern ambition, its crown slicing into the clouds, proud and impossible.

It shimmered in the morning light, not cold or sterile, but majestic, as though it had grown from the earth with purpose.

"It looks like a cathedral," she whispered.

"A cathedral of commerce," Francisco replied, a reverent smile playing on his lips. "A symbol of what can be built when imagination is given structure. That," he added, eyes gleaming, "is what happens when a man dares to dream without apology."

Carmen stared up at the spire, her thoughts swirling like the smoke rising from the chimneys below. The building didn't just defy gravity, it defied limitation.

And in that moment, she felt something shift inside her. Not just awe, but possibility.

The gangway creaked beneath their feet as Carmen and Francisco disembarked, stepping into the pulsing heart of New York City.

Carmen's senses were immediately overwhelmed by the clang of trolley bells, the rumble of carriages and motorcars over cobblestone streets, the thick perfume of roasted peanuts mingling with coal smoke and sweat.

Immigrant families bustled through Ellis Island's final gates to build their futures, men in tailored suits shouted to each other in clipped English, and newsboys darted through the crowd crying out headlines while waving papers above their heads. Every corner hummed with possibility.

Francisco hailed a hansom cab with practiced ease. Carmen, meanwhile, turned slowly, taking in the city's towering buildings and ceaseless motion. A streetcar passed, ringing its bell. Children clung to their mothers' skirts. Shop windows glittered with imported silks and gleaming typewriters.

The motion, the noise, the sheer abundance—it all pressed against her at once. Her head spun with it, the enormity of the place both dazzling and overwhelming.

"It's… faster than I imagined," she murmured, more to herself than to anyone else.

Francisco smiled. "New York doesn't wait for anyone. But that's part of its magic. It rewards those who keep up, and those who dare to stay ahead."

As the cab pulled away from the harbor and into the veins of the city, Carmen leaned her head against the windowpane.

She watched as the city unfolded in layers: tenements and townhouses, soaring buildings and open parks, languages she recognized and others she didn't.

It was a city stitched together by difference. And in that strange tapestry, for the first time in a long while, she felt the flicker of freedom.

Here, no one knew her name, no one whispered behind her back. Here, it didn't matter where she'd come from, only that she'd arrived.

The following days in New York unfolded like pages in a dream Carmen hadn't dared to write.

Francisco led her through the wide, electrified streets of Manhattan, past the elegant carriages clattering down Fifth Avenue, into bookstores that smelled of leather and ink, through Central Park where they strolled in the rain beneath the shelter of Francisco's umbrella.

They wandered museums, paused before Rembrandts and Rodins, and dined in candlelit restaurants with velvet booths and menus written entirely in French, where the *maître d'*, with a flick of his eyes, noted her modest attire and discreetly guided them to a table tucked near the back.

For a girl who stitched skirts by her gas lamp in the heart of Barrio Sur, it felt like stepping into another world: dazzling, distant, and not quite hers.

She watched the women sweep past in the latest fashions, their gowns cut from fine fabrics, their steps assured on the crowded streets. Impossibly grand hats perched atop their heads, feathers swaying as though the city itself bowed to them.

In the shop windows, Parisian styles gleamed beneath the glass: velvet cloaks trimmed with fur, leather gloves in perfect rows, silk blouses in colors richer than anything she had ever touched. Each display seemed more extravagant than the last, a world measured not in stitches and hours but in wealth and spectacle.

Carmen's chest tightened. For a moment, she felt like a seam had been ripped open between who she was and who she was expected to be, and the edges did not quite match.

As they passed the gilded windows of a department store on Broadway, Francisco stopped, gesturing toward a mannequin draped in a sweeping emerald gown.

"You should have something like this," he said, admiring the display.

Carmen stopped abruptly on the sidewalk, her gaze fixed on the gown behind the glass.

It shimmered like liquid silk, stitched to fit a woman who never once had to survive by eating yesterday's rice, never scraped mold from her bread, never sewn hems by candlelight until her fingers bled.

Francisco, still speaking, didn't notice the shift in her posture until she turned to face him fully.

"So, do you think if I wear the right dress they'll forget where I come from?"

Francisco blinked, taken aback. "That's not what I-"

"I already feel like a stranger in this city. And now you want to buy me a costume so I can play a part in it too?"

There was a pause, thick with noise from the street and the thrum of something fragile between them.

"I know you meant well," she added, quieter now, "but I'm not here to be bought, I hope you know that. I won't be your ornament, Francisco. I won't be something you polish and parade around."

His face softened, but she wasn't finished. "I don't want to be bought into your world with silk and sympathy. I'm not just some stray you found out in the rain."

Francisco held her gaze, then slowly nodded. "You're right," he said. "Forgive me."

"If I wear a dress like that, it'll be because I bought it myself. On my own terms."

Francisco was silent for a moment, the hum of the city weaving around them, carriages clattering, distant horns, the rhythm of footsteps and ambition.

He took a slow breath. "I didn't offer you the dress to buy you, Carmen," he said, his voice low and deliberate. "It's just that whenever I see something beautiful, I want to share it with you."

Her gaze flickered, wary, unreadable.

He took a step closer, his tone softening but steady. "I know you're not some lost soul needing rescue. You're a tempest. A reckoning. I've never met a woman with more fire stitched into her bones."

He held her eyes, unwavering.

"I would never take away your right to stand on your own," he continued gently. "Not now. Not ever."

He hesitated, just long enough for the air between them to thicken. "You didn't come this far to be rescued, Carmen. I know that. You came to rise on your own terms. I see it in everything you do." He exhaled. "All I want is to walk beside you while you do. That's all."

Carmen stood still, her breath catching somewhere between her ribs and her throat.

Something in his words hit a place she rarely let anyone touch, a part of her stitched shut by years of surviving, of being underestimated, of being told to be grateful for scraps. She had expected flattery, maybe even guilt. But not this.

Not to be seen like that.

The fury that had burned in her chest moments before didn't disappear, but it softened, folding inward like a blade she no longer needed to wield.

She looked at Francisco now, not as a man offering her a gift, but as someone offering her space. A place beside him, not beneath him.

And yet, the old reflex tugged at her still.

The fear of becoming a kept thing. Of confusing affection with dependence. Of losing herself in something that, while beautiful, might still cost her the independence she'd bled for.

Her fingers curled slightly, nails pressing into her palm. She didn't look away.

"I don't need a dress," she said finally, her voice quieter now. "But maybe I'll let you walk beside me. For as long as you understand that I walk on my own."

She let the silence hang for a beat, then added, more gently, with the faintest curve of her lips:

"And maybe I'll let you carry the umbrella."

That evening, the city glistened beneath a steady drizzle, its cobblestones and lamplit streets shimmering like spilled champagne.

Carmen's shoes clicked softly against the wet pavement as she walked beside Francisco, their footsteps moving in sync through the humming crowd on Broadway Street.

He held the umbrella above them, but the frigid rain still curled the edges of her hair. She didn't mind. There was something oddly thrilling about it, this dance of damp sidewalks and bright marquees, the scent of rain on stone, the flicker of carriage lamps slicing through the mist.

Francisco guided her forward with gentle certainty, his walking stick tapping lightly against the ground. He took Carmen's hand, his grip warm and steady as he guided her through the lively throng of umbrellas and laughter that filled the rain-slicked streets.

As they reached the edge of the bustling square, the grandeur of the Knickerbocker Theatre rose before them, its ornate facade gleaming in the drizzle, every window alight, every column draped in velvet banners. The marquee pulsed like a heartbeat above the entrance.

Francisco slowed, then paused across the street, letting the moment bloom. He turned to Carmen, slipping his arm around her waist, and pulled her in close with that familiar glint of mischief lighting his eyes.

"Look there, *querida*," he murmured, his voice rich with contentment.

He pointed up to the theater's flashing marquee with his walking stick, a smile playing on his lips. Carmen followed his gaze and felt her heart skip a beat as Francisco translated the words, illuminated in bright lights as they moved along the marquee:

Paul Rubens' The Sunshine Girl – Premieres Tonight!

She gasped softly.

"You didn't," she murmured.

Francisco smiled beneath the brim of his hat. "Oh, but I did."

With a touch of theatrical flair, he reached into the inner pocket of his coat and pulled out two elegant tickets, their gold trim catching the glow of the marquee lights.

"It premiered in London last year to rave reviews," he said, glancing at her with warmth. "I couldn't think of a more perfect way to spend our evening."

Her eyes widened, a rush of warmth blooming in her chest as she realized that he must have planned this for weeks. The only thing she loved more than books and tango was the theater. The hush just before the curtain rose, the swell of music, the thrill of stories springing to life, of characters breathing and breaking beneath golden lights. It wasn't just imagination, it was where fantasy met flesh.

She slipped her hand into the crook of Francisco's arm, her eyes dancing as they approached the box office. Around them, the rain softened the edges of the world, turning streetlamps into halos and strangers into shadows.

As they stepped through the gilded doors of the Knickerbocker Theatre, Carmen felt the air leave her lungs in a hush of awe.

The air inside shimmered with soft opulence, like stepping into a dream woven in velvet and gold. Crystal chandeliers glimmered overhead like frozen constellations, casting a golden glow over sweeping staircases and velvet-draped balconies.

Rich red carpets muffled their footsteps, and gilded railings coiled like vines along the grand staircase. The scent of old wood, wax, and perfume lingered in the air, heady and theatrical.

Francisco offered her his arm as an usher in crisp uniform led them gracefully down the aisle to their seats near the front. Carmen lifted her chin, trying to steady the flutter in her chest as they passed rows of women swathed in silk and sequins, their perfume hanging in the air like a challenge.

Carmen wore the same simple evening dress she had worn the first night she had met Francisco: soft, understated, and sewn with her own hands. She felt the glances of the women around her, their eyes scanning with polite disdain.

But she held her head high.

Every stitch of her dress held a story. It was hers, honest and earned, woven with quiet pride.

Carmen's fingertips brushed the plush velvet upholstery as she sat, overwhelmed by the sheer grandeur of it all.

The house lights were dimming, and the orchestra below began to tune, the violin strings rising like a soft breath before a kiss.

She glanced over at Francisco. He wasn't looking at the stage. He was watching her, as though the only show worth seeing tonight was the wonder in her eyes.

As the house lights dimmed and the orchestra struck its first triumphant chord, Carmen's senses ignited. A hush fell over the audience like the soft drawing of a velvet curtain, and then, suddenly, the stage sprang to life.

Light flooded the set, bathing the performers in a golden glow. Costumes shimmered with every movement, silks and sequins catching the light like a thousand stars. The music swelled, jubilant and whimsical, as dancers burst onto the stage with a flourish of movement, their feet tapping in perfect rhythm, their smiles impossibly bright.

Carmen leaned forward in her seat, her eyes wide, her hands clasped tightly in her lap. Laughter rippled through the theater, lines delivered with impeccable timing drawing delighted gasps from the crowd. But Carmen barely noticed the audience around her. Her world had narrowed to the spectacle unfolding before her.

The heroine twirled across the stage, singing something hopeful and jubilant, and something inside Carmen stirred. She felt as though the theater itself were lifting her above the world she knew, away from workrooms and whispered judgments, into a realm where dreams danced freely.

Francisco glanced over at her, catching the light in her eyes. She didn't see him. Not yet. She was too immersed in the music, in the unfolding magic, her soul caught in the rhythm of something vast and alive.

And for a moment, sitting beneath the glittering chandeliers of a New York stage, Carmen forgot everything else.

Suddenly, the orchestra shifted, and the unmistakable pulse of a tango rose from the pit, spirited and lively.

She turned to Francisco then, with a look of surprise. In the dim glow of the theater, he was already watching her, a quiet pride softening his features. He said nothing, only nodded once, as if to say *You see? Even here, your world has found a way in.*

Tango had crossed oceans.

It had slipped through the cracks of old-world ballrooms and into the glittering heart of Broadway, hips swaying, violins sighing, its soul intact. Carmen felt it in her chest, the rhythm she had known since childhood now unfolding in satin and spotlight before strangers who had never walked her streets.

The music swelled into a bright, brassy flourish as the actors took to the stage in a spirited burst of choreography. Dressed in exaggerated gaucho hats and twirling handkerchiefs, they launched into song:

"Wouldn't it be jolly
If we took a little holi-day
Away from here?

We might go
to Montevideo,
You know, or Valparaiso!"

Their voices rang out in cheerful harmony, feet tapping in a merry approximation of tango steps, more vaudeville than *milonga*. The audience laughed, enchanted by the exotic flair and playful spectacle.

Carmen blinked, a half-smile tugging at her lips. The sight was almost comical to her, an exuberant, foreign fantasy of her homeland that felt more like costume than reflection. The rhythms were there, yes. But the soul of it, the ache and intimacy she knew so well, had been replaced with sparkle and satire.

Still, she didn't feel offended, only amused.

She glanced at Francisco. He leaned slightly toward her, raising a brow with a crooked smile that said: *they mean well.*

Carmen leaned back in her seat, a soft smile playing on her lips.

She couldn't fault the English performers for their earnest attempt. After all, tango wasn't just a dance, it was a story that spoke of lives lived in the margins, of hunger and heartbreak and desire coiled tightly into a single step. It wasn't something so easily captured in the bright lights of the polished and precise Broadway stage.

But still, she admired the effort. To see the tango performed on such a grand stage, before a captivated audience hanging on every beat, filled Carmen with an unexpected swell of pride.

This wasn't the crumbling courtyard of a *conventillo* or the smoky floors of the *Madreselva*, but here it was, their music, their stories, reaching across an ocean and finding a home in unfamiliar hearts.

She thought about the power of art to leap across borders, dissolve divisions, and speak truths that no translation could mute. It didn't matter where you came from or what language you spoke; something in the music, the movement, the words always reached you.

Maybe Francisco was right.

Maybe the world wasn't so vast or fractured after all.

Maybe it was just a constellation of scattered hearts, all beating toward the same rhythm, one they'd always known, deep down, without ever needing to be taught.

And just like that, a quiet truth took root inside her.

Her voice, her art, her beginnings, they weren't meant to stay hidden. *They belonged wherever she had the courage to carry them.*

And somewhere between the footlights and the final bow, Carmen understood. This wasn't the end of her story. This was only the beginning.

Chapter 13

Montevideo welcomed them home with a blaze of light. The sky, wide and cloudless, stretched over the Río de la Plata like a silk sheet warmed by gold. After the gray chill of New York, where winter's breath had clung to their coats and fogged their windows, the sun here felt like a balm, a soft and generous reminder of how far they had come.

Carmen lay back on a striped towel on the shore of Piriápolis, her legs dusted with fine sand, the skirts of her swimming costume hiked just enough to let the breeze kiss her knees.

Beside her, Francisco reclined under the shade of a woven parasol, deeply immersed in some important-looking papers.

"Is it always this warm in March?" she asked, eyes closed, letting the sun draw lazy shadows across her face.

He smiled without looking over. "Not always. But the city seems to be celebrating your return."

Carmen laughed softly, then fell quiet, listening to the rhythm of the waves lapping the shore. There was something sacred in the simplicity of it. No stage lights, no salons, no sideways glances, just the warmth of her homeland, the hush of the sea, and the steady pulse of the earth beneath her.

A shadow stretched across the sand, cutting the sun's warmth for a moment. Carmen lifted her head and shaded her eyes with her hand.

"Don Francisco," came a familiar voice, smooth and sure, "I had a feeling I'd find you enjoying your kingdom by the sea."

Francisco sat up, brushing sand from his trousers. "Carlos," he greeted warmly. "You're just in time. Sit. The sun is generous today."

Carmen turned as the man lowered himself onto a folding sling chair with practiced elegance. Tall, with a thin, painter's brush mustache, and dressed in a linen suit that somehow defied the wrinkles of the beach, Carlos exuded the effortless confidence of someone who knew how the world worked, and how to bend it.

Francisco gestured toward her. "Carlos, allow me to properly introduce you. This is Carmen Ruiz, a dear friend of mine, and a brilliant new literary voice."

Carlos gave her a nod, removing his straw boater hat in greeting. "A pleasure, *Señorita* Ruiz."

Francisco leaned back on his elbows, the sun catching the silver at his temples as he smiled in Carlos's direction.

"Carmen," he said, his voice easy with affection, "this is Carlos Bonavita. Carlos oversees all my projects, keeps everything from falling apart when I'm off chasing poetry and mad dreams."

Carlos chuckled modestly, but Carmen didn't miss the glint of pride behind his eyes.

Francisco went on, "Carlos is more than just my foreman, he's more like a son to me. He's been with me since he was barely out of school. There's no one I trust more with my affairs. If something ever happened to me, I'd sleep easy knowing it was Carlos at the helm."

Carlos gave her a wink. "Don Francisco's being generous, as always. I just try to keep the trains running on time."

Carmen studied him for a beat. "I think I recognize you, actually. From the Madreselva. You were there with Francisco that night."

Carlos's brow lifted slightly in surprise, then smoothed into a smile. "Ah, yes. So the mysterious muse wasn't a figment after all."

Carmen smiled coolly but said nothing. She remembered the way he had looked at her that night. Not unkind, but curious, calculating. As though she were a page he hadn't yet decided whether to read or tear out.

Francisco, oblivious to the tension, leaned back against his chair with a sigh. "Carmen's work is starting to get real attention. You'll be hearing her name in more than just cafés soon, Carlos."

Carlos raised an eyebrow, tilting his head as he looked at her anew. "Then I look forward to being proven behind the times."

As the sun climbed higher over the water, glinting off the waves, the conversation between the two men shifted, their tones tightening into focus.

"I've been reviewing the numbers again," Francisco said, brushing sand from his trousers as he reached for the leather portfolio he'd brought along. "Tourism is steady, but not growing fast enough. We need more traction if we want the investors to stay patient."

Carlos nodded, squinting against the sunlight. "I agree. We've done all we can with the current infrastructure. We need a new angle."

They began tossing around ideas: new signage, exclusive resort packages, even a luxury coach service from Montevideo.

Carmen, who had been quietly sipping her *mate* and watching the shoreline, finally chimed in.

"Why not extend the railway?" she said casually, then sat up straighter. "So people who don't own cars, people like me, like most of Montevideo, can actually come here? Make the beach accessible to everyone, not just the wealthy."

The men paused.

Francisco turned to her slowly, a grin blooming across his face like a sunrise. He reached out, cupped her cheek with sun-warmed fingers, and kissed her forehead.

"My darling girl," he murmured. "I knew I loved that brilliant mind of yours."

Carlos gave a low whistle. "That... might actually work." He leaned forward, brushing sand off his notebook. "She's right. If we could extend the rail line at least as far as Pan de Azúcar, we'd be halfway there. A spur line to Piriápolis could change everything."

Francisco nodded thoughtfully, already envisioning it. "We'd need permits, engineers, and a compelling proposal for the ministry. But if we can frame it as a public benefit, bringing in working families, stimulating the local economy…there's a case to be made."

Carmen's eyes lit up. "You could even pair it with a local fair, or festival. Something for the people. Not just investors."

Carlos looked at her, impressed. "You've got a head for this. Ever consider city planning?"

She laughed, brushing wind-tousled curls from her face. "I spend enough time trying to plan my own life."

Francisco chuckled, his gaze warm. "Well, you've just helped shape mine."

He turned back to Carlos, energized now. "Let's draw up a preliminary proposal. Talk to the municipal engineers. And Carmen, if you've got any more revolutionary ideas in that beautiful head of yours, I'm all ears."

She smiled, suddenly feeling like more than a guest in his world. She felt like a force within it.

That night, the three of them huddled over maps and sketches at a candlelit café near the Hotel Colón, the warm murmur of the city just beyond the windows. Waiters floated by with trays of espresso and pastries long gone cold as diagrams were drawn and redrawn, rail lines extended in pencil, then ink, then certainty.

By midnight, the plan had taken form; messy but alive, scrawled across napkins and notepads, filled with promise.

When they were finally done, Carlos signaled the waiter and ordered a bottle of champagne.

Francisco raised his glass first, his eyes never leaving Carmen.

"To the woman who saw what we hadn't. Vision doesn't always wear a suit or speak in numbers. Sometimes it wears salt-kissed curls and asks the right questions."

Carlos clinked his glass to hers. "To Carmen. For reminding us who we're really building for."

Carmen smiled, flushed but radiant. The fizz tickled her lips, the bubbles rising like her heart.

That night, under the soft golden lights of the café, she wasn't just a seamstress, or a dancer, or a girl from Barrio Sur.

She was a woman shaping futures.

Later, after Carlos had taken his leave and the streets had softened into quiet shadows, Francisco sat back in his chair, watching Carmen beneath the café's flickering amber lights.

The clink of cutlery had faded, the world narrowed to just the two of them and the low hum of something unspoken.

"You do something to me," he said, his voice hushed but certain.

Carmen looked up, one brow raised. "Do I?"

He leaned forward slightly, elbows on the table, eyes locked on hers.

"Yes. And it's not just… the way you move, or the way you laugh when you forget to be guarded. It's the way your mind works."

She blinked, unsure how to respond. A faint flush touched her cheeks.

"You don't have to flatter me, Francisco."

"I'm not," he said gently, his dark eyes heavy with longing. "I'm only telling the truth. Carmen Ruiz, you astonish me."

And for a moment, neither one of them looked away.

"Come," he said, offering his hand. "I want to take you somewhere."

They drove up the winding road in his car, the headlights carving golden paths through the dark as the silhouette of a castle crested into view, rising like a dream between the hills.

Carmen had only heard whispers about it: Piria's mysterious lair, spoken of in half-joking tones by port workers and curious women at the seamstress's table. A fortress tucked away somewhere deep in the countryside, where the alchemist magnate disappeared to when the world became too loud. She'd assumed it was more myth than truth, a romantic exaggeration stitched into the legend of the man.

She never thought it was actually real.

Now, as they crossed the threshold, her breath caught at the vaulted ceilings, the carved woodwork, the flickering sconces lining the stone halls.

Francisco guided her into the great room, where a fire had already been lit in the hearth, casting a warm, golden glow across the space. Without a word, he moved to the phonograph and placed the needle gently on a vinyl record. The familiar hiss of static gave way to the slow, aching strains of a tango.

As the first notes crackled softly from the phonograph, he crossed the room toward her, his hand extended with quiet intent.

"No orchestra tonight," he murmured, a hint of a smile playing on his lips. "No audience. Just you and me."

She didn't hesitate.

Carmen stepped into his arms, the music folding around them like smoke.

Francisco drew her close, one hand at her back, the other cradling her hand. Carmen moved into him easily, her cheek brushing his as they began to sway; slow, deliberate, breathless.

This tango was different. It wasn't for show. It wasn't born from defiance or flair. It was quiet, full of memory and unspoken promises. A conversation in steps, in held glances and half-smiles.

Her body melted into his rhythm, and his into hers. They danced not to impress, but to remember. To feel. To say what words never could.

When the final note faded into the night, Francisco rested his forehead against hers, their breath mingling in the warm dark.

"We've come a long way," he whispered.

Carmen closed her eyes and smiled. "And we're just getting started."

He traced the line of her cheek with reverent fingers, as though memorizing her face in the firelight, as her dress slipped softly from her shoulders and fell silently to the floor.

Outside, the wind stirred through the trees, but inside, time had folded in on itself; quiet, golden, suspended.

Their bodies moved together not with urgency, but with the slow ache of something inevitable. Every touch was a vow. Every sigh, a letting go.

It wasn't lust that consumed them, but something older, something truer. A communion of flesh and soul, fire and faith.

Her pulse drummed in harmony with the music still echoing faintly in the corners of the room.

Before the hearth, wrapped in the glow of embers, they came together like elements transforming. His kiss, the flame; her breath, the gold.

Alchemy.

And when sleep finally stole over them, they lay curled in the quiet aftermath, a tangle of limbs and longing, the fire still flickering at their feet.

They had crossed the threshold.

Not just of love, but of becoming.

Something deeper had been lit within them, something that would not stay contained.

And far below the castle, the winds of change had already begun to stir.

Chapter 14

The scent of sea salt had barely faded from her hair when Carmen stepped off the trolley in the Ciudad Vieja. The sky was the same soft gray as when she'd left, but something about it felt smaller now, more enclosed. The familiar clamor of vendors, clanging streetcars, and distant guitar strains greeted her like an old song, but this time, it didn't carry her in its rhythm.

Her shoes hit the cracked pavement of Barrio Sur with a dull thud. Home. The streets she knew like her own skin. And yet, as she passed the weathered façades and shuttered windows, a quiet weight settled in her chest. Everything was just the same as she'd left it, but she wasn't.

Her mother didn't rush to greet her. There were no hugs, no tears. Just a stern nod from the kitchen and the sound of laundry being wrung out in the sink.

Carmen set her bag down beside the door and glanced around the small, dim apartment.

The starchy smell of boiling potatoes filled the air. A radio murmured quietly from the corner.

Her mother barely looked up from the laundry basin.

"So, *la señorita* finally returns," she said flatly, wringing out a blouse with an audible snap.

Carmen bit back a sigh. "I brought you something." She held out a small parcel, a tin of English tea from New York.

Her mother gave it only a cursory glance. "Tea won't pay the rent," she muttered, turning back to the wet blouse in her hands. The fabric twisted beneath her grip, droplets falling like punctuation to her silence.

"You think you're someone now, don't you? Parading around with your rich man. Wearing perfume and airs." She shook her head. "You've forgotten where you come from."

"I haven't forgotten anything," Carmen replied, her voice quiet but steady.

"Oh no?" Her mother's eyes narrowed as she turned to look at her. "Then tell me, why do you drift through this house like a ghost? Why do you look at us like we're a chapter you've already torn from the spine and left behind?"

Carmen didn't answer.

And still, she knew that something inside her had grown too wide to fit back neatly into place.

In her bedroom, she stared at the familiar cracks in the ceiling. The air was heavy, and the silence carried a quiet cruelty. Her suitcase sat at the foot of the bed, still half-packed.

She lit the stub of a candle and pulled out her notebook.

She opened it slowly, fingers grazing the pages like a prayer. The velvet chairs, the lights of New York, the glow in Francisco's eyes as he watched her speak, already felt like memories from another life.

She dipped her pen and began to write:

March 1913—

I thought I could carry both worlds in my chest, but now they press against one another like iron doors swinging shut.

Here, I am the same girl I always was, yet no longer one they recognize. My hands still know the weight of a sewing needle. My feet still know these streets. But my heart…my heart walks boulevards lined with gold.

Is it betrayal to want more? To dream beyond these walls?

They say I've changed, as if it were a curse.

But change is not a sin. Silence is.

I won't shrink just because they're more comfortable with the smaller version of me.

She paused, staring at the ink drying into permanence. Then she flipped to a blank page and added, quietly:

I am not their shame. I am not their story. I am my own.

The candle flickered low, shadows dancing on the walls like ghosts of the past. Carmen blew it out and crawled into bed with the quiet certainty of someone who, despite everything, would not stop rising.

The next morning, Carmen returned to work at the atelier, the scent of starch and fabric dye grounding her like a slap to the face. Gone were the gleaming chandeliers and velvet box seats of New York.

Here, the only velvet came in bolts stacked high against the back wall, waiting to be cut, measured, and stitched into gowns for women with far more means and far fewer calluses.

She tied on her apron with fingers still stained with ink. The rhythm of the place hadn't changed. The hiss of the iron, the hum of needles, the scrape of chairs across worn wooden floors. But something within her had shifted.

"You're late," said Sylvia from the far end, already bent over her station, dark circles beneath her eyes.

Carmen gave a tight smile. "The streetcar got held up. Some kind of jam near the port."

Sylvia didn't look up. "You should've left earlier then. These hems aren't going to stitch themselves."

Carmen bit her tongue, took a breath, and sat down at her station, the hum of the machines already rising like a swarm. She knew better than to push back, especially not today.

Sylvia looked up briefly, her eyes flicking over Carmen's clothes. "Back from your grand adventure, then?"

Carmen didn't answer. She just nodded silently, threading her needle with steady fingers and began to sew, letting the needle drown out the sting in her throat.

Each pull through the fabric was a silent question.

Each hem, a thread binding her back to earth.

The world she had seen felt impossibly far away, but it still lived in her bones, and somehow, she would find a way to thread the two halves of herself into something whole.

Francesca sidled up beside Carmen at the long worktable, her arms full of fabric bolts and her braid slipping loose over one shoulder. She cast a quick glance at Sylvia across the room before lowering her voice.

"So," she whispered, nudging Carmen lightly with her elbow, "was it everything you dreamed? New York? The lights, the shops, the fashion?"

Carmen allowed herself a small smile, the first real one all morning. "It was… another world. Like something from a book I never thought I'd get to live inside."

Francesca raised an eyebrow as she pressed a seam flat with her iron. "How'd you convince Sylvia to let you go, anyway?" she asked, her voice low but teasing.

Carmen gave a soft huff, threading her needle with careful precision. "I didn't. I begged. Swore I'd make up the hours, and promised to work overtime to finish the orders for that big opening gala for *La Divorciata* at the Teatro Solís in June."

"So, how about Piria? Is he really as mysterious as they say?" Francesca leaned in, eyes wide with wonder.

Carmen hesitated, eyes flicking down to the fabric in her lap. "He's… complicated. Brilliant. Kind. But the world he lives in…it's a stage, Francesca. And I don't really know if I belong in the story."

Francesca didn't even pause her rhythm, the hiss of the iron filling the space between them like punctuation.

"Well, you don't have to belong to anyone's story but your own," she said simply, as if stating a fact about the weather.

That caught Carmen off guard. Her needle paused mid-stitch.

Francesca shrugged, her tone light but sincere. "Just don't forget you've got your own pages to write. With or without him."

Carmen gave her a grateful look, the corner of her mouth lifting. "You're wise for someone who still calls buttons 'fussy little devils.'"

Francesca grinned. "Wisdom and chaos can coexist. You taught me that."

Their shared laughter was brief, but it softened the edges of the day.

"So, where is he now?" Francesca asked, her voice low over the steam of the iron.

"Paris," Carmen replied, eyes fixed on her needle. "He had to leave again. On business."

The sewing machines hummed like anxious thoughts, relentless and loud, while Sylvia's clipped orders cut through the air with the precision of a blade.

Carmen kept her head down, her fingers moving steadily over fabric, grateful for Francesca's quiet companionship. Francesca didn't treat her like a cautionary tale or offer kindness laced with thinly veiled pity. With her, there were no whispered judgments, just small, shared silences that felt like reprieve.

Meanwhile, the days blurred into one another in Francisco's absence.

The weeks unfolded like bolts of heavy cloth; slow, unwieldy, and impossible to see beyond.

At the dress shop, the hours dragged beneath the relentless hum of sewing machines and the sharp hiss of irons.

Carmen arrived with the first blush of dawn and stayed long after the others had gone, stitching in silence until the windows were cloaked in night. She worked with quiet fervor, trying to make up for the time she'd lost, thread by thread, hour by hour.

She stitched bodices and hems with practiced precision until her fingers throbbed, but her mind wandered far beyond the thread, across ocean crossings and velvet-draped theaters, to the memory of Francisco's hand resting gently in hers.

But in her world, no one had time for reverie.

Dreams, after all, didn't keep the lights on.

"Water heater's gone cold again," her mother barked from the kitchen one evening. "And I suppose it'll be up to me to fix it. Like everything else."

Carmen bit her tongue, placing her bag on the hook by the door. "I'll look at it after dinner."

But her mother was already muttering. "You go gallivanting off, chasing some fantasy, and leave this house falling apart."

At night, Carmen lay awake listening to the sounds of the *barrio*, the distant bark of a dog in the alley, her mother's footsteps pacing like a metronome in the adjacent room.

She wanted to write, but every time she opened her notebook, the words snagged on the edges of doubt and the heavy load of her own exhaustion.

Her thoughts felt heavy, like laundry left too long in the basin: drenched, muddled, and impossible to wring out.

One morning, just as Carmen was carefully wrapping a rush order in brown paper, a sharp knock echoed through the back room of the workshop.

Sylvia stood in the doorway, her gaze fixed on her clipboard, not even bothering to look up as she tapped her pencil against the margin with clipped impatience.

"There's a letter for you," she said, nodding toward the front table. "Special delivery."

Carmen wiped her hands and hurried over. The envelope was thick, addressed in Francisco's unmistakable hand. She turned it over, heart fluttering at his signature wax seal.

She tucked it into her satchel, waiting until she got home to read it.

Later, seated in the window's glow with the candle light spilling across the pages, she unfolded his words slowly, like something sacred.

April 1913 –

Mi Querida Carmencita,

Paris is blooming.

The chestnut trees are thick with pink blossoms, and every street seems to exhale poetry. There are musicians beneath every bridge, lovers on every bench, and the scent of warm bread drifting through morning air like something holy. But none of it, not the Seine at dusk, not the soft golden light across Montmartre, not even the booksellers along the quays, has held me as spellbound as the thought of you.

I carry you with me in every quiet moment. In the hush before sunrise, when the city is still a whisper. In the candlelit cafés, where I imagine you reading aloud some new verse, your voice turning syllables into silk.

They say spring is for lovers, but what I feel for you cannot be contained by a season. It is not a budding thing. It is rooted, fierce, and full of fire. I miss your mind. Your wild courage. The way your laugh can undo me. And your hands…always creating, always mending. I would give anything to have them resting against mine right now.

I saw a gown in a window on the Rue de Rivoli that reminded me of you: not for its luxury, but for its simple, innate elegance. It had the quiet dignity of someone who knows their worth. I wanted to send it, but I could already hear your voice in my head: "I don't need fine dresses to be unforgettable."

And you're right. You don't.

Come to me soon; I can send for you. Or wait for me. But either way, know this: you are in every poem I've written since I left. And in every line, I fall for you all over again.

Yours always,
— F.

She pressed the letter to her chest and closed her eyes. It should have soothed her. Instead, it left her aching.

Because while he wrote of Paris and poetry and possibilities, she was still here, patching leaks in her mother's crumbling roof, stitching hems for women who wouldn't deign to say her name, and boiling water over a temperamental stove just to take a bath.

Too tired, even, to write.

Not because the words weren't there, but because her hands were too busy surviving.

That Sunday, while scrubbing laundry in the courtyard, her cousin Rafael appeared at the gate.

"Any news from the alchemist?" he asked, arms crossed, brows knit in that older-brother way of his.

Carmen rolled her eyes. "Please Rafa, give me a break."

Rafael softened, walking towards her through the gate. "I'm just looking out for you, *prima*. I just don't want to see you consumed by a world that's built on smoke and mirrors."

She paused, dropping the skirt she was scrubbing into the wash basin, water dripping from her arms.

"You think he's lying to me?" she asked, drying her hands on her apron, more like a challenge than a question.

He shook his head. "I think he believes everything he says. But men like that… they live in their own worlds, Carmen. Castles, salons, secret handshakes. I worry what happens when the magic fades and you're left in a place that doesn't speak your language."

Carmen nodded, her gaze falling back to the basin.

"I know," she murmured.

She plunged her hands into the soapy water, scrubbing the hem of the skirt with renewed focus, as if she could erase the doubt with each motion. The fabric clung to her knuckles, suds rising like breath, the silence between them filling with everything she wasn't ready to say.

"They're missing you at the Madreselva," he said casually, though his voice held a thread of something deeper. "Nico's been asking. Says it's not the same without your sharp eyes watching every couple like you're memorizing their steps for a revolution."

Carmen gave a faint laugh but didn't look up. Her hands moved mechanically.

"Tell him I've been at Sylvia's mercy," she said, wiping her brow with her forearm. "We've got a massive order due for the opera opening at Teatro Solís next month. It's been dawn to dusk, every single day."

Rafael took a step closer. "That's not what I mean. I'm not talking about the *milonga* or the dress shop."

She paused.

"I mean you, Carmen. You've been… distant." He touched her shoulder gently. "Just promise me you'll keep your eyes open. And that you won't forget who you are, even when they try to dress you in something else."

She managed a grateful smile. "I won't. Don't worry."

But later that night, as Carmen held a spool of gold thread up to the lamplight, a chill crept through her; the quiet fear that maybe she was already starting to lose herself.

Not all at once, but stitch by silent stitch.

Chapter 15

The morning sun slanted through the window of Carmen's modest kitchen, casting golden light over the worn wood of the table where she and Rafael sat, the *mate* gourd passing between them in quiet ritual. Steam curled lazily in the still air as Rafael flipped through the crinkled pages of a newspaper.

For a while, the only sound was the faint clink of the *bombilla* against ceramic. Then, with a dry scoff, Rafael folded the page and slid it across the table toward her.

"Have you seen this?" he asked, his tone sharp with disbelief, though his eyes were more amused than angry.

Carmen set down the *mate* gourd and smoothed the paper open. Her eyes skimmed the bold headline first, then narrowed as she scanned the article beneath:

Tango: A Mark of Societal Decay, Says American Theologist.

Below that, the words bristled with arrogance:

Campbell Morgan, famed theologist, has condemned the tango as a symptom of moral degeneration, claiming it reflects the regression of human behavior from man back to ape.

Carmen let out a bitter laugh, incredulous. "Of course. God forbid the poor, the Black, the immigrant, the passionate create something beautiful without it being blessed by the pulpit or paraded through a parlor first."

Rafael leaned back, the *mate* gourd cradled in his hands. "To them, we're animals. Barely civilized. Can you believe it?"

Carmen folded the newspaper slowly, deliberately, as if the ink itself might stain. "They don't fear the dance," she murmured. "They fear what it stands for. What it refuses to bow to."

Rafael took a long sip, watching her carefully. "They don't want to understand, Carmen. They want to own it. To tame it, and us with it."

Carmen said nothing. Her thoughts wandered to New York, with its glittering towers, its velvet-draped theaters, the way the women had eyed her dress as though it had reeked of something provincial. She had stood tall. And yet, beneath the silk and lights, she had felt the sting.

Her gaze drifted to the window. A clothesline fluttered gently in the late morning breeze, and somewhere beyond it, someone was humming a tango low and slow.

How strange, she thought. That something born of resilience, of longing, resistance, and grit, could be mistaken for degeneration.

That something so alive could be seen as a sign of decay.

After Rafael left, she sat in silence for a long moment, the echo of their conversation still humming in her ears like a distant *bandoneón*.

The water for the *mate* had gone cold and the flavor of the *yerba* was washed out.

She gathered the empty dishes and set them in the washbasin, her hands moving on instinct while her thoughts drifted further away.

There was still a weight in her she couldn't shake, a splinter lodged between who she had been and who she was becoming.

Carmen wiped her hands on a dish towel and reached for her shawl. She couldn't stay cooped up in that kitchen, not when her soul itched with unrest.

Outside, the streets of Montevideo pulsed with ordinary life: vendors shouting, laundry flapping, a stray dog darting between alleys, but to Carmen, it all felt unfamiliar now. Or maybe she was the one who had changed.

She slipped through a narrow alley, her boots echoing softly against the damp cobblestones.

As she neared Plaza Matriz, the mournful, beckoning cry of a *bandoneón* rose like smoke through the chill.

Drawn by the music, she stepped into the square and paused.

Beneath the bare weeping fig trees, their branches etched like veins against the winter sky, a pair of dancers moved in perfect, breathless tension. Each step was deliberate, each pause electric, as they glided across the timeworn stones of the plaza in a silent dialogue of closeness and control.

Their bodies clung together in that familiar tango hold while soft clouds of breath rose and vanished between them.

A small crowd had circled around, bundled in scarves and heavy coats, the chill of winter pressing in. Faces tilted toward the music, as if hoping to draw a little warmth from its slow-burning ache.

The *bandoneón*'s melody wrapped around them like a blanket, tender and frayed, offering comfort against the cold.

Carmen eased herself onto an empty bench at the edge of the square, the wood frigid beneath her. Her fingers were stiff from the wind, but she didn't mind. The tango always stirred something deep in her, an ache that lived just below the ribs.

When the music slowed, then faded, the dancers bowed, quickly putting on their coats. The crowd offered a smattering of applause, but Carmen stayed still. Instead, her fingers reached instinctively for the little notebook tucked into her bag. She opened it with care, as if afraid the moment might vanish too quickly.

There, beneath a pewter sky and the breath of distant violins, she began to write:

June 1913 –

Today, I watched the dancers in the plaza, unbothered by the gaze of tourists or the hiss of judgment.
Their bodies told truths the world tried to silence. There was something holy in it. Something ancient and untamed.

And I realized:

No theologian, no foreign tongue,
no society that fears its own desire,
can ever erase what was born from ache and rhythm.

Tango is not a regression.
It is a resurrection.
And I, too, am learning how to rise.

She stared at the last line for a long moment, her pen hovering in the still air. Then, with a quiet breath, Carmen turned to a fresh page.

The crisp paper waited—blank, expectant.

She touched the pen to the margin and began again:

Tango

Tamer of shadows on worn stone,
you summon the lovers in silence,
feet tracing the edge of a wound.

Eyes half-lidded, breath held hostage,
they circle each other like prayers
never meant to be answered.

Your rhythm is an old confession,
a threat sweetened by seduction,
a vow stitched with the sting of goodbye.

He grips her like a question
only he dares to answer;
she folds into him,
not out of weakness,
but out of knowing
that surrender can be sovereign.

Cruel, beautiful tango,
you devour without apology,
leaving only the ghost of perfume
and the sweet ache of longing
to prove we ever danced at all.

The following night, Carmen sat beside Rafael on the weathered stone steps of the Hotel Solís, the two of them sharing a battered thermos and worn out gourd of *mate* that still radiated warmth between sips.

A briny breeze drifted in from the bay, sharp with the tang of salt and cold enough to slip beneath their collars, curling like a whisper through the narrow streets of the old city.

Across the plaza, the grand facade of the Teatro Solís shimmered in gold and gaslight, its colonnade alive with the whirl of silk skirts, polished shoes, and gloved hands.

The opera gala for *La Divorciata* had drawn Montevideo's elite like moths to flame. Black carriages pulled up in quick succession, each one depositing another finely dressed couple into the glittering stream of arrivals. Carmen watched them pour into the theater, the glow of chandeliers catching the satin of gowns she recognized intimately.

"There," she murmured under her breath. A blue velvet with pearl buttons down the back. She remembered every stitch, every time the thread had snapped in her hand.

"And that one," she added, nodding at a crimson gown with a train that swept across the stone like a sigh. "I bled on that hem."

Rafael took a slow sip of *mate* and passed the cup to her. "You made half that room look like royalty."

Carmen stared at the entrance of the theater, at the women who had never once looked her in the eye as they'd come for their fittings.

"I made them unforgettable," she said. "And they don't even know my name."

Rafael was quiet a long moment. Then, simply: "But they could."

She turned to look at him, the noise of the city behind them and the music beginning to swell inside the theater.

"You could've been in there," he added, not unkindly. "If only you'd just let him put you in a pretty box and tie it with a ribbon."

Carmen shook her head. "No. That's not the stage I want to be on."

The light from the theater flickered across her face, and for a moment, she looked more like fire than shadow.

Rafael leaned forward on the step, his elbows resting on his knees, eyes scanning the gala crowd across the plaza. "So... when's the alchemist coming back?"

Carmen didn't answer right away. She traced her finger along the rim of the *mate* gourd before handing it back. "I don't know. He wants me to join him in Paris... or wherever he is next."

Rafael raised an eyebrow, glancing sideways at her. "So, are you going to go?"

She exhaled through her nose, slow and uncertain. "I don't know."

"Carmen." His voice was gentle now, stripped of teasing. "It's *Paris*. You know you want to."

She rubbed her palms together for warmth. "It's not that simple. I can't keep missing work. Sylvia's barely letting me breathe as it is, and my mother's still behind on the rent. If I leave again, everything would fall apart."

Rafael nodded slowly, but said nothing.

"And besides," she added, softer now, "I've fought too hard for my independence. I don't want to lose myself in someone else's world. I love him, but…"

"You're not a kept woman," Rafael finished for her. "And you never will be."

Carmen looked out at the theater again, at the women emerging like painted dolls from glossy carriages she had only ever seen from the outside.

"No," she said. "I won't."

But the moment the words left her lips, a shadow flickered through her chest. Because deep down, she feared she was already slipping. Losing pieces of herself in the quiet spaces between who she was and who she was becoming.

Carmen didn't sleep that night.

The echoes of the Teatro Solís still lingered in her mind: the swell of music, the bright cascade of laughter, the shimmer of gowns she had stitched with throbbing fingers but never worn herself.

Yet beneath the sting of that memory was something else. Not envy. Not defeat. But a quiet clarity, like the pale hush of dawn before the world wakes.

She wouldn't lose herself just to fit into a world that had never made space for her. It would have been easy, too easy, to let Francisco dress her up like a doll, for her to pen soft, pretty little verses about birds and blossoms, the kind the world would find palatable.

Ladies weren't meant to write about hunger, loss, defiance. They weren't supposed to rage or bleed on the page.

And yet that was the truth of her voice. That was her fire.

And she wasn't about to smother it just to keep others warm.

And so, she wrote.

She sat at the kitchen table long after her mother had gone to bed, a single candle flickering beside her. The worn leather of her journal lay open, its pages filled with sketches of moments, impressions, pieces of her heart.

But for the first time, she wasn't just writing to survive the day.

She was writing to shape something.

A collection.

Stories, essays, and poems rooted in the lives of the women she knew: the seamstresses, the laundresses, the girls with calloused hands and untold desires. Women made of rhythm and resistance, sorrow and spark.

She would tell their stories the way they deserved to be told. Not polished or pitied, but pulsing and real.

By sunrise, Carmen had filled three new pages. And for the first time in weeks, she felt like she wasn't waiting for a door to open.
She was building one.

A few days later, just as the late afternoon sun began to spill gold across the tired floor of the kitchen, there was a knock at the door.
Carmen wiped her hands on a dishtowel and opened it to find a courier standing there with a sealed envelope. No words, just a polite nod before he disappeared down the street.
The envelope was thick, elegant, with Francisco's distinctive seal. She carried it to the table with trembling fingers.

Inside was a letter.

June 1913 –

My Dearest Carmen,

I've just returned from a meeting with an editor here in Paris, a woman with a sharp eye and a sincere passion for new voices. I showed her some of your writing. Not all of it, just enough to make her lean forward in her chair and ask, "Who is this woman?"

She wants to meet you. No promises, only possibilities. But the kind that don't come around often.

Say yes. Come walk these crooked streets with me. Let the world hear you.

Always yours,

—F.

Carmen folded the letter slowly, her pulse unsteady. Outside, a breeze stirred the laundry on the line.

Maybe she would go to Paris after all.
But she wouldn't be going for Francisco.
She'd be going for Carmen Ruiz:
the voice of the South, ready to be heard.

Chapter 16

The air in Paris was different. Warm, fragrant, with chestnuts roasting on corner carts and something else Carmen couldn't name. Possibility, maybe. The kind of possibility that hummed under cobblestones and flickered in the golden haze of the Seine.

Carmen stepped off the train with her satchel clutched to her chest and her heart thudding loud enough to drown out the hiss of steam from the engine.

Gare Saint-Lazare pulsed around her, a blur of travelers and announcements echoing in French overhead. She didn't understand the words, but she understood the rhythm. Movement. Arrival. Becoming.

Outside, the city unfolded like a dream. Wide boulevards lined with sycamores, cafés bustling with cigarette smoke and laughter, flower stalls spilling color onto the gray stone.

The Eiffel Tower loomed in the distance, impossible and shimmering. It didn't feel real.

She was no longer in Barrio Sur patching her mother's roof or hemming dresses by candlelight. And yet, that girl was still with her, watchful, sharp, and stitched with caution.

New York had taught her how to move through the dazzle without losing her footing, but Paris asked something else. Paris asked her to surrender.

And still, that girl from Montevideo kept her laces tight.

Getting away hadn't been easy.

At the atelier, Carmen had approached Sylvia with her heart racing and a story carefully stitched together from threads of truth and omission.

"My aunt's ill," she had said quietly, not quite meeting Sylvia's eyes. "In Buenos Aires. She raised me like a second mother. I need to go…for a little while."

Sylvia had looked at her for a long moment, pinched lips and sharp eyes assessing whether this was the kind of lie that earned punishment or respect.

"You've already missed more days than I care to count," Sylvia finally said, fingers never stopping their work. "But you've also put in more hours than any girl I've ever trained. Go. Just don't expect your seat to be waiting for you when you come back."

Carmen had nodded, accepting the price. Whatever waited for her in Paris, she knew she couldn't stay in Montevideo patching together a life out of fear.

She didn't know if she'd return to the dress shop. Or to any version of herself that belonged to someone else's pattern. But she had to find out.

A cabriolet whisked her away through the arrondissements of Paris, past gilt theaters and shuttered windows and lovers kissing unashamedly in public.

Francisco was waiting outside a townhouse in Montmartre, a smile blooming slowly across his face as she stepped out.

"*Bienvenue, ma chérie,*" he said, and took her hand like it belonged to him.

Carmen looked up at the sky. The clouds parted just slightly, and for the first time in weeks, she let herself believe again in what might come next.

Paris unfolded before her like a dream half-remembered and somehow more vivid than real. Where New York had roared—brash, vertical, electric—Paris whispered. It hummed beneath her skin. The buildings curved in soft elegance, their cream façades blushing the sweet color of *rosé* at dusk. Bouquinistes lined the Seine with their crates of weathered books. Musicians played violins in the Métro tunnels.

Francisco took her by the hand as if he were reintroducing her to the world. They walked through the Jardin du Luxembourg where statues peered out from the hedges like guardians of forgotten poems.

They drank wine and made love with the windows open. They sipped espresso at cafés where Voltaire had once sat and argued about God and beauty. They wandered into art salons and old libraries, Carmen awed and unsure, always clutching a notebook like armor.

"You belong here," Francisco assured her one morning as they walked past the Sorbonne, ivy curling over its stone bones.

"I don't even speak the language," Carmen replied, though she'd started picking up words.

"But you speak truth," he answered. "That's the only language that matters."

The following afternoon, Francisco led her to a small editorial office, tucked between a bakery and a bookshop on a quiet *rue* off the Seine.

Inside, the air was thick with heat and the smell of ink and paper. A fan turned lazily in the corner, stirring warm air that did little to relieve the summer swelter.

The editor, a sharp-eyed woman with a husky voice and ink-stained fingers, raised a brow as she flipped through Carmen's newest work.

"She writes with teeth," the editor murmured, dabbing her brow with a linen handkerchief. "Like she's bitten the world and spit it back in verse."

She set the manuscript down with a sigh and looked at Carmen over the rim of her glasses.

"You've got talent," she said. "But my readers…well, they prefer gentler fare. Society pieces, romantic sketches, profiles of charming salons. The kind of thing that smooths out the rough edges."

Her tone softened just slightly. "Stick to delicate subjects. You'll sell more that way."

Carmen blinked. For a moment, she said nothing. Her heart pounded in her ears. She had crossed an ocean for this. She had risked her job, sewn dresses until her fingers bled, lied to Sylvia, and left her mother scraping coins for rent. And now, this stranger was telling her to sand down her voice, to write pretty things about parties and lace?

Her voice, when it came, was low and tight. "Thank you for your time," she said, gathering the pages as if they were fragile. As if she wasn't shaking inside.

Outside, the air was no cooler. The Paris streets blurred as she walked blindly beside Francisco, her disappointment wrapped around her like a second skin. She barely heard him speaking; about editors, about salons, about next steps. His voice sounded far away.

If the editor had already read some of her work, why summon her all this way, only to offer rejection disguised as advice?

A flicker of doubt crept in. Why had Francisco brought her here? Had he known she would be asked to trim herself down to something pretty and palatable?

Her heart gave a small twist.

But she pushed the thought aside, unwilling to believe that everything she'd built between them could be so easily cheapened.

No, Francisco had always seen her. He had believed in her voice when even she had struggled to. Still, the thought lingered.

Finally, she stopped walking.

"Which of my writings did you show her?" she asked quietly, not looking at him.

Francisco turned, brows knitting in surprise. "I gave her a few of your more romantic pieces. I thought they'd be more accessible… easier for her to connect with."

Carmen let out a soft, incredulous laugh. Not bitter, but close. "Of course."

He reached for her hand, but she pulled it back.

"I risked everything to be here, Francisco," she said, her voice trembling. "And you gave them the safest version of me."

Francisco's expression shifted. Regret, perhaps, or something dangerously close to guilt.

"Carmen, you have to start somewhere," he said gently. "To get your foot in the door. This was just the first step, *mi vida*, but don't worry," he said, reaching for her hand, "you'll find your place, you just need time."

Carmen kept walking in silence, notebook clutched tight in one hand, the echo of his words settling somewhere in her chest. Neither comfort nor insult, but a quiet resolve. She nodded, but it was stiff. Hollow.

Inside, the words unsettled her: *accessible, easier, start somewhere.* As if her truth needed to be softened, reshaped, made smaller to fit through someone else's doorway.

But she said nothing. Not yet. The silence between them stretched, not angry, just full.

Back in Montmartre, she opened her notebook again. She sat by the window as Paris shimmered outside: gold-tipped rooftops, the distant clang of a bell tower, the faint perfume of lilacs drifting up from a courtyard below.

She didn't blame Francisco. Not really. But she couldn't help the quiet ache that curled inside her. Romantic sketches. Delicate subjects. That wasn't the world she knew, nor the one she wanted to write.

She closed her eyes and let the memory of home settle into her bones: the thrum of sewing machines, the hiss of irons, the laughter of women hanging laundry in courtyards, her mother's voice singing half-forgotten lullabies into a pot of boiling stew.

That was *her* Paris. The grit beneath the gloss.

She dipped her pen in ink.

And began again, not with flowers or perfumed salons, but with the truth.

With blood and callouses.

With everything she had been told not to say.

No soft sketches. No romantic vignettes.

Words with teeth.

Because some women were born to be muses.

And others, she knew, were born to set the world on fire.

I walk the line between lacquered salons
and shadowed alleys that remember my name,
one hand dusted in chalk,
the other in ash.

They tell me: be still.
Be lovely. Be small.
Let lace cover your defiance.
Let pearls weigh down your voice.

But I have danced in borrowed shoes
and run barefoot through storms.
I have stitched dresses for women
who've never said my name with kindness,
and still, I stitched.
Still, I danced.

I am not your gentle muse,
your glass figurine behind velvet rope.
I am the heat in the forge,
the ink that stains fingers red.

Yes, I carry both hunger and grace.
Yes, I want love, but not a leash.

I want to belong,
but not at the cost of my fire.

So let them whisper
that I do not belong.

I was never meant to fit their mold.
I was meant to break it.

Later that evening, she and Francisco wandered into a cabaret tucked beneath the amber glow of Montmartre's lamplight. The dining hall was a swirl of silk and perfume, of crystal glasses clinking and low laughter rising like smoke. A small orchestra played in the corner, and on the lacquered floor before them, couples danced.

Tango.

Or at least, a version of it.

Carmen watched with a tightened jaw as the dancers moved, fluid, theatrical, dripping with exaggerated seduction. The women's legs kicked high, their backs arched excessively, their dresses slit too far up the thigh. Men led with affected flair, all swagger and showmanship. The crowd cheered at the dips and the twirls, enchanted by the exoticism of it all.

"This isn't tango," Carmen murmured, barely audible over the lilting strains of the orchestra.

Francisco turned to her, brow lifted. "It's all the rage here. The French are absolutely enchanted."

She shook her head slowly, eyes fixed on the dance floor, where couples moved with exaggerated flair. "Yes, but they've taken it and distorted it. They took its soul and filled it with something... foreign."

"You know the French, anything that whispers of liberation, especially the sexual kind, and they worship it. Once the Cardinal of France condemned the tango, calling it sinful, suddenly everyone in Paris wanted to tango in the streets…and with fewer clothes."

"But the tango was never meant to be about *sex*," Carmen said, her voice barely above the clink of silverware. "Tango is about grief, struggle, longing, freedom. About the silence between the notes. Not all this…"

She couldn't find the word, but Francisco understood. He reached out to touch her hand.

"You'll find that the tango is evolving with the soul of each city and the spirit of its dancers, *mi vida*. Here in Paris, it's becoming a dance of romance and seduction. You should see the way the Russians dance it."

Francisco said with an eyebrow raised, swirling the wine in his glass. "It's all sharp angles and control. Almost militant in its intensity."

She looked down, her finger circling the rim of her glass in slow, thoughtful motion.

The dancers spun faster, a blur of limbs and gartered fishnets, their movements drenched in lust and abandon. The crowd roared in approval, intoxicated by the display.

"They've made it a spectacle," Carmen said quietly, more to herself than to him. "Just like they want to do to us."

She paused, the music swelling in the background, foreign and ornate.

Francisco's gaze followed hers, lingering on the display before them. "Yes," he said evenly, "because spectacle is easier than truth. Easier to consume. Most people would rather be entertained than be transformed through feeling."

Later, as the laughter faded and the clatter of cutlery gave way to the hush of midnight streets, Carmen sat beside the open window of the flat, her notebook resting on her knees. Below, Paris buzzed softly, a city that never truly slept.

She thought of the dancers at the cabaret: provocative and practiced, but hollow somehow. The tango they danced was seductive, provocative, almost staged for the male gaze.

It wasn't born of the dirt-floored tenements of Montevideo, or the sweat and grief of the *milonga*. It had lost its ache. Its soul.

She picked up her pen.

They've taken the tango and lacquered it in perfume.
Smoothed its edges.
Lifted its skirt for spectacle.
And now they ask me to do the same.
Be gentle. Be soft.
Write nice things in cursive.

But the real tango limps, leans, bleeds.
It is a wound pressed into rhythm.
And so am I.

She paused, the ink still wet, her breath caught somewhere between fury and clarity.

They could twist the dance. They could rewrite the rules.

But she would not let them rewrite her.

Chapter 17

Loving a powerful man was like dancing on the edge of a blade: exhilarating and unpredictable, demanding balance, silence, and surrender.

But being in the arms of someone who held the world in his hands came at a price, and Carmen was beginning to count the cost with every careful step.

At first, it had felt like a miracle: the sudden departures, moonlit dinners, letters scented with distant cities and pressed petals. But the shine of enchantment dulled when set against the ticking hands of reality.

Carmen's once seamless balance between her duties at the dress shop and her spontaneous adventures with Francisco began to unravel.

Each trip she took with him meant missed shifts, frayed patience from Sylvia, and whispered comments from the other seamstresses. Her needle no longer danced with the same focus, and her returns were often met with narrowed eyes and half-forgotten trust.

She had built her life on precision, on showing up, on following through. But Francisco's world spun on whim and wonder, indifferent to time clocks and deadlines.

He beckoned her with champagne and star-strewn skies. The dress shop demanded early mornings, stiff collars, and aching fingers.

And somewhere between the two, she began to feel herself splitting, pulled between the grounded life she'd fought for, and the glittering unknown that Francisco seemed to hold just beyond her reach.

The familiar scent of starch and machine oil clung to the air as Carmen stepped back into the atelier, the morning light spilling in through the tall windows.

The hum of sewing machines and the quiet rustle of fabric had once felt like home. Now, they buzzed with a nervous energy she couldn't quite place.

Sylvia didn't look up at first. She was bent over a bodice, her fingers moving with expert precision. But when she finally did lift her head, her gaze was cool and unwavering.

"Carmen," she said flatly. "Step into my office, please."

The chatter quieted around them. Francesca caught Carmen's eye briefly, offering a faint nod of support.

Carmen followed Sylvia into the small, glass-walled room at the end of the workroom, her pulse quickening with each step.

Sylvia closed the door behind them and folded her arms.

"You've missed several weeks. Again." Her voice was clipped, professional, but undercut with something sharper. "And every time you disappear, the rest of us have to scramble to meet deadlines. I've covered for you more than once, but this is becoming a disruption to the entire operation."

Carmen opened her mouth, but Sylvia held up a hand.

"You're talented. One of the best I have. But this shop isn't a place you come and go from as you please. This isn't a salon or a dance hall, Carmen. It's work. And we've been drowning in it."

Carmen swallowed, guilt threading through her ribs like a corset pulled too tight. She nodded slowly, eyes steady.

"I understand," she said quietly. "And I'm sorry."

Sylvia didn't soften. "If you want to keep your position, I need a decision. Either you're with us, or you're not. No more half-in, half-out."

Outside, the machines had resumed their rhythmic drone, but to Carmen, everything felt still.

She had danced through castles and Parisian salons. But this—this was her reckoning.

Carmen nodded, a wave of anxiety rising in her chest. She felt torn down the middle, as if one version of herself had already begun to outgrow the other.

"I understand, Sylvia," she said softly. "I'll do whatever it takes to make it right. You have my word."

Sylvia's gaze didn't soften. "Good. Because going forward, I expect no more absences. If your personal affairs continue to take priority over your responsibilities here…" she paused, letting the words hang, "then perhaps it's time you find employment elsewhere."

Carmen swallowed hard and nodded again, the sting of the warning settling deep. There was nothing left to say.

But inside, something had shifted. She wasn't sure if it was fear, or the start of resolve.

Later that week, as she and Francisco lay entwined in the golden hush of his hotel suite, Carmen stared up at the ceiling.

Her body was still, but her thoughts churned, threads knotting tighter with each passing minute.

The suite glowed with the fading light of day, sunlight slipping through gauzy curtains in soft ribbons of gold, casting shadows across the rumpled sheets. The air was dense with the scent of linen, skin, and the lingering warmth of their shared breaths.

But within her, a quiet storm gathered. Love, yes, but also a creeping sense of unease.

The more time she spent in Francisco's world, it seemed, the more hers began to blur at the edges.

She lay against Francisco's chest, her fingers tracing idle patterns through his chest hair. For a moment, everything was still; the world outside, the ticking of the clock, the thrum of uncertainty in her chest.

"I need to tell you something," she said quietly, not lifting her head.

Francisco tilted his chin toward her. "*¿Qué pasó, mi vida?* Tell me."

She hesitated, then exhaled. "I'm starting to feel… overwhelmed. I've missed so much work, and Sylvia's been patient, more than I expected. But I can't keep disappearing for weeks. I'm afraid I'm pushing my luck."

He didn't speak right away. His fingers moved gently through her hair, but the silence between them stretched just enough to sting.

"I love being with you," she added, her voice soft but firm. "But there's still a part of me that needs to stand on my own two feet. I can't risk losing that."

Francisco finally nodded. "I understand, *Carmencita*. Truly."

But neither of them moved, and in the quiet between heartbeats, something unspoken lingered; neither surrender nor distance, but the delicate pull of two worlds still trying to live inside one woman.

After a moment of silence, he reached out to gently stroke her hair, his touch reassuring.

"*Mi amor*," he said, his voice low and steady, "I would never want our time together to come at the cost of your peace, or your purpose."

Carmen exhaled, the knot in her chest loosening just slightly. She had feared that her worries would seem small in his world of grand plans and borderless living; that he wouldn't understand the quiet weight of obligation, of clocking hours in a place where her name was just ink on a schedule.

Francisco turned to her then, his eyes holding hers with a gentle intensity, as if he could feel the storm still flickering behind her calm.

"Carmen," he said gently, turning to face her more fully. "Tell me, is your work at the dress shop truly fulfilling?"

She hesitated, eyes tracing the golden slats of light that striped the sheets. "It's not that simple," she murmured. "I have a responsibility… to my mother, to my family. If I lose that job, I wouldn't be able to help her. And that's not something I can just turn away from."

Francisco nodded slowly, his voice thoughtful. "So the seamstress work, it's not your calling, but merely a means to an end."

Carmen looked down, her fingers twisting in the linen. "It's survival," she said. "My real passion is the page, my writing, you know that. That's where I feel most like myself." She paused, a wry smile touching her lips. "But ink doesn't pay the rent."

He was quiet for a moment, studying her. "No," he said finally. "But denying yourself doesn't feed the soul either."

Carmen sat up slightly, pulling the sheet around her, the warmth of his words at odds with the quiet fire rising in her chest.

"I need you to understand something," she said, her voice firm despite its softness. "I can't—won't—depend on you. Or anyone."

Francisco shifted beside her, his brow furrowed. "It's not dependence, Carmen. It's partnership."

But she shook her head. "Maybe. But I need to know I can still stand on my own, Francisco. I've spent too long fighting for my own freedom, and I can't just give that up because life feels easier when I'm with you."

She turned to him, her eyes steady. "I love what we share. But I need to be able to walk beside you, not behind you. Not as someone you have to carry."

Francisco looked at her for a long moment, then nodded with quiet respect. "And that," he said, brushing a strand of hair from her cheek, "is one of the many reasons I love you."

Carmen exhaled, not with relief, but with the weight of knowing the path ahead would not be easy, but it would be hers.

Francisco reached out and tucked a loose strand of hair behind her ear, his fingers lingering for a moment with quiet tenderness.

"I promise, *corazon*," he said, voice smooth as velvet, laced with something unreadable. "You have nothing to worry about. Just follow your own path and leave the rest to me."

There was something in his tone, firm but not forceful, loving without possession, that loosened the knot in her chest. She didn't fully understand what he meant, not yet. But in that moment, it was enough.

As the weeks wore on, Carmen poured herself into her work at the dress shop, stitching with quiet urgency, determined to earn back the time she had lost.

Sylvia's eyes followed her everywhere—sharp, unblinking, always just over her shoulder. Every seam was scrutinized, every hem inspected, as if waiting for the smallest slip to justify her lingering disapproval. She seemed to expect more from Carmen than ever before: longer hours, tighter deadlines, fewer mistakes. There was no room for fatigue, no margin for error.

By the time Carmen trudged home each night, the sky already bruised with darkness, the day's labor was far from over. House chores awaited her like unpaid debts, piling up alongside her exhaustion. She moved through them in a haze, her limbs aching, her mind dulled.

Too tired to dance.

Too tired to write.

Too tired to even be herself.

The weight of responsibility pressed down on her like a second skin, and slowly, the spark that once lit her soul slowly began to flicker.

Carmen returned to the atelier one morning expecting the usual: the hum of machines, the hiss of steam, and Sylvia's clipped voice directing the room like a conductor.

But instead, she was met with unfamiliar silence, broken only by the murmur of new voices and the clatter of unfamiliar shoes across the floorboards.

The air smelled faintly of men's cologne instead of starch and sweat. Sylvia was gone.

In her place stood an unfamiliar gentleman wearing suspenders and little round spectacles, clipboard in hand, already barking instructions to the seamstresses who looked equally confused.

Carmen stood frozen just inside the door, heart ticking faster.

One of the girls leaned toward her and whispered, "They said Sylvia stepped down. That the whole atelier's under new management now. Just like that."

Just like that.

Carmen's eyes narrowed slightly as she set down her bag and smoothed the front of her dress. A chill crept up her spine despite the warmth of the spring morning.

She couldn't help but wonder: *did Francisco have something to do with this?* Had he pulled strings in the background, silent and invisible, to make things easier for her somehow?

The thought unsettled her more than she cared to admit.

That evening, Carmen stood at the window of Francisco's hotel suite, watching the lights of the city flicker to life. The clink of cutlery from dinner still echoed faintly behind her, but she hadn't touched her food.

Francisco set down his glass of wine, sensing the shift in her silence. "Something's on your mind."

She turned slowly, arms crossed. "Sylvia is gone."

He arched an eyebrow. "You mean your employer at the dress shop?"

Carmen nodded. "She didn't retire. She didn't get sick. She just… disappeared. And now there's a new manager, new protocols, new clients. Everything's changed."

Francisco leaned back in his chair, measured. "And you think I had something to do with that?"

She held his gaze. "Did you?"

A pause. Then, calmly: "Would it be so terrible if I had?"

Carmen's jaw tightened. "Yes. It would, Francisco. Because if you did, you didn't even consult me or even give me a warning. You went behind my back and rearranged my life like it was one of your business ventures!"

Francisco gave a small, rueful smile. "Carmen, *mi vida,* you've been under so much pressure lately. I couldn't just stand by and watch you unravel."

Carmen's eyes searched his face, trying to untangle sincerity from intention. "My mother told me you also had our roof repaired while we were in Paris. Without asking," she said quietly. "And now you've replaced my boss. What's next?"

Francisco stood now, his voice soft but firm. "*Mi amor*, I'm not trying to run your life. I just don't want to see your brilliance dimmed by work that doesn't deserve it."

He stepped closer, eyes locked on hers. "You say I should've consulted you first, but tell me…when would you have let me help? You constantly push me away, Carmen."

His hand brushed her arm, light as breath. "I'm not the enemy here. I've only ever wanted to see you thrive… even if that means making the hard decisions when you won't."

"I wasn't asking to be saved," she replied, a tremor in her voice. "I told you that."

He stepped closer, but she didn't move. "Carmen—"

She shook her head. "Do you know what it feels like to fight for a place in the world, only to realize someone's been quietly moving the walls behind you?"

Silence stretched between them.

"I need to know that my victories are mine," she said, her voice steady now. "Not gifts I didn't ask for."

Francisco's expression faltered, wounded but understanding. "I didn't mean to take anything from you."

"I know," she said. "But you did."

Francisco's hands found hers gently, grounding her. "Carmen, listen to me. What happened at the atelier, it wasn't meant to control you. It was to give you space. Space to breathe. To write. To become everything I already see in you. The new management has agreed to keep your position open indefinitely. No pressure. No clock ticking. You're free to come and go as you please, or not at all. Your pay will still be delivered to you. You get to choose."

She looked away, lips pressed into a thin line. It was tempting. The idea of writing without exhaustion. Of not trading ink for stitches. Of letting her voice come first, for once.

Still, a chill stirred inside her.

Maybe it was gratitude.

Maybe it was dread.

"What about Sylvia?" Carmen asked, her voice quieter now, but firm. The guilt pressed hard against her ribs. The thought that others might have paid the price for her indulgence left a bitter taste in her mouth. "She built that shop from nothing. And now, because I…because we-"

Francisco raised a hand gently, his expression calm but resolute. "Carmen, listen to me. Sylvia was not cast aside."

He took a step closer, his tone softening. "When we acquired the shop, I made sure she was compensated generously. More than fairly. She has the freedom now to open her own atelier if she chooses, or to rest if she prefers. She's earned that."

Carmen hesitated, her brow still knit with concern.

"As for the shop," he continued, "we've brought in a dressmaker from Rome, one of the finest. She'll take over as Head Seamstress. The clients will be in exceptional hands. You didn't ruin anything, Carmen. If anything, your talent helped elevate it."

But the weight didn't fully lift. Carmen nodded slowly, her thoughts still with Sylvia; her steady hands, her sharp eyes, her pride in her craft. Some things, Carmen knew, couldn't be paid for in coin.

Still, she said nothing more. Not yet.

"Well, what's done is done," she said softly, her voice thin with weariness. "I'll just have to make the best of it now, I suppose."

Francisco's arms wrapped around her, warm and certain.

She rested against him, letting her body be held, but not fully surrendering. A quiet unease stirred beneath her ribs, a tension she couldn't name aloud. How could love feel both like a refuge and a cage?

Even as she leaned into him, a truth gnawed at her. Every freedom bestowed without her asking felt like another thread pulled from the tapestry of her becoming. He meant well, she knew that. But kindness wrapped in control was still a kind of containment. And comfort, when not chosen, could feel like surrender.

Later, as she sat at her writing desk, listening to the familiar hum of the world, she wondered:

Was she drifting, slowly, into someone else's dream?

She took her journal out of the desk drawer, turned to a blank page, and began to write:

August 1913 –

Maybe that's what love is meant to be, I told myself tonight. A series of softenings. Maybe Francisco is right. Maybe this isn't control, but care. Not erasure, but partnership.

And doesn't partnership require compromise? A meeting in the middle? A blurring of lines?

But I keep wondering: how much ground can a woman give before she no longer recognizes the land beneath her feet?

I want to believe in the beauty of shared dreams, in two lives stitched together, not one swallowed by the other. But the line between devotion and disappearance feels so thin lately. Too thin.

Francisco's world dazzles. It's all vision and possibility, light and forward motion. I stepped into it because I believed in what we could build together. I still do. But sometimes I catch myself shrinking, tucking pieces of myself away just to keep pace. Just to keep the peace.

And I don't know if that's love.
Or if it's losing myself in someone else's dream.

—C.

She looked down at her ink-stained fingers, the callouses that came not from wealth or influence, but from work, from creation, from survival.

No, she thought. *Love should make room. Not just for dreams, but for the dreamer, too.*

The pen in her hand felt heavier than ever, a weight, a lifeline, a defiance.

She had to keep writing.

Even if no one read a word.

Even if it meant clawing her way back to herself, letter by letter.

Because if she stopped, she feared she might vanish. Not all at once, but in quiet, imperceptible pieces.

Chapter 18

It began as a whisper. A headline tucked beneath the fold of the newspaper *La Mañana*, hardly more than a murmur in the cafés of Montevideo: *Archduke Franz Ferdinand Assassinated in Sarajevo.*

Most skimmed it. A European affair, far from the balmy breezes of the Río de la Plata. But within weeks, the whispers sharpened. Austria-Hungary declared war on Serbia. Russia mobilized. Germany advanced. France responded. And then, suddenly, all of Europe was on fire.

Soon, the war was no longer a distant story, it was on every radio, in every paper, written in the worry lines on the faces of dockworkers and seamstresses alike.

Carmen wasn't sure what she believed. Only that something in the air had changed; like the moment before a storm breaks, when the birds go silent and the sky turns colors.

Her poems felt small now. Her dreams, distant.

Although Uruguay remained officially neutral, neutrality didn't mean indifference.

The streets of Montevideo grew quieter with each passing week, as the sons of Italian, Spanish, French, and German immigrants shipped off to serve the distant countries that still lived in their blood. Sidewalks once full of laughter now echoed with farewells. Mothers stood on doorsteps longer than usual. The cafés lost their clatter. A kind of hush settled over the city.

At first, it was curiosity.

People gathered outside the kiosks and newsstands, scanning headlines and maps with countries outlined in red. Men argued in cafés over alliances and causes. Schoolboys began collecting newspaper clippings, speaking of trenches and empires with the same awe they once reserved for football scores.

Then came the fear.

Imports slowed. Letters from relatives in Europe stopped arriving. Rumors rippled through the ports, of sunken ships, of young men conscripted abroad, of entire towns vanishing beneath artillery fire. Even those who had never left Montevideo suddenly felt tethered to a continent unraveling at its seams.

One morning, the usual rustle of newspapers over breakfast was interrupted by the sharp crack of Francisco slamming his fist on the table. Carmen looked up, startled, just as he rose from his chair with the crumpled pages clenched in his hand.

"Don't they have more pressing matters to attend to?" he snapped, eyes blazing with disbelief. "France and Britain have just joined the Russians in declaring war on the Ottomans, and we're standing on the brink of a global catastrophe, and *this* is what the Vatican chooses to denounce?"

He tossed the paper down.

Carmen reached for the discarded newspaper, smoothing the creases with careful fingers. Her eyes found the headline beneath the fold:

POPE DENOUNCES THE 'NEW PAGANISM'
Pastoral Letter Condemns Tango as a Threat to the Soul; Urges Parents to Shield Children or Risk Failing Their Divine Duty

Her stomach tightened.
She read on.

November 1914 –

The Holy See has issued a formal condemnation of the tango, denouncing the dance as a lewd and pagan spectacle, unworthy of Christian virtue and a danger to the moral fabric of society. The decree warns that tango promotes indecency, undermines the sanctity of family

*life, and leads the faithful astray. Parents, it cautions, will be held
accountable before God if they fail to shield their children from such
corrupting influences, thus neglecting their most sacred duty.*

Phrases like *moral corruption, sensual abandon, degeneration of
values* leapt off the page like accusations.

"They don't even know what it is," she muttered, half to herself.

He ran a hand through his hair, pacing now. "We're on the verge of
the unimaginable, and they're worried about ankles and embraces. As if
the collapse of empires could be blamed on a dance!"

There was something electric in his outrage, something personal. As
if this wasn't just about the dance, it was about the soul of a people, the
right to express beauty in the midst of chaos.

Carmen watched him, quiet but stirred. For once, he wasn't waxing
poetic or charming a room, he was furious. And she couldn't help but
agree.

She set the newspaper down slowly, her jaw tight. "They're afraid of
what they can't control," she said, voice low. "They always have been."

She looked out the window, at the muted streets of Montevideo. Even
the city felt changed; slower, as if holding its breath. Young men were
disappearing into steamships bound for Europe, and still, the powerful
found time to scold poor people for dancing.

Francisco let out a dry laugh, pacing the tiled floor. "It's not the tango
they're afraid of, but of what it stands for."

He turned, his gaze finding hers. "The tango doesn't threaten the
family and social life. It threatens their *illusion* of it. As if holiness only
lives in stillness," he muttered, shaking his head. "Meanwhile the world
burns. Men are dying by the thousands in trenches, and *this* is what they
choose to attack!"

Francisco's voice rose with conviction as he began to pace the parlor,
the tension in his shoulders rippling beneath his crisp white shirt. His
hands moved as if conducting a silent orchestra of frustration and hope.

"We cannot—must not—allow ourselves to be shackled by these
archaic beliefs any longer," he declared, his footsteps echoing on the
tiled floor. "These men, cloaked in holy robes and blind authority, they
fear what they cannot mold in their own image."

He stopped abruptly and turned to face her again, eyes blazing. "It *is*
fear, Carmen. Fear of change. Of liberation. Of the fire that art and
thought ignite in the hearts of those who dare to question the script."

She watched him, heart pounding, not just from his words, but from
the force behind them.

"It's always been that way," she said quietly. "What can we really do? We don't hold the power. Not against a global institution. Not against centuries of doctrine."

Her voice wasn't cynical, just tired. It held the weariness of someone who'd lived long enough to understand the cost of pushing back.

"It's time, Carmen," he continued, voice dropping but no less impassioned. "Time for a *new* era of enlightenment. One not dictated by crowns or crosses. A time when the people of this country can think, speak, and live according to their own conscience. Where we are no longer sinners for feeling, or heretics for *dreaming*."

Carmen crossed the room toward him, a feeling of dread stirring in her chest.

"Francisco," Carmen began, her voice tentative, "are you saying you would really go up against *the Church*?"

He turned to her, the fire in his eyes still burning, though his expression gentled as he reached for her hand and enclosed it in both of his.

"I wouldn't call it going against," he said softly. "But yes, I would question it. Challenge it, if I must. Carmen, you know I was raised with reverence for our traditions. But reverence is not the same as obedience. I believe people deserve something greater now. A faith that welcomes, not excludes. That listens, not silences."

Carmen looked down at their joined hands, her brows drawn. "I understand what you're saying," she murmured. "Truly. But this place, our people, they're built on customs, on rituals that have shaped them for generations. If you pull at the roots too quickly..." She hesitated. "Everything could fall apart."

Francisco shook his head gently. "Or something new might grow. Something honest. I don't want to burn down the old ways, Carmen. I want to clear a space for something more humane to grow alongside them."

She lifted her gaze to meet his, the weight of their worlds pressing between them like a fragile thread stretched thin.

A small bubble of fear rose in her chest, unspoken but unmistakable.

She'd seen that look in his eyes before: the blaze of conviction, the kind that burned bridges without a backward glance. And she knew, as surely as she knew the shape of her own name, that once Francisco set his mind on a mission, there was no turning him back.

"These are institutions, Francisco. Legacies. The Church. The State. Pillars that have never had their power questioned." She inhaled slowly, steadying herself. "You have to be smart. Strategic. Find a way to stir the waters without drowning in them. Because if they come for you, they won't come alone, and they won't stop with you."

As she spoke, Carmen felt a weight settle across her shoulders, a quiet heaviness born from the knowledge that Francisco's pursuit of liberation would demand sacrifice, and not all of it would be his.

"Just promise me one thing," she said softly. "Don't lose sight of the people you're trying to save. Even revolutionaries forget who they're fighting for."

Their eyes locked, the silence between them stretched taut, thick with everything unsaid.

His grip on her hand tightened just slightly, a silent vow. "That's why I need you beside me," he said. "You keep me grounded to the heart of everything."

Carmen's fingers didn't pull away, but they didn't tighten either. "Please just be careful, Francisco," she said softly. "Even the noblest visions can cast long shadows." Her gaze didn't waver. "And I've seen how easily you get lost in the light."

She meant every word. Francisco was brilliant, magnetic, relentless, the kind of man who believed the world could be reshaped by sheer force of will.

But brilliance had its blind spots. And she had seen, more than once, how easily he overlooked the wreckage left in the wake of his visions.

And this time, she wasn't sure she could be the one to pull him back.

Chapter 19

The clatter of stone echoed through the valley as workers hoisted great blocks into place, the sun blazing down on the hillside where Francisco's newest endeavor had begun to take shape.

Columns of rose-colored granite stood like sentinels, rising from the earth with quiet defiance; the bones of a church unlike any other.

Francisco stood a few paces ahead, surveying the construction with a glint of pride in his eye, his notebook open and fluttering in the wind like scripture.

To him, it was a temple not just of worship, but of awakening, a place where man and divinity could meet without fear or hierarchy.

Behind him, Carmen and Carlos Bonavita exchanged a glance.

Bonavita rubbed his jaw and muttered, "This land is limestone and wind. It's going to be hell to anchor those vaults if you keep pushing for a dome that size."

Francisco barely looked up. "Then we anchor it to the sky."

Carmen folded her arms, voice measured. "That's poetic. But Carlos is right. You're pushing this vision fast, Francisco. Too fast. People are talking…about the cost, about the meaning. Some think you're building a monument to yourself."

Francisco turned to her, eyes alive with a flicker of challenge. "Let them talk. This isn't for them. This is for what comes after them. A sanctuary outside dogma, outside fear. A new Eden."

"But even Eden had a serpent," Bonavita said dryly.

Francisco smirked. "Then let him come."

Carmen stepped forward, her voice softer now, more intimate. "*Mi vida*, I believe in what you're trying to build. But belief alone doesn't hold beams in place. And if you lose the people, the structure won't matter. A church without community is just a ruin waiting to happen."

Francisco's expression faltered for just a moment.

Then he closed his notebook and looked out at the rising walls. "Then we build the kind of place that draws the right people in."

And with that, he strode forward, trailing dust and dreams in his wake, leaving Carmen and Bonavita staring after him, the weight of vision and reality settling heavy between them.

Once Francisco was out of earshot, barking instructions to the masons across the scaffolding, Bonavita let out a long breath through his nose and leaned against a stack of timber. His brow, already furrowed from sun and age, creased further as he watched his boss disappear behind a cloud of dust and ambition.

"He hasn't slept," Bonavita muttered. "Not really. I've seen him out here before dawn, pacing like a madman being chased by something only he can see."

Carmen, standing beside him, didn't answer right away. Her gaze lingered on the unfinished structure, on the rough columns reaching toward heaven as if in desperate prayer.

"I know that look," she said finally. "That hunger. The way he speaks, the way he dreams, it's like he's on fire from the inside out."

Bonavita gave a low grunt of agreement. "Fire's beautiful. But it burns through the fuel it loves most."

Carmen turned toward him, her expression soft but taut with worry. "He wants so badly to make something pure. Something untouched by the corruption he sees everywhere. But I don't think he sees what it could cost him. What it could cost the people who care about him."

Bonavita scratched his stubbled chin. "I've been with him a long time. Built half his damn dreams. But this? This isn't a project. This is a crusade. And men don't come back from crusades the same."

They stood in silence for a beat, the wind catching bits of loose sand and prayer-dust around their feet.

"I just…" Carmen paused, swallowing down a knot in her throat. "I wish he'd let someone help carry the weight."

Bonavita nodded solemnly. "Then you'd better stay close, *Señorita* Carmen. You may be the only one who can."

Their eyes met, two souls bound by quiet loyalty to the same impossible man, and by the growing fear that he was building something not even he could control.

As construction on Francisco's new church pressed forward, Carmen's unease deepened as her fears proved all too prophetic.

What had begun as a daring act of passion, quickly ignited fierce resistance and unrelenting backlash from every corner of society.

The conservative establishment, rattled by the prospect of spiritual and political disruption, launched a ruthless campaign to discredit Piria's vision.

Newspapers fanned the flames, churning out slanderous headlines that painted him as not a modern thinker, but a madman dabbling in dangerous arts:

Piria's Folly or Pagan Temple? Unholy Structure Rises in Piriápolis: *Locals question the true nature of the new coastal sanctuary.*

Alchemist or Heretic? The Dangerous Mystique of Don Francisco Piria: *Religious leaders urge immediate investigation.*

A Madman's Monument? Critics Call for Halt to Piria's Blasphemous Edifice: *Conservative voices demand government intervention.*

Whispers turned to rumors, and rumors into a wildfire of fear.

In shops, bakeries, and on the dusty streets of town, the gossip grew louder by the day:

"I heard he imported stone from Italy...black marble. That's not for worship. That's for witchcraft."

"My cousin saw strange symbols etched into the foundation. Weren't Christian, that's for sure."

"Did you hear about the full moon ceremonies? Bonfires. Chanting. God forgive me, but I think he's trying to summon something."

"It's not a church, it's a trap. And once it's finished, we'll all be damned."

Even those who had once admired him began to shrink back in silence.

The Catholic clergy condemned the building as a "house of heresy," and from pulpits across the region, priests warned:

"The serpent does not enter through the door, it builds its own and calls it sanctuary."

And worst of all, some of the townspeople began to turn on each other, arguing over whether Piria was a genius or a blasphemer.

Children were forbidden to go near the construction site. A few locals claimed they'd heard strange music at night, or seen flickering lights dancing within the unfinished structure.

The press amplified it all:

Occult Symbols Discovered in Stonework: *Builder's apprentice mysteriously dismissed after questioning design motifs.*

Madman or Messiah? The Country Divided Over Piria's Vision

Through it all, Carmen watched from the margins, fear curling in her chest, not just for Francisco, but for the dream that once seemed so full of light.

Now, the town that bore his name hummed with suspicion, and the line between vision and delusion grew harder to discern.

Pamphlets circulated. Anonymous letters arrived. Longtime allies and investors began to distance themselves.

What began as a monument to progress now stood at the center of a storm: misunderstood, maligned, and increasingly isolated. And Carmen, watching it all unfold, could feel the tide turning against them.

Soon, Francisco's once-promising symbol of faith and community became a target for anger and frustration, as misunderstandings and prejudices fueled acts of vandalism and destruction.

Carmen, Francisco and Bonavita arrived at the site one morning just after dawn to survey the destruction. The air in Piriápolis was thick with sea mist, but it couldn't mask the acrid stench of smoke and the sting of shattered glass.

Carmen stepped out of the car first, her eyes scanning the devastation in silence. Francisco followed, jaw clenched, his boots crunching over broken tiles and discarded stones.

The once-pristine foundation of the church had been defaced with black paint, cruel words scrawled across the granite in frantic strokes:

Here Lies Blasphemy
Devil's Work
Alquimista Maldito

Francisco moved toward the main arch, his hand brushing against a section where a carving had been pried out and left shattered on the ground.

"They've destroyed the keystone," Bonavita said quietly from behind them, hat in hand. "And it wasn't just kids. They used tools."

Carmen knelt to examine the debris, her hands trembling. "This was deliberate," she said. "Calculated."

"I know who it was," Francisco muttered, fire sparking in his eyes. "They've gone after more than this. The school in Minas, the amphitheater near the baths… all vandalized. The statue of Dionysus in Las Flores? Gone. Toppled. And no one lifts a finger to stop it."

"People are afraid," Carmen said softly, rising to face him. "The papers, the church, the rumors… they've made you into something monstrous. Even those who once admired you are questioning everything."

"They never understood to begin with," Francisco spat. "They want miracles wrapped in tradition, change only when it looks like the past."

A group of workers stood off to the side, watching warily. Bonavita stepped forward. "They're scared, Don Francisco. Some are saying they won't return unless there's protection. Others are threatening to quit outright."

Francisco stared at the desecrated walls, his fists clenched. "They think they can destroy this with bricks and ink and cowardice. But they will not bury me."

Carmen reached for his arm, grounding him. "No," she said gently. "But you have to be smart. If you let your pride burn hotter than your vision, they'll destroy more than your buildings. They'll destroy you."

His eyes met hers then—stormy, desperate. For the first time in weeks, he looked truly lost.

"I thought I could build something eternal," he whispered.

"You still can, *mi vida*," she said. "But not alone."

Later that night, the sea murmured below the cliffs of Piriápolis, waves lapping against stone like a lullaby. The sky had turned a dusky gray, and the wind carried the scent of salt and ruin.

Inside the unfinished nave of the church, moonlight poured through the gaping ribs of the ceiling. Carmen stood near the altar, fingers grazing the edge of the broken stone, the distant sound of hammers and voices having long since faded into silence. Francisco sat on the base of a toppled column, his shoulders slumped, his eyes dark.

For a long while, neither spoke.

Then, quietly, Carmen broke the silence.

"You were trying to build something beautiful," she said. "Something lasting. I see that."

Francisco looked up at her, his face lined with fatigue. "Then why does it feel like I've only built a target?"

She walked over, kneeling beside him. "Because beauty, real beauty, terrifies people when it asks them to change."

He turned away, jaw tight. "They defile it because they can't understand it."

"No," she said gently. "They fear what they *almost* understand. What whispers to them that another way is possible."

He shook his head. "So you think I should abandon it? Shrink it down to something polite and acceptable?"

"No," Carmen replied. "But you have to know when to fight, and when to offer peace. Francisco… your vision is too far ahead. Too bold for a world still clinging to its fears. You can't force them to catch up all at once."

He was silent again, but listening.

She placed a hand over his. "What if you gave it to them?" she said. "Not as surrender, but as a gesture. A gift. Offer this church, your church, to the Vatican. Let them have it. Let them fill it with incense and Latin chants and gold crosses."

Francisco tensed, but she continued, voice steady.

"Let them have the walls. But the foundation? That will always be yours. You built it. You laid the stone. You'll have planted your vision right beneath their feet, and one day, they'll realize it."

He looked at her then, truly looked. "You think I should hand them my soul's work like a peace offering?"

"I think," she said, "if you don't, they'll burn it down. And you with it."

Francisco's gaze dropped to their joined hands. Her touch was warm, grounding. He pressed his thumb over her knuckles.

"And you?" he asked softly. "Would you still believe in me, if I did that?"

Carmen nodded, her voice barely above a whisper. "I'd believe in you if you had nothing left but a single brick. Because what you're trying to build isn't just a church. It's a legacy. And that's worth protecting, even if it means playing the long game."

He leaned in, resting his forehead gently against hers. "You're the only one who ever knows how to anchor me," he murmured. "When everything else slips away, it's you who brings me home."

She smiled, bittersweet. "That's because I'm the only one who's not afraid to see the man behind the myth."

And for a moment, in that half-ruined sanctuary, there was peace.

But peace, like prophecy, never lingers where flames have taken root, and as the world moved to smother what it could not grasp, Carmen soon felt the fire they'd lit curling inward, slow and merciless, beginning to consume her.

Chapter 20

The sharp tang of salt hung in the air as Carmen stepped off the streetcar and onto the cracked cobblestone streets of Barrio Sur. The sweltering summer heatwave was merciless, but it was not the heat that made her skin prickle. It was the silence; the heavy, unnatural kind that settles just before a storm.

She hadn't taken more than a few steps when the stares began. Sharp. Lingering. A group of women gathered outside the bakery fell quiet mid-conversation. One clutched her rosary tighter. Another muttered something under her breath. Carmen kept her chin high.

"*Bruja!*" someone hissed from across the street.

The word struck like a stone.

She passed Doña Lidia's corner stoop, where she'd once played as a child, and saw the old woman make the sign of the cross, her eyes narrowing to slits.

Then came the first true blow: a wad of spit, hot and sudden, landing on the hem of her skirt.

Carmen froze. Her hands clenched at her sides.

"You've brought shame on this *barrio*," the woman sneered. "On all of us."

The others said nothing, but their silence was louder than words. Condemnation pressed in on her from every direction, thick and suffocating. She didn't cry. She didn't speak. She simply walked on, her heels clicking against the cobblestones like defiance.

But deep inside, something cracked.

She had braced herself for consequences, but nothing could have prepared her for the cruelty, the venom in every glance, the disgust that clung to her name like a bad stench.

And yet, the fire inside her refused to die.

It flickered, faint but unyielding.

At home, things were no better.

The moment Carmen stepped through the door, her mother's voice sliced through the air like a whip.

"Don't you dare step foot in this house. I've heard the rumors!"

"*Mamá*, I—"

"No." Her mother shot up from her chair, eyes wild with fury. "You let me speak. I will not have a devil worshiper under my roof!"

Carmen flinched as if struck. "*Mamá*, that's not—"

"Don't you lie to me, Carmen." Her mother's voice rose to a fever pitch. "I've read the papers. I've heard the neighbors. You're out parading with that *heathen*, while decent people whisper prayers for your soul!"

Carmen opened her mouth, tried again to explain, but her mother stormed forward, trembling with rage.

"You think this is a game? You think this is some romantic fantasy? That man is no prophet! He's a heretic, a corrupter, a curse! If you had any sense, you'd run while you still have the chance."

Tears welled in Carmen's eyes, but her voice held. "Please. Please, just listen. You're not being fair."

"Fair?" Her mother laughed, bitter and breathless. "What's not fair is watching my daughter throw herself into the arms of a man who mocks God, while I pray every night you'll come to your senses."

Carmen's voice cracked. "The rumors, they're not true. He's not what they say. He's not."

Her mother's eyes narrowed. "Then what is he, Carmen? Because I didn't raise you to bring this shame to our name. And yet here we are."

"He's a good man…and I love him," Carmen said softly, the words falling from her like a confession. "I love him."

The room went still.

"Love?" her mother hissed, as though the word itself was poison. "Love doesn't drag you from your faith. Love doesn't leave you scorned in the streets. Love doesn't cost you your *soul*, Carmen."

She pointed a trembling finger toward the door. "You want to live like that? Fine. But not under my roof. Either you leave him and return to the Church, or you pack your bags and go. Tonight."

Carmen stood frozen, her heart pounding against the walls of her chest. The scent of garlic and old incense filled her lungs. The kitchen, dim and familiar, suddenly felt foreign.

She swallowed hard, staring at the woman who had raised her, loved her, prayed for her… and was now casting her out.

A silence stretched between them like a final thread, and Carmen realized that whatever choice she made, something would be lost forever.

Carmen didn't speak. Her mother's words still rang in her ears, echoing in the silence that followed like the aftermath of a thunderclap.

She took a shaky step back, her hand still on the doorknob. Outside, the late afternoon sun shone over the *barrio,* just like any other day. Somewhere in the distance, a dog barked. A baby cried. Life went on, indifferent.

Inside, the house felt suddenly smaller. The table where they used to peel potatoes together. The worn chair by the window where her mother whispered rosaries in the dark. The crucifix above the door.

Everything familiar. And yet, Carmen felt as if she no longer belonged to any of it.

Her mother stood motionless now, arms crossed tight across her chest, not in defiance anymore, but in armor. Her jaw clenched, her eyes refusing to soften. The quiet between them was thicker than the shouting had been.

Carmen blinked slowly, and a tear slipped down her cheek. She wiped it away before her mother could see.

She swallowed hard, her throat tight with emotion. She met her mother's gaze, not with rebellion, but with quiet, aching defiance.

"I'd rather lose my soul a hundred times," she said, her voice steady but low, "than live my whole life too afraid to feel anything at all."

For a beat, the words hung heavy in the room, more wound than weapon.

Her mother's eyes flashed, but her voice came out cold, flat. "Get out."

"*Mamá,* please—"

"Get out!" she hissed, louder now. "And don't you dare come back here until you've seen the error of your ways!"

Carmen stood frozen for a moment, her breath caught between protest and surrender. Then, slowly, she turned away.

She gathered her things in silence, every motion a quiet grief. The shawl her grandmother had embroidered. A tattered notebook. The rosary she hadn't prayed with in years but still kept at the bottom of her drawer.

With each item placed into her satchel, she felt the weight of what she was leaving behind; not just a house, but a lifetime of familiarity, of small rituals and old love turned brittle.

Her hands trembled, but she didn't let herself cry. Not yet. Not in front of her.

She looked around once more, at the patched curtain, the faded photograph of her grandparents on the wall, the cracked linoleum beneath her feet, and tried to memorize it all. As if those things, too, might be something she would never see again.

With silent resolve hardening in her chest, Carmen slung her satchel over her shoulder and stepped out onto the stoop. The wooden door creaked shut behind her, clicking softly into place like the end of a chapter.

In the street, the shadows lengthened.

She didn't know where she would go. Only that she couldn't go back.

Carmen pulled her shawl tighter around her shoulders and started walking, her heels clicking softly against the worn cobblestones.

The evening air carried the scent of hearth smoke and simmering stew, the familiar perfume of the *barrio*, but tonight it felt distant, like something she'd been exiled from.

As she passed familiar houses, she kept her gaze low. Windows glowed with warm light, but behind them she imagined faces peering out, watching her pass.

The fallen daughter. The blasphemer. The one who had danced with devils.

She didn't blame them. Not entirely.

The street narrowed as she approached her aunt's home: an old, narrow house with a chipped wrought-iron gate and climbing bougainvillea spilling over the eaves.

She hesitated. This was where she had once come for extra sweets on Sundays, for comfort when her mother's moods turned sour. But things had changed. She had changed.

Still, she climbed the small stoop and knocked softly.

The door creaked open a crack, and a familiar face appeared, her cousin Leticia. Older now, and cautious.

"Carmen?" Leticia blinked. "What are you doing here?"

"I just..." Carmen faltered. "I didn't come to stay. I just wanted to talk to Rafael."

Leticia's eyes softened, but she didn't open the door any wider. "*Mamá* says we're forbidden to speak to you. I don't agree with her, but..."

Carmen nodded, swallowing the lump in her throat. "It's alright. I didn't expect anything more."

Leticia hesitated. Then she slipped something through the crack of the door—a small bundle wrapped in cloth. "*Pan con grasa*. I made it this morning. You should eat something."

Carmen accepted it without a word, her fingers brushing Leticia's for a moment before the door gently closed.

She turned back to the street, the bread bundle tucked under her arm, her bag heavy on her shoulder, her name heavier still.

"*Carmen?*"

She stopped and turned at the sound of his voice: familiar, steady, and laced with something heavier tonight.

Rafael stepped out onto the stoop, the door clicking softly shut behind him. He looked at her for a long moment, his expression tight with sympathy and something more fragile; helplessness, maybe. His eyes flicked over her, noting the tired curve of her shoulders, the bag clutched close to her side.

"You look like you've been walking around for hours," he said softly. His voice carried the weight of everything he couldn't fix.

Carmen gave a small, humorless laugh and looked down at the cracked sidewalk. "Well, she finally kicked me out," she said, barely above a whisper. "Told me not to come back until I repented."

Rafael nodded slowly, his jaw tightening. "I heard," he said. "People talk."

She glanced up at him. "Of course they do."

"I didn't believe half of it," he added quickly, stepping closer. "But I knew something was wrong when I heard my aunt was closing all the shutters like it was a funeral."

Carmen exhaled, long and shaky. "Feels like one."

Rafael was quiet for a moment, the setting sun casting a soft halo around them. "I'm sorry, *prima*."

She looked at him, eyes stinging. "Me too."

"*Mamá*'s not letting anyone even speak your name in the house," he said quietly, rubbing the back of his neck. Rafael glanced behind him, then back at her, lowering his voice. "She wouldn't even let me bring you out a plate of *guiso*. I had to sneak out just to come talk to you."

Carmen didn't flinch. Her face was pale, but calm. "I figured as much."

There was a pause between them, thick with memories of childhood, of laughter in alleyways, of whispered dreams beneath washing lines. Then Rafael asked, "Why aren't you with him? With Francisco?"

"He's in Rome," Carmen said, her voice low. "Trying to make peace with the Vatican. He thought it would help quiet things down. He told me to stay behind. Said it was too dangerous to travel, with the war going on in Europe."

Rafael looked at her for a long time. "And you agreed?"

"I didn't want to," she admitted, her voice cracking. "But I suppose he's right. Things are getting pretty bad over there. Rafa, he's not what people think he is…"

Rafael stepped closer, placing a hand on her shoulder. "You don't have to explain yourself to me, *prima*. Just… be careful. People around here…they're scared. And scared people do stupid things."

She nodded, the weight of his warning settling over her like a heavy coat.

"So, what now?" Rafael asked softly.

Carmen looked past him, down the length of the street where the gas lamps had begun to flicker to life, one by one, like the fireflies they used to chase as children.

Her voice was steady, but quiet. "I don't know," she said. "Nico's boarding house doesn't allow women, and Marí and Antonio…" She exhaled, the corners of her mouth tightening. "I doubt they'd welcome the walking scandal everyone's whispering about."

Rafael shifted uncomfortably on the stoop, rubbing the back of his neck. "I tried to talk to my mother," he said softly. "Tried to tell her this wasn't your fault. But she's scared. She's convinced if we associate with you, the church will mark us too."

Carmen gave a small, bitter smile. "So now I'm contagious."

"No," he said quickly. "Not to me." He stepped down from the stoop, standing beside her. "You're still you, Carmen. That's what kills me. I know you haven't changed. I know everyone else is just seeing you through a cracked lens."

She looked up at him, eyes glassy but dry. "You think I don't feel it? Every step I take through this *barrio* feels like a trespass."

Rafael's jaw tightened. "You shouldn't be walking around alone. Not right now. Come inside. Just for a little while. I'll try to sneak you into my room. I'll get Leticia to—"

"No." Carmen's voice was quiet but firm. "I won't force my way into where I'm not wanted."

He hesitated, then nodded. "Then let me at least walk you somewhere. Where will you go?"

She hesitated. "I thought maybe I'd take the train back to Piriápolis… see if Francisco's foreman will let me stay in Francisco's hotel suite while he's out of town."

Rafael sighed, pressing a hand to his chest as if to steady something inside. "You shouldn't have to do this alone."

"I'm not alone," she said, her voice laced with quiet defiance. "I have my own two feet. And the fire's still lit."

And with that, she turned toward the length of the street, the gaslight haloing her figure like the last ember of something sacred, still burning.

As Carmen neared the train station, the clatter of departing wheels and distant whistles filled the air, a mechanical symphony of people leaving, arriving, moving on. She pulled her shawl tighter around her shoulders against the evening chill, but it did nothing to ease the weight pressing against her chest.

Each step away from Barrio Sur felt heavier than the last.

She hadn't expected comfort. But she hadn't expected cruelty either. Not from her neighbors. Not from the old women who used to call her *muñequita* when she brought her mother's *torta fritas* to the chapel. And certainly not from her own blood.

Her mother's words still rang in her ears, harsh and final.

Devil worshiper. Shame. Get out.

They echoed like church bells, each syllable tolling another fracture in her heart.

What hurt the most wasn't the yelling, or even the exile.

It was how easy it had been for her mother to discard her.

Carmen had always imagined their love as something unconventional, yet unbreakable, like the threads in the seams she stitched, invisible but strong.

But now, she saw it clearly. Her mother's love had conditions, and Carmen had just broken them all.

She reached for her journal.

It had always been her refuge. A place untouched by judgment, by doctrine, by the eyes that followed her through the *barrio* like she wore sin on her sleeves.

The pages opened willingly, the spine bending like an old friend. Her pen hovered for a moment, then met the page:

The One Who Loved Me First

Who was she? The silent flame at my start,
the one who held my cries against her heart?

Who peeled the veil gently from my eyes,
then vanished, leaving echoes in the skies?

Who offered her breath so I might live,
and bore the wound that love alone can give?

Who gave me warmth, then faded into cold,
a story half-whispered, with no hand left to hold?

Whose lips were the first to bless my skin,
and yet, for me, would never kiss again?
Whose breast did I cling to in that fragile hour,
drawn to her heartbeat like a budding flower?

Was she a ghost, or memory half-spoken,
a bond unseen, yet never broken?

Who loved me first, so fierce, so true,
and left no name, no trace, no clue?

Was it fate, or mercy, or something unsaid?
Who could she have been?... Perhaps she is dead.

Carmen gazed at the poem, her fingers trembling ever so slightly as the ink dried. A tear slipped down her cheek, and before she could wipe it away, it landed on the page, smudging the final line.

She glanced up at the platform sign, watching the list of destinations flicker into place. Towns she'd only ever heard about in whispered stories or read in cheap novels suddenly felt like lifelines.

Places where no one knew her name. Where no one would spit at her feet or cross themselves as she passed.

For a flickering moment, doubt crept in.

Was I wrong? Was loving him worth all this?

But deep down, beneath the ache and the ruin, the answer glowed like an ember that refused to die.

Yes.

Because love, real love, wasn't always soft. It burned. It carved.

And sometimes, it called you to leave old versions of yourself behind.

As the train pulled in with a hiss of steam and steel, Carmen stepped forward. Not because she knew exactly where she was going, but because she knew she could never go back.

Chapter 21

The train hissed to a stop, its wheels screeching softly against the tracks as the coastal air slipped through the open windows. Carmen stepped onto the platform in Piriápolis, the very town whose birth she had once dared to imagine beside the man who had brought it to life.

The irony wasn't lost on her, that she had helped dream up the very train that now delivered her into her own exile.

The air smelled of salt and eucalyptus, tinged with the faint scent of iron from the rails. Waves crashed in the distance, steady and indifferent, as though the sea itself had no memory of the girl who once believed she could belong here.

She clutched the strap of her satchel tighter, her fingers numb from more than just the chill of the sea air. Behind her, the whistle gave a parting cry before the train lumbered back the way it came, toward the capital, toward the life she could no longer claim.

Ahead, the marble monuments glistened like ghosts in the afternoon light. The city of dreams Francisco had built from dust and vision loomed before her, beautiful and haunted.

And now, for better or worse, it would have to hold her.

The walk to the Hotel Piriápolis was long, though she had done it before.

The grand structure rose from the earth like a vision carved from ambition: limestone and marble, its façade a blend of neo-classical architecture and Latin pride. Francisco had once told her it was meant to be a symbol of possibility. Today, it felt like a relic of a dream that no longer belonged to her.

The bellboy at the entrance barely recognized her, but gave a courteous nod as she entered. The lobby echoed with quiet, the floor gleaming under her worn boots. Tourists had thinned since the scandals, and the vast space felt like a cathedral between devotions.

She made her way down the corridor past the dining hall and found the familiar office tucked beside the stairwell, the door slightly ajar. Inside, Carlos Bonavita sat behind his desk, hunched over blueprints with a pencil tucked behind his ear, muttering to himself in half-spoken calculations.

He looked up.

"Carmen?" Surprise flickered across his face. "What in the world are you doing here?"

"I—" she hesitated in the doorway, then stepped inside. Her voice caught in her throat. "Do you have a minute?"

Carlos stood, wiping ink from his fingertips, his eyes scanning her face with concern. "Of course."

She sat in the chair across from him, her satchel on her lap like a child clinging to a doll.

"My mother threw me out," she said quietly.

Carlos blinked, startled. "What happened?"

Carmen swallowed hard. "The rumors. The Church. People think I'm... dangerous. Blasphemous." Her voice was steadier than she felt. "I went home, and she told me to never come back."

Carlos leaned back in his chair, his expression softening. "I'm sorry, Carmen. That's... terribly cruel."

"Francisco told me it wasn't safe for me to go with him to Rome, so I stayed behind." She paused. "And....I have nowhere else to go," she admitted, a whisper now.

Carlos ran a hand through his thick hair, exhaling slowly. "You're safe here, alright? You hear me?"

She nodded, looking down at her hands.

"You're not alone in this, Carmen," he said at last, voice low and earnest. "We're all feeling it here too. The tourists have caught wind of the rumors in the papers, and our investors... they're backing out one by one. I had to let go of almost half our staff today."

Her heart clenched. She hadn't realized the damage had reached this far.

"This place was supposed to be a dream," she murmured.

"It still can be," he replied. "But right now... it's on fire."

They sat in silence, the gravity between them a quiet tether.

"I can help," Carmen said, lifting her chin. "Whatever you need. Clerical work, writing copy, helping with the books... even stitching linens, if it comes to that. I can't just sit by and do nothing, Carlos."

He studied her, the corners of his mouth twitching into something close to a smile. "You really are one of us now, aren't you?"

"I guess I always have been."

After a moment, he spoke again, more gently. "We'll figure something out. One day at a time."

She looked up, surprised by the warmth in his voice.

"You can stay in one of the empty staff quarters," he offered. "They're simple, but clean. And if you want to keep busy, I could use help organizing records. The hotel's not what it used to be, but it's still ours to keep standing."

Tears welled in her eyes, but she blinked them back. "Thank you," she said, and meant it.

Carlos gave her a lopsided smile. "You know, I always knew you had more grit than most of us. Francisco saw it, but he wasn't the only one."

For the first time in days, Carmen felt a flicker of steadiness return to her chest. Not joy, not peace, but something like shelter in an unrelenting storm.

Outside the window, the moon rose slowly over the hills, and the sea murmured softly in the distance.

As the days went on, the scent of salt and stone lingered in the air as Carmen stepped out into the morning light, the Hotel Piriápolis now a temporary refuge instead of a far-off dream.

She had begun helping at the front desk, sorting guest logs, tending to linens, and sweeping through the airy corridors where echoes of better days clung to the walls.

Carlos, though quiet by nature, had taken to checking in on her each day. He brought her fresh pastries from the kitchen, never said much, but always managed to say enough.

One morning, as they sat in the small staff lounge over lukewarm coffee, Carlos lowered his voice. "They're coming, Carmen. Not tourists. Real estate men from the capital. Government-backed, some of them. They're talking about nationalizing part of the land, claiming Francisco's holdings were illegal to begin with."

Carmen stiffened. "Illegal?"

"They're using the chaos, his disappearance, the Church scandal, all as leverage. Investors keep pulling out left and right. Some say the hotel won't survive the season." He rubbed his jaw, then looked at her with a weariness she hadn't seen before. "I've worked for Don Francisco since I was a teenager. I've built half this town with my own two hands. And now I watch men circle like vultures, waiting for the chance to tear it apart, piece by piece, brick by brick, like it was all just some foolish dream gone sour."

Carlos exhaled, rubbing his temple before continuing. "They smell weakness, Carmen. The rumors, the Church, the investors pulling out… it's blood in the water. And without Francisco here to stand guard, they think they can move in. Buy him out. Claim the land. Strip it for parts."

He looked up at her then, eyes weary but resolute. "That's the new threat. Not just bad press or angry priests. It's the men in suits with contracts and fake smiles. The ones who say they admire what he built, right before they try to gut it and call it progress."

Carmen stood up, a mix of anticipation and unease twisting in her stomach. "We can't afford to be passive now. This isn't just about saving buildings, it's about preserving the future we want for this place. If we let them take it, there's no going back."

Carmen looked at Carlos, a question rising to her lips. "Where are Francisco's sons in all of this? Don't they have any say? This is their legacy too."

Carlos let out a slow breath, his eyes darkening as if the mere mention of Francisco's family brought back a bitter memory. "His sons? They're all estranged, Carmen. There's no unity there, not anymore. The only one who bothers to keep tabs on his father is Francisco José…Pancho, as we call him. But don't be fooled by his name. He's nothing like his father."

Carmen raised an eyebrow, intrigued but skeptical. "What do you mean?"

Carlos reclined in his chair, his jaw tightening with barely contained frustration. "Pancho is a lost cause," he muttered, his voice heavy with contempt. "Expelled from one boarding school after another, thrown out of countless universities, all for drinking, violence, and sheer recklessness. Hell, he even shot at mice in the school dining halls like it was some twisted game. Now, the only time he bothers to show up is when he's looking for money. He doesn't care about the business, about the legacy Francisco spent his life building. He's only interested in what will drain it: money, liquor, women. He's spoiled, selfish, and greedy… a walking contradiction to everything Francisco hoped his legacy would be."

Carmen's stomach sank as she processed his words. She had hoped for more, for some kind of support, someone who would stand with Francisco's ideals. But it seemed the Piria name had been twisted by those who had never understood the heart of it.

"So, he's just out to take whatever he can?" she asked, her voice thick with disappointment.

"Exactly," Carlos replied, his voice colder now, tinged with disdain. "Pancho doesn't care about preserving his father's legacy. He only cares about what he can squeeze out of it. And that's the sad truth. If you're looking for support from him, don't bother."

Carmen sighed, feeling the weight of the situation press against her chest. "Then it's up to us. If anyone's going to fight for Francisco's vision, it looks like we're the ones who have to do it."

Carlos gave a small nod. "It seems that way. We're the only ones left who truly believe in what he built."

She stared at him for a moment, her mind racing. "Then we'll make them see. We'll make them remember why it matters."

Carlos looked at her, nodding. "You're right. It's time to start making our move."

Carmen looked up, her eyes sharp with clarity. "We need to get a telegram to Francisco right away," she said, her voice steady with purpose. "But we can't stop there. We need to take control of the narrative. Get a press release out, fast. If they want to tear down what he built, we'll remind them why they can't. We're not just fighting for our reputation, we're fighting for something real. For legacy. For truth. And we're going to make sure the world knows it."

Carlos watched Carmen, surprised by the sudden shift in her energy. The weight of the moment, the uncertainty, the very real threat looming over them was palpable; he could feel it. But here was Carmen, like a spark in the dark, lighting up with a plan.

She was right. They couldn't afford to wait.

He nodded, meeting her determination with his own. "You're right. I'll get the telegram ready."

Carmen was already reaching for a piece of paper and a pen, her movements swift, driven by a mind that refused to pause. As she wrote, Carlos sat at his desk, his focus divided between preparing the telegram and watching her, captivated by the determination unfolding before him. The room was thick with tension, but in Carmen, he saw an unwavering resolve. She was no longer just a bystander; she was becoming the voice, the force, the one who would stand unshaken in the face of this storm.

Carmen paused, looking up at him with a sharp gaze. "I need you to make sure we get this in the right hands. Call the press. Anyone who will listen. We don't just fight back, we show them why Francisco's work matters. Why it can't be erased."

As she wrote, her mind flashed back to Francisco's words: *There's no better weapon than the pen.* Her grip on the pen tightened.

This wasn't just a letter. It was a declaration.

She finished the note, her eyes scanning the words for strength. She handed it to Carlos. "This is our first move."

Press Release:

For Immediate Release

Defending a Legacy: A Stand for Vision and Integrity

March 1915—

Montevideo, Uruguay — In light of recent rumors and escalating threats to the visionary works of Francisco Piria, we stand resolute in defending not just the structures he built, but the values upon which they were founded. The recent surge of negative press, fueled by misleading reports and opposition from vested interests, marks a critical moment in our history, a moment we refuse to let pass in silence.

Francisco Piria's contributions to Uruguay are undeniable. His work is not just architecture; it is a living testament to innovation, culture, and the enduring power of vision. From the monumental buildings that have shaped the landscape to the transformative ideas that continue to inspire, his legacy is a foundation of progress that cannot and will not be erased by those who seek to undermine it for personal gain.

We recognize the challenges we face as we confront these malicious attempts to destroy what has been built, but we will not back down. To those who think they can buy his legacy, we say this: it is not for sale. To those who think they can strip it away for profit, we remind you that true progress is not measured by the dollar but by the lasting impact on a community, on a people, on a nation.

As we stand firm in defense of what Francisco Piria has developed, we also stand in solidarity with the values he championed: integrity, innovation, and the belief that great work endures beyond the material. This fight is not just about real estate or business interests. It is about defending the future he envisioned, a future that is built not on exploitation, but on respect, on vision, and on the truth of what was created.

We call on the press, on the people of Uruguay, and on those who believe in the integrity of progress to stand with us. The battle is far from over, but we will face it with unwavering strength, guided by the knowledge that what Francisco Piria built is bigger than any one individual or group, it is the legacy of an entire nation.

For further information, please contact:
Carlos Bonavita
La Industrial Francisco Piria S.A.
Hotel Piriápolis
Rbla. de los Argentinos 9003

End of Release

Carlos took the letter, his fingers grazing the edges of the paper. In that moment, he understood. Carmen wasn't merely offering help, she was stepping up, standing by him, ready to face whatever lay ahead.

His expression hardened with resolve. He met her gaze, his voice firm and unwavering. "I'll get on it, Carmen. We're not going down without a fight."

The press release went out late that morning, and within hours, the city began to stir. The words in the release spread like wildfire, circulating in newspapers, radio broadcasts, and word of mouth. At first, it seemed like any other story, another scandal, another controversy, but there was something different about this one.

Carmen sat in the dimly lit office of the Hotel Piriápolis, glued to the small radio in the corner, flicking between stations. The broadcast was all too familiar, yet something about the way it spoke to the public now felt charged, as if the tides were shifting.

A news anchor read the statement aloud, his voice steady but with an undercurrent of intrigue. "In a bold response to mounting rumors and corporate pressure, supporters of Francisco Piria have issued a public stand in defense of his legacy. The release, which claims that the magnate's architectural contributions are under threat from investors and opportunists, has garnered swift attention from both the public and press alike."

Carmen could feel her heart thumping in her chest. She wasn't sure whether it was the adrenaline or the weight of what was at stake. This was more than a defense, it was a declaration.

The anchor continued, "Public reactions have been mixed, with some voicing their concerns over the alleged 'power grab' while others praise the bravery of those choosing to defend Piria's vision."

Carlos walked in just as the broadcast switched to audio of a heated public debate outside the city's main square. People gathered, some shouting, some chanting.

"Seems like the storm's here, Carmen," Carlos said, his voice low but laced with a grim smile.

Carmen didn't answer immediately. She was lost in the voices she heard through the airwaves, the voices of people she once knew, now divided. Some were cheering to the statements of protest, while others murmured in disbelief. But it wasn't just the ordinary people who were talking. The whispers had reached the halls of power.

The broadcast cut to an interview with a well-known investor, his words cold and calculating. "I've always respected Piria's work, but these accusations, they're an inconvenience. This isn't just about ideals, it's about business. Progress doesn't wait for sentimentality."

Carmen clenched her jaw. She had expected no less from those who saw the world in terms of transactions, but hearing it spoken aloud made her blood run cold.

Yet, the press release had done exactly what she had hoped for, it had sparked the conversation. It had put the issue on the map.

A call came in, interrupting her thoughts. Carlos answered, his expression unreadable as he spoke with someone on the other end. After a few short exchanges, he hung up the phone and turned to her.

"Francisco's calling an emergency meeting with some key players. They're gathering their support."

As the news rippled through the city, Carmen felt a quiet certainty settle within her. This was only the beginning. The public's reaction was still raw, the lines between friend and foe still blurred, but one thing was undeniable: they were watching.

And though the storm would only grow fiercer, she knew one thing for sure: no matter how dark the road ahead, she couldn't let this unravel them. Not now. Not when everything was on the line.

Chapter 22

Weeks had stretched into what felt like an eternity since Francisco had left for Rome. Each day had seemed to drag on longer than the last, the absence of his presence hanging heavy in the air. Carmen stood at the edge of the platform, her breath forming misty clouds in the cold morning air. The familiar hum of the train tracks vibrated beneath her feet, but today, it didn't bring comfort. Instead, it carried the sharp, electric buzz of uncertainty.

She had been consumed by the whirlwind of scandals and public scrutiny, her focus divided, but now, as the train finally emerged on the horizon, all the questions that had been simmering in the back of her mind came rushing forward. What had he learned in Rome? Had the Vatican's cabinet offered him the peace he had been hoping for? Or had they crushed his last hope, leaving him to face the ruins of his ambition?

The train screeched to a halt, its doors creaking open with a sound that felt louder than it should have been. Carmen's heart quickened, the weight of expectation pressing down on her chest. She had been waiting for this moment, yet as it arrived, she couldn't shake the unease that had been growing with every passing day. The world had changed in Francisco's absence, and she couldn't help but wonder what kind of man would step off that train, whether it would be the man she once knew, full of vision and fire, or someone altered by the crushing weight of his dreams.

Carlos's words echoed in her mind, sharp and unrelenting: *Men don't come back from crusades the same.*

As the last of the train's wheels stopped turning, Francisco appeared. His figure was unmistakable, yet something about him felt different. His suit was immaculate, as always, but his face was the grimest she had ever seen. There was no spark in his eyes, no glint of the energy that used to radiate from him. Carmen felt a tightness coil in her chest. She knew, without a word, that the meeting with the Vatican had not gone well.

Carmen tightened her grip on the edge of the platform railing, the cold metal biting into her palms as she stared at the train. She didn't want to believe it, didn't want to accept the possibility that the man she had known, the man who had built an empire on hope and ambition, might not be the same after this. But deep down, she feared Carlos might be right. There was a part of her that had always known that the stakes of this journey were too high, that something might be lost along the way. Something irreplaceable.

She moved towards him, but he didn't meet her gaze. Instead, he fixed his eyes on the ground as he walked toward her, his shoulders heavy with a weight she could almost feel in the air.

"Francisco," she called softly, but he didn't answer right away.

After a long, agonizing pause, he came to a stop, his body tense as though every word required an immense effort to release. He looked at her, his expression tight, strained with the weight of his restraint. "It's over, Carmen," he said, his voice barely above a whisper. "I gave them everything. I presented the church to them as a peace offering, hoping that if I surrendered it, they would finally accept the project, accept my partnership. I thought... I thought it would be enough. But it wasn't. They denied me."

Carmen's heart tightened at the words. She had known the stakes of this endeavor, understood the weight of his dream. The church project wasn't just a structure, it was a symbol of his faith, his ambition, his desire to leave behind something greater than himself.

Francisco took a deep breath, the weight of his next words settling between them. "They've asked me to halt all work on the church... to cease construction entirely. In exchange, they've promised peace, a temporary ceasefire in this ongoing battle. A truce."

Carmen's eyes widened, a flicker of relief crossing her face. "But that's good news, Francisco. A truce means we can regroup, we can think clearly. It's a step forward."

He shook his head, his gaze drifting, lost in thought, as uncertainty clouded his features. "It's not that simple, Carmen," he murmured, his voice thick with frustration. "Demolishing the project would be admitting failure. What will I tell the investors? How can we make things right with them? It would be more than a setback, it would be accepting defeat."

Carmen met Francisco's gaze with quiet resolve, fully aware of the gravity of the situation. Yet, she knew there was more to this than the collapse of the church project. There was still a path forward, a way to turn this moment of defeat into a chance for rebirth.

Francisco let out a heavy sigh, his shoulders slumping as he walked toward the waiting carriage. Carmen followed closely behind, her steps light but deliberate, matching the weight of his silence. The horses shifted restlessly as they approached, the sound of their hooves on the cobblestone street a stark contrast to the heaviness between them.

As Francisco climbed into the carriage, his movements slow and deliberate, Carmen slid in beside him, her gaze never leaving his face. She watched him, waiting for him to speak, to let the thoughts swirling inside him find their way out.

"Francisco," she said quietly, breaking the silence that had enveloped them. "Making peace with the Vatican was the first step. You've already done that. You've shown them you're willing to compromise, that you're capable of putting aside personal ambition for the greater good. That alone will go a long way in rebuilding trust, not just with the Church, but with the investors, and with the public."

He exhaled sharply, his hands gripping the edge of the seat, as though the carriage itself was something solid to hold onto. "How do you figure?" His voice was rough, as though the words had been clawing their way out. "Everything I've worked for is falling apart. My vision, the entire city... It was never just about stone and mortar. It was meant to be something alive, something that pulsed with meaning. And now... now it's nothing but a dying creature, being torn apart by buzzards."

The carriage rolled forward, the streets passing in a blur. Carmen's throat tightened, the raw pain in his voice cutting through her. She moved closer to him, her hand gently resting on his arm, offering the only comfort she knew how.

"*Mi vida,* this isn't the end," she said, her voice calm, but firm. "You still have us. You still have your vision, even if it can't be built the way you imagined it."

His eyes flickered toward her, and for a brief moment, she saw the man she knew, the one who had dreamed up an entire city, who had once believed so fiercely in the future he was creating. But then, just as quickly, the light in his eyes dimmed, replaced by a bitter sadness.

He let out a small, humorless laugh, shaking his head. "Do I?" he murmured, his voice distant. "I've spent a lifetime building something, pouring every ounce of myself into it, only for it to all fall apart. I don't know anymore, Carmen. I'm too old for this. I don't know if I can keep going after this."

Carmen squeezed his arm, leaning in slightly as the carriage bumped over the cobblestones. "You can," she said, her words steady, unwavering. "You've done it before. You've rebuilt from nothing. You still have the strength, Francisco. You still have your vision. And this... this doesn't have to be the end."

The silence stretched between them again, but this time it felt different. The air was thick with possibility, with the weight of a choice yet to be made. Francisco sat back against the seat, his eyes staring out the window, lost in thought, while Carmen remained close beside him, a quiet anchor in the storm of his emotions.

As the city passed by, the future seemed uncertain, but Carmen knew one thing for sure: Francisco had always been a man who could rise from the ashes.

Carmen's hand remained firmly on Francisco's arm, her grip unwavering. She turned to face him fully, her voice firm, steady. "Whatever happens, Francisco, you have to keep going. You've created something meaningful, even if it's not in the form you thought it would take. Your legacy isn't just in this city. It's in what you've done, what you've changed, who you've inspired. Don't let this one setback define you."

Francisco didn't respond immediately. Instead, his gaze drifted to the passing cityscape outside the carriage window, the familiar sights of Montevideo slipping by unnoticed.

The weight of her words seemed to have no effect on him, as if they couldn't reach through the heavy fog of disappointment clouding his mind. The church, his great vision, had been his greatest hope for the people. And now, it was nothing more than an abandoned structure, a silent monument to what could have been.

His voice was barely audible, tinged with sorrow. "Maybe," he muttered, "but sometimes even the strongest dreams fade. And I wonder if I can still fight for a vision that no one else sees."

Carmen felt a tightness in her chest as the weight of his words hit her. He wasn't just questioning his vision; he was questioning his very purpose. The silence stretched between them, thick and heavy with unspoken fears, the weight of a battle they had both fought to the brink.

The carriage jolted as they turned down a familiar street, the cobblestones beneath them rattling. Carmen took a deep breath, looking out the window as she tried to steady her own thoughts. This wasn't the time to lose faith. She reached out and placed her hand on his, her fingers warm against the cold tension of his skin.

"You've lost everything before, Francisco," she said, her voice quiet but resolute, "and yet, you've always managed to rebuild. You'll do it again."

He didn't respond right away, but she could feel the shift in the air between them. A flicker of something, hope, perhaps, or recognition, moved in his eyes as he turned slowly toward her. His gaze softened, just for a moment, the raw vulnerability in his eyes a reminder of the man who had built everything from nothing.

"I've lost everything before, but this... this is different," he said, his voice almost a whisper. His fingers tightened around hers, as though seeking something to hold onto in the storm of his thoughts. "I was younger then. I've already given everything, Carmen. It's hard to imagine starting over."

Carmen didn't flinch at the weight of his words. She squeezed his hand gently, meeting his gaze with unshakable certainty. "You can rebuild. You've done it time and time again. This church was just one part of your dream. There are other ways. Other paths."

Her words hung in the air between them as the carriage continued its journey. Francisco sat still for a moment, his face a portrait of conflict. He closed his eyes, his brow furrowing as though trying to absorb the truth she had just spoken.

When he opened them again, there was a shift in his expression, subtle, but undeniable. The faintest spark of resolve flickered in his eyes, like a match struck in the darkness. His shoulders relaxed, the tension beginning to ease.

"Maybe you're right," he said quietly, his voice steadier now. "Maybe I can rebuild. I just... I need to figure out what that looks like now."

Carmen shifted in her seat, her fingers still wrapped around his. The words she needed to say lingered in her mind, but she knew now wasn't the time for hesitation. She had seen the way his gaze fell when he spoke of tearing it all down, and she couldn't let him walk away from this, no matter how bruised it had made him.

"Francisco," she began, her voice steady, "don't demolish the church. Halt the project, but don't tear it down. Leave the church standing."

He looked at her, a flicker of confusion passing across his face. "What do you mean? It's just a symbol of my failure now. What good will it do to leave it standing there?"

Carmen shook her head, her gaze unwavering as she met his eyes. "No. No, leave it. Tell the investors that the project is on hold, but don't erase what you've built. It's still part of your vision, part of who you are. You can't just wipe it away like it never happened."

The carriage rumbled along the street, the wheels turning steadily beneath them, but for a moment, everything around them seemed to stop. Francisco's expression softened, but the doubts still flickered in his eyes.

"Why?" he asked quietly, his voice full of vulnerability. "What does it matter if I leave it standing? It's just a reminder of everything that went wrong."

"No," Carmen said firmly. "Don't look at it as a reminder of your failure. See it as a reminder of your strength, of how far you've come, of the fight you're still willing to put up. Failure would be tearing it down. Instead, let it stand there, not as a monument to defeat, but as a symbol of pause, a temporary hold. A beginning, not the end. The world doesn't need to see you giving up."

Francisco stared at her, processing her words, his mind no doubt turning over the idea. The tension in his shoulders began to ease, a small glimmer of understanding in his gaze.

"I still don't know if I can ask the investors to wait," he said, his voice more uncertain now than before. "How do I tell them that the project is just... suspended? What do I say to them?"

"You tell them the truth," Carmen replied, her voice steady and certain. "That the project is temporarily on hold while you reconsider its future. You don't have to have all the answers now, Francisco. You just have to let them know that you're not giving up on it. Not yet."

He turned his gaze toward the window, watching the city pass by, the weight of his decision heavy on his shoulders. Carmen knew it wasn't an easy choice, but it was the right one.

"Do you think they'll listen to me now?" he asked, his voice tinged with doubt.

"I know they will," she replied confidently. "The public, the investors, they're all watching. They want to see that you can be trusted again, that you can lead with integrity. They need to know you've learned from this, that you've made a choice for peace, not just for your own ambitions, but for something bigger."

Finally, he nodded slowly, the faintest trace of resolve returning to his eyes. "Alright," he said, his voice steady now. "I won't demolish it. I'll try to hold them off. And...maybe you're right. Maybe this is just the pause we need. To figure out where to go from here."

Carmen smiled softly, a surge of quiet relief flooding her chest. Her heart felt lighter now, the burden of his doubts beginning to lift. "You don't have to figure it out alone," she said, her voice gentle yet filled with unwavering support. "You have me, Francisco. And you have Carlos. We'll figure this out together."

The silence that followed wasn't filled with the weight of defeat. It wasn't heavy with the pain of loss. Instead, it was filled with something else, something new. Something like hope.

The carriage rolled onward, carrying them through the heart of the city, its streets familiar, but now full of new potential. The church project had to remain abandoned for the time being, but Carmen knew that Francisco's true strength lay not in the buildings he had crafted, but in his ability to rise; the way he could rebuild himself from the rubble, time and time again.

The battle wasn't over. Not by a long shot. And this time, she would be standing beside him as he rebuilt, not just the city, but himself. Together, they would forge a new path forward, one step at a time.

Chapter 23

As time went on, the storm that had once threatened to consume everything had begun to lose its strength. Its winds no longer howled with the same fury, and its damage, while still visible, had stopped spreading. Slowly, hesitantly, the tide turned. Investors who had once fled in fear now began to trickle back, lured by the uneasy peace Francisco had forged with the Church and the quiet victories won in court—wins that prevented the nationalization of his life's work.

Yet the scars remained.

They showed in the guarded conversations between Carmen and Francisco, in the hesitations that lingered at the edges of decisions, in the shadows beneath their eyes. The worst had passed, but peace did not come without a cost.

In the stillness that followed the storm, a need for respite stirred, deep and undeniable. What they craved was not celebration, but stillness. Not victory, but rest.

They drove through the countryside, where the land rolled wide and open, and the sky stretched above them like a breath finally exhaled.

The noise faded behind them, replaced by the hush of wind through tall grass and the distant call of birds. Each mile they traveled softened something in them. The road curved gently through meadows dusted with wildflowers, and the sunlight filtered through the trees like grace.

Carmen rested her head against the window, watching the world slip by in a blur of nature, feeling a small flicker of peace that had eluded her for so long. She hadn't truly realized how much the weight of everything had affected her until now. The city, the pressure, the constant fight, it had all left her breathless.

Francisco sat beside her, his gaze fixed on the road ahead, but his posture was more relaxed than it had been in months. The tightness in his shoulders seemed to have loosened, his face less drawn, though the weariness still lingered in his eyes. They had both been through hell and back, and though the worst seemed to have passed, neither could shake the quiet knowledge that their journey was far from over.

The car bumped gently over a dirt road, and Francisco finally broke the silence. "I never realized how much I needed this," he said, his voice low but genuine, almost as if speaking to himself.

Carmen turned to him, her eyes soft. "We both did."

For a moment, neither of them spoke, the sound of the car's tires on gravel the only noise between them. It was a comfortable silence, one that had grown easier over time, even after all the turmoil. They had learned to find solace in each other, even when the world around them was in chaos.

As they turned off the main road and onto a winding country lane, Carmen relaxed into her seat. The air was rich with the sweet, loamy scent of wildflowers. Birdsong drifted through the trees like a lullaby woven into the wind. Rolling hills stretched into the distance, splashed with vivid blooms that swayed in the breeze like painted brushstrokes. Overhead, the sky unfurled in an endless sweep of blue, vast and unbroken, as if the world itself were holding its breath.

Francisco's gaze lingered on Carmen as the car wound its way through the golden countryside, the late afternoon sun brushing the fields with light.

His voice was warm, laced with quiet excitement. "I've been meaning to bring you to my country house for a long time," he said, his dark eyes gleaming with anticipation. "It's a place that holds a great deal of meaning for me. I think… once you see it, you'll understand why."

As the car wound its way up the narrow, rugged path, Carmen's anticipation swelled with each turn.

And then, she saw it.

Perched gracefully against the hillside, the house emerged like a vision conjured from a dream. The Tuscan-style cottage, bathed in honeyed sunlight, looked as though it had been carved from the landscape itself.

Its terra cotta roof glowed warmly beneath the open sky, and timeworn wooden shutters hugged each window like a quiet embrace from the past. Wildflowers nodded in the breeze, and vines curled up the stone walls with careless elegance.

It was everything she had imagined, and somehow, even more.

It was simple, secluded, and quietly beautiful; exactly what they needed. A place not just to rest, but to recuperate and recharge.

Carmen stepped out of the car, letting the crisp country air wrap around her like a shawl. She drew in a deep breath, and for the first time in what felt like forever, the weight of the city, the noise, the tension, the unspoken grief, all began to lift.

Peace settled in its place, quiet and steady. She exhaled slowly, fully, letting the serenity of the landscape wash over her like a balm she hadn't known she needed.

As they neared the front door, a flurry of colorful songbirds and little green parrots flitted joyfully through the trees, their wings like delicate petals fluttering in the breeze. Their cheerful songs filled the air, harmonizing beneath the vast expanse of brilliant blue sky.

Carmen stood for a moment, captivated, feeling a deep reverence for the serene beauty of the place. It was a sanctuary, untouched by the noise and chaos of the world, a place where the simple joys of life could be appreciated in their purest form.

Francisco gently pushed open the little arched wooden door, his hand extended in silent invitation, urging Carmen to step inside and explore. As they crossed the threshold, a wave of tranquility washed over her.

There was a quiet magic in the place, an immediate sense of belonging amidst the rolling hills and tranquil atmosphere.

The cottage's French windows were thrown wide, letting golden streams of sunlight flood in, mixing with the crisp, fresh country air.

The European oak floors glowed warmly beneath their feet, and the high ceilings gave the rooms an airy, open feeling, as though the house itself breathed in time with the landscape.

Upstairs, Carmen stood at the bedroom window, her eyes drawn to the picturesque panorama that lay before her. The lush greenery stretched endlessly, the trees swaying gently in the breeze, while in the distance, the imposing landmark of Pan de Azúcar rose against the azure sky. Its verdant slopes seemed to cradle the meadows below, a perfect blend of nature's embrace.

Beyond that, the view opened up to Francisco's grand castle, standing proudly amidst miles of rolling hills and vast green meadows, as far as the eye could see. It was a view so breathtakingly beautiful that it seemed almost surreal, like a dream come to life.

Carmen stood, mesmerized by the breathtaking view of the lush countryside, the afternoon air flowing gently through the sheer curtains of the bedroom window, carrying with it the scent of earth and new beginnings.

As she took it all in, Francisco approached quietly, his presence warm and steady. He reached out and gently took her hand in his, his touch grounding her.

"Carmencita," he began, his voice filled with sincerity, "I brought you here to thank you…for standing by me through everything. Through all the turmoil and uncertainty, you've shown me unwavering support and loyalty, even when the world seemed intent on tearing us apart." His voice faltered for a moment, emotion thickening the air between them. "I can't thank you enough for being here, for never wavering."

Carmen met his gaze, her eyes reflecting a complex mix of emotions: gratitude, understanding, and a quiet sadness. She squeezed his hand gently, her voice soft but firm.

"Mi vida," she whispered. "You know I've always believed in you, in your vision, no matter how many obstacles we've faced. I still believe in you, Francisco."

A small smile tugged at the corners of her lips, a silent promise that she was with him, always.

He gently stroked her hair, his touch tender, as his voice dropped to a soft, sincere murmur. "I know how much you've given up for me," he said, his eyes searching hers, soft but heavy with the weight of his words. "Your family, your home... everything you've known. You've sacrificed more than anyone could ever ask of you, and I can never truly repay that."

He paused for a moment, as if weighing his next words carefully. "But I want you to know, I see it. I appreciate it. Every part of you, every sacrifice you've made."

Carmen met his gaze, her heart heavy yet steady. She took a small breath, her fingers brushing his as she spoke, her voice soft but resolute. *"Mi amor,"* she said quietly, "I've never thought of it as a sacrifice. My family, my home, they'll always be a part of me, but this…" She paused, looking around them at the tranquility of the countryside, "this is what I choose. Being with you, standing by you through everything. That's what matters most to me. What we're building together, even through the chaos, that's where I'm meant to be."

Her eyes held his, unwavering. "I've never regretted it. Not once."

Francisco smiled tenderly and pulled her into his arms, holding her close as they stood in the serenity of the cottage, surrounded by the beauty of nature. "So, what do you think of the house?" he asked, his voice thick with anticipation, as if his heart rested on her answer.

Carmen's smile blossomed, her eyes lighting up with genuine admiration. "Oh, I love it," she said softly, her voice warm and full of affection. "It's so charming and cozy. A perfect retreat." She breathed in as the cool morning breeze swept through the window, tousling her hair, adding a sense of timeless tranquility to the moment.

"I'm glad you like it," he murmured softly, pressing a tender kiss to her forehead. "Carmen, *mi amor*," he whispered, his words full of affection. "This cottage once housed the manager of my vineyards, but I've long since retired my wineries."

He paused, his gaze softening as he looked at her, the love and trust in his eyes unwavering. "And now... it's yours, *Carmencita*," he said, his voice sincere and full of promise.

Carmen blinked, caught off guard, her heart skipping a beat. Her eyes searched his face, the weight of his words sinking in slowly. "Mine?" she asked, her voice barely above a whisper, a mix of surprise and disbelief. "What do you mean?"

"I want you to have it, *vida mía*, a place to call your very own. You can take the train here whenever you want. It's a place where you can write, find peace, and be inspired, whenever you need it. For you."

The weight of his words settled between them, and for a moment, Carmen simply stood there, overwhelmed by the unexpected gesture. Her heart swelled with emotion as she took in the significance of what he was offering. This place, this sanctuary, was his gift to her, a space where she could truly be herself.

She searched his face, her mind racing, the words catching in her throat. "Francisco..." Her voice faltered, a mixture of surprise, gratitude, and something deeper swirling within her. "You don't have to do this. You've already given me so much."

He smiled gently, his eyes filled with warmth and resolve. "*Mi amor*, I want to. This place isn't just an escape, it's a canvas for you to fill with your dreams, your words, your peace. A sanctuary where you can be yourself, without limits."

Tears welled in her eyes, though she blinked them away quickly, not wanting to let the moment slip through her fingers. She stepped forward, closing the distance between them, and placed her hand gently on his chest, feeling the steady beat of his heart beneath her palm.

"*Mi vida*," she whispered, her voice thick with emotion. "I don't even know what to say..."

Francisco smiled softly, his eyes full of tenderness. He reached out and gently wiped away the tear that had slipped down her cheek, his thumb brushing over her skin with a touch so tender it made her heart ache.

"Don't say anything, *mi cielo*," he said gently, his voice filled with quiet affection. "Just know that this house is a symbol of my love for you, and that it will always be here for you, no matter where life takes us."

Carmen's breath caught in her throat, and she closed her eyes for a moment, letting his words sink in. There, in the stillness of the countryside, surrounded by the simplicity and beauty of the world they had created together, she felt an overwhelming sense of gratitude, of peace.

With a quiet sigh, she leaned into him, resting her head on his shoulder. "I don't deserve all this," she murmured, her voice barely audible.

Francisco's arms tightened around her, offering her a quiet strength. "You do, Carmen. You deserve more than you know."

With a tender smile, he pressed a kiss to her forehead, letting his lips linger there before drawing her into a quiet embrace.

Overwhelmed, Carmen let her tears fall freely, her heart aching and full all at once. Resting her head against his chest, she looked out at the rolling hills beyond, their lush green slopes bathed in golden afternoon light. For a brief, fragile moment, it felt as though the world had paused just for her, offering a sliver of peace amid the storm.

Carmen felt something settle deep within her, a quiet revelation. Her sanctuary wasn't just the cottage tucked between the hills or the soft rustle of eucalyptus leaves in the breeze. It was him. The quiet steadiness of his presence, the way his arms wrapped around her like a shield from the world.

Here, she could breathe without bracing. Here, the noise of judgment and fear faded into nothing. In his embrace, she found space to be, to dream, to create, to simply exist without apology.

The weight of all they had endured seemed to dissolve into the stillness. Outside, the world teetered with uncertainty. But within the warmth of his touch, she felt anchored. Safe. Together.

Whatever came next, she knew they would meet it not as fugitives of the past, but as co-authors of what was still to come. Side by side. Flame and flint.

Chapter 24

The weeks stretched languidly by, each one unfolding like a quiet promise as Carmen and Francisco settled into the rhythm of their newfound haven.

Surrounded by the murmurs of wind through the branches and birdsong that rose like prayer, the world outside felt like a distant echo. The cottage was no longer just a retreat, it was a sanctuary. A love nest stitched together by stolen moments and unspoken understandings.

In the peaceful embrace of the countryside, far from judgment and noise, they breathed more freely, loved more gently, and rediscovered the sacred art of simply being.

Carmen would wake early, before the sun had fully risen, and slip out into the cool morning air. The earth was still, the world hushed in the pre-dawn light, and she would sit by the window with her *mate*, watching the mist roll over the hills, her mind quiet but full. It was in these moments, in the simplicity of nature, that she found clarity, a stillness she hadn't realized she'd been longing for.

Even Francisco, always tethered to the relentless pulse of the city, had found a kind of peace there. Each afternoon, as the sun dipped low and the sky turned a fiery red, they would wander hand in hand through fields of wildflowers, their colors vivid against the green backdrop.

Winding paths led them to hidden coves and quiet beaches, each turn revealing a secret corner of the world untouched by time. The landscape seemed to cradle them in its vast, unspoken grace, a gentle reminder that joy could be quiet, and love could bloom in stillness.

Evenings carried a quiet kind of magic. Back at the cottage, the warm glow of candlelight cast gentle shadows across their faces as they shared simple meals that tasted richer for the company. Their conversations flowed easily: stories, dreams, half-whispered hopes, each word exchanged like a cherished offering.

Beneath the hush of moonlight, they danced, slow and barefoot in the grass, swaying to a melody only they could hear. The sky above stretched wide and infinite, dusted with stars like scattered promises.

And for a little while, time held its breath. In that fragile hush between day and tomorrow, they were just two souls suspended in wonder. Grateful, weightless, and entirely, achingly alive.

But while the outside world seemed distant, a sense of unease still lingered beneath the surface. Francisco's earlier battles had not been easily forgotten, and though the tension between them had eased for a while, Carmen could sense the weight that still pressed on his shoulders.

He had never fully shared the burden with her, never told her the full extent of the struggles he had faced in the wake of the scandals, the deals, the compromises he'd had to make. But she could see it in the quiet moments, in the way his gaze would drift beyond the horizon when he thought she wasn't looking. In the way he sometimes pulled away in the still of the night, his thoughts far away, even as he lay beside her.

The cottage may have sheltered them from the world, but it couldn't keep the storm at bay forever. There were still whispers in the city, still rumors that threatened to undo everything they had fought for. The nationalization of his properties had been avoided, but Francisco's empire was still fragile, teetering on the edge of something far more dangerous.

There was still the question of his legacy, of the choices he had made and the ones he had yet to face. And Carmen knew, deep down, that no matter how peaceful their surroundings, the war was far from over.

One afternoon, as they sat on the veranda, watching the golden light of the setting sun bathe the landscape in warmth, Carmen could feel the silence stretch between them, a quiet tension that she couldn't ignore. Francisco's hand rested in hers, but his mind was clearly elsewhere.

"*Mi vida*," she began, her voice soft but tinged with concern, "You've been so distant lately. I feel like you're a million miles away. What is it? Please talk to me."

He hesitated for a moment, his eyes darkening as he looked at her. "I don't want to bring the weight of the world to our doorstep, Carmen. I've already put you through so much," he said softly, his voice laced with an unspoken regret.

"But the truth is…the battles aren't over. The people who've been waiting for me to fail, they won't stop. Not until they've taken everything."

Carmen felt a tightness in her chest, but she didn't look away. She squeezed his hand, her voice resolute. "Then we fight. Together."

Francisco met her gaze, and for the first time in weeks, there was a flicker of something in his eyes, something that hadn't been there before. A spark of resolve. But it was fleeting, and as quickly as it appeared, it was gone.

"I don't know how much more I can give, Carmen," he murmured, his voice tinged with exhaustion. "I've already given everything I have, and yet the world keeps coming. I'm afraid… of what's next."

Carmen leaned in, brushing a soft kiss against his cheek. "Whatever comes, *mi vida*, we face it together. I'm not going anywhere. We'll figure it out. One step at a time."

Francisco's eyes softened for a brief moment, but the sadness in them was undeniable. He gently pulled his hand away from hers, his face clouded with a mixture of frustration and regret.

Francisco's jaw tightened as he turned away, his gaze drifting toward the distant peak of Pan de Azúcar, like a man already measuring the weight of an impossible ascent. Silence hung between them before he finally spoke, his voice low but resolute.

"The Austrian investors there have pulled back. I have to go meet with them in Zurich. They're spooked, and not just by the numbers. Italy just declared war on Austria, and they've all fled to Switzerland. This war is spreading faster than anyone expected."

Carmen's brow furrowed. "Then let me go with you. I won't be in the way."

"No. It's not safe, Carmen," he said, his voice quiet, almost sorrowful. "The war is only getting worse. Russia's aggression is spreading, and it's becoming too dangerous for anyone to be there. I can't risk putting you in danger like that. You don't understand, Carmen, the situation in Europe is volatile. My investors, my allies, they're desperate to secure their assets, and I need to be there, not just for them, but for my own future. For ours. I can't afford to have you caught in the crossfire."

Carmen's chest tightened at his words, but she held her ground. "I understand, *mi amor*," she said softly, "but you have to understand something, too. I can't just let you carry this alone. This fight, this vision, it's not just yours anymore. Everything we've fought for is on the line. Think of all the people you've inspired. I can't just stand on the sidelines while it all burns."

She reached for him again, this time more forcefully, her hand grasping his as she searched his eyes, desperate for him to see how much she wanted to be there with him.

"I'm not asking you to fight it alone. Not again. Please, Francisco. Let me be there for you, to stand with you. Please don't shut me out."

His eyes softened again, the weight of her plea pressing down on him. But still, he shook his head, his voice firm though laden with sorrow. "No. It's too dangerous, Carmen. And if anything happened to you—"

"I can take care of myself," she interrupted, her voice trembling but resolute. "You're not the only one who's strong. I know what's at stake, and I'm willing to face whatever comes."

Francisco exhaled sharply, closing his eyes for a moment as if trying to fight the battle within himself. When he opened them again, there was a finality to his expression, a quiet resignation.

"No. I need you safe. And I need you here." He turned back to her, his expression unreadable. "This is a fight I have to face on my own. This isn't just about us anymore. It's bigger. And if I fail—" He cut himself off. "I can't drag you down with me in this, Carmen. I won't."

Carmen felt the sting of his words like a cold slap, her throat tight as she fought to keep her composure. But deep down, she knew the truth. There was nothing she could say to change his mind. He had made his decision.

"Just promise me one thing," she whispered. "Don't disappear into that war."

Francisco reached for her then, brushing a strand of hair from her face. "I'll find my way back to you," he murmured. "No matter how long it takes."

But as he kissed her forehead and pulled away, Carmen felt it, that hollow echo of separation already beginning to open like a chasm between them.

The days turned into weeks as Francisco set sail for Europe to fight his own kind of war.

Alone in the stillness of the countryside, Carmen found herself drifting into thoughts she couldn't easily silence.

The days, once filled with light and peace, now seemed to stretch endlessly before her, the quiet moments leaving space for doubts she hadn't expected. The cottage, which had become a sanctuary for them both, now felt like a cage, trapping her in a spiral of unspoken fears.

The letters from Francisco were sparse. They arrived only intermittently, leaving her to wonder whether the delay was due to the war, or if he had simply become too preoccupied to write. Each letter, when it came, felt more distant than the last, and the uncertainty of their connection left her questioning whether she was still a part of his world at all.

She unfolded Francisco's latest letter, her fingers trembling slightly as she read it once more, hoping to find something that might reassure her, but only finding the same impersonal tone that had begun to leave her feeling more alone than ever:

June 1916 —

Carmen,

I hope this letter reaches you, and finds you well, though I know the circumstances aren't easy. Zurich is bleak, and the days seem to stretch on endlessly with negotiations and discussions that never seem to reach a conclusion. I apologize for the silence; it's been more difficult than I anticipated to keep everything in motion here while still finding time to write.

The work here is consuming, but necessary. The investors are cautious, and with everything happening in Europe, their focus is scattered. The war continues to cast a long shadow over all of this, but I believe there is still a way forward. The board and I are pushing through the challenges, as we always do.

As for the situation back home, I trust you're managing. I hope you're finding opportunities to write during this time. It's been hard, I know, but we'll get through this.

I'll write again soon. Please don't worry.

Yours,

—F.

She stared at it, her fingers tracing the letters as though that might bring some warmth back to the coldness of the page. *I trust you're managing.* The words echoed in her mind, leaving behind an emptiness that ached where there should have been affection, understanding, something more than a rushed formality.

The silence in his words felt like a wall that grew thicker with each passing day. *Keep you updated.* Was that all she was to him now? An afterthought? A fleeting moment in the grand, urgent world he was so absorbed in?

Her heart tightened in her chest. She wanted to believe that he was just busy, that he was caught up in the whirlwind of his projects and the stakes that weighed on him. She had stood by him through it all, even when his ambition seemed to outpace her every hope. But this... this felt different. The absence of warmth, the lack of even a simple *"I miss you"* or *"I'm thinking of you"* unsettled her. Had it always been like this, or had something changed between them?

She folded the letter carefully, the edge still sharp from the many folds. Her fingers trembled slightly as she slid it back into the desk drawer. Was she foolish for holding on? For expecting him to come back the way he once was, full of fire and affection, wrapped in the intensity of their shared love?

She sat at the small wooden table by the window, her fingers absentmindedly tracing the rim of her *mate* gourd, the steam rising in delicate swirls, dissipating into the still air. The gentle hum of nature outside, the rustling of leaves, the occasional chirp of a bird, seemed distant, as if the world beyond the cottage was moving in a rhythm she could no longer follow.

Francisco's absence was a tangible thing, a hollow space beside her where his presence once filled the air with warmth and energy. The quiet moments that had once been a sanctuary now seemed to stretch on endlessly. Her eyes drifted across the room, landing on the fireplace where the embers still smoldered faintly, the soft crackling of the wood almost the only sound in the room.

Her mind began to wander, her thoughts circling back to the uncertainty of their future. She stood up suddenly, feeling restless, her footsteps echoing softly in the quiet space. She walked to the window, pulling back the curtain just enough to see the rolling hills beyond. The landscape before her was breathtaking, with verdant fields stretching endlessly toward the horizon, the sun casting a warm, golden glow over the land. Yet, it felt almost unreal, like a scene from a film that she could admire but never truly touch. Her fingers gripped the edge of the windowsill as she tried to steady her breath.

Francisco's promise to return felt distant, fragile. She could still hear his voice, low and sincere, as he had told her he would come back, that this separation was temporary, but what if the world outside had other plans? What if his battles in Europe took longer than expected? What if he didn't return at all?

Why wouldn't he let me go with him? The question tightened in her chest like a knot pulled too hard. She had stood beside Francisco through every storm, through rumors and ruin, through visions and victories. He knew how fiercely she loved him, how ready she was to face the fire with him. And yet, when it mattered most, he had told her to stay behind.

The thought clawed at her. Was it really about her safety? Or was it something else?

What if he's ashamed of me? The idea made her stomach twist. She tried to push it away, tried to remember the way he looked at her when they were alone, the way his hand lingered at the small of her back. But still, the doubt crept in.

He belonged to a world of fine suits and powerful men, of whispered deals and golden rooms. And she was a mere woman, one from narrow streets and hand-stitched dreams. She was not one of them, and maybe he had finally seen it too clearly.

Maybe love was never going to be enough to cross that divide.

Shaking her head, Carmen turned away from the window, pacing across the room. She stopped by the table where her journal sat, open but untouched. She had spent hours filling its pages with words of hope, dreams of a future with Francisco, but now those words seemed empty. The future felt too uncertain, too fragile. She picked up the pen, but the words wouldn't come. The knot in her chest got tighter.

She walked to the fireplace, crouching down to stir the fading embers. The flames flickered briefly before dying down again, leaving only the heat of the coals. She could almost feel the warmth of his touch, of his embrace, as she stood in the quiet room. There had been a time when their shared silences had been comforting, when the space between them had felt full. Now, it was filled with uncertainty.

Carmen stepped back, her mind racing, and moved toward the back door of the cottage. She opened it, the cool air rushing in, the smell of fresh grass and wildflowers filling her lungs. Without thinking, she stepped outside, her feet brushing the dew-covered grass. The landscape stretched out before her, peaceful yet daunting in its vastness.

She walked through the meadow, her thoughts a whirlwind. The sound of her footsteps on the grass was rhythmic, almost meditative, but the doubts continued to churn.

He asked me to stay behind, she thought bitterly. *He said it was too dangerous, that he couldn't protect me. But his words feel hollow now, like a curtain pulled over something I wasn't meant to see.*

What if he hadn't left her behind for safety, but for convenience? What if he really was ashamed? Ashamed to have a woman like her, unauthorized, uninvited, daring to take up space in a world that was never meant for her? A world of men in polished shoes and closed doors.

What if I've just been a distraction this whole time?

The thought slid into her mind like a cold blade.

Not a partner. Not an equal.

Just a beautiful pause between ambitions.

A muse to pass the time, not someone to build a future with.

Her mind felt like it was spinning in circles. She couldn't keep living like this, questioning everything, questioning *him.*

She turned back toward the cottage, her steps quickening with purpose. She had to pour it all out, empty the noise onto the page before it swallowed her whole.

Back at the small desk by the window, she sank into the chair. The late afternoon light cast golden shadows across the paper as she picked up her pen and began to write; raw, urgent, searching:

July 1916—

There are moments in this stillness, brief, breath-held silences between chores and clock hands, when I think I've found peace. But it never lasts. My mind begins to churn, turning over old doubts like stones in a stream.

Francisco said Europe was too dangerous. That the war, the politics, the Vatican, none of it was safe for me. But what if that wasn't the whole truth? What if that was just his way of leaving me behind?

Sometimes I wonder if I'm just a lull between his battles, a soft place for him to land before he takes flight again. A happy distraction, not a true companion. And if that's all I am... then what does that make the pieces of myself I've given him?

I can't shake the thought that maybe he's ashamed. Not of what we are, but of who I am. I come from a world he's long since risen above, one of calloused hands and patched skirts and borrowed books. I'll never glide effortlessly through the parlors and drawing rooms of

Europe. Maybe he knows that. Maybe that's why he didn't want me beside him.

Because I don't belong to that world. Not the way those polished women with their gilded names and inherited grace do.

But I don't want to believe that. I can't. What we've built, what we've survived, has to mean more than social standing or a name. I am not a passing infatuation. I am his partner. His equal.

And if I have to prove that by standing on my own two feet, if I have to face the storms alone, I will. Because I would rather walk into the fire than fade into the background of someone else's story.

Carmen set the pen down, the words feeling both freeing and heavy. She let out a slow breath, running her fingers over the paper. The act of writing had always been her way of finding clarity, but now it felt more like an act of survival, of fighting off the darkness that threatened to creep in.

She stood up, walking back toward the window. The wind had picked up, and the trees outside swayed gently in the breeze. It was quiet again, and for the first time since Francisco had left, Carmen allowed herself to truly listen to the stillness. Maybe this was her chance to find her own strength, to prove to herself that she didn't need anyone to validate her worth. She had already proven to herself that she was capable of standing on her own.

As the last rays of sunlight disappeared over the hills, Carmen stepped back from the window and closed her journal, her heart steadier now. She would wait for Francisco, yes, but she would also take the time to grow, to strengthen herself, so that when they were reunited, they would be more than just two people fighting the world together. They would be two whole souls, standing side by side.

She tucked the journal beneath her arm and turned toward the door, unaware that the storm gathering on the horizon would test everything she had just promised herself.

Chapter 25

The streets of Montevideo had grown colder in Francisco's absence, or perhaps it was simply the chill of uncertainty settling into Carmen's bones. The city moved around her as if nothing had changed, but everything had. The fire they had kindled together had turned to smoke, curling into corners she could no longer reach.

She walked with purpose, though her steps were heavy. Past shuttered storefronts and the smell of roasted peanuts and damp cobblestone, she made her way back to the one place that had once made her feel alive.

The Madreselva.

Its windows glowed amber in the gathering dusk, soft light spilling into the street like a quiet promise. As she reached the door, the familiar strains of a *bandoneón* curled around her like an embrace. Melancholy. Elegant. Full of ache.

The floorboards creaked beneath her heels as she stepped into the *milonga*, the scent of waxed wood and cologne curling into her senses like memory. It had been months since she'd set foot in the place. Months since she let music move through her instead of sorrow. But tonight, something unspoken had drawn her back.

Carmen hovered in the doorway, uncertain for a breath. Then Nico spotted her.

"Well, well," he said, polishing a glass behind the bar, the corners of his mouth lifting as she approached the bar. "*La musa* returns."

Carmen offered a small smile, the edges of it tight with unspoken thoughts. "I'm not here to make a scene," she replied, her voice trailing off as she searched for the right words. "I just needed..." She paused, unsure of how to finish the thought.

Nico nodded, understanding without explanation. "You don't have to say it. Tango always fills the spaces we don't have words for."

Carmen let the music wash over her, the longing, the weight, the slow, sweet burn of remembering who she was. Here, she wasn't scandal. She wasn't shame.

She was breath and blood and rhythm.

She was a woman trying to belong to herself again.

"It's been a while, *Carmencita*," he said, his voice warm but tinged with a hint of concern. "The place hasn't felt the same without you."

Carmen forced a smile, but it didn't quite reach her eyes. She had spent so much time lost in her thoughts, in Francisco's battles, that even the familiar hum of the Madreselva felt like a distant memory.

"I wasn't sure I'd ever come back," she admitted, her gaze dropping to the worn leather strap of her satchel before lifting to meet his eyes again. "I wasn't sure how I'd be received."

Nico gave a knowing nod, a hint of a smile tugging at the corners of his lips. He leaned against the counter casually, his eyes thoughtful.

"The gossip's quieted down a bit," he said, his voice low, but not without a certain warmth. "Once the bad press about Piria started to die down, people found something else to talk about. The war's been keeping everyone busy. It's all anyone's been focused on these days. You've been off the radar, *Carmencita*. People have more to worry about lately."

She exhaled a sigh of relief, though it was tempered by a twinge of unease. The weight of the scandal had felt endless, each day more suffocating than the last.

The thought of returning to the world she had once known, to the eyes of those who had judged her, had seemed daunting. But now, with the war overshadowing everything, she realized how much that pressure had faded from her life, if only for a while.

"So, I'm not the talk of the town anymore?" she asked, her voice teasing but laced with a quiet vulnerability she hadn't intended.

Nico chuckled softly, shaking his head.

"No, not really. I think they've mostly forgotten about the noise around Piria. He's not the headline anymore." He gave a slight shrug, his tone turning a little more serious. "It's funny how easily people forget when something new comes along."

Nico studied her face for a moment, his expression softening.

"You're always welcome here, Carmen. You know that, right?" He paused, a playful glint appearing in his eyes. "And, just for the record, I never thought you were a witch."

Carmen blinked, caught off guard by his humor, and then let out a soft laugh. "*Dios mío*, that rumor reached you too?"

Nico shrugged, a mischievous grin spreading across his face. "Well, you know how people are. They like to throw around accusations when they're bored, especially when it involves someone they don't understand." He raised an eyebrow, his voice light. "But I always figured you were more likely to curse them with your silence than with anything else."

Carmen chuckled, feeling the weight of the past few days lift just a little. "If I were a witch, I think I would've cast a spell for more peace around here," she said, her tone still teasing but with a touch of gratitude for the small moment of levity.

The joke hung in the air like incense. Soft, fragrant, and just a little bit protective.

Her gaze drifted around the room, taking in the familiar glow of the Madreselva before returning to Nico. "Has Rafael been around?" she asked casually, the edge of a smile playing on her lips. "Haven't seen him in a while. I was hoping to run into him."

Nico leaned on the bar, his expression shifting into something warm and amused. "Rafa? Yeah, he's been around, kind of slipping in and out. Keeping to himself more than usual." He paused, a hint of fondness in his voice. "But I imagine it's not the same without his favorite partner in crime."

She turned to scan the room, the old rhythm of the space drawing her in. And then, as if conjured by the pull of memory, a familiar tune began to play. For a moment, she allowed herself to be swept away in the music, her body moving subtly with the beat, her thoughts floating somewhere distant.

Her gaze flicked toward the small dance floor, where couples began to gather, the fluid motion of their bodies weaving in time with the music. She was still looking for Rafael, but he was nowhere to be seen. Perhaps he was off somewhere, lost in his thoughts or avoiding the chaos, as he often did.

Her gaze caught on a stranger standing at the edge of the dance floor. With a subtle nod, he extended an invitation to dance. No words, just a silent offer: to forget, to float, to lose herself in the music for a few stolen minutes.

Without thinking too much, she nodded back, her body already moving toward him, her feet taking the familiar steps she had once danced a hundred times before. As she approached, the man's eyes held hers, a quiet understanding between them.

His hand extended, waiting for hers. She placed her hand in his, and together, they stepped into the current of the music.

As they began to move, Carmen's body fell into the old, sacred language. Step, breath, pivot, pause. Her muscles remembered even what her mind had tucked away. She wasn't dancing to be seen. She was dancing to feel.

And for a few moments, nothing else existed. The ache of absence, the gossip, the bad press, was lifted. It was just the music, the movement, and the solace of being weightless in someone else's rhythm.

And as the music built toward its final cadence, Carmen turned her face just slightly, and caught sight of someone, at the entrance.

Tall. Familiar.

Rafael.

Rafael lit up the moment he saw her making her way across the floor, still glowing from the *tanda*.

When they embraced, it was without hesitation, tight and familiar, like no time had passed at all.

She pulled back slightly, her eyes soft with something between nostalgia and relief.

"Rafa," she said, her voice gentler than she expected. "It's been too long."

"Too long," he replied, his voice carrying a familiar edge, half humor, half something more. "You disappeared on me. I was starting to wonder if I'd have to come looking for you."

They settled into a quiet corner table, the *milonga* softening around them like a distant tide. For a moment, just being in each other's company brought a kind of comfort neither had realized they'd been craving.

Carmen set her satchel gently beside her chair and offered a small, uncertain laugh. "I guess I've been hiding in plain sight."

She studied Rafael more closely. He looked older somehow. Drawn, with shadows under his eyes that hadn't been there before. A quiet weariness clung to him, the kind that didn't come from lack of sleep but from carrying too much for too long.

"How have you been?" she asked, her voice low, tentative. There was distance between them now, and she was trying to find her way back across it.

Rafael leaned back with a sigh. His eyes drifted to the window for a beat before returning to hers.

"You know how it is," he said, his tone too light to be convincing. "My family's been… difficult. Everything's unholy. Even breathing the wrong way might summon the devil."

He tried to smile, but it faltered at the edges. The weight behind his words lingered between them like the bitter scent of burnt coffee.

Carmen nodded. The same heaviness had followed her like a shadow ever since her own mother's rejection. "I know," she murmured. "It's like we're stuck in a past that everyone else is trying to bury."

Rafael let out a breath through his nose, a crooked half-smile tugging at his mouth. "Yeah, well... not all of us get to run away to seaside sanctuaries when things go to hell." His tone was teasing, but the glint in his eyes betrayed something more. Resentment, maybe. Or hurt. That quiet ache he never let anyone name.

Carmen frowned, a pang of guilt pulling at her. "I wasn't running away, Rafael. I was just... figuring things out."

He didn't say anything immediately, but his eyes softened, and he nodded slowly. "I get it," he said, his voice quieter now. "It's hard to know who you are when the whole world is trying to tell you who you should be."

They both fell into a long silence, the kind that only old friends could share, one filled with unsaid words and shared understanding.

"And Francisco?" Rafael asked gently, his voice edged with concern. "Where is he tonight?"

Carmen's gaze faltered for a moment at the mention of Francisco's name, but she quickly masked it with a shrug. "You know him, always running off to save the world. He's in Zurich, making deals and trying to keep everything from falling apart. But…" She trailed off, looking down at her hands.

Rafael studied her closely. "But?"

Carmen's eyes flickered away for a moment before she spoke, her voice low. "But something's changed. He's… distant lately."

He tilted his head. "What's going on?"

"I don't know what's going on anymore. His letters are few and far between. And when they do come, they're all business now. No warmth, no questions. Just updates. And... well, his silence is louder than anything else."

Rafael sat back, studying her with an intensity that made her feel like he could read every thought in her head. "I'm sorry, Carmen," he said quietly. "I know you've been fighting for something, for him, for so long, but you deserve more than this. You deserve someone who's there for you, who sees you. Someone who stays."

His words hit her harder than she expected. She blinked rapidly, trying to keep the emotion from showing, but it was no use. The tears were welling up, and she didn't have the strength to hold them back anymore.

"I don't know what else I can do to prove myself to him," she whispered, her voice trembling at the edges. "He's everything to me. And I… I've done everything I can to show him that I'm strong enough to stand beside him. I was willing to do anything, become whatever he needed me to be. I thought he saw that."

Rafael leaned forward, his voice soft but firm. "You're not just *whatever someone needs you to be*, Carmen. You're you. And I know that, even if you've forgotten it for a while."

The sincerity in his voice cut through her, and she found herself staring at him, taking in the warmth and care in his eyes. "I wish I could see myself the way you do," she whispered.

"You will," he said simply, offering her a smile that was more comforting than any words could be. "Just give yourself time. You've spent so long trying to make sense of his world that you've lost sight of your own. But it's still there, Carmen. You're still there."

She nodded slowly, her heart aching but also strangely relieved.

Rafael leaned back in his chair, his eyes thoughtful as he looked at her. There was a softness to his expression now, a quiet understanding that she hadn't seen before.

"You know, Carmen," he began, his voice gentle but firm, "maybe you've been *too* caught up in Francisco's world. I get it, he's a force, a magnet. Everything he does pulls you in. But you've forgotten about your own world, the one that was there before him. The one where you were you."

Carmen looked down at her hands, feeling the weight of his words settle over her.

He was right, wasn't he? In all the years of fighting for Francisco, of standing beside him, she had lost sight of herself. She had buried her own hopes and dreams under his own ambitions for her, under his ideals, his endless projects, until she had become a shadow in her own life.

"You're right," she murmured, her voice steadying. "I've lost track of what I want. Who I am without him." She paused, taking a deep breath. "I can't keep living like this, always waiting for him to come back and fix everything."

Rafael studied her for a long moment before speaking again. "You're not lost, Carmen. You're just… far away from yourself. Maybe it's time to start looking inwards again. Remember who you were before all this. Remember the things you used to love, the things that made you you. I know it feels like everything's been torn apart, but you've got the power to rebuild yourself. Don't wait for someone else to do it for you."

His words hung in the air, and Carmen let them sink in, each one like a thread pulling her back toward herself. She had been so caught up in Francisco's vision, in the fight for something that seemed too big to ignore. But now, with Rafael's words echoing in her mind, she realized that she had given up so much of her identity in the process.

Rafael nodded, a small, encouraging smile tugging at his lips. "You know," he added with a more casual tone, "your mother's calmed down a bit. I hear things have settled down since Piria made peace with the church. Maybe it's time to reach out to her. You don't have to fix everything overnight, but a conversation... that could be the start of something."

Carmen blinked, surprised by his words. The idea of reaching out to her mother felt both daunting and fragile, like a thread that might snap if she pulled too hard. "Do you think she'd even want to talk to me?" she asked, the question heavy with months of unresolved tension.

Rafael's gaze softened. "I think it's worth finding out."

He leaned back in his chair, a thoughtful expression crossing his face as he watched Carmen absorb the weight of their conversation. After a long pause, he spoke again, his voice laced with a hint of excitement.

"You know, there's an outdoor *milonga* coming up in La Boca," he said, a spark of enthusiasm lighting his eyes. "At La Vuelta de Rocha, in Buenos Aires. They're having a tango competition. Fireworks, dancers, and some of the best musicians around. It's going to be a night to remember."

Carmen's brow furrowed slightly, intrigued by his sudden shift in topic. "Oh really?"

Rafael nodded, his grin widening. "Yeah, it's a big event. It's not just the competition, there's something magical about dancing under the stars, with the sounds of the *bandoneón* filling the air. The whole thing has this energy, this life, that you can't find anywhere else. I've been thinking... maybe we should check it out."

"I'm a little too out of practice for a competition," she said softly, her mind wandering to the days when she and Francisco would take to the floor together, lost in the music. But those thoughts quickly darkened, replaced by an unfamiliar pang of doubt. "I don't know if I'm ready for that... for all of it."

Rafael's expression softened. "You don't have to dive in headfirst, Carmen. Just come with me, enjoy the night. We can be spectators, watch the competition, feel the music, let ourselves be swept away by the crowd. No pressure."

Carmen met his gaze. He wasn't pushing her. He wasn't urging her to return to the life she wasn't ready for, wasn't asking her to dive back into the chaos and complication of what used to be.

No, Rafael was offering her a brief escape, a chance to breathe, to simply exist without the burden of her current reality, even if just for one night.

After a long moment, she smiled faintly. "Alright, I'll go. I guess I could use a change of scenery."

Rafael grinned, leaning back in his chair with satisfaction. "Good. I think it'll do you good to get away, *prima*. And besides, you never know what might happen when the music starts. You might just find your rhythm again."

As Carmen stood up, a flicker of excitement stirred within her. The idea of allowing the music to carry her away once again, this time in a new and different setting, felt like the first real step toward reclaiming herself. For the first time in a long while, she felt a freedom that had quietly been calling to her, a freedom she hadn't realized she needed so desperately.

Because sometimes, a dance isn't just a dance, but the beginning of everything that comes next.

Chapter 26

Carmen stood in the hush of the cottage, the amber light of dusk filtering through the windows, stretching shadows across the floor like echoes of all she hadn't said. She had spent the past few days in solitude, wrapped in the stillness that had settled over her like dust, each moment thick with memory. The weight of the past few months still clung to her, unresolved and raw. Yet, even without full clarity, something deep within her stirred. She knew she needed this, needed to step away to breathe, to break free.

She glanced around the cottage one last time, making sure she hadn't forgotten anything. Her small suitcase sat at her feet, packed with only the essentials. The familiar smell of the old wood, the earthy scent of the countryside, lingered in the air. It was a peaceful refuge, a place where she had allowed herself the space to breathe, to heal. But now, it was time to face the world again, to test her own strength, her own purpose.

Carmen moved to the kitchen, where she quickly scrawled a note on a piece of paper. Her handwriting was neat, yet there was something in the way the words flowed that spoke of the uncertainty that still lingered in her heart.

Francisco,

I've left for Buenos Aires. I'll be gone for at least a week, though I'm not sure when I'll be back. I'm with Rafael. Please don't worry about me. I'll be alright.

–C.

She read the note one last time, her fingers smoothing out the creases before she folded it carefully and placed it on the kitchen table, where he would be sure to find it. There was no urgency for him to read it, no need for him to rush back just to see her.

If he did happen to return and come across the note, it would be just another moment in the rhythm of their lives, another layer of distance between them, but one that would give her the chance to breathe freely, even if only for a week.

Taking a final look around the cottage, Carmen closed the door behind her, locking it with a quiet click. As she walked toward the waiting taxi that would take her to the train station, her heart beat a little faster. She wasn't sure exactly what she was searching for in Buenos Aires, but something inside her told her that it was time to find it.

As the taxi rumbled away down the dusty road, Carmen leaned back in her seat, eyes fixed on the receding coastline. The uncertainty that had once clung to her like a second skin now seemed to loosen its grip. For the first time in what felt like ages, she wasn't just running, she was moving toward something. Toward herself.

As she and Rafael finally stepped aboard the ferry bound for Buenos Aires, a crisp wind tugged at their coats, carrying the scent of salt and the promise of something unknown.

The hum of the engine vibrated beneath their feet, a steady rhythm that echoed her heartbeat. The Río de la Plata stretched wide and endless before them, its silvery surface catching the final gold threads of daylight like a mirror to the sky.

As the ferry pulled away from the shore, Carmen felt the subtle shift in energy—restless, electric. The low murmur of voices swirled around her, mingling with the rush of water and wind. There was something in the air tonight, something raw and alive.

Buenos Aires shimmered on the horizon like a mirage, a city pulsing with possibility, chaos, beauty. So close now. So ready to be touched.

And behind her, the quiet ache of Montevideo faded into dusk.

Rafael stood beside her, his gaze fixed on the city as it unfolded in the distance, the skyline sharpening with each passing minute. Though his stance was casual, there was a quiet electricity in him that Carmen could sense immediately.

"I heard Francisco Canaro's band is playing tonight," he murmured, leaning in to speak over the murmur of the other passengers. "And they say El Cachafaz is dancing."

Carmen turned to him, her interest instantly sparked. The glow in Rafael's eyes was unmistakable, a glimmer of reverence, even awe.

Benito Bianquet, known throughout the Río de la Plata as El Cachafaz, or The Rascal, had earned his nickname as much for his rebellious streak as for his brilliance on the dance floor.

A former street brawler turned living legend, he had climbed to fame with a flair that bordered on myth, defeating world-class dancers in fiery tango duels, seducing audiences with his unmatched precision, bold improvisations, and the raw emotion he poured into every step.

To witness him perform was to witness tango itself. Untamed, unapologetic, alive.

Carmen felt her face flush with excitement. The thought of seeing El Cachafaz in person, maybe even dancing in the same *milonga* as him, filled her with a restless thrill she hadn't felt in months.

A flicker of the girl she used to be stirred within her, the one who still believed in magic, in movement, in the power of a single night to change everything.

Rafael chuckled, his grin wide with mischief. "Who knows, *prima*?" he teased, nudging her gently with his elbow. "Maybe you'll even get a *tanda* with the legend himself!"

Carmen laughed, the sound light and genuine, caught up in his teasing. Of course she knew better. Don Benito, El Cachafaz, never danced with anyone but his fierce and formidable partner, La Francesita, Emma Boveda.

Everyone in the tango world knew her name. Her dancing was electric, her temper notorious, and her jealousy the stuff of whispered legend.

Carmen shook her head, a teasing glint in her eye. "I think I'll leave that dance to someone else," she said, a smile tugging at her lips. "I'm not sure I'd want to come up against La Francesita if I did."

Rafael laughed, his eyes sparkling with amusement. "*Ah,* La Francesita," he grinned, shaking his head. "I heard she once punched her fist through a window just to prove a point. And no one dared say a word about it afterward, not even Don Benito himself."

Carmen raised an eyebrow, intrigued and slightly impressed by the woman's reputation. "A window?" she repeated, a playful smile tugging at her lips. "I guess she really knows how to make an entrance."

Rafael nodded with mock seriousness. "Oh, she's not one for subtlety. Watch out for her, you might see her throw another punch or two, maybe even out on the dance floor."

The ferry eased into the dock, and as Carmen and Rafael stepped onto the cobblestones of La Boca, they were immediately swept into a whirlwind of color and sound.

The buildings, painted in bold, joyful hues, seemed to vibrate with energy, their windows glowing under strings of hanging lights. Street vendors called out over the crowd, their voices rising above the clamor; children darted between alleyways like streaks of laughter; and somewhere in the distance, the soulful cry of a *bandoneón* floated on the air, coaxing them deeper into the heart of the barrio.

Carmen paused, taking it all in. The scent of sizzling meat from nearby *parrillas* mingled with the sweetness of overripe fruit and the smoky tang of woodfire. The beat of dancing feet echoed against the walls, weaving with the music into something primal and alive.

La Boca didn't just live, it roared, pulsed, and demanded to be felt. Every corner whispered a story. Every shadow promised a secret.

And Carmen felt, in that moment, as though she had stepped into the rhythm of something bigger than herself.

Though she had been born into the chaotic pulse of Buenos Aires, Carmen had never truly lived its nights, never let herself be swallowed by their music, their mystery.

But now, as she walked beneath the flickering gaslights of La Boca, it was as if the city was blooming just for her. Her pulse danced to the rhythm of the cobblestones, each step crackling with a new kind of freedom.

Beside her, Rafael grinned, sharing her excitement. He nodded toward a crowded café where the air pulsed with the haunting chords of a *bandoneón*. In the center of it all, a couple moved as one, locked in a tango so raw, so precise, the world seemed to hush around them. Carmen stopped, breath caught in her throat, mesmerized. Their feet painted stories on the ground—sharp, elegant, intimate.

A slow smile spread across her lips as she felt the music thread its way into her chest, into her limbs.

The *conventillos* rose around them like proud sentinels, their walls splashed in bold strokes of yellow, red, and cobalt blue, each façade a living canvas etched with memory, culture, and quiet rebellion. In front of one building, a group of young people passed around a shared gourd of *mate*, their laughter spilling into the street like music. An elderly couple sat nearby on a stoop, swaying gently to the rhythm of a *bandoneón* drifting from an open window.

Carmen paused, drawn into the pulse of the moment. The air vibrated with life, layered with history, with longing, with the unmistakable heartbeat of tango. It wasn't just heard or seen. It was *felt*, as if the very city itself was alive with its rhythm..

"Feels different, doesn't it?" Rafael murmured, barely rising above the noise. "You can feel the tango in the pavement here."

Carmen nodded slowly, her eyes drinking in the scene. This city was not as conservative as Montevideo. In Buenos Aires, the tango wasn't just a dance, it was a language, a defiance, a soul. It spilled from the windows, clung to the walls, and echoed in every step across the square. The whole place moved to its rhythm. And for the first time in days, so did she.

As they neared the square at La Vuelta de Rocha, the hum of voices swelled into a vibrant chorus. A small stage stood at the heart of the plaza, washed in the warm, flickering glow of string lights that dangled above like captive constellations. The night sky deepened to a rich indigo as Carmen and Rafael slipped into the throng, the scent of wine, tobacco, and cologne thick in the air.

The renowned Canaro orchestra had begun to play, their soul-stirring melodies rising into the night like smoke, winding through the square and curling around every listener.

The *bandoneón* cried out its longing, the violins answered with aching beauty, and the deep, steady thrum of the double bass rooted it all to the earth. Carmen felt the music before she understood it, felt it in her bones, in the space behind her ribs.

Couples glided onto the cobblestones, their bodies locked in the sacred intimacy of tango. Shoes clicked in harmony, skirts swirled like whispers, and Carmen watched, breathless, as story after story unfolded in movement. Raw, aching, alive.

Rafael, catching her expression, leaned closer with a smile. "What do you think? Not bad for your first night in La Boca, *eh*?"

Carmen nodded slowly, as she took in the scene. "It's like the whole city is breathing in rhythm."

Suddenly, a hush rippled through the crowd, like a tide pulling back to sea. A commanding figure had stepped onto the dance floor.

Don Benito... El Cachafaz.

The name passed in whispers from couple to couple, reverent and awed. One by one, the other couples melted off the floor, clearing the space in a silent show of deference.

With a striking presence, Don Benito stood at the center of the square beside his partner, La Francesita. His expression was unreadable, his gaze sharp and unflinching.

There was nothing conventionally elegant about him, his pockmarked face, the heavyset frame, the stiff shoulders, but the crowd held its breath all the same.

Then the orchestra struck the first notes of *La Cumparsita*.

And he moved.

Not like a man, but like a force. Every step was a revelation: precise, daring, impossibly fluid. Carmen's breath caught as she watched the legend unfold before her eyes. There was no showiness, no wasted movement. Just pure, unfiltered tango.

He and La Francesita were no longer dancers, they were music made flesh. With each pivot, each pause, each impossible embellishment, they told a story of longing, defiance, and devotion, one too sacred to speak aloud.

Carmen and Rafael stood in awe. And for a moment, it was as if time had folded in on itself. The past, present, and future of tango all existed in the space between El Cachafaz's feet and the worn cobblestones of La Boca.

As the music of the sweet melody swelled to its climax, Don Benito ended with a flourish so bold and effortless it drew a wave of cheers and applause from the crowd.

Carmen and Rafael exchanged a look of shared admiration, both knowing they'd just witnessed something unforgettable.

The applause faded into a hum of anticipation as the band struck up once more, a new rhythm pulsing through the open night air. One by one, couples returned to the floor, slipping into each other's arms like it was second nature.

Rafael turned to her, his grin full of mischief, eyes glinting in the soft lamplight. "Well? What do you say, *prima*?" he asked, extending a hand toward her with playful ceremony. "Come dance with me."

Carmen hesitated. She hadn't danced, really danced, in so long. Not in the way she once did, with the freedom and fire that used to come so naturally to her.

Her eyes flicked to the dancers again, how effortlessly they moved together, their bodies in perfect harmony. But that night, a small voice of doubt clung to her like static.

"I don't know…" she muttered, the doubt creeping in. "I'm not sure I can compare to the talent on this floor."

Rafael let out a soft laugh, shaking his head in mock disbelief. "Are you kidding?" he said, his voice teasing. "The queen of the Madreselva, afraid to dance? If anyone can hold their own here, it's you."

Carmen raised an eyebrow, a small smile tugging at her lips despite herself. "The queen of the Madreselva, huh?" she said, amused by the title. "I guess I'll have to live up to that title."

Rafael gave her a playful nudge, his grin widening. "*Dale, prima.* No one's watching, except the entire city. No pressure, right?" He winked, the challenge hanging in the air.

Carmen felt it stir, something long buried but not forgotten. A flicker of the woman she used to be, before the rumors, before the exile, before love had rewritten all her certainties.

Her lips curved into a slow smile, the tension in her chest easing as the music spilled through the square like honey, sweet and irresistible.

Rafael extended his hand, no urgency in his gesture, just a quiet invitation. His eyes met hers, warm and steady, a tether in the chaos.

She hesitated, suspended in the space between who she'd been and who she was still becoming. But then she exhaled, squared her shoulders, and slipped her hand into his.

"Alright then," she said, her voice edged with something brighter. "Let's see if I still wear the crown."

Together they stepped into the tide of dancers, swept up in a current older than either of them. The music wrapped around her like an old friend, familiar and forgiving. As the first steps found her feet, Carmen felt the city breathe her back to life.

The music rose around them, a pulsing, honeyed ache that seemed to vibrate up through the cobblestones and into Carmen's bones.

She had danced the tango countless times, but that night, beneath the open sky of La Boca, with the crowd a living tide around them, everything felt charged. Raw. Slightly askew, like a dream unfolding too quickly to catch.

Rafael gave her a quick, reassuring smile before drawing her closer. "Just follow me," he murmured, his voice low, steady, sure.

She nodded, inhaling deeply as he led her into the first step. His movements were confident, seamless, and the moment their bodies fell into rhythm, a current passed between them. Familiar, grounding, yet touched with something new. Something fleeting and true.

As the music swelled, Carmen let go. Her feet moved of their own accord, tracing the steps she knew by heart. The crowd blurred, the square fell away. All that remained was the press of Rafael's hand at her back, the breath between movements, and the rhythm that held them both like a secret.

Carmen's doubts began to fade, replaced by the thrill of the dance, the freedom it gave her.

For the first time in what felt like forever, the weight of everything: Francisco, the uncertainty, the silence, lifted from her shoulders, swept away by the music. All that remained was movement, breath, and rhythm.

She felt the gaze of the crowd on them, some in awe, some in judgment, but it no longer mattered.

In that moment, it was just the two of them, bound together by the pulse of the tango, speaking a language no one else could hear.

The steps grew more intricate as the music swelled, the pulse of the *bandoneón* quickening like a heartbeat.

Carmen moved instinctively, her body attuned to Rafael's lead as if no time had passed at all. They glided across the worn stone with effortless grace, each spin and pivot drawing gasps from the gathering crowd. A laugh escaped her lips, light and unrestrained, as their feet clicked in sync. Sharp, sure, alive.

This was the Carmen she'd nearly forgotten. The woman who danced without fear, without apology. Untamed. Unburdened. Entirely herself.

As the tempo eased for a breath, Rafael leaned in with a teasing glint in his eye. "Not bad for the queen of the Madreselva," he said, a triumphant grin tugging at his mouth. "I knew you still had it in you."

Carmen's eyes twinkled with playful defiance. "You're not so bad yourself," she replied, her voice low, filled with the thrill of the dance. "Maybe I'll keep letting you lead…for now."

With a breathless laugh, they spun back into the rhythm, the dance lifting them higher as music and night swept them into the beating heart of La Boca.

Carmen's chest rose with exhilaration, her breath catching as the pulse of the tango surged through her. It coursed through her veins now; familiar, unrelenting, alive. Each step felt like a return, a remembering.

Beneath the string lights and among the *conventillos* painted in blues and ochres, surrounded by the warmth of a community that danced not for spectacle but for life itself, Carmen felt something settle within her. A quiet pride bloomed.

These streets, these rhythms, *this* was her origin.

Not in gilded ballrooms or marble halls where people wore masks and danced to put on airs, but there, on the worn cobblestones, in the scent of sweat and wine, in the humble cradle of the tango, was where she truly belonged.

And it had never let go of her.

That night, beneath the low light and the pull of the *bandoneón,* Carmen Ruiz was not merely dancing.

She was *becoming.*

Chapter 27

The sky had been threatening for days, thick with the kind of heavy gray that presses against your lungs and whispers of something more than just rain. Carmen and Rafael had tried to make the most of their time in Buenos Aires, visiting bookshops, slipping into cafés to escape the cold night air, catching glimpses of *milongas* through fogged-up windows, but by the third day, the heavens finally opened.

Torrents fell without pause, soaking the city in hours. Streets turned into rivers, and anxious voices echoed from every radio: *Caution. Flood Warnings. Avoid Roads.*

Their plans, like the avenues, were quickly washed away.

"I think that's our cue," Rafael said, peering through the dripping glass of the hotel window. He held their return tickets in one hand, already damp from the leak near the sill. "If we don't leave now, we might not get out for days."

Carmen nodded, her suitcase already half-packed. She'd felt the shift coming, not just in the weather, but in her spirit.

The city had offered a brief reprieve, a shimmer of distraction. But the world back home still waited—demanding, unresolved.

By dusk, they were boarding the ferry once more, bound for Montevideo. Carmen sat beside the window, watching the downpour smear the lights of Buenos Aires into watercolor streaks.

The boat groaned and rocked beneath them as the ferry began to move, carving a path through storm and shadow.

She didn't say it aloud, but part of her was uneasy. Something had changed. She could feel it. There was more waiting for her on the other side of the river, more than the headlines and the ruins of scandal. Something new. Something looming.

And it was coming faster than she could name.

The countryside air was sharp with the scent of wet earth as Carmen stepped out of the taxi in Piriápolis.

The rain had softened to a mist, blurring the hills with a dark shimmer. Her boots sank slightly into the gravel as she made her way up the winding path toward the familiar old cottage.

She was tired—bone-deep, soul-worn tired. Buenos Aires had offered only a fleeting distraction.

Now, back in stillness, her thoughts returned with a vengeance, loud and unrelenting, like footsteps echoing through an empty corridor. The ache of rejection began to gnaw at her once more: her mother's fury, Francisco's silence, a society all too eager to cast her out like a blemish it couldn't bear to acknowledge.

She crossed her arms tightly against her chest, as if to hold the pieces together. Rafael's departing embrace still lingered in her memory, a tender tether to something steady in a world that seemed to be unraveling beneath her feet.

As she climbed up the stairs and opened up the french windows to air out the bedroom, she paused. Something unusual flickered in the distance: warm light glowing against the silhouette of the hilltop.

Francisco's castle.

She hadn't expected to see it illuminated. Since he had left for Europe, the place had stood like a monument in mourning: dark, still, and impenetrable. But tonight, golden light poured from the windows like honey.

From the distance, she could hear faint music—string instruments, maybe, or a phonograph drifting something slow and classical into the mist. It wasn't a celebration, but it wasn't silence either.

Her brow furrowed.

Carmen stood there for a long moment, watching the castle burn quietly with unexpected life. Part of her wanted to run back into the shadows of the house and pretend she hadn't seen anything. The other part, a braver, more curious part, knew better. Something had changed. *Someone was there.*

Francisco hadn't told her he would be back. There had been no phone call. No telegram. Bonavita hadn't informed her of any event.

Her pulse quickened.

She went downstairs where she'd already checked the mailbox twice, maybe three times. Nothing. She noticed the note she had left was absent from the table, yet there was no note left for her in its place. And yet the air now buzzed with anticipation, as if something important were about to unfold, and she'd somehow missed the invitation.

Had he returned? Was he down there now, surrounded by diplomats and artists and old friends, acting as if she'd never existed at all?

A cold dread bloomed in her chest.

She hurried up the stairs, her heels striking the floorboards in sharp, echoing bursts. Breathless, she darted to the bedroom window, drawn by a need she couldn't name, as if to confirm the castle still shimmered in the distance, still aglow, and that she hadn't imagined it after all.

But as the lights sparkled below and the faint music swelled, Carmen stood in the shadows above, heart hammering, caught in a storm of uncertainty.

The questions came too quickly now, each one sharpening into doubt:

What if he'd come back and decided to leave her behind after all? What if her exile to the country house wasn't about generosity, but abandonment masked as benevolence?

For a moment, Carmen couldn't breathe.

It was as if the silence itself had teeth—sharp, merciless—gnawing at her edges.

The weight of everything descended at once: the exile, the unanswered questions, the aching sense of not belonging anywhere. It pressed into her chest like a closing door, stealing the air before she could even name the grief.

She had believed in their shared vision. She had believed in him.

And for the first time in weeks, she felt the terrifying pull of something she had fought so hard to suppress:

Abandonment. Betrayal. A grief that hadn't yet decided whether it would crack her open or burn her clean.

Her hands trembled as she moved to close the bedroom window, when the slant of evening light caught the edge of the mirror on the wall.

She paused.

There, reflected in the glass, was a woman she barely recognized.

Not because her clothes were wet and disheveled, though they were. Not because her eyes were tired, though they were, too. But because of what she saw in the stillness. A woman waiting. Sheltered. Dependent. Rootless.

And suddenly, it struck her with a force that stole her breath. She had become everything she once feared:

A kept thing.

Not a partner, not a creator, not the firebrand of her own destiny, but someone surviving in the shelter of a man's world.

Her hands dropped from the window. A wave of nausea rolled through her. Was this what all her sacrifices had been for? To end up tucked away, quiet and safe, while the world moved on without her?

Her fists clenched. She stepped back from the mirror.

No. She would not be a shadow of herself.

She pulled on her shawl, wrapping it tight against the drizzle, rain misting her cheeks like cold breath, and darted out the door, heart pounding as she headed toward the hill.

Carmen pressed onward, her dark curls whipped wild by the misty wind as she climbed the long gravel path up towards the castle. Each step struck the earth with quiet defiance, her breath steady, her eyes fixed ahead, even as the distant music, low and haunting, rose to meet her, growing louder with every stride.

As she neared the great stone entryway, laughter rose and fell like waves on the breeze, refined and careless. She stepped into the shadows, heart pounding.

The castle doors were open just enough to glimpse inside. Carmen leaned forward, peering in through the sliver between the hinges and the stone.

Candlelight flickered against the marble floors. Guests in silk and velvet milled about, clinking glasses and exchanging polite smiles.

And then she saw him.

Francisco stood near the hearth, bathed in golden light, his profile angled toward a woman whose elegance was so striking, so effortless, that it made her stomach drop.

The woman's gown shimmered like moonlight, and her laughter, a soft, melodic trill, floated effortlessly into the air between them.

Francisco leaned in to say something, and the woman touched his arm, her gloved fingers resting there a beat too long. In his hand, he held a delicate champagne flute, twin to hers, their rims kissing each time they toasted.

Carmen's hands shook as she gripped the stone of the castle walls. The chill from the evening wind curled beneath her shawl, but it wasn't the cold that made her shiver.

She didn't move, didn't blink. Just watched.

The man she had risked everything for—whose vision had swept her into a world of fire and ruin—looked, in that moment, like he belonged to someone else entirely.

Drawing a breath that trembled with restraint, Carmen stepped forward, each step deliberate, her soaked skirt clinging to her legs.

The elegant woman at Francisco's side turned first, her face flickering with polite alarm at the sight of Carmen—dripping rain, eyes blazing.

Francisco's gaze snapped to her, his eyes widening in disbelief. For a moment, his composure cracked.

"Carmen… I thought you were in Buenos Aires," he said carefully, his voice taut with surprise. "What are you doing here?"

She held his gaze, shoulders squared against the chill and betrayal. "I could ask you the same thing," she retorted, her tone low and steady—cutting, but calm.

"Please excuse us," Francisco said, tilting his head regretfully towards his guest. He took Carmen gently by the elbow, leading her into his study and shutting the door behind them.

Carmen stood at the threshold of Francisco's study, her arms crossed tightly across her chest. The room smelled of tobacco and leather-bound books, the faint trace of clove lingering from one of his imported cigars.

"Francisco, what is the meaning of this? You've barely written," she said, her voice low, edged with something brittle. "You haven't called. I've been sick with worry, wondering if you were ever coming back, if you were safe, if you were even *alive*. And now I find you here, smiling and laughing with another woman? What is all this? A party I wasn't supposed to know about?"

Francisco took a step toward her, his tone soft but urgent. "Carmen, *querida*, it was never my intention to keep you in the dark. Clarissa is here with her husband. It was all last minute, just a gathering for a few guests."

Carmen's eyes flashed, her voice tight with restrained fury. "I see, so you had time to arrange candles, music, champagne… but not even a moment to send for me? To telegram and tell me you were coming home? Why, Francisco? Why plan a last-minute celebration, of all things, *knowing* I wouldn't be here?"

Francisco exhaled sharply and leaned back, pinching the bridge of his nose. "It wasn't meant to be like this. I didn't plan—"

"That's exactly it," she cut in, her tone rising. "You didn't plan. You didn't consider me. Or maybe you did. Maybe it's just easier for you when I'm not around, no one to challenge you, no one to ask *why*. Is that it?"

Francisco stood, slow and deliberate, but Carmen didn't flinch. Her eyes held his, fierce and unblinking. The silence between them crackled like a wick. At last, Francisco crossed the room and reached for her hand, but Carmen stepped back.

"Don't bother," she said, her voice low but laced with bitterness. "I see it all so clearly now. I was never meant to belong in your world, was I, Francisco? I was always just another one of your projects."

He opened his mouth to speak, but she held up a hand.

"You know, at first, I told myself it didn't matter. The stares, the whispers. I convinced myself that all those women in their pearl-button gloves, the men in tailored suits, weren't really watching us. That it didn't sting when they looked at me, then at you, like they were trying to make sense of something unseemly."

"Carmen—"

"But it does matter. It matters when it happens every time we step into public. When you don't say my name. When the *maître d'* offers to seat us somewhere 'less conspicuous'. When I pay for something in a shop, and the clerk smiles and hands *you* the parcel, like I'm just your handmaid, like I'm invisible."

"I never wanted you to feel—"

"I know you didn't," she said, her tone softening, but her resolve firm. "And I've played along. I smiled through it. Let it go, again and again. I've spent a lifetime being underestimated, ignored. But I won't shrink to fit into places I was never invited. Not anymore. And I won't dress myself up in lace and diamonds just to be palatable either. I'm not your pet, Francisco, and I'm not an option."

She paused, her eyes narrowing slightly, her voice dropping to something more raw.

"Do they even know what I am to you?"

The question hung in the air, fragile and damning.

Francisco didn't answer right away.

Then, softly, "I don't think they know what to make of you."

A pause.

"Do you?"

His face, always so composed, flickered with something, uncertainty, maybe. Or shame.

"I know how I feel about you, Carmen," he said. "But feelings don't always translate into language the world is ready to hear."

"And what about the language *you* speak?" she asked. "Is your world the only thing that matters?"

The silence between them stretched, taut and trembling.

It was the first time Carmen wondered not if he loved her, but if he was brave enough to stand beside her when love became inconvenient.

"Just admit it," Carmen said, her voice sharp and unflinching. "All these years, and not once have you introduced me to your children, your family, or to anyone who *truly* matters to you. Why? Because you're ashamed. Ashamed to be seen with a girl like me, from Barrio Sur. A nobody."

The words rang out between them like a slap.

Francisco's jaw tightened, but he didn't interrupt. He stood still, his face straining beneath the weight of unspoken truths.

"I've given you everything I knew how to give," he said at last, his voice low with a kind of worn sincerity. "But… you don't understand how vicious my world can be, Carmen. The people closest to me—my children, my circle—they wouldn't just judge you. They'd stop at nothing to see you finished. They'd devour you. I only ever wanted to spare you from that kind of cruelty."

"So instead you kept me hidden?" she snapped. "Is that why you tucked me away in the countryside, far from everything and everyone? To hide me away like some dirty little secret?"

He stepped toward her, his tone softening. "No, Carmen. I just wanted to protect you."

"No, Francisco. You wanted to protect yourself. Your name. Your reputation." Her voice cracked.

He opened his mouth to speak, but she pressed on.

"You say you care. But if you care about me so much, if you want to protect my dignity, and my reputation matters to you even a little, Francisco, then answer me this: *then why haven't you married me?*"

Silence fell like a guillotine.

Francisco looked at her, something hollow and haunted flickering in his eyes, but no answer came.

Carmen's hands trembled at her sides, but she stood her ground. The silence between them was louder than any answer he could have given.

She swallowed hard. "That's what I thought," she whispered, her voice breaking.

Tears threatened to spill as she turned and walked away, the sound of her footsteps sharp against the floor. Behind her, Francisco called her name, but she didn't look back.

She stepped out into the rain, the cold wind lashing against her skin, each drop a bitter echo of everything left unsaid.

The gates of the castle loomed behind her, swallowed by mist as Carmen fled down the winding path, her rain-soaked skirts clinging to her legs, each breath ragged and sharp in her chest.

The rainstorm had passed, but with it, the last thread of certainty had unraveled inside her. Grief pooled in the hollows of her throat, hot and raw and unrelenting.

She didn't stop walking until her legs gave out beneath her.

Somewhere beyond the vineyards, past the perfume of wild jasmine and sea brine, she collapsed beneath a crooked ceibo tree. The moon hung overhead like a silent witness, casting silver across her trembling form.

Tears spilled without protest. Not for the loss of comfort, or even for the man whose name still ached against her ribs like a bruise, but for the version of herself she had let slip away. The girl who believed she could outrun history. Who believed that love could shield her from the ruin of reality.

For what seemed like hours, Carmen lay there, still, silent, undone.

This was her reckoning.

Not the dramatic fall from grace that the gossips had predicted, but the quiet, soul-rending collapse of belief. The crumbling of all the stories she had built around him. Around herself. Around the future they had imagined together like children daring fate.

Was it all a lie?

Or worse, had she been the lie all along? Shaped and reshaped to fit someone else's vision, until even her own reflection felt like a mask she could no longer wear?

A foolish part of her had waited—for footsteps, for a voice to come rolling across the plains, for him to come after her, to choose her at last.

But the truth settled over her like a damp shroud: Francisco Piria would never make a scene for her. Not in front of his guests. Not when dignity mattered more than love.

The moon shone overhead, indifferent.

And in that abyss of heartbreak and rage, something old and quiet stirred in her: the voice she had nearly forgotten. The one buried beneath devotion and delusion. The voice that had once whispered poems to the night sky. The voice of a girl who had dreamed not of castles, but of freedom.

It would take time. She didn't yet know who she was becoming. But she knew this: she would not be anyone else's unfinished project.

Not anymore.

She sat up slowly, the ceibo tree casting a protective shadow over her like a shroud. Her palms were raw, her body sore, but her spirit... her spirit, though dim, was still burning.

She would make her way forward.

But first, she would sit with the night. Let it speak. Let it strip her bare.

Because only in that sacred silence could she begin the long, slow alchemy of turning loss into light.

Chapter 28

The boarding house in the barrio of Porteño sat hunched between two taller buildings like a tired widow in mourning, its stucco façade cracked and fading, the iron gate groaning as Carmen pushed it open.

A brass plaque beside the door read *Casa de Huéspedes El Sol*, though the name seemed a cruel joke under the overcast sky.

It was a modest boarding house for working women—quiet, respectable, anonymous.

Carmen had boarded the midnight train out of Piriápolis without saying goodbye. Not to Bonavita. Not to anyone. Francisco hadn't come after her, just as she had predicted. That truth lodged itself deep in her chest, a quiet ache she tried not to name.

Heartbroken but resolute, she chose to disappear. Not forever. Just long enough to figure out who she was without him.

Inside, the air was heavy with the scent of boiled cabbage and stale tobacco. The landlady, a stout woman with a sharp chin and a pen tucked behind her ear, looked Carmen over with a mix of suspicion and weary indifference. Her name, according to the wooden sign behind the desk, was Señora Varela.

"You alone?" she asked, flipping through the pages of a thick, ink-smudged ledger.

Carmen nodded. "*Sí, señora*. I just need a place. For now."

"Five *pesos* a week. One meal a day. No gentlemen callers, and lights out by midnight." The woman's eyes didn't soften. "Room's on the third floor."

Carmen handed over what little she had, feeling the weight of the coin between her fingers before placing it on the counter.

The weight of her satchel pulled on her shoulder, heavier than it had felt earlier. It carried everything she owned now.

Señora Varela led her up the narrow staircase without ceremony. The wooden steps creaked beneath their feet, and faint music, possibly a tango playing on an old gramophone, filtered in from somewhere below.

The woman stopped at the end of the hall and unlocked a door with a long, jangling key. "Here."

The room was barely larger than a train compartment, with only enough room to hold a narrow cot, a chipped dresser, and a small writing desk pressed against a single, small window. The view looked out over rooftops interrupted by laundry lines and crumbling chimneys. A tiny radiator hissed quietly in the corner, as if exhaling a long-held breath.

Carmen stepped inside, setting her satchel down on the narrow cot, its iron frame creaking slightly under the weight. The room smelled of old linen and the faint metallic tang of solitude.

"It locks from the inside," Señora Varela added, gesturing to the simple bolt on the door. "Bathroom's down the hall. It's shared. Dinner is downstairs in the dining room at eight-thirty sharp. If you're late, you don't eat."

And with that, she turned and shuffled back down the hall, her footsteps swallowed by the moan of the old floorboards.

For a moment, Carmen didn't move. Just stood in the silence, listening to the unfamiliar rhythm of her new surroundings.

The room was small, but it was hers.

She had thought, briefly, of returning home, to her mother's house in Barrio Sur. Of begging forgiveness.

But the thought of slipping back into silence, of clipping her own wings for the comfort of familiarity, made something inside her recoil.

No. If she went back now, she might never find the strength to leave again.

She moved to the window and looked out. Laundry lines sagged between buildings, the scent of fried dough drifted from a vendor down the street, and children chased each other through puddles left by the morning rain. Life, indifferent and unbothered, went on.

She unpacked slowly. A change of clothes. A tin of writing supplies. Her worn journal. She placed them with care in the dresser drawers and on the desk, creating order where she could.

That evening, Carmen stood at the shared stove, the dented steel kettle rattling softly as it came to a boil.

The kitchen was a narrow, steamy space filled with the quiet rhythm of evening routines.

Women moved around her in a kind of practiced choreography: untying aprons, reheating leftovers, folding laundry in the corner. Some came in smelling of fish and sea salt from the port; others wore the faint perfume of retail counters and pastry shops. They all moved with a tired grace, their eyes avoiding contact, their silences heavy but not unkind.

No one asked Carmen her name. They didn't need to. In a place like this, silence was its own kind of respect, an agreement to let pain remain unnamed, a pact not to prod where the wounds still wept.

There, privacy was sacred. One didn't need to explain why you were there, only that you were.

She cupped her hands around the chipped porcelain mug and returned to her quarters. She stared at the rising steam, letting it blur the outlines of the room.

The future loomed ahead like an unlit corridor, every step uncertain, every turn unknown.

She had nothing now but her name, her hands, and a heart that still ached from the weight of betrayal.

Hunger stirred in her belly, sharp and insistent. It had been a long time since she had gone without, and the sensation felt like a cruel return to an old life she thought she had left behind.

She had a little money saved, but not much. What little she earned had always gone to her mother, for rent, for food, for the endless repairs that kept the pipes from bursting and the roof above their heads from collapsing.

For a moment she wondered if she had been foolish to never have accepted Francisco's help. The thought pressed down on her as she sat on the narrow iron cot, staring at the meager collection of belongings laid out before her.

Panic seeped in, steady as water through a cracked wall.

She was cut off now from everything she had ever known: her mother, her family, even the shadow of Francisco's name that had once given her both shelter and chains. For the first time in her life, she was completely and utterly alone.

What if she couldn't find work? What would happen once her measly *pesos* were all gone? Who was she, stripped of Francisco's orbit, stripped of her place in the life she had sacrificed so much to sustain? Years of her strength, her devotion, her silence had all been poured into his ambitions, until she no longer recognized the woman who remained.

The panic thickened, growing teeth, sinking them deep.

She had never felt more adrift. The walls pressed close, their stillness suffocating, her thoughts circling like restless birds with nowhere to land. She pressed her hands to her face, forcing herself to breathe, but the question lingered, raw and unrelenting:

Who am I now?

And then, unbidden, her mind turned to the one place that she ever felt remotely like herself: the Madreselva.

Without another thought, she gathered her satchel, slung it over her shoulder, and stepped out into the fading light.

The Madreselva was quieter than usual, the air thick with the scent of varnished wood and candle wax.

Carmen pushed open the door, the familiar creak of its hinges sounding louder than it should have.

Nico looked up from behind the bar, startled at first, then softening when he saw her.

"You look like hell," he said gently, setting down the glass he'd been polishing.

"I feel worse," Carmen muttered, sliding onto a stool.

Nico didn't press her, didn't ask right away. He just poured her a glass of Malbec and set it down in front of her.

"It's on the house," he said.

One glass turned into two, then three. Somewhere after the fourth, the words started to tumble out of her: about her mother, the betrayal, Francisco's silence, the hostility in Barrio Sur, the shame. Nico listened quietly, his hands still, his face unreadable.

"You ever feel like the whole world's spinning off its axis and you're just...stuck?" she slurred, her fingers tracing the rim of her glass. "It's like...everything I believed in is burning, and I don't even know if I'm supposed to save it or just watch it fall."

Nico placed a steadying hand over hers. "You're not supposed to do anything except survive. The rest comes later."

But Carmen was already fading into the fog of wine and heartbreak, her head resting against the bar, her words dissolving into silence.

Nico watched from behind the bar, concern etched deep across his brow as Carmen nursed yet another glass. Her usual spark had dimmed, dulled beneath the thick fog of drink and heartache.

He wiped his hands on a towel, then stepped closer, lowering his voice with quiet care. "Carmen," he said gently, the worry unmistakable in his tone, "maybe that's enough for tonight, don't you think?"

Carmen's words cracked through the dim bar like a whip. "Don't you tell me what to do, Nicolás," she snapped, her voice sharp with fury and something darker underneath. Her eyes burned, glassy with drink and defiance. "You know, everyone's always so worried about my *reputation*," she scowled, her mouth twisting bitterly. "Well guess what? To hell with my damn reputation. Just keep pouring, alright?"

Nico flinched slightly at the sharpness of her words, but said nothing. He'd known Carmen long enough to recognize when her grief had closed itself off to reason. With a quiet sigh, he turned back to the bar and wordlessly refilled her glass.

Each sip blurred the edges of her pain a little more. The weight pressing down on her chest began to lift, not from peace but from numbness, the kind that came with the slow unraveling of restraint. In that warm, woozy haze, her sorrow lost its shape, and with it, her sense of control.

The room swayed around her as she stumbled toward the dance floor, the soft glow of the Madreselva's lights flickering like candle flames in a storm.

She moved with reckless abandon, eyes locked on a handsome stranger who watched her with an amused smirk.

She circled him slowly, draping an arm over his shoulder, her hand trailing down the front of his shirt. The gesture was meant to feel seductive, but her motions were too loose, too sloppy. He grinned, mistaking her unraveling for invitation, and reached for her with greedy hands, pulling her against him in a crude mockery of the tango's sacred embrace.

Carmen's vision swam. She barely felt his touch, barely noticed the eyes fixed on her, the horrified glances, the murmurs sweeping through the club like a chill wind. The music played on, but it had lost its soul.

And still, she kept moving, not in rhythm, but in ruin.

The music throbbed like a pulse around them, thick with smoke and sweat. Carmen stumbled slightly in the stranger's grasp, the heat of his body pressed too close.

"*Che, linda,*" he murmured, his breath hot against her ear, "why don't we get out of here?"

His words slithered through her like oil, slick and unwelcome. A shiver shot down her spine, momentarily cutting through the haze that dulled her senses. But the drink had softened her judgment, her pride, her resistance.

Something inside her wanted to recoil. But something else, a darker, lonelier thing, wanted to self-destruct and disappear.

So she nodded.

It was not consent so much as surrender. To the night. To the numbness. To anything that might drown out the ache clawing at her ribs.

They slipped out the door and into the shadows, her heels striking unevenly against the cobblestones. The streets seemed to sway beneath her, tilting sideways as if the city itself had lost its balance. Her heart knew better. But her pain was louder.

And so, she let the night swallow her whole.

In the darkness of the boarding house room, she stood motionless, her soul hovering somewhere above her body, her head swimming as if detached from flesh.

She did not resist while the faceless stranger stripped her bare, taking away what little she still carried: hope, innocence, the fragile dignity she had fought to keep. In the dim cold of a bare boarding room, she was desecrated, effaced, undone.

When it was over, she was left hollow. Empty of resistance. Empty of tears. Empty of everything but silence.

Later, as the stranger slipped out of her room and disappeared into the chill of the night, the echo of his boots dragging across the worn hardwood left a sick, hollow feeling pooling in her stomach.

She sat up in her bed, clutching the thin sheet to her chest as the door clicked softly shut behind him.

She had wanted to forget, just for a night. To numb the ache of exile, of betrayal, of dreams turned to dust.

But now, in the cold light of sobriety, her heart felt splintered and raw.

The room smelled of sweat, cheap cologne and regret.

She swung her legs over the edge of the bed, feet meeting the creaky wood below. The silence pressed in on her, thick and unrelenting.

Shame gnawed at her like a silent animal, burrowing into the quiet spaces of her mind. She thought of her mother's words, of Rafael's wounded expression, of Francisco's absence, and of the girl she had once been, full of fire and conviction, who used to believe her body was a temple, her story a sacred thing.

Now, it all felt far away.

She buried her face in her hands, breath shaking.

"I've gone too far," she whispered into the stillness.

But no one answered.

Only the wind outside, rising through the alleyways of Montevideo like a chorus of ghosts, bearing witness to the girl who had once dared to chase destiny, and was now quietly, painfully, trying to find her way back.

Chapter 29

A sharp rap on the door shattered the stillness of the morning.

Carmen's eyes flew open, her head splitting with pain. The dim light slanted through the gauzy curtain of the narrow room of the boarding house, casting pale stripes across the faded floorboards. Her mouth tasted like smoke and regret.

What have I done? she thought, clutching her temples. Flashes of the night before came in waves: too much wine, blurred laughter, a warm hand on her back, a moment of reckless comfort that had gone too far.

The knock came again, louder now.

"*Señorita!*" came the clipped voice from the other side. "Open the door—*ya mismo!*"

Carmen struggled upright, stumbling toward the door. When she cracked it open, she was met with the pinched face of Señora Varela, the landlady, arms crossed over her starched blouse, lips pressed so tight they nearly disappeared.

"May I remind you, *señorita*, that there are *strict rules* in this house," the woman snapped. "Absolutely no gentlemen callers. None. This is a respectable boarding house for working women. Not the kind who work on their backs."

Carmen's cheeks burned. "I—*Señora*, I'm not—"

"I'm sure," Señora Varela cut in. "You're new, so maybe you didn't hear me when I went over the rules. So I'll give you this one warning. But if it happens again, you're out. This is not a brothel. If you're that kind of working girl, there's a *bordelo* in Villa del Cerro. You can check in there."

With that, she spun on her heel and marched down the hallway, her slippers slapping angrily against the floor boards.

Carmen closed the door slowly behind her, the weight of shame settling onto her shoulders like a wet cloak. Her head still throbbed, her heart even more so.

She leaned against the door, closing her eyes.

I'm finished, she thought.

Word had likely already swept through Barrio Sur like wildfire: Carmen Ruiz, drunk and disgraceful, throwing herself at men in some smoky dive like a common whore. A seamstress turned scandal, no better than a barmaid in a brothel. She could already hear the whispers, feel the stares.

She could never go back there.

She slid to the floor, her back against the cold doorframe, breath snagging in her throat as the silence thickened around her like fog.

And then the thought struck her like a blow: *What if word had reached Francisco?*

The possibility wrapped around her chest like iron bands.

A sob ripped through her chest before she could stop it, the sound raw and desperate.

She buried her face in her hands, but the weight of it all refused to let go.

The thought of Francisco, so proud, so principled, learning of the scandal made her stomach churn. It was one thing to disappoint her mother. It was another to think of completely losing the respect of the only person who had ever believed in her.

She had been reckless, but more than that, she had been *seen*.

And now, she feared she couldn't undo the version of herself the world had already chosen to believe.

A cold panic surged through her chest. She rose suddenly, her hands trembling as she gathered her things.

There was still time. Maybe. If she could just see him, explain, be heard. If she could look him in the eye and say the words that burned on her tongue, maybe she could stitch the pieces of her unraveling life back together.

Maybe she could still be forgiven.

She took the train, and desperately made her way up the long steps of the Hotel Piriápolis, her heart pounding with a fragile hope.

But when she reached the office, it wasn't Francisco who greeted her. It was Carlos Bonavita.

He looked up from behind his desk, and the lines of fatigue etched into his face told her everything before he spoke a word.

"Carlos," she said, her voice barely steady. "I'm looking for Francisco. Have you seen him?"

Carlos stood slowly, folding his hands in front of him. "Carmen," he said gently. "Don Francisco… he's gone. He set sail for Europe again this morning. He left word that he might be away for some time."

She blinked, unable to hide the blow. "But… he just returned. How could he have left again so soon?"

Carlos exhaled, clearly weighing how much to say. "He didn't tell me much. Only that there were matters in need of his attention abroad. Political matters, maybe personal ones too. All I know is, he left in a hurry, and said he wouldn't be accessible for a while."

Something buckled in Carmen's chest. The last thread of certainty she'd been clinging to had finally snapped.

She hesitated, then asked quietly, "Did he say anything about me?"

Carlos turned back to her, his voice gentler now. "Only that I should tell you that the deed to the cottage is in the kitchen cabinet, tucked behind the spice tins. And that the payroll from the atelier will continue arriving at your old address indefinitely."

A strange ache settled over her. She nodded once. "Thank you, Carlos. Please have the checks sent to my mother's address."

He blinked, surprised. "You don't want the money?"

Carmen managed a small smile, one heavy with quiet resignation. "I don't feel right taking his money. But… she could use it."

She didn't say the rest aloud—that maybe it was the last thing she could offer her mother. A gesture of love from a distance. A way to give without being allowed back in.

Carlos offered her a sympathetic smile. "Very well. I'm sorry I couldn't give you more information," he said softly.

"Thank you, Carlos. For everything," Carmen said softly, turning to leave.

"Carmen."

She stopped, glancing over her shoulder.

Carlos hesitated, then met her eyes with quiet earnestness. "Francisco… he has his own way of loving. Not with declarations or softness. He shows his love through acts of service, because that's how he understands care. Through legacy, not sentiment."

His gaze held hers, steady and searching.

"I know it can feel like overreach. Like control," he continued, "but I've never known his love to be empty. Just… difficult to carry."

Carmen nodded, the knot in her chest twisting tighter. Maybe she had misjudged Francisco after all.

She moved quietly through the late morning streets. The weight of her steps matched the heaviness settling in her heart. Each echo of her boots on the stone seemed to whisper the same aching question: *What have I done?*

As she neared the boarding house, a wave of regret washed over her, sharp and suffocating. She had pushed him away, convinced herself it was for the best; but now, with everything unraveling, the clarity she'd clung to felt paper-thin.

She paused at the gate, her hand resting on the rusted metal. The warmth of his embrace, the fire in his eyes when he spoke of building a better world, it all came rushing back like a tide she could no longer hold back.

And now, it was too late to take any of it back.

She pressed her forehead against the gate, eyes closing as a single tear slipped down her cheek. Whatever came next, she would have to face it alone.

Her steps were heavy as she climbed the stairs to her boarding room. The familiar creak of the floorboards followed her like a shadow, each groan a reminder of how far she had drifted from everything she once knew.

As she passed Señora Varela's door, she caught the faint scent of lavender and wood polish, the comforting hum of someone else's quiet life still moving forward.

Inside her room, the air was still, save for the hiss of the radiator in the corner.

Carmen lowered herself onto the chair beside the little writing desk, its surface scratched and worn, like her. She opened her journal, the pages already thick with ink and sorrow, and let her fingers hover over the paper.

She took a deep breath, then began to write:

August 1916—

I thought I was protecting myself.
That stepping away first would spare me the fall.
But love doesn't vanish just because you walk away.
It lingers.
Quiet. Stubborn.
Filling the corners of every day with echoes.

I told myself I was choosing freedom.
And maybe I was.
Because real freedom isn't the absence of love,
It's the courage to face it,
To carry it with grace, even when it hurts.
Francisco was many things.
Bold. Restless. A force of nature.
And through all of it, he believed.
In his vision. In something bigger.
In me.
And I...
I learned.
That fear can dress itself in logic.
That pride can mimic wisdom.
But also this:

We are allowed to change our minds.
To return, not to what was,
But to what might still be.
If he doesn't come back,
I'll still be whole.
Because I'm not waiting anymore.
I'm walking forward.
And today, beneath this vast celestine sky,
I'm not wondering what might've been.
I'm building what might still become.

She closed the journal slowly, her fingers lingering on the worn leather cover. The silence in the room no longer felt so heavy. It felt like a pause. A breath before the next beginning.

This wasn't the life she had imagined. But it was one she would try to shape for herself. Piece by piece. Day by day.

She would find work. She would write. And somehow, she would begin again; not as a daughter, or a lover, or a shadow of someone else's dream, but as Carmen Ruiz.

As herself.

Chapter 30

Life at the boarding house crept in like a new rhythm: awkward at first, then oddly familiar.

Each morning, Carmen rose to the scent of strong coffee and starch from the laundry room downstairs. The building was filled with working women like herself: teachers, seamstresses, telegraph operators, each one tucked into their own rhythm, their own quiet resilience. There was a comfort in that hum of shared purpose.

At first, she kept to herself, unsure how to exist in this new chapter. The wounds were too fresh. The rawness of exile, the weight of rejection still pressed against her ribs like a hand that wouldn't let go. It was a loneliness that didn't shout, but seeped; silent, relentless.

But life, even when unwelcome, had a way of pushing her forward, step by reluctant step.

And in time, what was once strange and unbearable settled into rhythm, until her new life became simply her life.

Downstairs, the bustle had already begun. Women boiled water for *mate*, ironed collars with quick flicks of the wrist, swapped gossip over piles of steaming laundry. Their laughter was too loud for the hour—sharp, breathless, defiant—as if trying to drown out the quiet ache that lived in all of them.

As Carmen entered the common room, the clatter stilled just enough. Heads turned. A spoon paused mid-stir.

Someone muttered under their breath. A pause, a glance.

Carmen smiled politely and lifted her chin, not with pride, but with the quiet resolve of someone who had nothing left to prove.

As Carmen wrestled with the temperamental little stove, the kettle stubbornly refusing to boil, a voice from nearby offered dryly, "That thing has a will of its own. Don't take it personally."

She turned to find a woman perched casually on the windowsill. She was about her age, maybe a little younger, with freckles scattered across her nose like constellations and a long auburn braid tossed over one shoulder. Her sleeves were rolled to the elbows, and a threadbare smock-frock hung comfortably on her frame. A notebook lay open in her lap, her fingers still poised with a pencil mid-thought.

Carmen gave a faint smile and nodded her thanks before turning back to the kettle, still sputtering its defiance.

A pause passed between them before the woman spoke again, gently, curiously. "So, you're a writer."

It wasn't a question so much as a quiet recognition.

Carmen hesitated. "I…what gives you that idea?"

The woman shrugged, not looking up. "You've got ink on your fingers." She nodded toward Carmen's hands. "Smudged between your thumb and forefinger. Same as my brother used to get when he scribbled his stories. He called it 'proof of dreaming.'"

Carmen looked down. The stain she hadn't noticed felt suddenly like a small, defiant badge. Her lips lifted slightly.

"I suppose I am," she admitted.

The woman finally glanced up, offering a half-smile that didn't quite reach her eyes. "Good. We need more dreamers around here. Especially the kind who don't scare easy."

A sliver of understanding passed between them; thin, but real. A thread.

"You must be new," she said, putting the notebook aside. "I'm Violeta."

"Carmen," she replied, turning toward her fully now. "Just moved in about a week and a half ago."

Violeta offered a crooked smile. "Well, welcome to the madhouse. It's not much, but the walls don't judge and the roof usually doesn't leak."

Carmen chuckled, the first real laugh she'd allowed herself in days. She glanced down at Violeta's smock, covered in paint speckles. "Are you a painter?"

"Mostly," Violeta nodded, gesturing toward the pile of sketchbooks on the windowsill. "But I've been dabbling in etching, too. I'm with a collective down near Parque Mario. Artists, writers, a couple of musicians. We trade ideas, complain about the world, drink too much *mate*."

Carmen's interest piqued. "That sounds… incredible."

Violeta studied her for a moment, then smiled again, this time softer. "You've got the hands of someone who makes things, too. What do you do?"

"I sew," Carmen offered quietly. "And I write. When life allows."

Violeta's face lit up. "Well, then you *must* come. We've been desperate for someone to help with costumes for the upcoming season at Teatro Solís. I don't think it pays much, but the company is rich in spirit. We're actually meeting tonight, if you're interested. I have a feeling you'd fit right in."

They talked. About tango, about books, about the beautiful nonsense of loving men who lived more in their heads than in the real world. And for the first time in weeks, Carmen laughed for the first time in what felt like years.

And just like that, the boarding house began to feel a little less like exile, and more like possibility.

That night, cloaked in darkness and the distant murmur of horse-drawn carriages, Carmen and Violeta slipped through the labyrinthine streets of Montevideo.

The air was heavy with sea salt, thick and damp against their skin, as the mist caught in the glow of gas lamps, turning them into halos of molten gold.

Violeta walked as if she owned the night. She carried herself proudly, chin lifted, stride unflinching, utterly indifferent to the weight of other people's eyes.

She had told Carmen enough stories of throwing fists with her brothers growing up in Salto that Carmen never doubted she could hold her ground if pressed. But it wasn't only her strength that struck Carmen, it was the ease with which she wore it. There was no apology in her step, no fear in her gaze.

Beside her, Carmen felt something stir. A spark of envy, yes, but also of inspiration. Violeta's spunk, her defiance, was like a lantern in the dark, and Carmen found herself wanting to walk in that light, if only for a moment.

They turned down a narrow alley, its cobblestones slick with fog, and descended the steps to a weather worn cellar door marked only by a faded chalk outline of a crescent moon.

Violeta knocked twice, paused, then once more. A breath, then the door creaked open.

Inside, the room breathed quiet resistance. Candlelight pooled in corners and danced on cracked plaster walls, casting shadows that felt alive.

A phonograph spun softly in the corner, letting a low, smoky tango curl through the air like incense. Artists sprawled across worn sofas, paint on their hands and fire in their eyes. Poets hunched over notebooks, their pages ink-stained and trembling. A violinist tuned her instrument between sips of wine.

There was no pretense here. No shame. No caution.

This wasn't merely a gathering. It was a sanctuary.

A haven for those who refused to kneel to the Church, to the state, to the rules that carved people into silence. It was communion by candlelight, rebellion with rhythm. The kind of place where truth was spoken not with fear, but with fire.

As Violeta greeted familiar faces with casual nods and warm handshakes, Carmen stood still, letting her gaze sweep slowly across the room.

A woman lounged in a velvet chair, reading a sonnet with a voice like smoke; sharp, slow, and strangely sensual. Nearby, a painter unveiled a raw canvas: a couple locked in tango, all jagged lines and unspoken longing. In the corner, a woman strummed a guitar with a cigarette balanced between her lips, her foot tapping softly, in time with something only she could hear.

A man appeared at Carmen's side, offering her a glass of red wine so dark it looked like ink.

"First time at El Espejo Azul?" he asked, a knowing smile tugging at his mouth.

Carmen shook her head politely at the glass of wine, still absorbing the scene. "Is it always like this?"

He glanced around, his expression turning thoughtful. "Only when the world tells us to be silent."

Violeta took Carmen's hand, weaving through the crowd with Carmen trailing just behind her, still slightly overwhelmed by the sheer eccentricity of the place.

When they reached a low velvet couch near the back wall, a woman stood up to greet them.

"Carmen," Violeta beamed, "this is Magdalena. She's one of the directors at Teatro Solís. Magda, this is the seamstress-writer I told you about this afternoon."

Magdalena was striking, if unconventional. Her linen smock was splattered with faint paint stains, cinched at the waist with a gauzy scarf in brilliant hues of orange and teal. A cloche hat perched precariously over her short black curls, and bold red spectacles framed her expressive eyes.

"Well now," Magdalena said, eyes twinkling and bangle bracelets jangling as she reached out to grasp Carmen's hands. "That dress is divine. Let me guess…French? No, no. Too clever. Too personal."

Carmen flushed slightly. "I made it myself," she said. "Sewed it, I mean."

Magdalena stepped back and gave a delighted gasp. "*You* stitched that? With those seams?" She leaned in, inspecting the craftsmanship along the bodice. "Marvelous. A seamstress with a mind for line and silhouette, how very rare."

Violeta smirked, a spark of mischief in her eyes. "She's not just a seamstress, you know. She writes too."

With that, she slipped away into the crowd, leaving Carmen flushed and caught in the echo of her words.

Magdalena arched a brow. "Do you now? What kind of writing?"

"Stories," Carmen said, then hesitated. "Journal entries, poetry sometimes. Observations, mostly."

Magdalena clasped her hands dramatically. "Exactly what we need. We've been searching for someone with a real voice, not just the usual dry copywriters. Someone who understands rhythm, atmosphere, story."

Carmen blinked, unsure whether to laugh or ask if she was serious.

"You wouldn't happen to have any samples of your work with you, would you?" Magdalena asked, already hopeful.

Wordlessly, Carmen dug into her satchel and pulled out her journal, the leather soft and worn, the pages bloated with ink and pressed flowers. She handed it over.

Magdalena opened to a random page and began to read. Her expression shifted as her eyes moved across the lines—first curious, then contemplative, and finally—enchanted.

After a long pause, she shut the journal and looked up, a spark lighting behind her red glasses. "Carmen, how would you feel about joining our creative team for the season? It's not glamorous pay, but the work is real. Rehearsals, previews, exhibitions. *Teatro* life. You'd be writing the copy that draws people to our performances."

Carmen stared, stunned. Somewhere deep inside, something fluttered to life. The kind of flutter that felt like destiny pulling at the thread of a new beginning.

"That'd be great," she said, breathless.

Magdalena's eyes lit up as she grinned. "Splendid. Thank heavens for Violeta and her eye for talent. I'm absolutely hopeless when it comes to writing copy, and I've been desperate for help. Come by the theatre tomorrow afternoon, around four. I'll be there."

Violeta reappeared beside her, eyes lit with urgency and a glint of something reverent. "Come, Carmen," she said, nodding toward the open space where chairs had been pushed back and candles flickered like tiny rebellions. "It's about to begin."

Carmen blinked, caught off guard. "What is?"

Violeta took her hand, warm and certain. Her voice dropped to a whisper, steady and sure.

"The *milonga*," she said. "This is how we *resist*."

The first haunting notes of a violin rose, slow and aching; a tango not of spectacle, but of soul. The melody curled through the air like smoke, heavy with longing, rebellion, and desire.

A hand reached for Carmen's, drawing her gently into the circle of light. Around her stood painters with ink-stained fingers, poets with sleepless eyes, dancers with bare feet that stamped out freedom in rhythm and fire.

They were misfits, dreamers, outcasts, and yet here, they were sovereign. Here, they refused to bow.

Carmen's breath caught. For a moment she had to pinch herself to believe it was real. Perhaps, after all, she was no longer wandering on the edges. Perhaps she was slowly, at last, finding her own place in the world.

And as the music rose around her, fierce and unyielding, Carmen allowed herself to believe, just for that night, that everything might yet work out.

As she moved, her body remembering what her spirit had never truly forgotten, something ancient stirred in her chest. This wasn't escape. It wasn't even resistance.

It was resurrection.

And this time, she would not be silenced.

Chapter 31

The months passed in quiet metamorphosis. Carmen's life, once bound by rules and expectations, began to shift into a rhythm all its own, one shaped by the thrum of rehearsal halls, late-night readings, and the soft rustle of parchment filled with ink and daring new ideas.

At the Teatro Solís, Carmen worked closely with Magdalena, immersing herself not just in the mechanics of stage production, but in the deeper alchemy of voice, story, and spectacle. What started as a modest role writing program notes and press releases, quickly evolved into something richer.

She found herself sketching costume ideas, refining dialogue, and staying late to breathe new life into tired monologues. The theater pulsed with creative energy, alive with possibility, and for the first time in what felt like forever, Carmen felt that same current crackling through her veins.

By day, she walked the wooden halls of the theater, her footsteps echoing like applause in empty auditoriums. By night, she returned to the boarding house, where she and Violeta would trade verses by candlelight, argue over politics and art, and dream aloud about new ways to speak truth through beauty.

She found herself surrounded by kindred spirits: painters, poets, composers, each of them a little strange, a little wounded, and yet brilliant in their own defiance.

Together, they made a world of their own, stitched from scraps of hope and ink and rebellion.

Carmen still carried her grief. The pain of exile, the ache of abandonment, and the sharp wound of Francisco's absence still hadn't faded. But she had begun, at last, to root herself in something new. Something of her own making.

And though she did not know it yet, change was on the wind once more. A shadow was gathering, quiet and steady, and certain to find them all.

The golden hour cast long shadows across the marble statues and stone path of Plaza Independencia as Carmen exited the Teatro Solís one afternoon, her satchel slung over one shoulder, still faintly dusted with chalk from the rehearsal board.

The sound of carriage wheels clattering on cobblestone mingled with the faint clinking of café glasses and the sharp trills of birds retreating to roost in the trees.

She moved slowly, not in a hurry to return to the boarding house just yet. The city seemed suspended in amber, Montevideo glowing in that soft, forgiving light that made even the chipped fountains look like sculpture.

As she crossed the plaza, the familiar cry of the newsdealer echoed above the hush of the square:

"Three ships sunk! Germany attacks Argentine vessels!"

Carmen stopped mid-step, the words catching like thorns in her chest. She turned, drawn to the vendor's wooden stand cluttered with ink-stained headlines and smudged pages flapping in the breeze. She reached for one of the broadsheets, her fingers trembling slightly as she scanned the blocky type:

LA MAÑANA — EXTRA: ARGENTINA COULD ENTER WAR AFTER GERMAN ATTACKS AT SEA

Buenos Aires, February 1917 — Tensions mount as Germany's policy of unrestricted submarine warfare has claimed three Argentine vessels. The unprovoked sinkings have sparked national outrage.

The crisis deepened further with the interception and publication of a German telegram containing grave insults directed at Argentine officials. The contents, widely circulated in the press, have provoked widespread condemnation and ignited a firestorm in diplomatic circles.

Sources confirm that Argentina now stands perilously close to declaring war on Germany, a dramatic shift that could alter the country's long-maintained stance of neutrality in the global conflict.

The paper crackled in her hands.

Voices buzzed around her now. Passersby whispered nervously, a man clutched a folded newspaper with white knuckles, a child innocently asked what "war" meant.

Carmen's mind raced. If Germany had attacked Argentinian ships, it meant the war was no longer a distant storm, it was now right at their doorstep.

A wave of unease rolled over her, mingling with the exhaustion from the day's work.

Carmen unfolded the crinkled periodical, her fingertips trembling slightly as she scanned the column about the war. But her breath caught when her eyes landed on a familiar name further down on the page.

Francisco Piria.

Her gaze froze. The headline screamed back at her in bold, merciless ink:

PIRIA, TYCOON, WEDS EUROPEAN HEIRESS IN PRIVATE CEREMONY

The world around her blurred, muffled into silence. She stood motionless, the paper suddenly heavy in her hands, as though it were made of stone.

Her blood ran cold as a rush of emotion surged within her: grief, confusion, a slow-burning fury.

Six months. It had only been six months since they had last spoken, since he had sworn that he cared about her, that he had only wanted to keep her safe. And now this?

How quickly he'd erased her.

Had she truly meant so little?

She had tried to bury the hope, to silence the foolish voice that had insisted that he would return. That one day he would return from Europe with his affairs in order, ready at last to seek her out, to take her hands in his, and to finally ask her to be his wife.

She had told herself to be practical, to be rational. Yet somewhere deep within, a stubborn part of her had still clung to that fragile, impossible hope.

And now, instantly, it shattered.

Her thoughts spiraled. Had he heard the whispers of her scandal with the stranger at the Madreselva? Had her indiscretion made her unworthy? Or had he always intended to leave her behind, just another chapter in his story, not the ending?

A bitter taste rose in her throat. She had bared her soul to him, offered him her whole heart, her belief, her trust. And now, he was gone; not in death, but in matrimony.

To someone else.

Tears burned at the corners of Carmen's eyes, rising fast and hot. She blinked them back with effort, refusing to allow herself to fall apart in the middle of Plaza Independencia, for all the world to see.

With trembling fingers, she folded the newspaper and tucked it under her arm, dropping a shiny *peso* onto the newsstand without meeting the vendor's eyes.

Panic fluttered in her chest, sharp and breathless. She needed somewhere—anywhere—to unravel, hidden from the prying eyes and muttered judgments of the city.

The boarding house was too far, and stumbling into the Madreselva in a mess of tears was out of the question, especially not after the last shameful, scandalous spectacle she had put on there.

Suddenly, her mother's house came to mind, just a few blocks away. If fortune was kind, it might be empty. A quiet corner, a fleeting refuge, long enough to steady herself and gather her thoughts.

Before doubt could take hold, she spun on her heel and left the square, her footsteps striking a sharp staccato against the cobblestones as she hurried toward the only place that felt within reach.

Returning to Barrio Sur after so many months felt like stepping into a wound that had never closed. Faces slid past her, familiar yet distant, their eyes narrowing, their mouths tight. No one greeted her. No one stopped. They only stared, as if scandal still clung to her skin like a bad stench. She hadn't expected a welcome, not after everything. Yet the silence of her neighbors cut deeper than any words, a quiet blade that only sharpened her pain.

She prayed the house might be empty, for a place to grieve unseen.

But of course, her mother was there. Carmen knew better than to hope for tenderness, for any gesture of comfort.

What she received instead was the sharp lash of a tirade, well-rehearsed and waiting, the kitchen walls closing in as her mother's voice rose.

This was the moment her mother had been waiting for: the chance to tell Carmen she had been right all along about Francisco, about the shame of it, about how far her daughter had fallen.

Carmen endured it only as long as she could. Then she fled, leaving behind her mother's scolding, the sweltering air of the tiny kitchen, and the hollow ache of knowing she no longer belonged at home.

She fled the house and made her way to the only place that had ever really felt like home: the Madreselva. At that early hour, she knew it would be nearly empty, save for Nico, who had long since grown accustomed to the company of the brokenhearted.

He had watched countless souls drown their sorrows in shadows and song, and she knew he would not flinch at hers.

Nico leaned against the counter, working a towel over a glass with practiced ease, as she slid onto the old familiar barstool. He studied her for a moment, his usual smirk gone, replaced with something steadier.

"You know, Carmen," he said quietly, "I've seen all kinds of people sit right where you are. Lovers, dreamers, plenty of poor souls gutted by love."

She looked up, caught off guard by his seriousness. "Yeah? And what have you learned from watching them?"

"That the love you're mourning…" Nico shook his head. "It's not about him. It's about you. What you felt, what you gave, that belongs to *you*. No one can take it away."

Carmen blinked at him, the words catching her off guard. "But why does love always have to end in heartbreak?" Her voice trembled. "Why does it have to be some sort of cruel joke?"

Nico set the glass down and leaned across the bar, lowering his voice. "Because, sometimes, people aren't *meant* to stay. They just pass through, spark something in you, and then they're gone. Doesn't mean it wasn't real. It just means that nothing truly lasts forever."

Her throat tightened. "I just feel so lost, Nico. Where do I go from here? It feels impossible to move on from this…"

"You don't *move on*, Carmen," Nico said firmly. "You carry it forward. You take what it gave you: the fire, the lessons, the strength, and you make something out of it. You write, you dance, you fight. Whatever the hell keeps you breathing. But don't just sit here waiting for a man who already showed you he won't come back."

He picked up her empty glass and set it aside, his eyes softening, just a little. "Maybe Piria wasn't meant to be your great love. Maybe he was just the one who showed you what you're capable of. The one who pushed you to stop hiding and become who you really are."

Carmen's eyes stung, but for the first time in weeks, she felt the knot in her chest begin to loosen. She managed a small, crooked smile. "You make it sound so simple."

Nico smirked faintly, returning to his glass. "Simple? No. But it's the truth."

She reached across the bar, squeezed his hand briefly, then let go.

As she stepped out into the evening air, she felt something shift.

The ache was still there, but now it burned with purpose. Francisco might be gone, but she still had her words, her dreams, her own stubborn will.

And for the first time in a long while, Carmen let herself believe there might still be a life ahead of her, one that belonged entirely to her.

The Río de la Plata stretched before her, its waters dull and gray, yet she knew that beyond the horizon, those same waters ran clear and blue. One day, she told herself, her life would find that brightness too.

The world may have been swallowed in conflict, but Carmen refused to let her flame die.

In the crucible of loss, she felt the ember of something stronger: resilience.

And in that ember lived the proof that love and creation could endure—defiant, unyielding, eternal, even in the darkest of times.

Chapter 32

The dark times certainly did come.

The young men that had sailed back to Europe to fight in the Great War, stirred by duty and loyalty to distant homelands, returned not as heroes, but as unwitting carriers of an invisible enemy.

By 1918, news of the influenza pandemic had slipped ashore like a shadow no one could keep out.

Hushed rumors of sickness soon spread through every *barrio*, every street, every home. Montevideo braced itself, not for the clamor of battlefields abroad, but for a quieter, more merciless war within its own walls.

Carmen saw it with her own eyes, neighbors shuffling through the streets with strange contraptions strapped to their faces: makeshift helmets fashioned from fish bowls or glass jars and leather straps, fans tied to their shoes in the hope that moving air might sweep away contagion. Some smeared their skin with pungent oils, others clutched garlic cloves or sprigs of herbs as talismans against death.

The city that once thrived on laughter, on music, on tango's embrace, now looked like a masquerade of fear.

As fear mounted, so too did the hand of authority. The government slowly imposed stricter measures with each passing week. At first it was schools, then theaters and churches, their doors locked and barred. Processions and festivals vanished from the calendar, and soldiers patrolled the streets to ensure curfews were kept.

And then came the decree that cut deepest: *milongas* were forbidden.

For Carmen, it was as if the heart of Montevideo had been stilled. The dance halls that once swelled with the pulse of the *bandoneón*, with laughter and breath and sweat, now stood hollow and silent. Posters announcing closures hung limply on doors, flapping in the wind like surrender flags.

To those in power, it was a matter of control, of order. But to the people, to Carmen, it was more than an inconvenience. It was the theft of expression itself, the severing of a lifeline that bound neighbors, lovers, and strangers together in shared rhythm.

What Francisco had once railed against, authority cloaked in the language of protection, she now saw unfolding around her, not in distant rhetoric, but in the very streets she walked.

The city no longer moved to music, but to fear.

Carmen slammed her notebook shut, her voice breaking the silence of the boarding house kitchen. "They've taken everything," she said, her tone trembling between sorrow and anger. "The theaters, the churches, the plazas, and now the *milongas*. We're not animals to be kept in cages. Do they not understand? The *milonga* is how we breathe. It's how we remember we're alive."

Violeta lifted her gaze from the canvas, charcoal smudges streaking her fingertips, her expression calm but unyielding. "Of course they understand," she said, her voice low, each word deliberate. "This isn't about safety, Carmen, it's about control. Look at the Espionage and Sedition Acts in the United States. They've made it a crime to speak against the war. Prison—for words."

She leaned forward, her eyes flashing in the lamplight. "And don't think it isn't reaching us. The moment Uruguay broke neutrality, when we seized the German ships in the port and leased them to the United States, we were no longer outside this war. We were inside it. And the first thing any government does in wartime is silence dissent."

Her voice grew more urgent. "If no one dares to gather, no one dares to speak. And when people stop gathering, they forget their power. But when they come together..." She tapped the table with the flat of her hand. "They remember their strength. They remember they can resist."

Carmen pressed her palms flat on the table, the wood cool against her skin. "But what good is strength if we're locked away? If every door we once entered is now chained shut?"

Violeta's gaze softened, but her words carried steel. "Strength doesn't disappear just because it's forced underground. It just changes shape. I still have my art, and you still have your words, Carmen. Write them. Let them remind people that silence is not the same as surrender."

Something in Carmen stirred, like an ember catching. She thought of the *milongas*, of the bodies moving as one, of music that refused to bow to anyone's command. If she couldn't dance, then perhaps her words could move in their place.

That night, Carmen lit a single candle in her small room at the boarding house. The flame wavered against the draft creeping in from the shutters, casting restless shadows along the walls. She sat at the narrow desk, notebook open, pen poised above the page.

For a long moment, she simply listened—to the silence of the city, to the distant coughs and muffled sobs that drifted up from the street. The absence of music was louder than any melody; it pressed against her chest, demanding to be named.

Her hand began to move:

They have silenced our gatherings, but they cannot silence the pulse that lives within us. They forbid the embrace, but they cannot forbid memory. Even in the stillness, the rhythm persists, like blood beneath the skin, like breath itself.

The words spilled faster, her pen scratching furiously. She wrote of the barricaded dance halls, the posters plastered across doors, the contraptions people wore to keep death at bay. She wrote of grief, but also of defiance, the unbroken thread of belonging that no decree could sever.

When at last she stopped, the candle had burned low, its wax spilling in pale rivulets down the brass holder. Her hand ached, her eyes burned, but her heart felt steadier than it had in weeks.

She closed the notebook gently, as though sealing something sacred. The silence of the city remained, but within it, Carmen heard something new: the first faint stirrings of resistance.

A week later, Carmen found herself descending the narrow steps into the cellar of El Espejo Azul. The café above had gone quiet since the mandates, its tables emptied, its piano covered in dust. But below, in the smoky half-light, life stirred.

Painters, musicians, poets, and dreamers had agreed to begin to meet in secret, huddled in shadows as though conspiring against the silence itself.

The air buzzed with restlessness. Violeta sketched faces in the corner, her charcoal sharp and angry. A violinist ran his bow in ghostly silence across the strings, miming the music he could no longer play aloud. A playwright muttered lines under his breath, words that would never see a stage.

"They are choking us," an actor said bitterly, slamming his fist against the table. "First the theaters, now the *milongas*. They want a city of the dead, obedient and voiceless."

The room bristled, voices overlapping as if each one was afraid to be drowned out by silence.

"I heard," muttered a gaunt young man hunched close to the lamp, his eyes shadowed with suspicion, "that this flu isn't even a virus at all. They say the soldiers were infected on purpose in the training camps, through vaccines for typhoid, for smallpox. Sent off already carrying it in their veins. Brought back to us not by fate, but by design."

A murmur rippled through the group. A poet stopped writing, eyes narrowing. "I've heard the same. And now the government claims it's for our safety, shutting the doors on every place where we might gather. Theaters, cafés, dance halls… all silenced. It reeks of something more than illness."

A murmur swept the table, uneasy and electric. The violinist lowered his bow, leaning in. "But why? What would they gain from poisoning their own men?"

The gaunt young man's eyes darted around the circle, then back to the flame of the lamp. "Not their men…our people. If everyone's afraid, if no one dares to gather, then no one dares to speak. No rallies, no protests, no whispers of reform. Just silence."

Violeta gave a sharp nod, her charcoal stick snapping in her grip. "Fear is the perfect leash. Make neighbors suspicious of neighbors, and you never have to raise a weapon. People will police themselves."

A hush followed her words, broken only by the crackle of the lamp. Carmen felt the truth of it shiver through her. The bans on gatherings, the shuttered *milongas*, the closed theaters—it wasn't just about illness. It was about control.

She looked around at the faces lit by the weak yellow glow, each marked by anger, doubt, and a gnawing hunger for something more. In that moment, the room itself seemed to pulse with defiance, as if their shared outrage had become its own form of resistance.

"You're right," someone chimed in, another writer with ink-stained fingers. "This isn't about health, it's about keeping us apart. No politics, no resistance, no ideas shared in whispers over wine. They want us isolated, obedient, easy to manage."

A hush fell, broken only by the scrape of Violeta's charcoal across paper. She looked up at last, her jaw tight. "And it's working. The people are afraid, afraid of each other even. They cross the street to avoid a cough, a sneeze. They've let fear make strangers of us all."

Her words settled like a weight over the table, and for a moment no one spoke. The anger in the room was real, but beneath it was something sharper: the realization that they were up against not just a sickness of the body, but a sickness of control.

Carmen, who had been silent until then, leaned forward. The light from the flickering candle caught the edge of her notebook, tucked under her arm. "Then let's give the people something stronger than fear."

The others turned toward her.

She swallowed, steadying her voice. "Not whispers, not secrets buried in notebooks. We'll light a fire under them. Spark the flame of rebellion through word on the street. We could write pamphlets. Something anyone can hold in their hands. If they forbid music and gatherings, then we fight with language. With truth. We remind the city that silence is not the same as surrender."

A charged hush followed. Violeta's eyes lit with approval, and one of the younger painters let out a low whistle.

"Pamphlets," he echoed, as though testing the word. "Distributed in the barrios, slipped under doors, left in cafés…"

"Exactly," Carmen said, a fire rising in her chest. "We don't need a stage or a dance hall to make ourselves heard. We just need ink, paper, and courage."

The group looked around at one another. Heads began to nod. The violinist finally set bow to strings and drew out a single, defiant note, soft but steady, the kind of sound that carried.

In that moment, Carmen knew: their resistance had begun.

The next night, El Espejo Azul transformed into a workshop. The tables, once cluttered with glasses and bottles, now held stacks of cheap paper, ink pots, and a single battered printing press someone had dragged in from a friend's shop. The hiss of the lanterns and the scratch of pen on paper filled the space, replacing the music they all longed for.

Carmen bent over her notebook, her handwriting sharp and deliberate as she copied the words of her manifesto. Violeta, sleeves rolled high, was already smudged with ink as she turned the crank of the press, pulling damp sheets free and laying them out to dry. The violinist, unable to keep still, tapped his bow against the wood in an impatient rhythm, as if to remind them all that resistance was also a form of music.

The press gave a final groan as Violeta tugged the damp sheet free. She shook it gently, then held it up in the lantern light. Ink still glistened on the words, the letters dark and defiant against the cheap paper.

With a grin, she crossed the room and placed it in Carmen's hands. "Here," Violeta said, her voice low but steady. "The first of many. Tell me if it sings the way you meant it to."

¡NO MÁS SILENCIO!

They say it is sickness.
They say it is for our protection.
But what is protection, if it steals our voices?
What is safety, if it chains our feet and forbids us from dancing?
They close the theaters.
They silence the musicians.
They forbid the milongas.
And what do they fear?
That we might gather.
That we might speak.
That we might remember we are stronger together.
Do not be fooled. Fear is their weapon. Division is their shield.
They want a city of the dead: obedient, voiceless, bent to their will.
But we are alive.
We will not bow.
We will not let them write our silence into history.
Let the word pass from hand to hand, from door to door.
Let our streets remember their heartbeat.
Let our people remember their strength.
The pen is our weapon.
The truth is our rhythm.
WE WILL NOT BE SILENCED.

Carmen's fingers trembled slightly as she scanned the words she herself had written, now multiplied and pressed into permanence. It felt different to see them here, no longer confined to her notebook but ready to live in the world, ready to be dangerous.

"Discretion will be everything," one of the older poets muttered, fanning the wet ink with his hand. "If they catch us distributing these..." He let the thought trail off, but the image hung heavy in the cellar.

Carmen straightened, ink staining the side of her hand. "Then we make it harder for them to catch us. We scatter. Each of us takes a bundle, leaves them where they'll be found. Cafés, markets, the tram stops. Even slipped under doors in the *barrios*."

Violeta smirked, wiping sweat from her brow. "Like planting seeds. And we'll see what grows."

The group exchanged glances, some nervous, some emboldened. For weeks they had been suffocating under decrees, under silence. Now, in the dim light of the hidden cellar, something had shifted.

Carmen gathered a handful of freshly pressed pamphlets, their edges still curling from the dampness of the ink. She held them like one might cradle a weapon, or a prayer. "If they've stolen our voices from the plazas," she said quietly, "then we'll put them back into the hands of the people."

Outside, the city lay in darkness, heavy with fear. But in the hidden basement of El Espejo Azul, resistance had found its first breath.

By dawn, the pamphlets had already found their way into the streets. Folded sheets tucked beneath bread loaves at the market, slipped under tram seats, wedged into doorframes where only the wind would discover them. Carmen had walked home with ink still staining her fingers, her heart hammering with the knowledge that her words were now loose in the world.

Within days, the city stirred. A laundress on Calle Yí read one aloud to her neighbors as they pinned damp clothes to the line; a group of dockworkers passed a copy between them, their faces grim but lit with recognition; a shoemaker tucked one into the pocket of every customer who entered his shop.

The authorities were swift to condemn. Newspapers loyal to the state called the writings "dangerous and incendiary". But the very effort to denounce the pamphlets only proved their reach.

People whispered the words in markets and on street corners, memorizing lines before burning the evidence.

Carmen watched it all unfold from the edges of the plazas and alleyways, her pulse quickening every time she saw someone's eyes widen as they read.

Fear was still there, palpable, clinging to every shadow, but it was joined now by something else. A restless stirring. A quiet defiance.

For the first time since the *milongas* had gone silent, Montevideo seemed to remember its heartbeat.

That evening, Carmen lingered by her desk, the last pamphlet from El Espejo Azul lying beside her notebook. She traced the edge of the page with her fingertip, marveling at how ordinary the paper looked;

thin, smudged, imperfect. And yet, somewhere in the city, these words were being read, carried, remembered.

She thought of the young men who had returned home from war. Their weapons had been rifles, their scars the kind the eye could see. Hers would be different: ink and paper, fragile in appearance but no less dangerous in their reach.

From the street below came the shuffle of footsteps, the low murmur of voices, and then, faintly, the sound of someone reading one of the pamphlets aloud.

Carmen froze, heart thrumming, straining to catch the cadence. A line she knew, her line, rose and broke against the night air like a tide.

She pressed a hand to her chest. For the first time since the music had been silenced, she felt the city's pulse again.

And yet, in that quiet, Carmen knew: her fight was far from over.

Chapter 33

The news reached Carmen on a gray morning, carried not by a letter, but by Rafael himself. He appeared at the doorway of the office at the Teatro Solís, his face pale, his usual quick words weighed down by something heavier.

"Carmen," he said, his voice catching. "It's your mother… she's fallen ill."

Her stomach knotted instantly. "Is it the virus?" she asked, the word bitter on her tongue.

Rafael shook his head. "No. Not the flu. It's her heart. She collapsed… last night. They say it was an attack."

For a moment, the air seemed to thin around her. Carmen gripped the edge of the doorframe to steady herself, her mind reeling.

The thought of her mother—so stern, so unyielding, a figure who had weathered storms of grief and poverty alike—struck down not by the plague that stalked the streets, but by the quiet rebellion of her own body, left Carmen shaken in a way she had not expected.

"She's alive," Rafael added quickly, reading the fear in her face. "But weak. They don't know if she'll recover."

Carmen drew a shaky breath, the rush of memory colliding with the present: her mother's scorn, her sharp words, but also the lullabies hummed long ago, the warmth of hands guiding her own at a sewing table. Whatever lay between them, the thought of losing her now cut deep.

"I need to see her," she whispered.

Carmen didn't pack a bag. She only slipped her notebook into her satchel, as if instinct told her she might need it, and followed Rafael through the streets.

The city was still gripped by silence, the emptiness of quarantine pressing in on every corner, but Carmen barely noticed. Her thoughts ran ahead of her feet, racing to the house she had once called home.

When they turned onto her mother's street, Carmen's breath caught. The house looked the same: the faded stucco, the familiar iron bars over the windows, but a heaviness seemed to hang over it, as though even the walls had bent beneath the weight of illness.

Rafael opened the door without knocking, and Carmen stepped inside. The air smelled faintly of boiled herbs, an attempt to mask the sharper scent of illness.

The front room was dim, the shutters drawn against the daylight, and somewhere deeper in the house Carmen heard the soft murmur of women's voices.

Her heart pounded as she made her way across the small main room to her mother's door.

And then she saw her: her mother, lying propped against pillows, her face pale, her breath shallow but steady. A shawl was draped over her shoulders, though sweat dampened her brow.

For an instant, Carmen froze in the doorway, her throat tight with everything she had not said, everything she had left behind.

Then her mother's eyes opened, clouded but sharp enough to recognize her.

"Carmen." Her mother's voice was thin, but it carried the same steel as ever. Her eyes, though rimmed with weariness, flicked over her daughter as if measuring the weight of her return.

Carmen stepped into the room, the floorboards groaning beneath her weight. Rafael stood just behind her, hat in his hands.

"*Mamá,*" she breathed, uncertain whether to move closer or hold back at the threshold.

Her aunt, keeping vigil at the bedside with a rosary wound tightly around her fingers, looked up sharply. Her eyes narrowed as they flicked between mother and daughter.

Rising stiffly, she leaned close enough for her words to sting. "She's weak," she hissed. "I hope to God you haven't come just to upset her."

Without waiting for a reply, she gathered her shawl and slipped from the room, pulling the door shut behind her until it clicked, leaving Carmen alone with the silence and the sound of the faint rasp of her mother's breathing.

The air was thick with the scent of eucalyptus and damp linen, but beneath it all lingered something rawer—the undeniable smell of frailty.

Her mother's eyes tracked her, sharp despite the pallor of her face. "You shouldn't have come," she said at last, her voice thin but edged.

Carmen's throat tightened. She forced herself another step forward. "I couldn't stay away, not knowing you weren't well…" Her words faltered, tangled in the years that lay between them.

Her mother shifted against the pillows, wincing, but she did not soften. "And when I was well? Where were you, *eh*?" she murmured, each syllable cutting despite her weakened breath. "Always too late, Carmen. Always only when it suits you."

Carmen's lips parted, a protest caught on her tongue. But she stopped herself. To argue with her mother now, in this room, felt like spitting into a well. The distance between them was not something a single conversation could mend.

Still, she couldn't let the silence be the last word. She drew a slow breath and steadied her voice. "I came because you're still my mother," she whispered. "Even if you can't see that it matters."

Her mother turned her head sharply, her eyes narrowing as if the sight of Carmen itself fanned the fire in her chest.

"The only thing you seem to care about," she spat, "is scribbling in silly notebooks, chasing foolish dreams. Your father was the same. Full of cheap talk, promises, ambition."

Her breath hitched, but she pressed on, the words gathering force like a storm. "I married him because I thought he'd lift us higher, give me more than the hard, narrow life I'd been born to. And what did he give me? Nothing but disappointment. Nothing but struggle. He ran off to Brazil like a coward, left me in a *conventillo* in Montserrat, with a child clinging to my skirts and nothing but empty promises in my pockets. And for what?" Her lips curled, voice sharp as glass. "Some bronze-skinned dancer with painted lips and no morals."

The room went still, heavy with the venom of it. Carmen stood frozen at the foot of the bed, the echo of her mother's words digging into her like thorns. Every syllable carried the weight of years, of betrayals she had never lived but now had to bear, as though her mother's anger had been waiting all along for a vessel to pour itself into.

Her mother paused and turned her head towards the window, as if the past might still be glaring back at her through the glass. Then, with a sigh edged in resentment, she went on.

"I could've married Ernesto Rivera. His family had land. His mother liked me. I could've had a proper life. But no, I had to fall for a dreamer. A drunk. A boy with nothing but a guitar and a lot of promises."

Carmen kept her eyes lowered, her lips pressed tightly together. She had endured this same rant more times than she could count, and yet each repetition cut anew.

"Do you think I wanted this life?" her mother pressed on, her breath uneven. "To be abandoned, left to raise a child alone? To live with the shame, the gossip? I wanted more, Carmen. I wanted you to have so much more."

Her voice wavered then, softening at the edges though the bitterness still ran beneath it like an undertow. Carmen felt a wave of sorrow rise within her, mingling with her own frustrations, her own grief. She knew the sharpness came from her mother's pain, yet knowing did nothing to dull the sting.

"I don't want you to end up like me," her mother whispered, her tone straining between warning and plea. "I want you to be wise, to make better choices. But you… you're so stubborn, so determined to follow your heart, even when it drags you to ruin."

Carmen drew in a long breath, trying to steady the tremor in her chest. Then, with quiet resolve, she stepped forward and lowered herself into the chair at her mother's bedside. Hesitant at first, she reached for the frail hand resting atop the coverlet.

"*Mamá*," she began gently, "I know you want the best for me, but I have to live my own life. I have to find my own way, even if it means making mistakes. I can't live my life in fear, afraid to love, afraid to take risks, just because of what happened to you. I'm not you. My life is different."

Her mother's eyes snapped back to her, dark and sharp despite the pallor of her face. She pulled her hand away, leaving Carmen's palm empty and cold.

"Different?" she scoffed, her breath hitching with the effort. "That's what every foolish girl believes, until life grinds her down. Until she's left with nothing but regrets." Her voice cracked as she coughed weakly, then hardened again. "You think you're stronger than I was? Wiser? Don't fool yourself. The world doesn't bend for women like us, Carmen. It breaks us. And when it does, there's no one there to gather the pieces."

The words struck like a lash, heavy with bitterness and a truth born of pain.

Carmen's throat ached with the weight of silence. She stared at her empty hand, then lifted her eyes to the frail figure on the bed. The words broke from her before she could stop them, trembling, urgent.

"*Mamá*... please," she whispered. "I know I've disappointed you. I know I've made choices you don't understand. But everything I've done, it's because I want a life that feels like my own. Not borrowed. Not bound. My words, my work... they're all I have. They may seem foolish to you, but they give me purpose."

Her voice broke, but she pressed on, her desperation spilling into every syllable. "I don't want to lose you without you ever believing in me. Just once, *just once,* can you see me not as a mistake, not as a burden, but as your daughter? Can't you be proud of me, even a little?"

The plea hung in the dim air of the room, fragile and exposed, like a candle struggling against the dark.

For a moment her mother simply stared at her, the room heavy with the weight of their words. Her mother's face remained hard, her eyes narrowing with a coldness that illness had not managed to soften.

"Foolish girl," she whispered, though her voice carried something more fragile beneath the bitterness—resignation, perhaps, or even fear. "You ask too much," she murmured, her voice brittle but steady. "I could never be proud of what I cannot respect."

Then, with a weary shake of her head, she turned her face once more toward the window. "You'll see, Carmen. One day, you'll see that I was right."

The silence that followed was crushing. Carmen's plea hung unanswered between them, dissolving into the stillness of the room. She felt the sting of tears pressing at the corners of her eyes but refused to let them fall.

Her hand clenched tight in her lap, aching for the touch she had reached for, the tenderness she had always begged for desperately, but never received.

In that moment, Carmen understood with painful clarity: the approval she had chased her whole life would never come.

The only sound was the faint rattle of her mother's breathing, steady and unrelenting, a wall Carmen would never break through.

At last, she rose, her chair scraping faintly against the floorboards. She lingered one last heartbeat in the doorway, willing her mother to call her back, to soften, to offer even a scrap of blessing.

But the only sound was her mother's labored breath, steady and unyielding.

That was the last time she ever saw her.

When the news of her mother's death reached her days later, Carmen could only clutch the edge of her desk, the grief crashing over her in waves.

First Francisco, now this. The twin losses hollowed her, leaving her adrift. She had lost the only man she had ever loved, and now even the hope of reconciliation with her mother was gone, snatched away with finality.

Grief clung to her like a second skin. The city outside seemed a blur of shadows and silence, its mourning bells echoing her own.

For the first time, she felt truly untethered, as though the ground beneath her had been swept away.

Grief hung heavy on her chest, and the silence of the city offered no escape. Where once she might have lost herself in dance, she now poured her anguish into words, filling page after page with fragments of memory, protest, longing.

Her small room became both prison and sanctuary. At times she wept as she wrote, her tears staining the ink; at others her hand raced furiously, as though the act of writing could keep despair from swallowing her whole. The words were raw, jagged, unrefined, but alive.

What began as an attempt to soothe her own sorrow soon grew into something larger. She wrote not only of loss, but of the city's silence, of neighbors shuttered away in fear, of the authorities' grip tightening under the guise of protection. Her grief bled into defiance. Her solitude became a voice for all who could not speak.

Even without the familiar voice of the *bandoneón*, Carmen discovered rhythm again, in the flow of ink, in the rise and fall of sentences, in the steady insistence of her own heart refusing to break completely.

One night, her candle guttering low, she pressed her pen harder to the page and let the words spill out like a cry:

> *They have silenced the music,*
> *yet still I hear it—*
> *in the shuffle of feet along empty streets,*
> *in the cough that rattles through thin walls,*
> *in the breath of the grieving*
> *who refuse to forget.*
>
> *They cannot ban rhythm;*
> *it lives in our blood.*
> *They cannot forbid memory;*

it lives in our bones.

If they bolt the doors of the milonga,
we will dance in the streets—
in words smuggled like lanterns,
in dreams that pulse against the dark,
in the very act of standing unbroken,
of refusing to bow.

And when the music rises again,
as it always will,
the world will remember
that silence was never enough
to stop us all from moving.

She set down the pen, her hand shaking, ink smudged on her fingertips. The passage was uneven, rough, but it burned with a truth she could no longer contain.

For the first time since her mother's death, Carmen felt her chest loosen, as though she had pulled something heavy from her ribs and given it form.

She leaned back, staring at the passage until the letters blurred. Outside, the night lay hushed and heavy, but she knew her words were alive now, waiting.

And somewhere deep inside, Carmen understood: the heart must be broken open for light to enter, the seed must split before it blooms, the traveler must lose her way to discover new roads.

Pain was not only a wound, it was the chisel that shaped her, the fire that refined her.

This, she realized, was the alchemy of living: to take sorrow and transmute it into strength, to turn grief into wisdom, and loss into a language that might light the way for others.

For the first time in a long while, she felt she was no longer only surviving her story, she was transforming it.

Chapter 34

The city did not heal overnight, but little by little, life began to return. Shops reopened their shutters, their doors flung wide to let in sunlight and cautious customers. Church bells rang again on Sundays, though the pews still carried the emptiness of loss. And at night, faint strains of music, hesitant at first, then bolder, began drifting back into the plazas where silence had reigned for months.

For Carmen, the return to normalcy came with a quiet astonishment. Her words, once confined to the privacy of her notebook and the secrecy of pamphlets passed hand to hand, had now taken root in the wider world.

A local periodical, *La Voz del Pueblo*, had published a few of her essays, pieces that spoke not only of grief and survival but of resilience, of the need to claim joy even in the face of fear.

She had seen her name in print for the first time, black ink against white paper, and it startled her. Not vanity, never that, but a strange, electric sense that she was no longer invisible.

People were reading her. Neighbors whispered about her words in doorways, a shopkeeper had pressed her hand with quiet thanks, and even strangers in the market nodded in recognition when her eyes met theirs.

The city was finding its rhythm again. And so, in her own way, was Carmen.

One warm afternoon, she made her way to *Café Olimpia*, a narrow corner establishment that had become a quiet haven for artists, journalists, and students.

Its windows were flung open to the street, letting in the chatter of passersby and the smell of roasting coffee.

The café had survived the closures, and now, as life cautiously returned, it pulsed once more with conversation and smoke.

Inside, the tables were crowded with papers, ink-stained fingers, and the hum of restless ideas. Painters argued over perspective, poets recited verses half-formed on napkins, and a young guitarist plucked absent chords in the corner as though tuning the air itself.

It was here, in this unruly sanctuary, that Carmen first saw him.

Gastón.

He entered as though the room had been waiting for him.

Tall, loose-limbed, smudges of dried paint still clinging to his cuffs. His hair fell across his forehead in the careless manner of men too occupied with their visions to glance at their reflections.

His accent was unmistakably Parisian, though someone whispered he had just moved from Buenos Aires recently.

He moved with a looseness, a lazy elegance, an ease so foreign to Montevideo that it felt almost indecent in a city bound tight with propriety and whispers.

When he laughed, the whole table seemed to lean toward him, as if the sound itself carried life.

Carmen, listening from her corner, found herself drawn in despite herself. There was no guardedness in him, no calculations or veiled insinuations, only candor, sharp and bright.

Later, when they were introduced, Gastón took her hand without hesitation, studying her face as if she were a portrait he might one day paint.

"So," he said, with a smile that felt like a dare, "you are Carmen. They told me you write. That means you are dangerous."

She laughed. *Dangerous.* No one in Montevideo called her that. There, she was infamous, scandalous, even blasphemous. Yet never dangerous.

Somehow, the word in his mouth felt like liberation.

Gastón was tall, broad-shouldered, with the kind of athletic frame that seemed shaped by both movement and ease. His jaw was square and handsome, softened by the boyish openness of his dark eyes. Those eyes betrayed every flicker of emotion, as though they had never learned the art of disguise.

He was arresting, yet genuine. Charming, yet utterly candid. And what made him all the more dangerous to Carmen's composure was the sense that he had no idea how attractive he truly was.

Carmen tilted her head, the faintest smile tugging at her lips.

"I'm only dangerous to those who mistake silence for obedience," she said, her voice low and amused, like a secret shared in confidence.

She let the words hang in the air, testing him, the way he had tested her. And when his smile deepened, as though he relished the challenge, she felt a spark leap between them, quick and electric.

Gastón didn't let go of her hand right away, and though the gesture might have been too forward from anyone else, in him it felt disarming rather than presumptuous. It was as if he were testing the weight of her presence, anchoring her name in memory.

"Your eyes," Gastón said, studying her, "you have the most incredible eyes. Full of fire and sadness. Writers, painters, dancers… we are all cursed, *no?* We feel too much. We carry it in our bodies until we explode it into the world. *Boom*." He flung his free hand outward as if releasing sparks into the air.

Carmen laughed, startled by the sheer audacity of him.

It wasn't a performance meant to impress her; it was who he was. He spoke with every word unfiltered, delivered as if the world were a sketchbook and conversation was just another brushstroke.

He leaned closer, lowering his voice as if confessing a secret. "Cursed or not, it is the only way to live. Otherwise, *pfft*"—he made a dismissive gesture, tossing his head so that a curl of hair tumbled across his forehead—"one dies long before the body does. Don't you agree?"

The room around them hummed with low conversation, clinking glasses, the scratch of a match striking a cigarette. Yet Carmen felt oddly suspended, as though she and Gastón spoke in a different register, one just out of tune with the rest of the café.

Gastón was alive in a way that made the air itself vibrate, and unlike Francisco, there was no carefulness in him, no guarded attempt to conceal his truth.

Before Carmen could reply, Gastón snatched a napkin from the table and a bit of charcoal from his coat pocket. "Don't move," he ordered, grinning like a boy at play. "I must capture the *dangerous Carmen* before she disappears again."

He began sketching her face with quick, feverish strokes. His hair fell into his eyes as he drew, smudging his fingers until they were blackened. Then he shoved the napkin toward her, a half-formed portrait, wild and alive with lines. "*Voilà!* You see? You are impossible. Already escaping me."

Carmen laughed despite herself, shaking her head. He was unlike anyone she had ever met. Impulsive, irreverent, as though the rules of the world did not apply to him.

Where Francisco had been commanding, Gastón was unstudied. Francisco's presence had always filled a room with certainty, but there had always been a guardedness beneath it, a shadow that suggested he was trying to keep parts of himself hidden.

Careful, always careful. As though he were erasing his own past with every step forward.

Gastón was the opposite: unruly, uncontained, spilling over the edges of himself as though life were too small to hold him.

He had a very Parisian way of saying exactly what he meant, his candor cutting through pretense like a blade through silk.

To Carmen, it was startling, almost intoxicating. Here was a man who carried no masks, no whispered insinuations, no careful diplomacy. Only honesty, bright and unflinching.

And perhaps that was why, in Gastón's presence, the weight of her past seemed to slip away.

He knew nothing of the stories that trailed her like smoke, nothing of Francisco, or her mother, or the betrayal of her own community. Around him, she was simply Carmen; no explanations, no apologies, no shame.

For once, she was not someone's wayward daughter, nor Francisco's scandal.

In that crowded café, with this mercurial Frenchman who looked at her as if she were the most fascinating thing in Montevideo, she was simply what she had always longed to be: an artist among artists.

Gastón leaned across the table, lowering his voice into something conspiratorial. "Do you know what I think?" His eyes glinted, boyish and dark, almost fevered with mischief.

"What?" Carmen asked, tilting her head, leaning in without realizing her guard was loosening in spite of herself.

"Montevideo is a city of locked doors. But you," he tapped her hand, leaving a smear of charcoal across her skin, "you are the key. I can tell. Keys always look restless."

She laughed, glancing at the smudge he'd left behind, as though he had branded her in some secret language. "Restless?" she teased. "And what does a key unlock, *monsieur*?"

"Everything," Gastón said without hesitation, his grin reckless. "Doors, hearts, cages…even heaven itself, if you dared. A woman like you could walk right up to the gates and God would have no choice but to let you in."

Carmen arched an eyebrow, amused. "Careful. You'll have me accused of blasphemy, and it wouldn't be the first time."

"Bah!" Gastón waved his hand dramatically. "Blasphemy is just another word for freedom. Besides, if God disapproves, He should learn to paint. Then perhaps He'd understand."

Carmen shook her head, laughing, unable to help herself. "You are impossible."

"Good," he shot back, his voice low, dark eyes gleaming. "Impossible is the only interesting thing to be."

Her pulse quickened. Gastón spoke in sparks, in laughter, in wild, unfiltered fragments that demanded no defense.

He left her no space to retreat behind silence, no time to measure the propriety of her words. He pulled her forward, out of herself, into something alive.

"Tell me, dangerous Carmen," he pressed, leaning closer, close enough that she could smell the faint trace of turpentine clinging to his shirt. "When you write, do you write to unlock yourself, or to lock everyone else out?"

The question startled her, too intimate, too precise. But she smiled, refusing to give him the satisfaction of rattling her completely. "Maybe both," she said slowly. "It depends who's knocking."

"Then I will knock." His words came like a challenge, but his smile was boyish, almost tender beneath the mischief.

Carmen shook her head, smiling despite herself. No one in Montevideo spoke this way. Gastón spoke as if life were a game to be played, a secret to be shouted, a fleeting spark to be caught before it disappeared.

And for the first time in a long time, she wanted to play along.

They lingered over the table as the café thinned, their voices threading between the clatter of cups and the low murmur of other conversations.

Gastón sketched her again and again—on napkins, scraps of paper, even the back of his own sleeve—each drawing more careless than the last, each one alive with a fevered energy.

Carmen laughed at his exaggerations, but each time he slid the sketch toward her, she felt as though he had stolen something private and set it down in lines of charcoal for the world to see.

When at last she rose, shawl pulled close around her shoulders, he caught her hand one final time. His fingers were smudged with black, his touch warm and unhesitating. "Do not vanish," he said softly, his eyes holding hers with an intensity that startled her.

Carmen tried to laugh, to brush it off. "I'm not so easy to lose."

But Gastón only smiled, boyish and unguarded, as though he already knew something she had yet to admit. "Good. Then I will find you."

She stepped out into the night, the lamps spilling golden light across the cobblestones. Behind her, the café door shut with a thud, but his presence clung to her like smoke, like a song half-remembered. Every careless laugh, every outrageous word still echoed in her ears.

And as she walked into the darkened streets of Montevideo, she knew she would see him again. She wanted to.

Perhaps she had already decided she wouldn't resist.

Chapter 35

The Roaring Twenties arrived, and with them, a city transformed. Montevideo shook off the shadows of war and plague and stepped into a new rhythm—faster, bolder, unashamed.

Jazz mingled with tango in the cafés, hemlines crept higher, and young women dared to bob their hair and laugh too loudly in public. The old ideals of restraint and silence gave way to something more electric, a hunger for life that pulsed through every street.

For Carmen, the twenties arrived like a long exhale after years of holding her breath. The suffocating ideals of the pre-war era began to loosen their grip, and with the decade's first stirrings came a new sense of possibility.

The city was shifting, pulsing with change—and she felt herself shifting too.

When an editor from El Espejo Azul offered her a regular column in *Imparcial: diario independiente de la tarde*, Carmen stepped into a freedom she had long craved. She was a published author at last, and she could give herself wholly to her craft, letting her words move beyond the margins of her notebooks and into the beating heart of the city.

She spent long days writing—essays, stories, poems—and long nights in the company of painters, musicians, and actors who, like her, were determined to push against the boundaries of the old world.

At *El Espejo Azul* and in smoky cafés, ideas sparked and collided, growing into something neither private nor safe, but daring and alive.

For the first time, Carmen felt not like an outsider clawing for a place at the table, but like a voice among voices, a part of a movement bigger than herself.

The current of ideas, laughter, and passion carried her as if she had always belonged there.

And in that warmth, in the freedom of being seen and heard without censure, another thought stirred, one she had long pushed aside.

For the first time in years, the thought of love rose quietly to the surface, fragile but alive, like a bloom breaking through forgotten soil.

Her gaze drifted to Gastón beside her, his laughter ringing above the din, and she felt a spark of something fragile but undeniable.

What had begun as long afternoons of shared conversation, soon blossomed into something deeper, as Carmen and Gastón's friendship grew into a connection that pulsed far beyond the salons and cafés of Montevideo.

Their bond was not built on spectacle, but on the quiet certainty that they understood one another, each carrying wounds and dreams that the other could hold without judgment.

Together they left the city behind for Piriápolis, settling into the little whitewashed cottage Carmen had once retreated to in lonelier times.

Now it brimmed with life. Windows were thrown open to the sea breeze, canvases leaned against the walls, and the table was always set for more guests than it could comfortably hold.

Work and life folded easily into one another, dissolving the line between creation and companionship. Gastón's brushes and Carmen's notebooks often mingled on the same surface, their days punctuated by bursts of inspiration and evenings of celebration.

They hosted dinners that spilled late into the night, where wine loosened tongues and spirited debates about art, literature, and philosophy rose and fell like music.

In time, the cottage became more than a home, it was a refuge, a gathering place, a heartbeat for their circle of artists and dreamers.

Friends and colleagues alike crossed its threshold not just to share food and drink, but to be part of something larger: a space where ideas flourished freely, and where Carmen, at last, felt utterly alive.

When the last of their friends had drifted out into the night, the cottage grew quiet except for the restless hum of the cicadas outside.

Empty wine bottles gleamed in the candlelight, crumbs scattered across the table, as though the echoes of laughter still lingered in the air.

Carmen slipped off her shoes and moved into the small adjoining room, where Gastón had set up his easel by the window. The breeze stirred the curtains, carrying with it the salt and warmth of summer.

He was waiting for her there, palette in hand, his eyes steady and soft. "Stay just as you are," he murmured, as though speaking to a muse rather than a lover.

With only the flickering lamplight for company, Carmen let her dress fall to the floor, pooling at her feet. She held herself still, not with shame, but with a quiet defiance, the same defiance that had carried her through rejection, through grief, through the silencing of her city. To sit naked before Gastón was not surrender; it was reclamation.

He studied her with reverence, not hunger, his brush moving in deliberate strokes across the canvas. Outside, the breeze rustled in rhythm with his brushstrokes, as if nature itself kept time with the creation unfolding in the little cottage.

Carmen's gaze drifted to the half-finished canvas where her body began to take form: lines and color, yes, but also strength, softness, truth.

"Do you like what you see?" Gastón asked quietly, not looking up from his work.

Her lips curved into the faintest smile. "For the first time in my life," she whispered, "I do."

Gastón set his brush down for a moment, tilting his head as he studied her in the wavering lamplight. "Carmen," he said quietly, almost absently, as though the thought had slipped from him unplanned, "how did you end up here, in this little cottage in the countryside? Alone, before I came?"

The question landed like a stone in her chest. Memories pressed at the edges of her mind: nights of grief, when silence had been her only companion. She felt the words rising, bitter and heavy, but she could not bring herself to offer them.

Instead, she arched her back slightly, the curve of her body catching the candlelight. A faint, knowing smile played across her lips as she leaned toward him, her voice dropping to a low murmur. "Do you really want stories tonight?" Her hand slipped to the collar of his shirt, tugging him closer. "Or something sweeter?"

His breath hitched, the question dissolving on his lips as she pressed against him, guiding his hands away from the canvas. As Gastón's question dissolved beneath her touch, Carmen felt the familiar rhythm take over: the tilt of her head, the graze of her lips against his ear, the heat of her body pulling his closer. It was a role she knew well, one she had learned along the way: how to distract, how to redirect, how to keep him from pressing too hard against her softest places.

Seduction became effortless, almost instinctive, like slipping into a well-worn costume. When she was desired, she was untouchable. When his breath quickened against her skin, he could not ask about the past, nor prod at wounds she had no wish to reopen.

She could give him passion, and in return, he would not demand confession.

The half-finished painting stood forgotten by the window as Carmen drew him into her, covering silence and sorrow alike with heat, with touch, with the practiced certainty that she knew how to keep the past at bay, at least for tonight.

But as his hands moved over her body, another truth stirred uneasily within her chest. For all its power, this shield of hers was also a prison. It kept the questions at bay, but it also kept her hidden.

Gastón saw her beauty, her allure, but not the ache she carried, not the grief that still haunted the corners of the little white cottage. And wasn't that what she feared most? To be seen too clearly?

She closed her eyes, clinging to the fire of the moment, to the way it silenced everything else. Yet even in the intensity of his embrace, a voice deep inside whispered that she was not escaping at all, only postponing.

Later, when the rush of heat had ebbed, the room settled into stillness. The candle burned low, its wax pooling along the brass holder, and the night breeze carried the faint sound of crickets chirping. Gastón lay beside her on the rumpled coverlet, his arm draped across her waist, his fingers tracing idle patterns along her skin.

"You're incredible, Carmen," he murmured, his voice thick with drowsy warmth. "The world has no idea what it's been given in you."

She turned her face away, staring at the shadows trembling along the cottage wall. The words should have filled her, but instead they pressed against the hollow place she carried deep inside.

He didn't know. He couldn't know. He saw her passion, her laughter, her brilliance in the moment, but not the grief that had driven her here, not the wounds that still ached like deep bruises.

Carmen forced a small smile, running her hand along his chest. "You make me sound like a mystery," she teased softly.

"You are," he said, pressing a kiss to her temple. "And I want to spend the rest of my life discovering you."

The tenderness in his tone caught her off guard. Her chest tightened, her throat thick. She wished she could give him the whole of her—every truth, every fracture, every shadow—but she couldn't bring herself to open that door. Not yet. Perhaps not ever.

So she kissed him instead, gentle and lingering, letting silence take the place of the words she couldn't speak.

And as Gastón drifted toward sleep, Carmen lay awake in the dark, wrestling with the secret ache that passion could only ever quiet, never erase.

Quietly, she slipped from the bed, pulled her shawl around her shoulders, and settled at the small writing desk by the window. The air smelled of salt and turpentine, remnants of their evening, the unfinished canvas still waiting on the easel.

She opened her notebook, the familiar scratch of pen against paper steadying her. At first the words stumbled, hesitant, but soon they poured forth:

I give him my body so I do not have to give him my past. He sees fire and thinks it light, but he does not see the ashes it hides. I let him discover the surface, the curve, the laugh, the touch, because to uncover the rest would be to risk breaking what we have. Desire shields me, but it also binds me. How long can love survive if it knows only half the truth?

She stopped, staring at the ink as it bled through the page. Her chest felt lighter for having put the ache into words, yet heavier knowing the truth of them.

Behind her, Gastón stirred, murmuring her name in his sleep. Carmen closed the notebook gently, hiding the words away before he could wake.

It was easier to be his muse than to be fully known.

Weeks blurred into months, each day at the cottage steeped in sunlight, laughter, and the constant hum of creation. Gastón painted feverishly, his canvases alive with color and form, while Carmen filled notebook after notebook with stories, essays, and fragments of verse. Together, they hosted friends, walked the shore at dusk, and built a life that seemed, to all who looked upon it, idyllic.

When Gastón asked her to marry him, it was not with spectacle or grand flourish, but in the intimacy of their home. One evening, as the lamplight flickered against the walls, he took her hand in his, his eyes clear and earnest.

"Carmen," he said softly, "you are my anchor, my muse, my home. Share the rest of your life with me."

The words filled the room with a warmth she could not deny. And yet, beneath that warmth, a shadow lingered. She thought of Francisco, of the passion and ruin he had left in his wake. She thought of her mother, gone now, her disapproval echoing still in memory. And she thought of the parts of herself she had never given away, the parts she kept buried in the pages of her notebooks.

Gastón did not pierce her soul the way Francisco once had, yet his love was steady, unwavering. He wanted her not for what she might become, but for who she already was. He asked for no transformation, no compromise. In his presence, there was no demand, only acceptance. Their lives had braided together with ease, the quiet comfort of companionship woven into each passing day.

Carmen smiled, her throat tightening. She said yes.

Gastón pulled her into his arms, his joy spilling out in laughter and kisses. To him, it was a promise fulfilled, a future secured. To Carmen, it was both gift and compromise, a vow she wanted to believe in, even as she knew she could never give him the whole of her heart.

That night, while Gastón celebrated with wine and plans, Carmen slipped away to her desk. In the quiet, she opened her notebook and wrote a single line:

I will be his wife, but part of me will always belong to the silence.

She stared at the words until the ink seeped into the paper, then closed the book and pressed her hand against its cover, as though sealing away the truth she could never speak aloud.

Gastón's laughter still drifted faintly from the other room, warm and full of hope.

Carmen leaned back in her chair, letting her gaze drift past the lamplight to the dark window beyond. The wind whispered through the sierras, low and eternal, a sound older than any promise. There was solace in it, the reminder that long after vows were spoken, long after her words turned to dust, the hills would remain. Steadfast. Unmoved.

And so would she.

For in her heart she knew: whatever future awaited her, whatever ring she might wear, she would always belong first to herself.

Chapter 36

The days in Piriápolis slipped by with an ease Carmen had never known. She and Gastón were married at last. The ceremony was a simple civil ceremony, but the vows they exchanged carried a weight that lingered.

In the stillness that followed, Carmen found herself steadied by the quiet certainty of their life together in ways she hadn't expected.

She found herself thinking less of what had been lost and more of what might yet be built: the little cottage alive with laughter, evenings of wine and music, the thought of a family someday. For once, the past seemed to release its grip.

But peace, she had learned, was a fragile thing.

The telephone rang late one afternoon, its shrill cry cutting through the cottage like a blade. Carmen frowned, wiping her ink-stained hands on her handkerchief as she rose from her desk. Calls were rare, and rarer still when the hour was so still.

As she lifted the receiver, she almost regretted ever having the thing installed. The cottage had once been a sanctuary from interruptions, now even silence could be broken.

"Hello," she said into the receiver.

On the other end of the line, there was a pause—brief but heavy—before a voice came through the crackling static. Deep. Familiar. Impossible.

"Hello, Carmen."

Her breath caught. The sound jolted through her veins, collapsing the years between them into nothing. For an instant she wondered if her mind was playing tricks, conjuring ghosts. But then it came again, steady and undeniable.

"Are you there?"

Her throat tightened around his name. "*Francisco?*" she whispered, scarcely believing it.

"Yes," he said, his tone weighted with something she couldn't quite read. "It's me. I know it's been a long time…"

Silence stretched, broken only by the faint crackle of the line—and from the other room, the quiet, rhythmic sweep of Gastón's brush against canvas.

Carmen's pulse quickened. A thousand questions crowded her mind, but none would form on her tongue. All she could do was clutch the phone to her ear, her breath shallow, as if bracing for whatever might come next.

"I don't know why I waited this long to call. Perhaps because…" he went on, words tumbling out between the static, "I didn't know if I had the right. But the truth is, I've been thinking of you…more often than I should admit."

Her grip on the receiver tightened, but still she said nothing. She pressed her free hand against the desk, steadying herself. From the next room, she heard Gastón humming absently, the faint sound of a tango song playing over the radio, sounds of the life she had built, fragile and real.

Francisco's breath crackled faintly across the line. "I need to see you, Carmen. Just once. There are things I cannot say here, things I should have said long ago."

His words struck her like a blow, sharp and impossible to ignore.

Carmen swallowed hard, her voice unsteady when it finally emerged. "Francisco, you can't just call here after all this time, out of the blue, like nothing happened."

The pause that followed was heavy, the static on the line filling it like a veil.

"I know," he said at last, his tone subdued. "I don't expect you to forget. I don't expect you to forgive. But the truth is, Carmen, I don't know how many years I've got left, and I can't just leave things as they are." He drew in a breath, audible even through the crackle.

Carmen closed her eyes, her mind torn between past and present. From the other room came the soft scrape of Gastón's chair, the brush whispering across canvas.

She pressed the receiver tighter to her ear, her breath unsteady. "Francisco…" Her voice faltered, then hardened with quiet resolve. "It's too late for this."

For a moment, nothing but static filled the line. Then his voice returned, lower, laced with something between sorrow and defiance. "Perhaps for forgiveness. But not for truth."

Her chest tightened. She had no answer. The weight of the years lay between them, heavy as stone.

Francisco's voice cut back through, lower now, almost pleading. "All I ask is for one meeting, Carmen. Just one. Then you'll never have to hear from me again, if that's what you want. But I can't just let the years end with silence."

Carmen's heart clenched. A thousand memories pressed in, jostling against the fragile peace she had built. Part of her longed for closure, for an end to the questions that still haunted her in quiet hours. But another part recoiled, terrified of reopening wounds that had only just begun to scar.

She drew in a sharp breath. "Francisco… you don't know what you're asking," she said, her voice low, unsteady. "I have a life now. A different life. Let's leave the past where it belongs…in the past."

Her words hung there, firmer than she felt inside. The silence on the line stretched, broken only by the faint crackle of static. For a moment she thought—hoped—he might relent.

But then Francisco's voice returned, softer, steady. "Some things refuse to stay buried, Carmen. You and I both know that."

Her fingers tightened around the receiver, her silence stretching until it felt like the whole world hung in the balance. Finally, against the warning in her chest, she exhaled.

"One meeting," she said at last, each word heavy, reluctant. "That's all I can give you. Nothing more."

On the other end of the line, she heard his exhale, ragged with relief. "That's all I ask," he said softly. Tomorrow afternoon. Three o'clock. There's a café in la Ciudad Vieja, on the corner of Sarandí and Ituzaingó. Quiet, discreet. Will you meet me there?"

Carmen closed her eyes, cradling the phone to her ear. The old streets of the Ciudad Vieja rose unbidden in her mind: the crumbling façades, the shadows cast by narrow alleys, the weight of history in every stone.

"Yes," she whispered, though the word tasted of both dread and inevitability.

"Thank you, Carmen," Francisco murmured. "Until tomorrow, then."

The line clicked, leaving her alone in the silence of the cottage, her heart pounding with the knowledge that by this time tomorrow, she would be face to face with the man she had sworn never to see again.

Carmen lowered the receiver, her hand trembling as it met the cradle. The faint crackle of the line died away, leaving only silence, and the uneasy thrum of her heart, caught between past and present.

Their rendezvous was set in a quaint café tucked away in a quiet corner of the city. As she approached the entrance, her heart fluttered nervously in her chest, unsure of what awaited her in this reunion with her past.

She pushed open the door, and the warm scent of coffee and anise met her at once. The room was dim, the walls lined with shelves of old bottles and tarnished mirrors, a space where voices seemed to soften on instinct.

And there he was.

Francisco sat at a corner table, back to the wall, hat resting on the chair beside him. His frame was leaner now, his hair streaked with more silver, but his presence had not diminished; if anything, it had sharpened with age. He rose as she entered, his dark eyes fixing on her with that same unsettling intensity she remembered.

He rose from his seat as she approached, his eyes reflecting a mixture of emotions: sadness, regret, and perhaps a hint of hope.

Her breath tightened in her chest, but she crossed the floor with measured steps until she stood before him.

For a long moment they simply looked at one another, neither speaking, the air thick with unspoken words and memories.

Then, at last, Francisco inclined his head, his voice carrying low across the space. "Carmen."

Her name, spoken by him after all this time, landed in her chest like a stone thrown into still water. She drew in a steadying breath, forcing her feet to carry her forward until she stood before him, every step a mix of dread and inevitability.

"Francisco," she managed, her tone cautious, almost guarded. "Five years is a long time."

A faint smile touched his lips, though his eyes held something darker. "Too long."

He gestured to the chair across from him, and as she sat, the clink of porcelain and the faint hiss of the espresso machine filled the silence between them. As they settled into their seats, there was a moment of quiet between them, the weight of their shared history hanging in the air.

"Thank you for meeting me, Carmen," Francisco said, his voice soft, threaded with a sadness that seemed to echo the years between them. "It's good to see you."

She gave the smallest of smiles, though uncertainty lingered in her eyes. "Yes… it's unexpected, to say the least. I really thought I'd never see you again."

Francisco inclined his head, his expression somber. "I heard you were married," he said gently. "I want you to know that I'm truly glad for you. You deserve all the happiness in the world."

"Thank you," she murmured, her voice little more than a whisper. After a beat, she added, forcing a brittle smile that betrayed her contempt. "I hope things are well with you and your marriage."

Silence followed, dense and unyielding, as their eyes met. A quiet acknowledgement passed between them, a mutual understanding of the complexities of their past, the weight of unspoken words hanging heavy in the air.

The waiter set down two small cups of coffee, their steam rising between them like a fragile veil. Neither reached for them right away.

Carmen folded her hands in her lap, her back straight, her expression carefully composed. "You said there were things you needed to explain," she said at last. Her voice was calm, but each word seemed weighed before it left her mouth.

Francisco leaned back slightly, studying her face as though reacquainting himself with its lines. "Five years is a long time," he murmured. "Long enough for truths to sour into stories… and for stories to harden into judgments."

Her gaze flickered, sharp but steady. "And which am I supposed to believe? The truth? The stories? Or the silence you left behind?"

He exhaled through his nose, not defensive but resigned. "I won't pretend silence wasn't a choice. It was. At the time, I told myself it was necessary."

"Necessary," she echoed, tasting the word with bitterness. "That's a convenient word for abandonment."

The words landed between them with quiet finality. Francisco didn't flinch, but his eyes lowered briefly, as though acknowledging a blow he knew he had earned. He reached for his cup then, more to steady his hand than to drink, and said quietly, "I never stopped thinking of you, Carmen. But what I carried… I couldn't bring it to your door."

She pressed her lips together, the ache in her chest growing sharper. "And yet here you are now."

Francisco's dark eyes lingered on her, heavy with unspoken weight. When he finally spoke, his voice was quiet, stripped of its usual authority. "Carmen... I asked you here because I owe you something I should have given long ago. An apology." He drew in a breath, meeting her gaze with a sincerity that caught her off guard. "For what happened between us. For the pain I caused. I made mistakes, and I carry them still. For that, I am truly sorry."

Her lips parted, her voice wavering when it came. "Francisco... I appreciate your apology," she said softly, shaking her head as though trying to steady herself. "But it's done. It's past."

He leaned forward, urgency in his eyes. "No. You need to understand. I should have been honest with you from the beginning. About my intentions. About the battles I was fighting."

She said nothing, only watched him, her gaze steady, unreadable.

He sighed, his shoulders slumping as though the admission itself cost him. "After the scandal with the church, I lost nearly everything. Investors pulled away, and I was standing at the edge of complete ruin. I couldn't bear to pull you down with me. And instead of telling you the truth, I thought I was protecting you. But in doing so..." He paused, his jaw tight, then shook his head. "I only hurt you more."

His voice lowered, threaded with a sadness she had never heard in him before. "I kept you away from my family for a reason. My son, Pancho...he's ruthless, violent, hungry for power. He would have blamed you, seen you as an obstacle. And obstacles, to him, are crushed."

Carmen drew in a slow breath, her throat tightening. "I understand," she whispered, though her voice trembled with the ache of old wounds. "But why didn't you write? Why didn't you call? You vanished, Francisco. I was left with nothing but silence."

He dropped his gaze, his hands tightening against each other as though he could wring the truth out of them. At last, he exhaled, and the weight in his shoulders seemed to sink him. "Marrying María Emilia was... a business decision. Her family's fortune kept my ventures from collapsing completely. It was the only option I had left at the time, a bargain I felt forced to make." His voice faltered, then steadied again, heavy with regret. "I didn't know how to tell you. So I chose the coward's way. I let you leave. I thought if I just let you go, it would be easier. For both of us."

Carmen let out a breath she hadn't realized she was holding. The words stung, but in some small way, she had always known.

"Easier?" she repeated, her voice barely above a whisper. "Easier for whom, Francisco? Because it wasn't easy for me. I waited. I searched the papers for any mention of you. I convinced myself I meant nothing to you, that I was foolish for believing otherwise."

He sighed, his shoulders sagging. "That's not true. You mean more to me than you know, Carmen, you must know that."

Carmen shook her head, blinking away the heat rising behind her eyes. "Then why didn't you come back?"

Francisco hesitated. "Because I was afraid," he confessed. "Afraid that my world, my name, my past, my enemies, would ruin you. Carmen…you're so young, you deserve to be free to create a beautiful life of your own choosing, not to be dragged down into an old man's problems."

Her chest ached at his words, but she refused to let them sway her.

"Do you have any idea how much worse it was, not knowing? All you did was leave me to wonder," she said, her voice trembling. "To suffer alone, not knowing why. Do you know what it's like to wake up every morning, hoping for a letter that never came? Searching for a face that never appeared? Do you know how many nights I wondered if I had ever meant anything to you? If you had just been playing a game?"

Francisco reached out hesitantly, his fingertips brushing against hers. "Never," he said, his voice hoarse. "It was never a game for me, Carmen. What I've felt for you was always real."

She swallowed hard, her heart warring with her pride and her pain.

"Then why not let me decide for myself what I wanted?" she whispered. "I wasn't afraid. I would have gladly stood and fought beside you."

Francisco gazed at her for a long moment, something unreadable in his gaze. Then, in a voice barely above a murmur, he said, "Because I loved you too much to let you make that mistake, Carmen."

She studied him, searching his face for the truth. The lines of worry, the hint of regret in his dark eyes. He had suffered too.

"Love…true love," Francisco said slowly, his gaze steady, "is freedom. When you come across a rare, magnificent bird, you don't clip its wings and lock it away for your eyes alone. You let it fly—higher, farther—because that's its nature. And you love it all the more for the flight, whether it returns to you or not."

Carmen met his gaze, and for the first time in years, she felt a stillness settle inside her. The pain of their past remained, the uncertainty of the future lingered, but there was a quiet solace in simply letting go. In that moment, she knew that forgiveness was its own kind of freedom; understanding, its own kind of peace.

They sat together in silence, the weight of unspoken years suspended between them. The past would always live within them, but it no longer had to bind them.

"Francisco," she said at last, her voice steady, though tinged with gentleness. "I forgive you. Truly. My life is different now—Gastón and

I are happy. And maybe… maybe things happened the way they were supposed to."

She released a slow breath, her heart lighter than it had felt in years. This was not a reunion, nor the rekindling of an old fire. It was something quieter, humbler: the recognition that what they once shared had mattered, that it had shaped them both, even if only for a season.

Carmen understood then that love—real love—was never about possession or sacrifice. It was about trust. About choice. And the choice she carried forward was her own.

Francisco's gaze softened, the tension in his shoulders easing just slightly. "I'm glad, Carmen," he said quietly. "It means more than you know to hear that you've found your happiness. You truly deserve nothing less."

He hesitated, then added, almost reluctantly, "That's why I'd like to present you with a wedding gift, in celebration of your new happiness."

Carmen frowned, wary. "A gift?"

His lips curved faintly, but it wasn't quite a smile. "I've commissioned a house. In Montevideo. For you and your husband." He let the words linger. "It will be yours when it's finished. Solid, beautiful. A place worthy of you."

Carmen's breath caught. "Francisco…" Her composure slipped, the sheer enormity of it pressing down on her. "I can't. It's too much."

He shook his head. "It's all I have left to give. I know I can't undo the past—or buy forgiveness with stone and mortar. But I can give you this. A place that's yours. A place to live, to write, to dream, without fear of it ever being taken from you."

Her eyes stung, though she forced the tears back. "I don't even know what to say," she whispered. After a pause, she added, almost to herself, "What will I tell Gastón?"

A trace of a smile touched his face. "Tell him it is a gift from your old friend Francisco Piria. A toast to the felicity and prosperity of your new marriage. Nothing more."

Carmen nodded slowly, her throat tight. "This is… generous beyond words. Thank you so much, Francisco."

For the first time since they'd sat down, the silence between them felt different—less suffocating, edged with a fragile kind of peace, though still heavy with all that could never be reclaimed.

Francisco inclined his head, his eyes softening. "You're more than welcome, Carmen. I know you'll want to speak with your husband first. My attorneys will be in touch when the time is right." Rising from the table, he offered her one last steady look, a faint smile that carried both farewell and release.

They parted quietly, no dramatic words, no lingering embrace, just the solemn acknowledgment of what once was, and what now could never be.

Stepping out of the café into the late afternoon light, Carmen drew a long breath. She felt lighter, as though some long-shadowed weight had finally eased. She was grateful—for closure, for the chance to move forward with her marriage, for the peace that came with letting go.

And yet, beneath that gratitude, a quiet ache remained. She knew she would always hold a place for Francisco in her heart, not as the man he might have been, but as the echo of a love that had shaped her, left its mark, and made her who she was.

But far out across the Río de la Plata, beyond the calm surface glittering in the light, dark clouds were already gathering. The wind carried a faint, briny edge, and gulls wheeled low over the water as if uneasy. A storm was coming, one that would not be so easily weathered.

Chapter 37

The storm came without mercy.

In the early hours of August 23, 1923, Montevideo was swallowed by *El Temporal*—the Río de la Plata, restless and swollen, rose up against the city like a beast unchained. Waves hurled themselves over the *rambla*, smashing against stone and dragging whole sections of the promenade into the gray, foaming water.

The wind howled through the streets, ripping tiles from rooftops and bending trees until they splintered. Windows rattled, doors shuddered on their hinges, and families huddled in darkness as the city trembled under the force of rain and sea.

By daylight, chaos reigned. Fishing boats lay shattered along the shore, tossed like toys by the waves. The port groaned with wreckage; carts overturned in the flooded streets. Whole neighborhoods were left in ruins, their houses drowned in mud and saltwater.

Montevideo had weathered storms before, but never one so merciless, never one that left the city so utterly broken in its wake.

From the sierras of Piriápolis, Carmen first heard the storm as a low, endless roar rolling in from the Atlantic. By the time news reached her, carried by shaken travelers and torn newspapers, Montevideo had been reduced to chaos.

Barrio Sur is gone, they whispered. Swept beneath the tide.

Her stomach twisted as she read the reports—entire blocks reduced to wreckage, boats piled like kindling against the seawall, homes swallowed whole. The streets where she had once played, the plazas where music spilled into the night—all of it had been taken by the water.

Carmen gripped the paper with trembling hands. The words swam before her eyes, each line another wound reopened.

She pressed the paper flat on the table, her breath shallow, her heart pounding with a grief so sharp it was almost disbelief. Barrio Sur was no longer a place she could return to, not even in memory.

Her thoughts raced. *Rafael. Nico. Tía. The cousins.* Were they alive, or had the water swallowed them too? The paper gave her no answers, only vague reports and numbers that turned lives into statistics. The telephone lines had been dead for days, the silence on the wires only feeding her dread.

She pushed back from the table, the decision already made. She couldn't sit in Piriápolis, waiting for scraps of news. She had to see for herself, to walk those streets, to find their faces among the living—or not at all.

Once the railways were cleared, three days later, she boarded the early train, her heart heavy as the black smoke trailed behind them toward Montevideo. The carriage rattled and swayed, crowded with weary faces, men clutching tools, women holding children close, all drawn back to the city by the same need: to know what had survived, and what had not.

When she arrived, the air itself seemed to carry the storm's memory—damp, raw, and tinged with salt. Streets were still slick with mud. The smell of brine and broken wood hung over everything. Soldiers and policemen patrolled the port, directing carts piled with rubble. Families picked through what remained of their homes, their movements slow, stunned.

She made her way south, each step harder than the last, until the familiar streets of Barrio Sur opened before her. Only, they were no longer streets, just fractured stones and gaping emptiness. Roof tiles and beams jutted from the muck, tangled with seaweed. A wall leaned drunkenly where a row of houses had once stood, its plaster smeared with silt.

As she turned a corner, her heart stopped. There, where her mother's narrow house had once clung stubbornly to the block…was nothing. She staggered forward, her shawl slipping from her shoulders, and pressed a trembling hand to her mouth.

Her mother's house was gone. Not even a doorway remained, only a scatter of bricks sinking into mud, washed clean of the life they had once contained. Carmen stood frozen, her breath shallow, staring at the place that had once held her childhood.

For years she had carried her mother's absence, that hard, unresolved ache. Now even the walls that had held their quarrels, their silences, their fleeting moments of tenderness, were gone. Erased, as if they had never stood at all.

Now there was nothing but wreckage and sea.

Her throat tightened, and she wrapped her shawl tighter around her shoulders as if to hold herself together. For the first time, she understood with piercing clarity: the storm had not just taken the *barrio*, it had taken the last trace of her mother's presence on this earth.

A sound rose in her throat, neither sob nor cry, but the hollow gasp of someone who had lost the last tether to a world that no longer existed.

Carmen sank down onto a half-toppled step, her shoes sinking into mud. Around her, the shouts of neighbors rose—grief and disbelief mingling with the crash of waves still battering the shore. She buried her face in her hands, letting the tears come. This time, she didn't care who saw her cry.

When at last she pulled herself up from the rubble, Carmen forced her feet to carry her forward. Instinctively, she turned toward Rafael's street, each step a prayer that some part of her world had survived the storm's wrath.

The further inland she walked, the less ruin she saw. Fallen branches littered the streets, roofs bore scars, windows gaped open where glass had been shattered, but the bones of the houses still stood. The devastation of the shore gave way to damage that was bruising, not fatal.

Her aunt's house, tucked behind a line of broad, wind-battered trees, was still standing. Its shutters were askew, and the garden lay in tatters, but the walls were solid, upright. Relief flooded through her as she lifted the latch and stepped into the courtyard.

Inside, Rafael was hauling buckets of water across the tiled floor, sweeping out the mud that had seeped in during the storm. He looked up at her entrance, his face drawn with exhaustion, but when he saw her, his eyes widened with disbelief before softening into relief.

"Carmen," he breathed, setting the bucket down with a splash. He crossed the room in two strides, pulling her into a rough embrace that smelled of damp wood and sweat. "*Gracias a Dios*—you're alright."

Carmen clung to him, her voice breaking. "Everything is gone, Rafa. *Mamá*'s house—it's all gone."

He pulled back just enough to meet her eyes, his own dark with grief. "I know. We've heard. Half the *barrio* is washed into the river." He shook his head slowly, the weight of it pressing into his shoulders. "But we're here, Carmen. We're still standing, thank God."

"Rafa," she asked hesitantly, her voice thin, "what about the others? Marí, Antonio… Nico?"

Rafael rubbed a hand across his brow before answering. "Marí and Antonio are safe. Their house took a beating, but it's standing. They're staying with cousins until the roof is repaired." He paused, his gaze dropping to the floor. "Nico…" His jaw tightened. "Nico's alive, thank God. But, Carmen—the Madreselva…it's gone."

Carmen froze, her breath catching in her throat. "No…" she whispered, shaking her head. "Not *La Madreselva*."

"The storm took it. Walls caved, the floor ripped to pieces. Nothing left but debris and broken bottles washed into the street." His voice wavered with the enormity of it. "They tried to save what he could, but… it's finished. The bar, the music—everything washed away."

Carmen pressed a hand to her mouth, her chest aching. She could see Nico in her mind's eye, his easy smile behind the counter, his dramatic flourishes, the warmth he created within those candlelit walls. To think of it swallowed by the storm was almost unthinkable.

She whispered, half to herself, "Poor Nico…"

Rafael nodded heavily. "He's not himself, Carmen. He's lost. That place was his heart. Without it…" He didn't finish the thought, only stared into the mud-streaked floor as if the silence might spare them both the truth.

Rafael's gaze remained fixed on the muddy floor, as though the words themselves were too heavy to lift. Finally, he spoke again, his voice low.

"It's terrible, Carmen…" Rafael's voice was low, almost hoarse. "La Giralda didn't survive the storm either."

Carmen froze, her breath catching. "No… not La Giralda too."

He gave a heavy nod, his face etched with grief. "The whole corner gave way. Walls crumbled straight into the street. There's nothing left to salvage." His voice cracked, just barely. "All those nights, the music, the food, the laughter…it's all just rubble now."

Carmen closed her eyes, the memories rushing back in vivid fragments. It felt like losing pieces of her own heart. Her mother's house, The Madreselva, La Giralda, places that had been more than buildings, places she had called home, places that had given her belonging, joy, escape—now erased as though they had never existed.

It was almost too much to bear. Memory and rubble collided in her chest, leaving her hollow, aching. Yet she knew she could not turn away. She had to see it for herself, the wreck of the *Madreselva*. The place where she had once found the courage to dance, to write, to defy the narrow mold the world had cast for her.

If it was gone, then she would say goodbye with her own eyes. Only then, perhaps, could she carry its spirit forward within her.

She made her way through the battered streets, following the familiar path toward the corner where the Madreselva had once stood.

When she arrived, her heart stopped. The building was gone— nothing but a heap of broken beams, shattered bottles glinting in the muck, and a gaping void where laughter and music had once spilled into the night.

And there, amid the wreckage, sat Nico.

He was hunched on an overturned crate, a cigarette dangling between his fingers, the smoke rising listlessly in the damp air. His once-proud waistcoat was rumpled and stained, his hair plastered to his forehead. He stared at the ruins as if he were trying to will them back into being.

"Nico," Carmen called softly.

He looked up at her, and for the first time since she had known him, his eyes held no spark. Only emptiness. He gave a bitter laugh, dry and humorless. "*Carmencita,*" he rasped. "Welcome to the graveyard." He gestured broadly to the wreckage around him. "Here lies the Madreselva."

Carmen's throat tightened. She stepped carefully over the rubble until she was close enough to touch him. "I'm so sorry, Nico," she whispered.

Nico took a long drag from his cigarette and exhaled, his gaze fixed on the broken timbers. "*Sorry* doesn't build walls. *Sorry* doesn't pour wine. *Sorry* doesn't bring back the music." He flicked the cigarette into the mud, grinding it out beneath his heel. "It's all gone, Carmen."

Her chest ached at the despair in his voice. She reached for his shoulder, steadying him with the only thing she could offer: her presence. "Not everything," she said softly. "You're still here."

Nico gave a hollow laugh, shaking his head.

"And for what? Without the *Madreselva*, I don't know who I am anymore." He stopped suddenly, his voice low, ragged. "I'm no tailor, no dockhand. All I know is pouring drinks, spinning stories, filling a room with laughter. Who's going to hire a barkeep with nothing to his name but ashes?"

He stood abruptly, pacing the length of the debris-strewn street, his boots splashing in the muck. "Maybe I'll end up on the docks, hauling crates till my back breaks. Or maybe I'll waste away in some sleazy cabaret, serving lecherous drunks."

Carmen watched him, her heart breaking at the sight of him so undone. He had always been the one to lift others, to tease, to charm, to make light of even the darkest corners. But now, stripped of his refuge, he looked like a man with no map, no compass, adrift in the wreckage of his life.

Carmen stood there for a long moment, watching him unravel against the backdrop of the ruins. Her heart ached with every word, every gesture of despair. Finally, she found her voice.

"Nico," she said gently, stepping closer, "listen to me."

He turned toward her, his expression raw, eyes rimmed red with sleeplessness.

"You're not nothing. You're one of the finest bartenders I've ever known—and more than that, you're the soul of every room you walk into. People don't come for the drinks, they come for you. For your laughter, your stories, your warmth." She placed a hand on his arm, firm but kind. "That isn't gone. It never could be."

He let out a bitter breath, his shoulders slumping. "Fine words, *Carmencita*. But words don't pay rent."

She pressed on, refusing to let the darkness close over him. "I know someone who can help. Carlos Bonavita—he manages the Hotel Piriápolis. It's thriving, full of tourists and aristocrats, and they're always looking for good staff. I could speak to him, Nico. I could ask him to give you a position behind the bar."

For the first time, his eyes flickered with something other than despair—uncertain, but not hopeless. "The Hotel Piriápolis..." he murmured, almost to himself. "That's no corner cantina, Carmen. That's a palace."

She smiled faintly. "All the better. A place worthy of you."

Nico's mouth twisted, caught between disbelief and the faintest hint of a smile. "And if he says no?"

Carmen's lips curved, steady and sure. "He won't," she said. "Carlos owes me a couple of favors. He'll listen."

For a moment, Nico just stared at her, as though weighing whether to believe. His shoulders eased a fraction, the despair in his face softening under the flicker of hope she had placed there. He ran a hand through his damp hair and gave a low, shaky laugh.

"*Madre mía, Carmencita…* always turning up with a trick up your sleeve." His eyes dropped back to the wreckage, but now his voice carried a thread of something different; uncertain, fragile, but alive. "Maybe… maybe you're right."

Carmen squeezed his arm gently. "I know I am."

For a long moment, he said nothing, his eyes fixed on the ruins as though he couldn't yet believe her. But when he finally turned to her, a flicker of something fragile, maybe hope, moved behind his tired gaze.

And Carmen, looking past the broken beams and mud-streaked streets, felt the truth of her own words. Montevideo had always been a city of tides; rising, falling, returning stronger. Though the storm had swallowed whole blocks and washed away its music, the day would come when the streets would hum again, when new walls would rise brighter than the old.

The city, like its people, would endure. And in time, it would return, greater than it had ever been.

Chapter 38

Montevideo rose again.

Brick by brick, street by street, the city that had been battered by storms and loss rebuilt itself with a fierceness that mirrored the spirit of its people. The broken walls were mended, new avenues opened, and electric light spilled brighter than before across the cobblestones. Music returned to the plazas, laughter echoed through the cafés, and once more the *milongas* swelled with dancers, as if the city itself had remembered how to breathe.

By 1930, Montevideo no longer felt like a provincial capital on the edge of the Río de la Plata, it felt like the center of the universe. Preparations were underway for the Centennial of Uruguay's Constitution, and with it, the city's grandest undertaking yet: hosting the very first World Cup.

New stadiums rose from the dust, colossal monuments of concrete and ambition. Hotels filled with visitors, boulevards bustled with parades and fireworks, and a heady mix of nationalism and celebration electrified the air. Uruguay was no longer a small republic between two giants, it had placed itself on the world's stage.

For Carmen, the city's transformation was as disorienting as it was dazzling. Montevideo had grown taller, louder, grander than she remembered. Yet beneath the swell of brass bands and banners, she still felt its heartbeat, the resilience of a people who had faced ruin and built something greater in its place.

Of the new infrastructure rising across the country, none loomed more grandly than Francisco Piria's latest venture: the Argentino Hotel in Piriápolis. Conceived with his characteristic audacity, the hotel was to be unlike anything anyone had ever seen, holding rank as the largest hotel in all of South America, an edifice of ambition that seemed to anchor Piriápolis to destiny itself.

Even half-finished, it dwarfed everything around it; the modest cottages, the winding streets, even the sea itself seemed to bow to its enormity.

Carmen could not deny its magnificence. The sheer audacity of it stole her breath, the way Francisco had once more bent the land, and the will of others, to align with the vision in his mind. The Argentino stirred something she could not name: pride in her country, awe at its scale, and yet unease too, a shadow edging her admiration, as if she already sensed this would be Francisco's final *pièce de résistance*.

She lingered on the promenade until the light shifted, the stone glowing gold beneath the sinking sun, before at last turning away, her steps heavy against the familiar path home.

A week later, the post arrived. Among the usual envelopes and notices lay one that felt different, unlike the rest: thick, cream paper bearing an elegant seal embossed with Francisco's distinctive emblem. Carmen's fingers hesitated on the flap, already certain of its contents.

The card inside was thick as a tile, edged in gold. An engraving of the hotel swept across the top—terraces like stacked waves, windows glittering in precise rows, a fountain tossing white water into the summer light.

At the top, in elegant script:

Señor y Señora Berton

You are cordially invited to attend the Grand Opening Luncheon of the Argentino Hotel - Piriápolis, Christmas Eve, 1930

Below, in fine print:

Luncheon will be served in the Great Hall at noon, with orchestra accompaniment and a promenade along the gardens to follow. Dress: Formal Summer Attire.

At the bottom, a flourish of ink not belonging to the printer but unmistakable in its hand:

May this day be yours as much as mine. —F.

Carmen stared at the card, its golden borders catching the light. A Christmas luncheon, ceremonial, glittering with formality, yet the personal note beneath struck with the intimacy of a whisper. She passed it to Gastón, who had just set down his palette knife, the smell of turpentine still clinging to him.

He wiped his fingers on a rag, took the card, and read it without comment. Then he glanced up, one quick look that said he already knew who had sent it.

"Are we going?" he asked simply.

Carmen's eyes lingered on the engraving of the Argentino, the impossible ambition made stone. Her pulse quickened as though the very weight of the invitation pressed into her chest.

"We should," she said quietly, placing the card gently on the table.

Gastón gave a slow nod. "Then we'll go," he said, a note of practicality in his tone. "Looks like you'll need a new dress, and a hat to shade you from the summer sun."

Carmen smiled faintly, though unease trembled beneath it. She folded the invitation back into its envelope and laid it on the table, beside the vase of eucalyptus sprigs. The card was for them both. And yet, the single line of ink made her wonder who, exactly, it was meant for.

Christmas Eve arrived, and the whole town buzzed with anticipation. The streets of Piriápolis, once sleepy and sparse, now pulsed with the clamor of motorcars, the train, and visitors in their finest summer linens. Carmen and Gastón joined the current, walking arm in arm up the wide, freshly paved avenue that led to the hotel.

The Argentino towered above them, dazzling white against the sky, its terraces alive with flags and garlands that rippled in the warm Atlantic breeze. An orchestra spilled notes from the open windows, bright violins mingling with the salt air. Carmen felt her chest tighten as she took it in. So immense, so commanding, it dwarfed the Hotel Piriápolis in its size.

A line of impeccably dressed attendants stood at attention along the grand steps of the Argentino Hotel, their posture straight, their expressions calm and assured. In their pressed white jackets and gleaming shoes, they looked less like staff than part of the architecture itself: polished, deliberate, exacting. Every detail of their uniforms spoke to the hotel's promise of refinement, each crease a quiet declaration of luxury.

As the first guests approached, the formation stirred to life. Smiles bloomed, practiced yet warm, and hands extended in gestures that felt both welcoming and precise. With a graceful nod here, a murmured word there, the staff ushered the arrivals across the threshold, seamlessly directing them through the soaring marble vestibule and into the gilded halls beyond.

Tours unfurled like choreography, silver trays raised and lowered, doors opened at just the right moment, voices low and steady as they revealed glimpses of the Argentino's splendor: the ballroom, the sweeping terraces, the polished dining rooms set for a feast. Every movement was timed to perfection, as though the hotel itself had rehearsed this moment for years, waiting for its grand unveiling.

Inside, the Great Hall glittered with light. Chandeliers spilled brilliance across polished marble floors, while long tables shone with silver and crystal, each surface catching the gleam like water. The air was thick with the mingled scents of roasted meats, citrus, and the briny freshness of fish pulled that morning from the sea.

Servants in immaculate white jackets wove through the crowd with practiced grace, champagne flutes winking on their trays. Every detail announced extravagance: fine linens brought from Italy, silver cutlery wrought in Germany, crystal glassware from Czechoslovakia that shimmered like ice in the sun. Even the furniture, heavy, elegant pieces crafted by Austrian woodworkers, seemed chosen not merely for comfort but to impress upon every guest the weight of permanence and wealth. It was an atmosphere not just of celebration, but of command, an opulence that insisted on being noticed.

Gastón leaned close, whispering with a half-smile, "This is less a luncheon than a coronation."

Carmen gave a faint laugh, though unease threaded beneath it. Around them, dignitaries, journalists, and families from Montevideo mingled, their voices rising in a tide of chatter. Everywhere she turned, the Argentino announced itself—not just a hotel, but a statement.

As they moved further inside, Carmen's gaze swept the room. She felt the press of heat, the hum of excitement, and beneath it all, an undercurrent she could not quite name. For a moment, she thought she glimpsed Francisco across the hall, his figure unmistakable in the crowd, but the sight was gone almost as soon as it appeared.

Gastón touched her arm gently, guiding her toward their table. "Come. Let's see what kind of feast ambition serves."

Carmen managed a small nod, her lips curving though the smile did not quite reach her eyes. Her pulse quickened, an uneasy flutter she could not name, whether awe at the grandeur around her, or dread at what she might yet face. Because somewhere in that vast, opulent room was the woman who now bore Francisco's name, the woman who had stepped into his life at the very moment Carmen had loved him most, when the intensity of it had nearly consumed her. The thought pressed against her chest like a weight, reminding her that even in splendor, some shadows could not be escaped.

Carmen and Gastón were seated near the center of the grand hall, their table offering a commanding view of the festivities. The chandeliers above shimmered like constellations, their light scattering across crystal and polished silver. They exchanged quiet smiles, leaning close as the first course was set before them; delicate hors d'oeuvres of fish and citrus, fragrant with herbs. The room buzzed with anticipation, laughter and clinking glasses weaving into a hum that seemed to pulse with the promise of history in the making.

As the waiters retreated and conversation lulled, Francisco Piria rose from his seat at last. At once, the hall was still. He stood tall, his dark suit gleaming under the lights, pride radiating from him as tangibly as the grandeur of the building itself. And yet, Carmen's eyes caught what others might have missed, a flicker of weariness at the edges of his expression, the faint shadow of years carved into his face. His presence was still formidable, his voice still rich and commanding, but the fire that once consumed him seemed tempered, dimmed by time.

"Ladies and gentlemen, esteemed guests," he began, his words carrying effortlessly through the hall, "today marks a momentous occasion, the grand opening of the *Argentino Hotel*, a vision brought to life through hard work, dedication, and an unwavering commitment to excellence."

He paused, surveying the crowd, letting the weight of his words settle.

"This hotel is more than just a building. It stands as a testament to the spirit of innovation and progress that defines our beloved country. It is a symbol of our nation's hospitality and our commitment to providing the finest accommodations for travelers from near and far."

His gaze swept the room, warm and steady, touching each table as though each guest were a vital part of his triumph.

"I am immensely proud of what we have accomplished here today, and I am deeply grateful to each and every one of you for your support and contributions. Together, we have created something truly remarkable, a place where luxury meets tradition, and where every guest is welcomed with open arms."

He raised his glass in a toast, his voice ringing out with sincerity. "To the *Argentino Hotel*, may it stand as a beacon of hospitality and a testament to the enduring spirit of Uruguay. *Salud!*"

The hall erupted in applause and the rise of countless glasses, the sound like a wave breaking against the marble walls. Carmen raised her own, the taste of champagne sharp on her lips, though her thoughts lingered on the flicker of weariness she had glimpsed in his eyes.

As the applause swelled and glasses clinked, Carmen's gaze swept the glittering hall. For a moment, she let herself be carried by the current of celebration—the music striking up, the waiters pouring fresh champagne, Gastón leaning close with a smile meant to steady her.

And then she saw her.

María Emilia stood near the far end of the room, close to the dais where Francisco had resumed his seat. Draped in a gown of pale silk that shimmered like water, she carried herself with the poise of someone accustomed to being watched.

It was not jealousy that gripped Carmen so much as recognition. Here was the woman who bore Francisco's name, the woman who had stepped into the space Carmen once thought her own. And though the hall brimmed with music and chatter, Carmen felt a silence open inside her, sharp and heavy.

She forced her eyes away, back to Gastón, who lifted his glass again with cheerful abandon. She mirrored him, the bubbles stinging her tongue, while in the corner of her vision María Emilia's presence lingered like a polished blade catching the light.

As the applause faded and the guests returned to their seats, Carmen rose quietly. She murmured something to Gastón about the powder room, and slipped away before he could protest.

The hall gave way to the vast marble lobby, its soaring ceilings painted with frescoes of sea and sky. The light from the chandeliers shimmered across the polished floor, catching on gilded banisters and the great bronze doors. Carmen slowed her steps, letting the hum of the dining room fade behind her.

She paused before a column, fingers grazing the cool stone, and let herself drink in the space. For a moment, she felt the pull of memory— the early days of Piriápolis, when Francisco's dreams seemed impossible yet intoxicating, when she too had believed she might build a world with words as he built with stone.

"Carmen."

His voice cut through the silence. Low, familiar, and closer than she had expected. She turned sharply, her breath catching. Francisco was approaching from the corridor, his dark suit impeccable, his expression carefully composed.

"Francisco…" The name slipped from her in a whisper, unbidden, as if it had been waiting on her tongue all along.

Standing face to face, she saw immediately what the brilliance of the dining hall had masked.

He was not well.

His once-vigorous face had grown hollow, his skin tinged with an unhealthy pallor. The strong planes of his features were etched more deeply than she remembered, each line a map of trials endured, responsibilities carried too long, dreams wrestled into being at great cost. His eyes, once lit with restless fire, now held a shadowed weariness, a vulnerability he could not entirely disguise.

It startled her. This was not the boundless man she had known, the one who had once seemed capable of bending the world to his will. The formidable spirit was still there, but dimmed, tempered by years and burdens that no triumph could erase.

And yet, despite everything, Carmen felt a sudden swell of tenderness. Compassion rose in her chest, unguarded, as though some invisible thread between them still pulsed with life.

Whatever else lay between them, he was part of her story, woven through her joys and her sorrows, and seeing him so diminished reminded her of the bond they had once shared, fragile but indelible.

For an instant neither of them spoke, the sounds of the celebration drifting faintly from beyond the doors. Then he inclined his head, a smile hovering at the edge of his lips.

"I was hoping I might find you," he said quietly. "Just for a moment. Away from the crowd."

Carmen drew in a steadying breath, her voice careful, her expression measured. "Yes…I also wanted to speak to you and offer my congratulations. Francisco, what you've built here is remarkable." She hesitated, her eyes searching his face, unable to ignore the pallor beneath his smile. "I hope you're well," she added, her words carrying a note of genuine concern she hadn't intended to reveal.

Francisco's smile faltered, the pride in his expression shading into something more fragile. "I feel blessed, Carmen," he said at last, his voice low, almost weary. "Though I'd be lying if I didn't wish the years were kinder. Time," he added with a faint chuckle, "is no man's friend."

They stood facing one another in the vast marble lobby, the murmur of the luncheon muffled behind the doors. For a moment, his gaze caught hers with such quiet intensity that it seemed to strip the grandeur from the room, leaving only the two of them.

"It means more than I can say that you came today," he murmured, his tone weighted with sincerity.

Carmen felt her breath catch, her voice softening despite herself. "I always believed in you, Francisco. Despite everything. What you've done here…it's more than legendary. I'm just glad I could be here to see it."

He searched her face, and something wistful stirred in his eyes. "Do you remember the first time I brought you here? To Piriápolis, before any of this?"

Her lips curved in a small, reluctant smile. "Of course I do. I remember thinking it was like stepping into a dream."

Francisco's shoulders eased, a trace of warmth flickering across his features. "That day…it reminded me why I built it at all. Not for monuments, not for glory, but for the chance to see wonder reflected back at me. Through your eyes."

Carmen lowered her gaze, her heart tightening. There was tenderness in his words, but also regret, a truth unspoken, pressing at the edges of the silence between them.

Francisco's voice lowered, as though the walls themselves were not meant to hear. "You know, Carmen… you were more a part of all this than my own children ever were. They see only the stone, the money, the power it might bring. But you—" He paused, his eyes searching hers. "You saw the vision from the very beginning. That first day, when I walked you along these hills, before the foundations were ever laid, you understood. You saw it as I did. Perhaps even more clearly than I could."

His gaze softened, a mixture of pride and sorrow in its depths. "It gave me strength, knowing someone believed in what I dreamed. No one else ever did, not like you. Not with the same heart."

Carmen's chest tightened. The words reached her like a hand across years, across all that had been lost. And for a fleeting moment, she saw him as he had been then, restless, driven, eyes alight with impossible dreams, and herself beside him, young and unguarded, believing too.

Carmen's smile deepened, though it trembled at the edges, her heart swelling with a tenderness she hadn't expected. "That day changed everything for me," she said quietly. Her gaze held his, steady and unflinching. "I'll always be grateful to you for opening that world to me, for showing me beauty and possibility I might never have known without you."

Francisco's expression softened, the pride slipping into something more vulnerable. "No, Carmen," he murmured, his voice carrying the weight of years. "It's I who should thank *you*. Success, wealth, buildings—they're hollow without someone who sees them, truly sees them. And you did. From the very beginning, you understood."

He hesitated, his eyes shadowed with regret. "It should have been you," he said finally, almost to himself. "You've been more to me than you can ever know. Through you I learned to see beauty in the ordinary, to hold fast to small moments, to believe in wonder again. Whatever else I've built, whatever storms I've weathered…you were the light in it, *Carmencita*. And I will carry that with me always."

They shared a moment of quiet reflection, the weight of their shared experiences hanging in the air between them.

Carmen felt a swell of emotion in her chest. In that moment, she realized the depth of their connection, of the way they had influenced each other's lives in profound ways.

They lingered in silence, the weight of years threading between them. Carmen's heart ached with tenderness and sorrow, stirred by the depth of his words.

"I want you to know," Francisco said at last, his voice low but unwavering, "that no matter what happens, I will always be here for you. You can count on me, Carmen, now and always."

He reached for her hand, his touch warm but fragile, and she let it rest in hers. For a moment, the din of the hotel seemed to fall away; there was only his gaze, steady yet shadowed, and the quiet truth neither dared to name.

Gratitude swelled in her chest, mingled with a grief she couldn't explain. For even as he spoke of always, she felt it: the strange, unshakable sense that he was saying goodbye.

And standing there in the golden light of the Argentino's lobby, Carmen understood: whatever time remained, their bond had already outlived circumstance. It was carved into her life, indelible as stone.

But as he released her hand, she knew with a certainty that chilled her: this was the last parting before the true farewell.

Chapter 39

Only three years after the triumphant unveiling of his beloved Argentino Hotel, the news came that shattered Carmen's heart. Francisco Piria was gone.

The words reached her like a blow she could not brace against. For all his weariness, for the shadows she had glimpsed in his eyes that day in the hotel lobby, some part of her had believed he would endure forever; that his restless spirit, so relentless and unyielding, could not simply fade. Yet now the inevitable had come, stark and final.

The newspapers spoke of his empire, of the monuments he left behind: the Argentino, the castle, the avenues of Piriápolis, the grand designs that had reshaped Uruguay's landscape. But to Carmen, the loss was not stone or legacy. It was the silencing of a voice that had once called her into a wider world, the dimming of a fire that had set her own heart alight.

She sat with the paper spread before her, unable to read the words through the blur in her eyes. All she could see was his face in that lobby, the fragile warmth of his smile, the weight in his hand as he pressed it over hers, the sense, unshakable now, that he had already been saying goodbye.

Carmen did not join the crowds who gathered for his funeral. She could not bring herself to stand among dignitaries and strangers, to listen to speeches of empire and legacy as though he had been only stone and wealth. Instead, a few days later, when the town had quieted and the mourners dispersed, she went alone.

The path to the mausoleum was still littered with wilted flowers, their perfume faint beneath the salt wind. The hill rose steeply, and with every step Carmen felt the weight of memory pressing closer. When at last she reached the gates, she paused, her breath shallow, her heart unsteady.

The marble façade loomed before her, cold and immense, yet it was the inscription that caught her eyes:

"I and She"

For decades, people had whispered that he had chosen the words out of arrogance, that Francisco had always put himself first, even here, even in death.

A final mark of ego, they said. Carmen stood in the silence and knew better. They would never know. She alone remembered the truth he had once told her: that he was too superstitious to write *She and I*, unwilling to tempt fate by suggesting his wife would be the first to pass away. He had believed then that he would go first. That he would be the first to depart.

Carmen stepped closer, her fingers brushing the cold marble as though they might warm under her touch. The world around her was hushed, only the distant hiss of the sea and the sigh of the wind through the cypress trees.

She thought of him not as the grand figure of the papers, not as the magnate or the alchemist or the builder of cities, but as the man who had once taken her hand in a crowded lobby, weary yet sincere, and told her she could always count on him. As the man whose fire had lit her own.

"I and She," she whispered, the words trembling on her lips. "And now only she remains."

Tears welled, but she let them fall. In the quiet of that hilltop, with only the stone and the sea to witness her, Carmen said goodbye.

The silence of the mausoleum lingered with her long after she returned home.

That night, she left her lamp burning late, pages open before her but her pen unmoving. The weight of absence pressed too heavily against her chest for words to come.

The telephone rang. Its shrill cry startled her from the quiet, and for a moment she hesitated, as if afraid of what new sorrow it might deliver.

She lifted the receiver.

"Hello?" Carmen's voice was barely a whisper.

"Carmen…it's Carlos Bonavita." The familiar timbre of his voice came through the crackling line, softer than she remembered, weighted with fatigue. "I hope I'm not disturbing you."

Her breath caught, sadness blooming in her chest. "No," she said gently. "Not at all. How are you holding up, Carlos?"

There was a silence, the kind born not of hesitation but of shared sorrow. When he spoke again, his words carried the same heaviness she felt. "It hasn't been easy," he admitted quietly. "For any of us." A pause, then his tone shifted, tender, almost fatherly. "I just wanted to hear your voice, to check on you. I know how hard this must be."

Carmen closed her eyes, her throat tightening at his kindness, at the loneliness beneath it that mirrored her own.

"I was hoping," Carlos added after a moment, his voice steady but gentle, "perhaps you might meet with me tomorrow morning."

There was no pressure in his words, only the quiet strength of someone who needed company as much as he offered it.

Carmen agreed, though her heart carried the weight of anticipation, a mixture of dread and solace in equal measure. Before they said goodbye, the two settled on a time. They would meet the next morning, at the café inside the Hotel Piriápolis.

The next morning dawned with a pale, washed-out light, the kind that made the sea and sky seem almost indistinguishable. Carmen dressed simply, her black shawl drawn tight, and made her way down the familiar road toward the Hotel Piriápolis.

The grand façade loomed as she approached, its white walls softened by the mist. She remembered the first time she had come here, the sense of awe, the promise of escape. Today, the place felt quieter, as though grief itself had settled into its halls.

Carlos was already waiting in the restaurant, seated near the tall windows that looked out toward the gray sweep of the Atlantic. His broad shoulders seemed heavier than she remembered, his once-quick smile subdued. Yet when he saw her, he rose immediately, extending his hand with a warmth that cut through the chill.

"Carmen."

"Carlos," she murmured, her voice low, and took his hand. For a moment, neither of them sat. They simply stood, holding each other's gaze, two people bound by the same loss.

When they did sit, the silence stretched comfortably at first. The waiter brought coffee, its rich scent filling the air, and a plate of warm medialunas, though neither reached for them right away.

"It feels strange, doesn't it?" Carlos said finally, his voice roughened by fatigue. "The world goes on as though nothing has changed. Guests still come and go. The band still plays at night. But for me…" He shook his head. "For me, everything feels emptier."

Carmen's hands tightened around her cup. "Yes," she whispered. "I feel that too. He was…larger than life. And now—" Her voice caught, but Carlos gave a small nod, as if finishing the thought for her.

"Now there's just silence," he said.

For a long while, they sat with that silence, watching the waves crash against the shore below, each of them lost in memory yet strangely comforted by the other's presence.

The clatter of dishes and the low murmur of other patrons faded into the background as Carlos leaned forward, his hands clasped around his coffee cup as though drawing strength from its warmth.

"Thank you for coming, Carmen," he said, his voice steady but touched with fatigue. "I know this isn't easy."

Carmen nodded, her shawl pulled close, the silence between them thick with unspoken grief. "It helps," she admitted softly, "to sit with someone who knew him as I did."

Carlos's gaze lingered on her, a flicker of hesitation in his dark eyes. Then, with a quiet breath, he said, "Carmen, there's something you need to know. Before Francisco passed, he…he took certain legal measures."

Carmen's heart lurched. She leaned in, her pulse quickening, her eyes fixed on his face. "What is it?" she whispered, unable to steady her voice.

Carlos set his cup down with care, as if afraid of shattering the moment. "In his Last Will and Testament," he said slowly, "Francisco claimed *you* as his daughter…"

The words struck her like a bell: sharp, resonant, impossible to ignore. For an instant, she thought she had misheard, but the gravity in Carlos's expression left no room for doubt.

Carmen's breath caught, her chest tightening. "His…*his daughter*?" she repeated, as though tasting the word for the first time.

Carmen's emotions swirled, crashing against one another like waves in a storm. Disbelief, sorrow, gratitude, even a strange sense of betrayal—each rose and fell in her chest as Carlos's words sank in. She gripped the edge of the table as though the weight of it might sweep her away.

Her throat tightened, a lump rising so sharply she could hardly breathe. "But… why? Why would he—"

Carlos reached across, his hand warm and steady against her arm. "I believe he wanted to find a way to ensure you'd be cared for after he was gone," he said softly. "This wasn't just about money, Carmen. It was about recognition. About what you meant to him. You mattered to him…more than you realize."

Carlos gave her a long, searching look, then spoke with quiet finality. "He wanted the world to see what he already knew: that he loved you. And under the law, under the *herederos forzosos* system, you are now his legal heir."

The words rang in her ears, too large to hold.

Carlos continued, his voice careful but firm. "It means your rights surpass even those of a wife. Inheritance flows first to the blood, Carmen. By naming you, he gave you more than acknowledgment. He gave you place. He gave you legacy."

Carmen sat frozen, her breath shallow. The café seemed to tilt around her—the clink of cups, the smell of roasted coffee, the view of the restless sea beyond the windows—all impossibly ordinary in the face of such an extraordinary truth.

"His *heir*…" she whispered, the phrase barely audible, as though saying it aloud might undo her.

And in the silence that followed, she felt both the crushing weight of responsibility and a fragile, piercing thread of belonging, binding her to him still.

She had always known, deep in her bones, that she and Francisco were never meant to marry, that their story could never have ended in a tidy, domestic happiness.

But in his own inscrutable way, he had made sure she would be cared for, remembered, even after his voice was silenced.

Carlos's hand tightened slightly on her arm, pulling her back to the present. His eyes, usually so steady, held a flicker of warning. "You must understand, Carmen," he said quietly. "The others—his family—they won't accept it easily. Not the will. Not you."

Her stomach turned at the thought, the weight of his words pressing down harder than the inheritance itself.

"But," Carlos continued, his voice firm with conviction, "I'll stand with you. Francisco entrusted this to me, and I'll honor that. You won't face them alone."

Carmen drew a long, unsteady breath. For a moment her chest tightened with dread, the image of Francisco's family descending upon her like vultures circling fresh prey. But then, from somewhere deep within, another feeling stirred—a spark that refused to be smothered.

Her chin lifted ever so slightly. "Then let them come," she said, her voice low but steady. "He wanted this. He named me. And I won't let them erase that."

Carlos studied her, a faint, approving glimmer softening his tired features. "Good," he murmured. "That's the Carmen I knew Francisco believed in."

The words steadied her further, anchoring her resolve. Whatever battles lay ahead, she would not shrink from them. Francisco had claimed her as his legacy, his heir, and she would carry that truth like a shield.

The confrontation came sooner than she expected.

Two days later, Carmen arrived at Francisco's offices in Montevideo, summoned under the pretense of reviewing some papers. The moment she stepped through the tall oak doors, she felt the air thicken—charged, brittle, waiting to snap.

They were already gathered around the long mahogany table: María Emilia, draped in black silk, her pearls gleaming like armor; Pancho, Francisco's son, his jaw tight, his eyes sharp with barely contained fury; and two of Francisco's nephews, whispering in low voices that cut off the instant she entered.

"*Ah*," Pancho said, rising just enough to acknowledge her, his tone laced with disdain. "So the *heiress* arrives." He spat the word as though it burned his tongue.

María Emilia's fan snapped open, fluttering once before she spoke, her voice cool and precise. "Señorita *Ruiz*," she began, deliberately using her former name. "We were just discussing the will. Surely, you understand it must be some mistake. A clerical error, perhaps."

Carmen felt her pulse quicken, but she remembered Carlos's words, his hand steady on her arm. She straightened her back, lifting her chin. "No mistake," she said evenly. "He named me. In his own hand. The notary confirmed it."

Pancho leaned forward, his fists pressing into the table. "He was not in his right mind. My father was unwell, clouded. To give away what belongs to his family—to a *seamstress* from Barrio Sur?" His voice rose, vibrating with anger. "We will contest this. And we will win."

Carmen's stomach twisted, but she held his gaze. "Contest what you will. The law is clear. As are his wishes."

The room bristled with hostility, María Emilia's fan stilled, Pancho's glare narrowing to a blade. But beneath their fury, Carmen felt it: her own resolve hardening like steel, the flicker of defiance now a steady flame.

The tension hung thick in the air, Pancho's glare fixed on her like a predator ready to strike. Carmen's palms pressed flat against her skirts beneath the table, her heart thundering, but she refused to look away.

The heavy doors creaked open. Carlos Bonavita stepped inside, his presence filling the room with the quiet authority of a man who had nothing to prove. He closed the doors behind him, his gaze sweeping over the gathered family before settling on Carmen.

"Ah, good," Carlos said evenly. "I see the conversation has begun." He walked to Carmen's side without hesitation, resting a reassuring hand on the back of her chair before turning to face Pancho and María Emilia. "I thought it best to be present, as Francisco entrusted me with the execution of his will."

Pancho scoffed, his lip curling. "Perfect. Another one of Father's pets come to meddle."

Carlos didn't flinch. "I was more than that," he said flatly. "I was his confidant, his partner in many ventures, and in the final years, one of the few men he trusted. And I can tell you this—he was of sound mind when he wrote that will. The notary can attest, as can I. He knew exactly what he was doing."

María Emilia's fan trembled slightly before snapping shut. "And you expect us to believe that he would pass over his own wife and sons, for some woman from the *streets*?"

Carlos's eyes hardened. "Believe what you like. The document speaks for itself. The law favors direct descendants, and Francisco made it clear who he recognized as such. Carmen is not just a beneficiary, she is his direct heir."

Carmen felt a surge of strength at his words, a steadiness she hadn't known she was capable of. Still, she braced herself as Pancho's chair screeched violently against the floor, his fists clenched at his sides.

"This is not finished," he growled, his voice a promise as much as a threat.

The room fell silent. Even María Emilia's fan stilled, her gaze fixed coldly on Carmen as though weighing her.

Carlos shifted slightly closer, a solid presence at Carmen's side, but said nothing more. There was no need. The air itself carried the unfinished battle, thick with threat and inevitability.

Carmen drew in a breath, steadying herself, the echo of Pancho's words lingering like storm clouds gathering just beyond the horizon.

This was only the beginning.

Chapter 40

That same year, in 1933, the rumble of boots replaced the rhythm of the *bandoneón*.

The coup struck Montevideo like a thunderclap. Parliament dissolved overnight, the new dictatorship tightening its grip on every corner of daily life. Voices of dissent were silenced, papers censored, gatherings forbidden. And once again, the *milongas*—those sacred nights of music and release—were outlawed, branded subversive by men who feared what it meant when people dared to move together.

For Carmen, it was as if history had circled back upon itself. She remembered the influenza years, when fear had emptied the dance halls. But this time it was not sickness—it was power, pressing its knee against the city's throat. The streets felt different now: watchful, hushed, as though even the walls might betray you if you spoke too freely.

But Carmen was no longer the uncertain girl of Barrio Sur, hiding her notebooks beneath her bed. She had a voice, and she knew how to wield it. With her essays, published quietly under pseudonyms, slipped into sympathetic presses, and copied hand to hand, she fought back. Each sentence she wrote was a refusal: a defense of memory, of art, of the right to gather and speak.

"Where there is silence, tyranny thrives," she wrote in one essay. *"But a single voice raised against it can remind the people of their strength. And when voices join, no decree can still them."*

The pen became her protest, her weapon, her means of resistance. What others whispered in secret, Carmen laid down in ink. And through her words, she carried the spirit of the *milonga* into another arena: fierce, unyielding, and alive, even in the shadows of repression.

But Carmen did not write only against the state. The same fire that drove her to defy the dictatorship fueled her fight against her personal adversaries.

Francisco's family had not relented; in salons and newspapers, they sought to diminish her, to paint her as an opportunist, a fraud, an interloper who dared to claim what was not hers.

Carmen answered not with slander, but with clarity. She wrote of inheritance not in terms of land or wealth, but of vision, of spirit, of the truths that bind lives together beyond bloodlines and signatures. Her words, though veiled, were unmistakable.

"To claim legacy is not to grasp at gold," one essay declared, *"but to guard the fire of another's vision, to carry it forward so it does not die. Those who fight hardest to silence such guardians often betray their own fear, that they themselves have no light to pass on."*

In a city hushed by censorship and fear, Carmen's defiance cut sharp and clear. Each essay was an act of rebellion, against the generals, against the whispers of Francisco's kin, against the suffocating weight of silence.

And with every word she sent into the world, Carmen felt again what she had always known deep down: they could ban the dance halls, they could seize the papers, they could strip away titles and property. But they could not strip her of her voice.

The winter light slanted pale through the tall windows of the Hotel Piriápolis, as Carmen sat at a corner table in the café, her notebook open before her, the scent of ink and coffee mingling with the salt drifting in from the sea. She had been there for hours, her pen scratching steadily across the page, the words flowing in quiet defiance.

She didn't notice him until his shadow cut across her paper.
Pancho.

He stood over her, broad-shouldered, his expensive coat brushing the edge of the table, his jaw set like stone. The murmur of conversation in the café seemed to dim, the clink of silverware muffled, as though the air itself tightened around them.

"So this is how you honor him," he said coldly, his voice low enough that only she could hear. "Scribbling poison into notebooks. Whispering your lies into print."

Carmen set her pen down deliberately, closing the notebook but keeping her hand resting on it, as if to shield it from him. Her eyes rose to meet his without flinching. "I only write truth, Pancho. If that stings, perhaps you should ask yourself why."

His lips twisted into a bitter smile. He leaned closer, breath sour with wine. "You think your little essays will shield you? They won't. This world belongs to those strong enough to take it. Keep meddling in my affairs, dragging my father's name through your ink, and you'll learn what regret feels like."

Fear flickered in her chest, but she forced her voice to stay level. "Regret comes from silence," she replied evenly. "And I will not be silent. Your father's wishes are not yours to rewrite."

Pancho pulled out the chair opposite and sat down, his glare burning with contempt. "You think you can waltz in here and claim what's mine? You're nothing but a parasite. Everyone knows it." His voice dripped venom, though his own reputation—lavish nights spent in brothels, his fortune squandered on women and drink—was hardly a secret in Montevideo.

Leaning in, his tone sharpened to a growl. "You're playing a dangerous game. Push me further, and you won't like the consequences."

With a casual gesture meant to terrify, he slipped a pistol from his coat and laid it on the table. Its cold metallic gleam caught the light, sending a chill through Carmen's spine.

Her breath snagged, but she steadied herself, fingers tightening on the edge of her notebook. She would not let him see her falter. Slowly, she met his gaze head-on. "I don't respond to threats, Pancho. Not yours, not anyone's. Whatever bitterness you carry toward your father, it isn't mine to bear. He made his wishes known. And I intend to honor them."

For an instant, his hand tightened on the gun, his eyes blazing. Carmen thought he might lash out then and there, right in the café. Instead, with a snarl, he snatched the pistol back into his coat and rose abruptly.

"Careful," he muttered darkly. "Words can be buried just as easily as people."

He strode out, leaving a wake of silence behind him. Only then did Carmen exhale, realizing she had been holding her breath, the echo of his threat clinging to her like smoke.

Carmen barely slept that night. Pancho's words haunted her still: *words can be buried just as easily as people.* The cold gleam of his pistol lingered in her mind like a phantom. Yet beneath the fear, another fire had been kindled. She could not, would not, be silenced.

The next morning, she dressed with care, pulling her shawl tight around her shoulders, her notebook tucked under her arm like a shield. Carlos met her at the steps of the courthouse, his steady presence a quiet reassurance.

"They'll try to rattle you," he warned softly, his hand brushing her arm as they entered. "But don't let them. Remember—you're not here to prove yourself to them. You're here to honor him."

The courtroom was crowded, thick with the smell of ink, wool, and damp stone. Journalists hunched in the gallery, their pens poised like daggers. Curious onlookers whispered, craning their necks for a better view of the seamstress from Barrio Sur who dared stand against Piria's kin.

At the center table, María Emilia sat rigid in her widow's weeds, pearls gleaming against her black dress like drops of ice. Beside her, Pancho leaned back in his chair, arms crossed, a smirk playing at his lips as though the outcome were already his.

When the questioning began, the prosecuting attorney broke his silence, his voice cutting across the chamber like a whip.

"You waltz in here claiming to be the daughter of the late Francisco Piria," he sneered, "but where is the proof? Where's the evidence for these absurd claims?"

All eyes turned to Carmen.

She rose slowly, her shawl slipping back as she steadied herself. The room seemed to shrink around her, the murmurs fading, the scrape of quills falling still. Her voice, when it came, was steady, deliberate, iron beneath silk.

"I may not have the conventional proof you seek," she began, her voice clear and calm, "but I have something far stronger. Truth. Francisco Piria was a father to me in every way that mattered. And more than that, he acknowledged me. He put his name to it. His will is his word, and his word was his bond. Tell me, who are *you* to question his integrity?"

A murmur rippled through the chamber, but the opposing counsel only leaned forward, his lip curling. "*Señorita,* you expect us to believe you were anything more than a passing fancy? The whole city knows what's being said about you."

Carmen's jaw tightened, but her voice remained steady. "The last time I checked, *Señor*, gossip holds no weight in matters of inheritance." She let her gaze sweep the room, meeting the eyes of the lawyers, the judge, even her enemies. "This is not about rumor. This is about principle. Francisco Piria entrusted me with a part of his legacy, and I will not allow it to be denied or diminished."

Her words struck with quiet force. She took a breath, her voice deepening, carrying through the chamber. "To dismiss his wishes is not merely to rob me, it is to betray him. To trample the very legacy you claim to defend. I will not stand by while his memory is twisted into something small, petty, or self-serving. If you want to honor Francisco Piria, then honor the truth of his word."

The silence that followed was thick, unsettled. Even the opposing counsel faltered, his sneer trembling at the edges. Carmen remained immovable, her spine straight, her eyes unyielding—more than a claimant now, but the living embodiment of his will.

The judge leaned forward, his gavel tapping lightly against the desk. "Enough," he said, his tone cutting through the chamber. His eyes fixed on the opposing counsel first, cool and unyielding, before turning to Carmen. "*Señorita*, the court has heard you. The words of the deceased, laid forth in his hand and witnessed by law, stand as evidence. This court will not dismiss them on the basis of gossip or hearsay."

A ripple of reaction swept through the benches—shock from some, indignation from others—but Carmen felt her breath return in a slow, steady tide. For the first time since the trial had begun, the balance had shifted.

Pancho's smirk faltered, just enough for her to see it.

And in that moment, Carmen understood: thought the fight was far from over, she had won more than a reprieve. She had won the court's ear.

The gavel struck once more, echoing through the chamber like a heartbeat. The session adjourned, but Carmen remained standing, her chin lifted, her resolve unbroken.

For the first time since the storm of his death began, she felt the weight of Francisco's absence settle differently—not only as grief, but as strength.

His word had carried her this far.

Her own voice would carry her the rest of the way.

Chapter 41

The legal battles dragged on, winding through the courts like a slow, relentless storm.

Carmen stood by the tall, arched windows of the stately home in Montevideo that Francisco had once bestowed her; a gift that now felt less like a blessing than a contested battleground.

In her hands, she cradled a watering can, tipping it gently over the trailing ivy that climbed the carved stone of the grand hall. The quiet ritual had become a kind of refuge, a way of imposing order where so much in her life felt uncertain.

As she lost herself in the tranquil ritual of watering her plants, her gaze drifted beyond the windowpane, outside to the front gate. Her heart skipped a beat as she suddenly saw Nico entering, slowly making his way up the front walk.

But it was not the Nico she remembered: no easy grin, no quick wave. His shoulders slumped beneath the weight of something unsaid, his steps slow and deliberate, as if each one dragged against him. Even from a distance, Carmen could feel the heaviness radiating from him, a solemnity that pressed against the glass and unsettled her heart.

Carmen's hands trembled. She set the watering can aside, ivy forgotten, as a chill of foreboding swept through her. Crossing the hall, she flung open the heavy oak door. The late afternoon light was bruised and fading, the air carrying the weight of some unspoken doom.

At the end of the path, Nico approached slowly, hat in his hands. The easy warmth she so often associated with him was gone. His gait was heavy, his eyes hollow, as if he bore a burden too great to carry.

Her heart lurched. Grief still raw from Francisco's death only weeks earlier surged to the surface, colliding with dread. "Nico," she called into the gathering twilight, "what's the matter?"

He climbed the steps with deliberate slowness, his voice thick with sorrow. "Carmen… something's happened. There's something you need to know." He paused, searching her face, then gestured toward the hall. "Can I come in?"

Inside, they sat across from one another in the drawing room, the silence pressing in like a tide. Carmen's hands twisted in her lap. "Please, Nico," she urged, "what is it? Just tell me."

He drew a long breath, steadying himself. "It's Carlos, Carmen…Bonavita," he said at last, his voice low. "He—he took his own life today. At the Hotel Piriápolis."

Carmen gasped, the words striking her like a blow. "What? …Carlos?" Her throat closed around his name. "But—but why?" Tears brimmed, spilling before she could wipe them away.

Nico hesitated, then delivered the second blow. "It's even more tragic, Carmen." Nico said, shaking his head, sadly. "Before he took his own life, Carlos got into a dispute with Piria's son, and it ended in a duel. Pancho... he was also killed."

Carmen pressed a hand to her mouth, unable to breathe. The weight of it—the man Francisco had trusted like a son, and the son himself—both gone in a single day.

Nico's hands tightened around his hat, the brim twisting between his fingers. His voice was low at first, but as he spoke, the images seemed to gather weight, filling the drawing room.

"It started this morning," he said. "The little train from Montevideo came in late. Sparks from its chimney caught in the weeds along the tracks. Within minutes, flames were licking up the hillside. The wind off the sea turned it wild. You could smell it before you saw it, burning brush, acrid smoke, that sharp bite that clings in your throat."

Carmen's chest tightened as he continued.

"The workshops were in chaos. Men shouting, buckets sloshing, the sound of horses screaming in their stalls. I saw Carlos and Pancho burst out from opposite sides of the yard, straight into each other's path. The fire lit the sky behind them, turning their faces into shadows against the blaze."

Nico swallowed hard. "They were shouting before they were even close enough to hear themselves. Carlos was red with fury—he accused Pancho of wasting time, of standing idly by while the fire spread. Pancho snapped back that the men on hand were city officials, not his to command. Their voices cut through the roar of the flames, each word sharp as gunfire. I swear the fire fed on their anger."

Carmen gripped the arm of her chair, knuckles white.

"They squared off right there, smoke whipping around them, sparks in the air like fireflies. Carlos called him a spoon-fed egotist, too big for his britches. Pancho barked back, calling him an old fool clinging to scraps of power. And then—" Nico's voice broke for a moment. "Then the guns came out. Like instinct. Like breathing. You could smell the powder even before the shots rang."

He lowered his gaze. "The crack split the air. Two, maybe three. Echoes tangled with the thunder of the fire. And when the smoke cleared… Pancho was on the ground. Carlos stood over him, his face… empty. Not proud. Not even angry anymore. Just hollow."

Nico drew a ragged breath. "He walked away from the yard like a man already dead. Came straight to the hotel bar. Ordered a double whisky, neat. Downed it like water. He looked at me, eyes blank, and all he said was: '*I killed Pancho.*'"

The words hung heavy in the air.

"I tried to stop him," Nico confessed, his own eyes wet. "I ran after him. But before I reached the door… the shot came. Just one. The sound rattled the glass, and then—silence. Nothing but the fire outside, and the smell of smoke and gunpowder clinging to everything."

His voice cracked, the memory too raw. "Carmen, it was like watching the whole empire crumble in a single morning. Francisco's dream, everything he built—it's like it died with them both."

Carmen pressed her palms into her knees, tears streaming down her face as she tried to anchor herself against the storm.

Francisco gone. Bonavita gone. Pancho gone. One by one, the men who had carried the weight of Piria's dream had vanished, leaving only ashes behind. What had been built with vision and audacity now unraveled under greed, pride, and neglect, like a grand tapestry fraying thread by thread.

Outside, Piriápolis still smoldered. Streets once alive with laughter and music sagged beneath the weight of emptiness. Shopfronts were shuttered, façades dulled and streaked with soot. The resort town that had once stood as a testament to Francisco Piria's immortal dream was collapsing into a husk of itself—more memory than place, more ruin than vision.

For thirteen long years, Francisco's inheritance lay snarled in the courts, a monument not to his genius but to human folly. More than fifty heirs—children, grandchildren, great-grandchildren—each clawed for their piece of the estate, their voices raised in endless petitions, their tempers flaring in mediation rooms and court chambers. The litigation dragged on like a disease, devouring resources, bleeding the estate dry. What had begun as a dream of wealth and legacy became a spectacle of ambition and spite.

When the dust of the inheritance battles finally settled, it left behind no victors, only ruins. No triumph, only a bitter lesson: that the relentless pursuit of fortune can strip away what is most fragile and irreplaceable: harmony, dignity, and peace of mind.

Carmen often found her thoughts drifting back to that Christmas Eve in the grand lobby of the Argentino Hotel, when Francisco had spoken with a rare tenderness. *Life is not in possessions or fleeting triumphs,* he had told her, *but in the bonds we nurture, in the love we give and receive.*

Those words had become her compass, even as they were lost on those who should have understood them most. His own family, blinded by greed, had picked apart his empire until there was nothing left but bones and ashes.

And yet, as Carmen stood at the window of her home, watching the last embers of daylight bleed into the darkening skyline, a quiet resolve crystallized within her. If they had torn Francisco's legacy to shreds in the courts, she would gather it anew—not in contracts or titles, but in spirit.

His dream would not be left to decay, nor his name reduced to a footnote in someone else's victory. Not while she still drew breath.

Chapter 42

It was 1958—twenty-five years since Francisco's passing.

Carmen stood once more within the halls of the Argentino Hotel, though the circumstances were irrevocably changed. Once, she had walked these marble floors at Francisco's side, his dream unfurling around them like a living thing. Now she stood alone, not as a guest, but as author of three published books, and the President of *La Industrial Francisco Piria S.A.*, the steward of his empire and the keeper of his legacy.

The hotel still shimmered beneath its towering chandeliers, its marble floors gleaming beneath the soft glow of candlelight. Yet there was a subtle wear to its edges now, a quiet testimony to all it had endured. Tonight, though, it breathed again, alive with music, verse, and the electric pulse of defiance.

Carmen had poured months of effort, influence, and relentless determination into bringing the Inter-American Poetry Conference to Piriápolis—a gathering of poets, dreamers, and revolutionaries whose voices echoed from every corner of the continent.

When it came time to decide how to honor them, she refused the sterile predictability of speeches and stiff formalities. Instead, she envisioned something alive, something that pulsed with the same spirit of defiance and creation that had shaped both Francisco's vision and her own journey.

She chose a *milonga*. A night where words and bodies would move in harmony, where poetry would weave itself through the haunting strains of the *bandoneón*, and where Francisco's legacy could be remembered not in silence, but in rhythm, music, and fire.

As the first sigh of the *bandoneón* filled the air, couples drifted onto the dance floor, their bodies moving as one beneath the chandeliers. Carmen lingered at the edge of the *salón*, her gaze sweeping over diplomats and poets, dancers and dreamers, their laughter mingling with the haunting strains of music.

For a fleeting moment, she felt him there. Francisco. As if he were watching from some shadowed corner, his dark eyes glimmering with that familiar mix of pride and mischief.

Her heart swelled with pride and grief in equal measure. This was not merely an event. It was a vow: that even in the wake of ruin, art and beauty would endure. That Francisco's vision, so fraught and brilliant, would not be lost to history.

Drawing a steadying breath, Carmen stepped forward. Her heels clicked softly against the marble, and the room gradually stilled. Murmurs faded into silence as poets and dignitaries turned toward her, their expectant faces glowing in the warm light.

Carmen felt the weight of every gaze, and beneath it, the ghost of his presence—Francisco's voice, his fire, his relentless belief in the power of dreams.

And for the first time in years, she felt ready to speak not only for him, but for herself.

She placed one hand lightly on the back of a carved wooden chair, grounding herself before she spoke.

"*Buenas noches*," she began, her voice clear yet warm, carrying easily across the hall. "Tonight, we gather not only to celebrate poetry, but to honor the spirit that lives within it. The same spirit that builds cities, ignites revolutions, and breathes life into all acts of creation."

Her gaze swept the room, lingering on the musicians, the dancers poised at the edge of the floor, the poets seated like watchful sentinels.

"When Francisco Piria founded *La Industrial*, he believed in more than brick and mortar, more than commerce and profit. He believed in weaving beauty into the very fabric of our lives. He believed, as poets do, that imagination can shape the world."

Carmen's voice softened, and a flicker of vulnerability passed through her expression. "Many of you knew Francisco as a visionary, a builder, a dreamer. I knew him as all of those things, but also as a man who lived as fiercely as he dared to dream. His life, like a tango, was filled with soaring triumphs and devastating falls, with moments of dizzying passion and haunting silence."

She paused, letting the words settle like dust in sunlight.

"And so, may this night remind us," Carmen said, lifting her chin, "that even in times of hardship, art endures. That beauty is not a luxury, but a necessity. And that, like the tango, life demands that we keep moving, even when the music changes."

With a subtle gesture, she turned to the musicians, who lifted their instruments as if waking from a dream. The first aching notes of the *bandoneón* filled the hall, rich and haunting, wrapping the room in an invisible embrace. Carmen stepped back, her heart swelling as dancers glided forward to claim the floor.

She pressed a hand to her chest, steadying the ache that would never fully leave her. Their story had ended in sorrow, yes, but like the final, lingering chord of a tango, its resonance endured: haunting, beautiful, impossible to forget. Whatever love had been lost, whatever ruin had followed, Francisco's vision had not died. Tonight, beneath the glittering lights of the Argentino Hotel, it was hers to keep alive, hers to carry forward.

And as she stood there, a fragile ember stirred within her, small but unyielding. Fire, she had learned, was not only a force of destruction. It could also purify, it could clear the ground for what was still to come. Someday, she knew, Piriápolis would rise again—not as it had been, but as something new, something reborn.

A phoenix, rising from the ashes.

www.ingramcontent.com/pod-product-compliance
Lightning Source LLC
Chambersburg PA
CBHW030735310726
48969CB00005B/1227